THE JOB

THE JOB

AN AMERICAN NOVEL

BY
SINCLAIR LEWIS

*Introduction to the Bison Book Edition
by Maureen Honey*

University of Nebraska Press
Lincoln and London

Copyright 1917, 1945 by Sinclair Lewis
Introduction to the Bison Book Edition copyright © 1994 by the
University of Nebraska Press
Manufactured in the United States of America

First Bison Book printing: 1994
Most recent printing indicated by the last digit below:
10   9   8   7   6   5   4   3   2   1

Library of Congress Cataloging-in-Publication Data
Lewis, Sinclair, 1885–1951.
The job: the American novel / by Sinclair Lewis; introduction to the
Bison Book ed. by Maureen Honey.
p.   cm.
ISBN 0-8032-7948-5 (pa)
1. Women white collar workers—New York (N.Y.)—Fiction.
I. Title
PS3523.E94J6   1994
813'.52—dc20
93-43084
CIP

Reprinted by arrangement with the Estate of Sinclair Lewis.

∞

CONTENTS

INTRODUCTION

By Maureen Honey

Published in 1917, *The Job* is Sinclair Lewis's second novel and the first to receive positive critical attention. It begins a trilogy about women's emancipation in the first two decades of the twentieth century.[1] *Main Street* (1920) would concern the restricted existence of a small-town wife, and *Ann Vickers* (1933) would focus on a suffrage activist who earns a Ph.D., has an abortion, marries at age forty, and then falls in love with a married man. Lewis himself divorced his first wife during this period and in 1922 married journalist Dorothy Thompson, a New Woman figure of the sort he wrote about.

The Job has been called a Horatio Alger story cast in feminine terms and so it is, but it grew out of a literary movement determined to shatter the "poppy-flavored novels" that Lewis castigates in his narrative.[2] Considering himself a realist writer, Lewis, like his contemporaries Edith Wharton, Henry James, Theodore Dreiser, and William Dean Howells, wished to penetrate the surface conventions of American life and expose its darker side. They were all part of an intellectual movement of rebellion against Victorian prudery and relentless propriety that, in their minds, dangerously obscured the painful reality of many people's lives, particularly those of women. By the second decade of a new century, they had made significant inroads into American literature, changing its melodramatic conventions and presentation of ideal character types into a recognizably modern picture of how people really behaved.

Lewis was attracted to the muckrakers, progressives, and bohemians of his time, joining socialist Upton Sinclair's New Jersey colony in 1906 and moving to New York to be a writer. As is evident in *The Job,* Lewis saw the underbelly of industrializing America, its exploitation of workers both native born and immigrant. He wanted to expose the misery of ordinary people like his heroine, Una Golden, and satirize the callousness, self-importance, and shallowness of her employers. Balancing this realistic exposé and seemingly in contradiction to it is the novel's upbeat ending. The unrealistic denouement can be explained partly, however, by the optimism of progressives like Lewis toward corporate development.[3] As a progressive, Lewis believed that the tendency of capitalism to focus on profits needed to be redirected toward a cooperative venture between workers and owners in order to create a better world. The jarring perorations to Big Business that appear in the novel are typical of reformist thought before World War I in that they posit a potential for eliminating war, poverty, and class stratification in modern capitalism. Una Golden's quest to be a businesswoman, therefore, is cast as a noble, idealistic journey toward the betterment of all humanity. It was a perspective that would be battered by World War I and ultimately destroyed by the Great Depression, but in 1917 many intellectuals who considered themselves realists were able to create models of utopian change. Una Golden's success, while echoing Horatio Alger fantasies, is meant to transcend the notion of individual triumph by standing as an emblem for a future America of equality, good will, and fairness.

The Job is a hybrid novel, combining as it does the muckraking and progressive traditions—a modern quest for authenticity and realism with the Victorian desire for uplift. It is a transitional piece that captures for us the amalgam of anger and optimism, rebellion and innocence characterizing Lewis's generation. It is daring enough to mention alcoholism, venereal disease, and petting while giving us a heroine who divorces, considers adopting a baby as a single woman, and has women friends who drink and smoke. At the same time, Una's sexual desires are frozen even as she explores her attractions, and she melodramatically walks away from a date who buys her a glass of sherry at a restaurant. For all her urban sophistication, Una Golden is a proper Victorian lady in many ways, just as the drifters and womanizers to whom she is drawn are, deep down, looking for a good woman to get them into shape. Similarly, the novel courageously tackles anti-Semitism and supports union organizations like the I.W.W. At the same time, it sidesteps the dramatic strikes that occurred in the story's time frame, such as those in Lawrence, Massachusetts (1912), Paterson, New Jersey (1913), and New York City, where in 1909 young Jewish women like Una's friend, Mamie Magen, led one of the largest walk-outs in American history, "The Uprising of the 20,000," a strike that lasted three months. Though the novel is set in New York and spans the years 1905–1915, there is no mention of these events, nor do we hear of the Triangle Shirtwaist Fire of 1911 that claimed scores of young women's lives or the large Wobblie-led marches of strikers through Manhattan in 1914. Una Golden is somewhat insulated from this social ferment by her class status—as an office worker, she is less exploited than a garment worker—but the author's focus on the deadening routine of women's work and sympathy for labor organizers make the omissions noticeable. For all his iconoclasm and progressive views, Lewis's perspective here is solidly middle-class and shaped by reformist rather than revolutionary impulses.

The way in which *The Job* forges new ground in an uncompromising fashion is its promotion of women's rights. Lewis is championing more than the right to vote by creating his narrative around the fortunes of a clerical worker, a largely invisible character in literature at the time despite the burgeoning number of such women in the labor force.[4] He takes great pains to assure us that Una Golden is an ordinary woman, "undramatic as a field daisy," and that she begins her quest for independence without knowing what a feminist is. By emphasizing the quotidian nature of his heroine and the crushing boredom of her secretarial jobs, Lewis subtly enlarges the reader's understanding of feminism from a narrow concern with the vote to a more radical critique of women's restricted role in the workplace and in the family. Moreover, he broadens the image of a feminist from that of a militant activist to a midwestern daughter trying to support her mother in a world controlled by male chauvinists. Finally, he demonstrates that a woman can transform herself from an apolitical, shy waif who dreams of being a corporate president's secretary to an articulate, confident real-estate developer who negotiates a salary ten times her beginning wage.

Tellingly, Una's growth stems from her awakening connections to other women, since she has been conditioned to consider men as the raison d'être. When she starts her business course at age twenty-four, Una notices three men students and becomes friends with one of them but sees the other women there "as a mass." She lunches with a sister stenographer during her first job at the *Motor and Gas Gazette* but the relationship is a shallow one. Her attention is taken up with a desk editor, Walter Babson, who fascinates her with his tales of adventure and his irreverent views on contemporary life. He represents what she cannot exercise as a woman with his freedom of movement, his sexual philandering, his editor status, and sense of command. Walter seemingly fears nothing or no one and while it is clear that he needs to find his bearings, he makes Una feel the comparative dullness of her life at eight dollars a week in a three-room flat with her mother. When she moves to a boarding house after her mother dies, Una again focuses on a man who lives there, even though he leads a somewhat seedy existence and repels her, rather than on her female librarian neighbor.

It is not until half-way through the novel that Una begins to seek the company of and identify with other women. She is fed up with the stale routine at an architect's office, and her vow to improve the quality of her life is intertwined with her desire to make women friends who are doing that. She succeeds by moving to the Temperance and Protection Home for Girls, where she meets Mamie Magen, a Jewish socialist for whom office work is a welcome alternative to the tuberculosis-infested sweatshops of the lower East Side. She also gets to know Esther Lawrence, a stenographer and feminist critic of the treatment of women in the work force. They educate Una about the world she inhabits in a way men failed to do and give her courage to assert herself at work. They also accompany her to concerts, art galleries, and the theatre, where she experiences cultural enrichment. It is through Mamie that Una gets her first good job at a real estate office and it is another woman, Beatrice Joline, who inspires her to sell real estate. By this time she is married to the n'er-do-well Eddie Schwirtz, who believes women belong in the home. At first Una listens to his reactionary rhetoric; then she begins to argue with him about women's rights after her exposure to women like Mamie, Esther, and Beatrice. She works her way into sales, supervises development of a new property on the North Shore of Long Island, divorces her drunken gambler of a husband, and plans to adopt a child at age thirty-four.[5] By the autumn of 1915, when the novel ends, Una marches in a suffrage parade and experiences "solid joy in her office achievements, in her flat, . . . and feeling comradeship with thousands of women." Una has broken out of the circumscribed nuclear family she was taught to replicate and entered an empowering community that reinforces her right to a satisfying public job.

At the end of *The Job,* Una's career success is coupled with romantic rewards as well. Walter Babson fortuitously returns to the very office Una has just joined, declares his love, and promises a marriage of comradeship: "We can both work, keep our jobs." They will have it all—fulfilling work, an equal relationship, and parenthood. This is quite a fantasy, even today, and it certainly was a less than realistic scenario in 1917 when *The Job* was published. To understand why Lewis ended his muckraking, realistic novel with a feminist pot of gold, it helps to look not only at the optimistic premises of the Progressive Years but at the fiction being published in national magazines when Lewis was beginning his writing career. These magazines were the primary source of popular fiction for women between the years 1910 and 1930.[6] Although many of the stories in them reinforced traditional courtship and marriage patterns, a significant proportion reflected the new ideas being debated in American society over woman's proper place. After key suffrage victories in Washington

(1910), California (1911), and four other states in 1912–13, magazines began to take a more positive view of women's rights and ran stories about quasi-feminist characters who put work at the center of their lives and looked for men who could accept relationships of equality.[7] The work-centered romance became a staple of women's popular fiction during the 1910s and lasted well into the 1930s, reflecting in part the interest of many women in nondomestic roles.[8]

The staple conventions of the work-centered romance show a small-town midwestern heroine leaving her stifling parental home for a metropolis, typically New York City, seeking a place for herself with the help of other women. Frequently she begins her journey upon the death of a parent, uses a mother's or aunt's inheritance to get started, and determines to be a successful businesswoman or artist. She finds the city both exhilarating and lonely, yet grows through meeting its challenge to exist outside the safe but limited realm she has known all her young life.[9] The employers and suitors she meets along the way often try to discourage her from dedication to a meaningful vocation, but she generally meets one man who loves her enough to respect her desire to have an identity outside the family. He is a man of some character with sufficient emotional security and modern sophistication to welcome a marriage of comradeship rather than insist on the old Victorian arrangement. Typically, the men she encounters are businessmen or artists themselves, equally dedicated to success of a meaningful sort, and they come to understand that women and men are basically alike on this score.

Although *The Job* was never serialized in a national magazine, it features many of the characteristics shared by the work-centered romances of its day. Una Golden leaves Panama, Pennsylvania, with its limited options and heads for New York only when her father dies, an event that transforms her from dutiful daughter to family head in charge of her own destiny and the welfare of her mother. It is an event that ushers in a new sense of self: "Her father's death had freed her; had permitted her to . . . be regarded as useful. Instantly—still without learning that there was such a principle as feminism—she had become a feminist, demanding the world and all the fullness thereof as her field of labour." The death of the father frees the New Woman to create a life of her own, and Una follows the pattern. She also must endure a series of trials that test her mettle and her belief in a new world that needs women's talents to run properly. Una suffers discouragement after discouragement in her quest for autonomy but keeps fighting for her dream and, like many in her fictional peer group, she is rewarded for her pluck and perseverance.

Sinclair Lewis was careful to set his heroine apart from the mainstream characters so popular with a mass audience—Una, we are told, has "thick ankles," wears rimless eyeglasses, and is "anaemic" in appearance. Furthermore, the text states that she is not a genius, artist, or actress, all typical heroines in the New Woman mold. The narrative violates as well formulaic prohibitions against the heroine's getting a divorce, having a child out of wedlock, or experiencing sexual desire (which is probably why it was not published in a mass-circulation magazine).[10] Nevertheless, the framework for the story is a familiar one from the period and the happy ending in particular places *The Job* squarely within the parameters of the work-centered romance. Given that Lewis operated in a literary market that featured New Woman types succeeding in their quest for love and work, it makes sense that he would have ended his story in this way.

The Job stands for us today as a reminder that contemporary feminist issues have been alive in American life for a very long time and that male writers, as well as female, were sympathetic to them in the early years of the twentieth century.[11] Although Una Golden's fate is not representative of most women's, it is typical of a literary trend that posited new roles for those entering the post-Victorian era. The optimism of this generation would prove to be unwarranted, but the narratives it created live on for us still as portraits, not of innocence lost, but inspiration regained.

NOTES

1. An analysis of this trilogy is provided by Nan Bauer Maglin in "Women in Three Sinclair Lewis Novels," *Massachusetts Review* Vol. 14, No. 4 (Autumn 1973): 103–18.

2. D. J. Dooley, *The Art of Sinclair Lewis* (Lincoln: University of Nebraska Press, 1967), p. 41.

3. Henry F. May describes this movement in great detail in *The End of American Innocence: A Study of the First Years of Our Own Time, 1912–1917* (New York: Alfred A. Knopf, 1959).

4. By 1910, the number of office workers who were women had grown to 37.7 percent, and from 1900 to 1920 the percentage of women in the labor force who were clerical workers went from 2 to 12 percent. Alice Kessler-Harris, *Out to Work: A History of Wage-Earning Women in the United States* (New York: Oxford University Press, 1982), pp. 9, 148.

5. For a discussion of the frequency and nature of divorce at this time, see Elaine Tyler May, *Great Expectations: Marriage and Divorce in Post-Victorian America* (Chicago: University of Chicago Press, 1980); and William O'Neill, *Divorce in the Progressive Era* (New Haven: Yale University Press, 1967).

6. By 1923, the number of magazines in the United States had grown to around three thousand with a combined per-issue circulation of 128,621,000, and it was by including a large amount of fiction that editors propelled the circulation of industry giants into the millions. Theodore Peterson, *Magazines in the Twentieth Century* (Urbana: University of Illinois Press, 1964), pp. 58–59, 126.

7. This subject is explored in detail in my anthology of magazine fiction, *Breaking the Ties That Bind: Popular Stories of the New Woman, 1915–1930,* ed. Maureen Honey (Norman: University of Oklahoma Press, 1992).

8. A good discussion of this post-Victorian trend is provided in Lee Ann Kryder, "Self-Assertion and Social Commitment: The Significance of Work to the Progressive Era's New Woman," *Journal of American Culture,* Vol. 6 (Summer 1983): 25–30; see also Sandra Gilbert and Susan Gubar, "Soldier's Heart: Literary Men, Literary Women, and the Great War," *No Man's Land: The Place of the Woman Writer in the Twentieth Century,* Vol. 2 (New Haven: Yale University Press, 1989) and Rosalind Rosenberg, *Beyond Separate Spheres: Intellectual Roots of Modern Feminism* (New Haven: Yale University Press, 1982).

9. The importance of work and an urban environment to the emancipation of women is explored in Margaret Gibbons Wilson, *The American Woman in Transition: The Urban Influence, 1870–1920* (Westport, Conn: Greenwood Press, 1979).

10. Mark Schorer describes Lewis's successful efforts to get his other stories published in periodicals at this time in *Sinclair Lewis: An American Life* (New York: McGraw-Hall, 1961), p. 233.

11. Other male writers in Lewis's day like Theodore Dreiser, George Weston, Clarence Budington Kelland, and Booth Tarkington created New Woman characters and treated them in a positive way.

Part I

THE CITY

THE JOB

CHAPTER I

CAPTAIN LEW GOLDEN would have saved any foreign observer a great deal of trouble in studying America. He was an almost perfect type of the petty small-town middle-class lawyer. He lived in Panama, Pennsylvania. He had never been "captain" of anything except the Crescent Volunteer Fire Company, but he owned the title because he collected rents, wrote insurance, and meddled with lawsuits.

He carried a quite visible mustache-comb and wore a collar, but no tie. On warm days he appeared on the street in his shirt-sleeves, and discussed the comparative temperatures of the past thirty years with Doctor Smith and the Mansion House 'bus-driver. He never used the word "beauty" except in reference to a setter dog—beauty of words or music, of faith or rebellion, did not exist for him. He rather fancied large, ambitious, banal, red-and-gold sunsets, but he merely glanced at them as he straggled home, and remarked that they were "nice." He believed that all Parisians, artists, millionaires, and socialists were immoral. His entire system of theology was comprised in the Bible, which he never read, and the Methodist Church, which he rarely attended; and he desired no system of economics beyond the current platform of the Republican party. He was aimlessly industrious, crochety but kind, and almost quixotically honest.

He believed that "Panama, Pennsylvania, was good enough for anybody."

This last opinion was not shared by his wife, nor by his daughter Una.

Mrs. Golden was one of the women who aspire just enough to be vaguely discontented; not enough to make them toil at the acquisition of understanding and knowledge. She had floated into a comfortable semi-belief in a semi-Christian Science, and she read novels with a conviction that she would have been a romantic person "if she hadn't married Mr. Golden—not but what he's a fine man and very bright and all, but he hasn't got much imagination or any, well, *romance!*"

She wrote poetry about spring and neighborhood births, and Captain Golden admired it so actively that he read it aloud to callers. She attended all the meetings of the Panama Study Club, and desired to learn French, though she never went beyond borrowing a French grammar from the Episcopalian rector and learning one conjugation. But in the pioneer suffrage movement she took no part— she didn't "think it was quite ladylike." . . . She was a poor cook, and her house always smelled stuffy, but she liked to have flowers about. She was pretty of face, frail of body, genuinely gracious of manner. She really did like people, liked to give cookies to the neighborhood boys, and—if you weren't impatient with her slackness—you found her a wistful and touching figure in her slight youthfulness and in the ambition to be a romantic personage, a Marie Antoinette or a Mrs. Grover Cleveland, which ambition she still retained at fifty-five.

She was, in appearance, the ideal wife and mother— sympathetic, forgiving, bright-lipped as a May morning.

THE JOB

She never demanded; she merely suggested her desires, and, if they were refused, let her lips droop in a manner which only a brute could withstand.

She plaintively admired her efficient daughter Una.

Una Golden was a "good little woman"—not pretty, not noisy, not particularly articulate, but instinctively on the inside of things; naturally able to size up people and affairs. She had common sense and unkindled passion. She was a matter-of-fact idealist, with a healthy woman's simple longing for love and life. At twenty-four Una had half a dozen times fancied herself in love. She had been embraced at a dance, and felt the stirring of a desire for surrender. But always a native shrewdness had kept her from agonizing over these affairs.

She was not—and will not be—a misunderstood genius, an undeveloped artist, an embryonic leader in feminism, nor an ugly duckling who would put on a Georgette hat and captivate the theatrical world. She was an untrained, ambitious, thoroughly commonplace, small-town girl. But she was a natural executive and she secretly controlled the Golden household; kept Captain Golden from eating with his knife, and her mother from becoming drugged with too much reading of poppy-flavored novels.

She wanted to learn, learn anything. But the Goldens were too respectable to permit her to have a job, and too poor to permit her to go to college. From the age of seventeen, when she had graduated from the high school—in white ribbons and heavy new boots and tight new organdy—to twenty-three, she had kept house and gone to gossip-parties and unmethodically read books from the town library—Walter Scott, Richard Le Gallienne, Harriet Beecher Stowe, Mrs. Humphry Ward, *How to Know the Birds, My Year in the Holy Land, Home Needlework,*

[5]

Sartor Resartus, and *Ships that Pass in the Night*. Her residue of knowledge from reading them was a disbelief in Panama, Pennsylvania.

She was likely never to be anything more amazing than a mother and wife, who would entertain the Honiton Embroidery Circle twice a year.

Yet, potentially, Una Golden was as glowing as any princess of balladry. She was waiting for the fairy prince, though he seemed likely to be nothing more decorative than a salesman in a brown derby. She was fluid; indeterminate as a moving cloud.

Although Una Golden had neither piquant prettiness nor grave handsomeness, her soft littleness made people call her "Puss," and want to cuddle her as a child cuddles a kitten. If you noted Una at all, when you met her, you first noted her gentle face, her fine-textured hair of faded gold, and her rimless eye-glasses with a gold chain over her ear. These glasses made a business-like center to her face; you felt that without them she would have been too childish. Her mouth was as kind as her spirited eyes, but it drooped. Her body was so femininely soft that you regarded her as rather plump. But for all her curving hips, and the thick ankles which she considered "common," she was rather anemic. Her cheeks were round, not rosy, but clear and soft; her lips a pale pink. Her chin was plucky and undimpled; it was usually spotted with one or two unimportant eruptions, which she kept so well covered with powder that they were never noticeable. No one ever thought of them except Una herself, to whom they were tragic blemishes which she timorously examined in the mirror every time she went to wash her hands. She knew that they were the result of the indigestible Golden family meals; she tried to take comfort by noticing their prevalence among other girls; but they kept startling her anew; she would secretly touch them with a worried forefinger, and wonder whether men were able to see anything else in her face.

You remembered her best as she hurried through the street in her tan mackintosh with its yellow velveteen collar turned high up, and one of those modest round hats to which she was addicted. For then you were aware only of the pale - gold hair fluffing round her school-mistress eye-glasses, her gentle air of respectability, and her undistinguished littleness.

She trusted in the village ideal of virginal vacuousness as the type of beauty which most captivated men, though every year she was more shrewdly doubtful of the divine superiority of these men. That a woman's business in life was to remain respectable and to secure a man, and consequent security, was her unmeditated faith—till, in 1905, when Una was twenty-four years old, her father died.

§ 2

Captain Golden left to wife and daughter a good name, a number of debts, and eleven hundred dollars in lodge insurance. The funeral was scarcely over before neighbors—the furniture man, the grocer, the polite old homeo-pathic doctor—began to come in with bland sympathy and large bills. When the debts were all cleared away the Goldens had only six hundred dollars and no income beyond the good name. All right-minded persons agree that a good name is precious beyond rubies, but Una would have preferred less honor and more rubies.

She was so engaged in comforting her mother that she scarcely grieved for her father. She took charge of every-thing—money, house, bills.

Mrs. Golden had been overwhelmed by a realization

that, however slack and shallow Captain Golden had been, he had adored her and encouraged her in her gentility, her pawing at culture. With an emerging sincerity, Mrs. Golden mourned him, now, missed his gossipy presence—and at the same time she was alive to the distinction it added to her slim gracefulness to wear black and look wan. She sobbed on Una's shoulder; she said that she was lonely; and Una sturdily comforted her and looked for work.

One of the most familiar human combinations in the world is that of unemployed daughter and widowed mother. A thousand times you have seen the jobless daughter devoting all of her curiosity, all of her youth, to a widowed mother of small pleasantries, a small income, and a shabby security. Thirty comes, and thirty-five. The daughter ages steadily. At forty she is as old as her unwithering mother. Sweet she is, and pathetically hopeful of being a pianist or a nurse; never quite reconciled to spinsterhood, though she often laughs about it; often, by her insistence that she is an "old maid," she makes the thought of her barren age embarrassing to others. The mother is sweet, too, and "wants to keep in touch with her daughter's interests," only, her daughter has no interests. Had the daughter revolted at eighteen, had she stubbornly insisted that mother either accompany her to parties or be content to stay alone, had she acquired "interests," she might have meant something in the new generation; but the time for revolt passes, however much the daughter may long to seem young among younger women. The mother is usually unconscious of her selfishness; she would be unspeakably horrified if some brutal soul told her that she was a vampire. Chance, chance and waste, rule them both, and the world passes by while the mother has her games of cards with daughter, and deems herself unselfish because now and then she lets daughter join a party (only to hasten back to mother), and even "wonders why daughter doesn't take an interest in girls her own age." That ugly couple on the porch of the apple-sauce and wash-pitcher boarding-house—the mother a mute, dwarfish punchinello, and the daughter a drab woman of forty with a mole, a wart, a silence. That charming mother of white hair and real lace with the well-groomed daughter. That comfortable mother at home and daughter in an office, but with no suitors, no ambition beyond the one at home. They are all examples of the mother-and-daughter phenomenon, that most touching, most destructive example of selfless unselfishness, which robs all the generations to come, because mother has never been trained to endure the long, long thoughts of solitude; because she sees nothing by herself, and within herself hears no diverting voice. . . .

There were many such mothers and daughters in Panama. If they were wealthy, daughter collected rents and saw lawyers and belonged to a club and tried to keep youthful at parties. If middle-class, daughter taught school, almost invariably. If poor, mother did the washing and daughter collected it. So it was marked down for Una that she should be a teacher.

Not that she wanted to be a teacher! After graduating from high school, she had spent two miserable terms of teaching in the small white district school, four miles out on the Bethlehem Road. She hated the drive out and back, the airless room and the foul outbuildings, the shy, stupid, staring children, the jolly little arithmetical problems about wall-paper, piles of lumber, the amount of time that notoriously inefficient workmen will take to do "a certain piece of work." Una was honest enough to know that she was not an honest teacher, that she neither

2   [9]

loved masses of other people's children nor had any ideals of developing the new generation. But she had to make money. Of course she would teach!

When she talked over affairs with her tearful mother, Mrs. Golden always ended by suggesting, "I wonder if perhaps you couldn't go back to school-teaching again. Everybody said you were *so* successful. And maybe I could get some needlework to do. I do want to help so much."

Mrs. Golden did, apparently, really want to help. But she never suggested anything besides teaching, and she went on recklessly investing in the nicest mourning. Meantime Una tried to find other work in Panama.

Seen from a balloon, Panama is merely a mole on the long hill-slopes. But to Una its few straggly streets were a whole cosmos. She knew somebody in every single house. She knew just where the succotash, the cake-boxes, the clothes-lines, were kept in each of the grocery-stores, and on market Saturdays she could wait on herself. She summed up the whole town and its possibilities; and she wondered what opportunities the world out beyond Panama had for her. She recalled two trips to Philadelphia and one to Harrisburg. She made out a list of openings with such methodical exactness as she devoted to keeping the dwindling lodge insurance from disappearing altogether. Hers was no poetic outreach like that of the young genius who wants to be off for Bohemia. It was a question of earning money in the least tedious way. Una was facing the feminist problem, without knowing what the word "feminist" meant.

This was her list of fair fields of fruitful labor:

She could—and probably would—teach in some hen-coop of pedagogy.

She could marry, but no one seemed to want her, except

old Henry Carson, the widower, with cartarrh and three children, who called on her and her mother once in two weeks, and would propose whenever she encouraged him to. This she knew scientifically. She had only to sit beside him on the sofa, let her hand drop down beside his. But she positively and ungratefully didn't want to marry Henry and listen to his hawking and his grumbling for the rest of her life. Sooner or later one of The Boys might propose But in a small town it was all a gamble. There weren't so very many desirable young men—most of the energetic ones went off to Philadelphia and New York. True that Jennie McTevish had been married at thirty-one, when everybody had thought she was hopelessly an old maid. Yet here was Birdie Mayberry unmarried at thirty-four, no one could ever understand why, for she had been the prettiest and jolliest girl in town. Una crossed blessed matrimony off the list as a commercial prospect.

She could go off and study music, law, medicine, elocution, or any of that amazing hodge-podge of pursuits which are permitted to small-town women. But she really couldn't afford to do any of these; and, besides, she had no talent for music of a higher grade than Sousa and Victor Herbert; she was afraid of lawyers; blood made her sick; and her voice was too quiet for the noble art of elocution as practised by several satin-waisted, semi-artistic ladies who "gave readings" of *Enoch Arden* and *Evangeline* before the Panama Study Circle and the Panama Annual Chautauqua.

She could have a job selling dry-goods behind the counter in the Hub Store, but that meant loss of caste.

She could teach dancing—but she couldn't dance particularly well. And that was all that she could do.

She had tried to find work as office-woman for Dr. Mayberry, the dentist; in the office of the Panama Wood-

Turning Company; in the post-office; as lofty enthroned cashier for the Hub Store; painting place-cards and making "fancy-work" for the Art Needlework Exchange.

The job behind the counter in the Hub Store was the only one offered her.

"If I were only a boy," sighed Una, "I could go to work in the hardware-store or on the railroad or anywhere, and not lose respectability. Oh, I *hate* being a woman."

§ 3

Una had been trying to persuade her father's old-time rival, Squire Updegraff, the real-estate and insurance man, that her experience with Captain Golden would make her a perfect treasure in the office. Squire Updegraff had leaped up at her entrance, and blared, "Well, well, and how is the little girl making it?" He had set out a chair for her and held her hand. But he knew that her only experience with her father's affairs had been an effort to balance Captain Golden's account-books, which were works of genius in so far as they were composed according to the inspirational method. So there was nothing very serious in their elaborate discussion of giving Una a job.

It was her last hope in Panama. She went disconsolately down the short street, between the two-story buildings and the rows of hitched lumber-wagons. Nellie Page, the town belle, tripping by in canvas sneakers and a large red hair-ribbon, shouted at her, and Charlie Martindale, of the First National Bank, nodded to her, but these exquisites were too young for her; they danced too well and laughed too easily. The person who stopped her for a long curbstone conference about the weather, while most of the town observed and gossiped, was the fateful Henry

Carson. The village sun was unusually blank and hard on Henry's bald spot to-day. *Heavens!* she cried to herself, in almost hysterical protest, would she have to marry Henry?

Miss Mattie Pugh drove by, returning from district school. Miss Mattie had taught at Clark's Crossing for seventeen years, had grown meek and meager and hopeless. *Heavens!* thought Una, would she have to be shut into the fetid barn of a small school unless she married Henry?

"I *won't* be genteel! I'll work in The Hub or any place first!" Una declared. While she trudged home—a pleasant, inconspicuous, fluffy-haired young woman, undramatic as a field daisy—a cataract of protest poured through her. All the rest of her life she would have to meet that doddering old Mr. Mosely, who was unavoidably bearing down on her now, and be held by him in long, meaningless talks. And there was nothing amusing to do! She was so frightfully bored. She suddenly hated the town, hated every evening she would have to spend there, reading newspapers and playing cards with her mother, and dreading a call from Mr. Henry Carson.

She wanted—wanted some one to love, to talk with. Why had she discouraged the beautiful Charlie Martindale, the time he had tried to kiss her at a dance? Charlie was fatuous, but he was young, and she wanted, yes, yes! that was it, she wanted youth, she who was herself so young. And she would grow old here unless some one, one of these godlike young men, condescended to recognize her. Grow old among these streets like piles of lumber.

She charged into the small, white, ambling Golden house, with its peculiar smell of stale lamb gravy, and on the old broken couch—where her father had snored all through every bright Sunday afternoon—she sobbed feebly.

She raised her head to consider a noise overhead—the faint, domestic thunder of a sewing-machine shaking the walls with its rhythm. The machine stopped. She heard the noise of scissors dropped on the floor—the most stuffily domestic sound in the world. The airless house was crushing her. She sprang up—and then she sat down again. There was no place to which she could flee. Henry Carson and the district school were menacing her. And meantime she had to find out what her mother was sewing —whether she had again been wasting money in buying mourning.

"Poor, poor little mother, working away happy up there, and I've got to go and scold you," Una agonized. "Oh, I want to earn money, I want to earn real money for you."

She saw a quadrangle of white on the table, behind a book. She pounced on it. It was a letter from Mrs. Sessions, and Una scratched it open excitedly.

Mr. and Mrs. Albert Sessions, of Panama, had gone to New York. Mr. Sessions was in machinery. They liked New York. They lived in a flat and went to theaters. Mrs. Sessions was a pillowy soul whom Una trusted.

"Why don't you," wrote Mrs. Sessions, "if you don't find the kind of work you want in Panama, think about coming up to New York and taking stenography? There are lots of chances here for secretaries, etc."

Una carefully laid down the letter. She went over and straightened her mother's red wool slippers. She wanted to postpone for an exquisite throbbing moment the joy of announcing to herself that she had made a decision.

She *would* go to New York, become a stenographer, a

secretary to a corporation president, a rich woman, free, responsible.

The fact of making this revolutionary decision so quickly gave her a feeling of power, of already being a business woman.

She galloped up-stairs to the room where her mother was driving the sewing-machine.

"Mumsie!" she cried, "we're going to New York! I'm going to learn to be a business woman, and the little mother will be all dressed in satin and silks, and dine on what-is-it and peaches and cream—the poem don't come out right, but, oh, my little mother, we're going out adventuring, we are!"

She plunged down beside her mother, burrowed her head in her mother's lap, kissed that hand whose skin was like thinnest wrinkly tissue-paper.

"Why, my little daughter, what is it? Has some one sent for us? Is it the letter from Emma Sessions? What did she say in it?"

"She suggested it, but we are going up independent."

"But can we afford to? . . . I would like the draymas and art-galleries and all!"

"We *will* afford to! We'll gamble, for once!"

CHAPTER II

UNA GOLDEN had never realized how ugly and petty were the streets of Panama till that evening when she walked down for the mail, spurning the very dust on the sidewalks—and there was plenty to spurn. An old mansion of towers and scalloped shingles, broken-shuttered now and unpainted, with a row of brick stores marching up on its once leisurely lawn. The town-hall, a square wooden barn with a sagging upper porch, from which the mayor would presumably have made proclamations, had there ever been anything in Panama to proclaim about. Staring loafers in front of the Girard House. To Una there was no romance in the sick mansion, no kindly democracy in the village street, no bare freedom in the hills beyond. She was not much to blame; she was a creature of action to whom this constricted town had denied all action except sweeping.

She felt so strong now—she had expected a struggle in persuading her mother to go to New York, but acquiescence had been easy. Una had an exultant joy, a little youthful and cruel, in meeting old Henry Carson and telling him that she was going away, that she "didn't know for how long; maybe for always." So hopelessly did he stroke his lean brown neck, which was never quite clean-shaven, that she tried to be kind to him. She promised to write. But she felt, when she had left him, as though she had just been released from prison. To live with him, to give him the right to claw at her with those desiccated hands—she imagined it with a vividness which shocked her, all the while she was listening to his halting regrets.

A dry, dusty September wind whirled down the village street. It choked her.

There would be no dusty winds in New York, but only mellow breezes over marble palaces of efficient business. No Henry Carsons, but slim, alert business men, young of eye and light of tongue.

§ 2

Una Golden had expected to thrill to her first sight of the New York sky-line, crossing on the ferry in mid-afternoon, but it was so much like all the post-card views of it, so stolidly devoid of any surprises, that she merely remarked, "Oh yes, there it is, that's where I'll be," and turned to tuck her mother into a ferry seat and count the suit-cases and assure her that there was no danger of pickpockets. Though, as the ferry sidled along the land, passed an English liner, and came close enough to the shore so that she could see the people who actually lived in the state of blessedness called New York, Una suddenly hugged her mother and cried, "Oh, little mother, we're going to live here and do things together—everything."

The familiar faces of Mr. and Mrs. Albert Sessions were awaiting them at the end of the long cavernous walk from the ferry-boat, and New York immediately became a blur of cabs, cobblestones, bales of cotton, long vistas of very dirty streets, high buildings, surface cars, elevateds, shop windows that seemed dark and foreign, and everywhere such a rush of people as made her feel insecure, cling to the Sessionses, and try to ward off the dizziness of the swirl of new impressions. She was daunted for a moment, but she rejoiced in the conviction that she was going to like this madness of multiform energy.

The Sessionses lived in a flat on Amsterdam Avenue near Ninety-sixth Street. They all went up from Cortlandt Street in the Subway, which was still new and miraculous in 1905. For five minutes Una was terrified by the jam of people, the blind roar through tunneled darkness, the sense of being powerlessly hurled forward in a mass of ungovernable steel. But nothing particularly fatal happened; and she grew proud to be part of this black energy, and contentedly swung by a strap.

When they reached the Sessionses' flat and fell upon the gossip of Panama, Pennsylvania, Una was absent-minded —except when the Sessionses teased her about Henry Carson and Charlie Martindale. The rest of the time, curled up on a black-walnut couch which she had known for years in Panama, and which looked plaintively rustic here in New York, Una gave herself up to impressions of the city: the voices of many children down on Amsterdam Avenue, the shriek of a flat-wheeled surface car, the sturdy pound of trucks, horns of automobiles; the separate sounds scarcely distinguishable in a whirr which seemed visible as a thick, gray-yellow dust-cloud.

Her mother went to lie down; the Sessionses (after an elaborate explanation of why they did not keep a maid) began to get dinner, and Una stole out to see New York by herself.

It all seemed different, at once more real and not so jumbled together, now that she used her own eyes instead of the guidance of that knowing old city bird, Mr. Albert Sessions.

Amsterdam Avenue was, even in the dusk of early autumn, disappointing in its walls of yellow flat-buildings cluttered with fire-escapes, the first stories all devoted to the same sort of shops over and over again—delicatessens, laundries, barber-shops, saloons, groceries, lunch-rooms. She ventured down a side-street, toward a furnace-glow of sunset. West End Avenue was imposing to her in its solid brick and graystone houses, and pavements milky in the waning light. Then came a block of expensive apartments. She was finding the city of golden rewards. Frivolous curtains hung at windows; in a huge apartment-house hall she glimpsed a negro attendant in a green uniform with a monkey-cap and close-set rows of brass buttons; she had a hint of palms—or what looked like palms; of marble and mahogany and tiling, and a flash of people in evening dress. In her plain, "sensible" suit Una tramped past. She was unenvious, because she was going to have all these things soon.

Out of a rather stodgy vision of silk opera wraps and suitors who were like floor-walkers, she came suddenly out on Riverside Drive and the splendor of the city.

A dull city of straight-front unvaried streets is New York. But she aspires in her sky-scrapers; she dreams a garden dream of Georgian days in Gramercy Park; and on Riverside Drive she bares her exquisite breast and wantons in beauty. Here she is sophisticated, yet eager, comparable to Paris and Vienna; and here Una exulted.

Down a polished roadway that reflected every light rolled smart motors, with gay people in the sort of clothes she had studied in advertisements. The driveway was bordered with mist wreathing among the shrubs. Above Una shouldered the tremendous façades of gold-corniced apartment-houses. Across the imperial Hudson everything was enchanted by the long, smoky afterglow, against which the silhouettes of dome and tower and factory chimney stood out like an Orient city.

"Oh, I want all this—it's mine! . . . An apartment up

there—a big, broad window-seat, and look out on all this. Oh, dear God," she was unconsciously praying to her vague Panama Wesley Methodist Church God, who gave you things if you were good, "I will work for all this. . . . And for the little mother, dear mother that's never had a chance."

In the step of the slightly stolid girl there was a new lightness, a new ecstasy in walking rapidly through the stirring New York air, as she turned back to the Sessionses' flat.

§ 3

Later, when the streets fell into order and became normal, Una could never quite identify the vaudeville theater to which the Sessionses took them that evening. The gold-and-ivory walls of the lobby seemed to rise immeasurably to a ceiling flashing with frescoes of light lovers in blue and fluffy white, mincing steps and ardent kisses and flaunting draperies. They climbed a tremendous arching stairway of marble, upon which her low shoes clattered with a pleasant sound. They passed niches hung with heavy curtains of plum-colored velvet, framing the sly peep of plaster fauns, and came out on a balcony stretching as wide as the sea at twilight, looking down on thousands of people in the orchestra below, up at a vast golden dome lighted by glowing spheres hung with diamonds, forward at a towering proscenic arch above which slim, nude goddesses in bas-relief floated in a languor which obsessed her, set free the bare brown laughing nymph that hides in every stiff Una in semi-mourning.

Nothing so diverting as that program has ever been witnessed. The funny men with their solemn mock-battles, their extravagance in dress, their galloping wit, made her laugh till she wanted them to stop. The singers were bell-voiced; the dancers graceful as clouds, and just touched with a beguiling naughtiness; and in the playlet there was a chill intensity that made her shudder when the husband accused the wife whom he suspected, oh, so absurdly, as Una indignantly assured herself.

The entertainment was pure magic, untouched by human clumsiness, rare and spellbound as a stilly afternoon in oak woods by a lake.

They went to a marvelous café, and Mr. Sessions astounded them by the urbanity with which he hurried captains and waiters and 'bus-boys, and ordered lobster and coffee, and pretended that he was going to be wicked and have wine and cigarettes.

Months afterward, when she was going to vaudeville by herself, Una tried to identify the theater of wizardry, but she never could. The Sessionses couldn't remember which theater it was; they thought it was the Pitt, but surely they must have been mistaken, for the Pitt was a shanty daubed with grotesque nudes, rambling and pretentious, with shockingly amateurish programs. And afterward, on the occasion or two when they went out to dinner with the Sessionses, it seemed to Una that Mr. Sessions was provincial in restaurants, too deprecatingly friendly with the waiters, too hesitating about choosing dinner.

§ 4

Whiteside and Schleusner's College of Commerce, where Una learned the art of business, occupied only five shabby rooms of crepuscular windows and perpetually dusty corners, and hard, glistening wall-paint, in a converted (but not sanctified) old dwelling-house on West Eighteenth Street. The faculty were six: Mr. Whiteside, an elaborate pomposity who smoothed his concrete brow as though he had a headache, and took obvious pride in being able to draw birds with Spencerian strokes. Mr. Schleusner, who was small and vulgar and *déclassé* and really knew something about business. A shabby man like a broken-down bookkeeper, silent and diligent and afraid. A towering man with a red face, who kept licking his lips with a small red triangle of tongue, and taught English—commercial college English—in a bombastic voice of finicky correctness, and always smelled of cigar smoke. An active young Jewish New-Yorker of wonderful black hair, elfin face, tilted hat, and smart clothes, who did something on the side in real estate. Finally, a thin widow, who was so busy and matter-of-fact that she was no more individualized than a street-car. Any one of them was considered competent to teach any "line," and among them they ground out instruction in shorthand, typewriting, bookkeeping, English grammar, spelling, composition (with a special view to the construction of deceptive epistles), and commercial geography. Once or twice a week, language-masters from a linguistic mill down the street were had in to chatter the more vulgar phrases of French, German, and Spanish.

A cluttered, wheezy omnibus of a school, but in it Una rode to spacious and beautiful hours of learning. It was even more to her than is the art-school to the yearner who has always believed that she has a talent for painting; for the yearner has, even as a child, been able to draw and daub and revel in the results; while for Una this was the first time in her life when her labor seemed to count for something. Her school-teaching had been a mere time-filler. Now she was at once the responsible head of the house and a seer of the future.

Most of the girls in the school learned nothing but shorthand and typewriting, but to these Una added

English grammar, spelling, and letter-composition. After breakfast at the little flat which she had taken with her mother, she fled to the school. She drove into her books, she delighted in the pleasure of her weary teachers when she snapped out a quick answer to questions, or typed a page correctly, or was able to remember the shorthand symbol for a difficult word like "psychologize."

Her belief in the sacredness of the game was boundless.

CHAPTER III

EXCEPT for the young man in the bank, the new young man in the hardware-store, and the proprietors of the new Broadway Clothing Shop, Una had known most of the gallants in Panama, Pennsylvania, from knickerbocker days; she remembered their bony, boyish knees and their school-day whippings too well to be romantic about them. But in the commercial college she was suddenly associated with seventy entirely new and interesting males. So brief were the courses, so irregular the classifications, that there was no spirit of seniority to keep her out of things; and Una, with her fever of learning, her instinctive common sense about doing things in the easiest way, stood out among the girl students. The young men did not buzz about her as they did about the slim, diabolic, star-eyed girl from Brooklyn, in her tempting low-cut blouses, or the intense, curly-headed, boyish, brown Jew girl, or the ardent dancers and gigglers. But Una's self-sufficient eagerness gave a fervor to her blue eyes, and a tilt to her commonplace chin, which made her almost pretty, and the young men liked to consult her about things. She was really more prominent here, in a school of one hundred and seventy, than in her Panama high school with its enrolment of seventy.

Panama, Pennsylvania, had never regarded Una as a particularly capable young woman. Dozens of others were more masterful at trimming the Christmas tree for

THE JOB

Wesley Methodist Church, preparing for the annual picnic of the Art Needlework Coterie, arranging a surprise donation party for the Methodist pastor, even spring house-cleaning. But she had been well spoken of as a marketer, a cook, a neighbor who would take care of your baby while you went visiting—because these tasks had seemed worth while to her. She was more practical than either Panama or herself believed. All these years she had, without knowing that she was philosophizing, without knowing that there was a world-wide inquiry into woman's place, been trying to find work that needed her. Her father's death had freed her; had permitted her to toil for her mother, cherish her, be regarded as useful. Instantly—still without learning that there was such a principle as feminism—she had become a feminist, demanding the world and all the fullness thereof as her field of labor.

And now, in this fumbling school, she was beginning to feel the theory of efficiency, the ideal of Big Business.

For "business," that one necessary field of activity to which the egotistic arts and sciences and theologies and military puerilities are but servants, that long-despised and always valiant effort to unify the labor of the world, is at last beginning to be something more than dirty smithing. No longer does the business man thank the better classes for permitting him to make and distribute bread and motor-cars and books. No longer does he crawl to the church to buy pardon for usury. Business is being recognized—and is recognizing itself—as ruler of the world.

With this consciousness of power it is reforming its old, petty, half-hearted ways; its idea of manufacture as a filthy sort of tinkering; of distribution as chance peddling and squalid shopkeeping; it is feverishly seeking effi-

3   [25]

ciency. . . . In its machinery. . . . But, like all monarchies, it must fail unless it becomes noble of heart. So long as capital and labor are divided, so long as the making of munitions or injurious food is regarded as business, so long as Big Business believes that it exists merely to enrich a few of the lucky or the well born or the nervously active, it will not be efficient, but deficient. But the vision of an efficiency so broad that it can be kindly and sure, is growing—is discernible at once in the scientific business man and the courageous labor-unionist.

That vision Una Golden feebly comprehended. Where she first beheld it cannot be said. Certainly not in the lectures of her teachers, humorless and unvisioned grinds, who droned that by divine edict letters must end with a "yours truly" one space to the left of the middle of the page; who sniffed at card-ledgers as new-fangled nonsense, and, at their most inspired, croaked out such platitudes as: "Look out for the pennies and the pounds will look out for themselves," or "The man who fails is the man who watches the clock."

Nor was the vision of the inspired Big Business that shall be, to be found in the books over which Una labored—the flat, maroon-covered, dusty, commercial geography, the arid book of phrases and rules-of-the-thumb called "Fish's Commercial English," the manual of touch-typewriting, or the shorthand primer that, with its grotesque symbols and numbered exercises and yellow pages dog-eared by many owners, looked like an old-fashioned Arabic grammar headachily perused in some divinity-school library.

Her vision of it all must have come partly from the eager talk of a few of the students—the girl who wasn't ever going to give up her job, even if she did marry; the man who saw a future in these motion pictures; the shaggy-haired zealot who talked about profit-sharing (which was a bold radicalism back in 1905; almost as subversive of office discipline as believing in unions). Partly it came from the new sorts of business magazines for the man who didn't, like his fathers, insist, "I guess I can run my business without any outside interference," but sought everywhere for systems and charts and new markets and the scientific mind.

§ 2

While her power of faith and vision was satisfied by the largeness of the city and by her chance to work, there was quickening in Una a shy, indefinable, inner life of tenderness and desire for love. She did not admit it, but she observed the young men about her with an interest that was as diverting as her ambition.

At first they awed her by their number and their strangeness. But when she seemed to be quite their equal in this school of the timorously clerical, she began to look at them level-eyed. . . . A busy, commonplace, soft-armed, pleasant, good little thing she was; glancing at them through eye-glasses attached to a gold chain over her ear, not much impressed now, slightly ashamed by the delight she took in winning their attention by brilliant recitations. . . . She decided that most of them were earnest-minded but intelligent serfs, not much stronger than the girls who were taking stenography for want of anything better to do. They sprawled and looked vacuous as they worked in rows in the big study-hall, with its hard blue walls showing the marks of two removed partitions, its old iron fireplace stuffed with rubbers and overshoes and crayon-boxes. As a provincial, Una disliked the many Jews among them, and put down their fervor for any

[27]

sort of learning to acquisitiveness. The rest she came to despise for the clumsy slowness with which they learned even the simplest lessons. And to all of them she—who was going to be rich and powerful, directly she was good for one hundred words a minute at stenography!—felt disdainfully superior, because they were likely to be poor the rest of their lives.

In a twilight walk on Washington Heights, a walk of such vigor and happy absorption with new problems as she had never known in Panama, she caught herself being contemptuous about their frayed poverty. With a sharp emotional sincerity, she rebuked herself for such sordidness, mocked herself for assuming that she was already rich.

Even out of this mass of clerklings emerged two or three who were interesting: Sam Weintraub, a young, active, red-headed, slim-waisted Jew, who was born in Brooklyn. He smoked large cigars with an air, knew how to wear his clothes, and told about playing tennis at the Prospect Athletic Club. He would be a smart secretary or confidential clerk some day, Una was certain; he would own a car and be seen in evening clothes and even larger cigars at after-theater suppers. She was rather in awe of his sophistication. He was the only man who made her feel like a Freshman.

J. J. Todd, a reticent, hesitating, hard-working man of thirty, from Chatham on Cape Cod. It was he who, in noon-time arguments, grimly advocated profit-sharing, which Sam Weintraub debonairly dismissed as "socialistic."

And, most appealing to her, enthusiastic young Sanford Hunt, inarticulate, but longing for a chance to attach himself to some master. Weintraub and Todd had desks on either side of her; they had that great romantic virtue.

propinquity. But Sanford Hunt she had noticed, in his corner across the room, because he glanced about with such boyish loneliness.

Sanford Hunt helped her find a rubber in the high-school-like coat-room on a rainy day when the girls were giggling and the tremendous swells of the institution were whooping and slapping one another on the back and acting as much as possible like their ideal of college men— an ideal presumably derived from motion pictures and college playlets in vaudeville. Una saw J. J. Todd gawping at her, but not offering to help, while a foreshortened Sanford groped along the floor, under the dusty line of coats, for her missing left rubber. Sanford came up with the rubber, smiled like a nice boy, and walked with her to the Subway.

He didn't need much encouragement to tell his ambitions. He was twenty-one—three years younger than herself. He was a semi-orphan, born in Newark; had worked up from office-boy to clerk in the office of a huge Jersey City paint company; had saved money to take a commercial course; was going back to the paint company, and hoped to be office-manager there. He had a conviction that "the finest man in the world" was Mr. Claude Lowry, president of the Lowry Paint Company; the next finest, Mr. Ernest Lowry, vice-president and general manager; the next, Mr. Julius Schwirtz, one of the two city salesmen—Mr. Schwirtz having occupied a desk next to his own for two years—and that "*the* best paint on the market to-day is Lowry's Lasting Paint—simply no getting around it."

In the five-minute walk over to the Eighteenth Street station of the Subway, Sanford had lastingly impressed Una by his devotion to the job; eager and faithful as the glory that a young subaltern takes in his regiment. She agreed with him that the dour J. J. Todd was "crazy" in his theories about profit-sharing and selling stocks to employees. While she was with young Sanford, Una found herself concurring that "the bosses know so much better about all those things—gee whiz! they've had so much more experience—besides you can't expect them to give away all their profits to please these walking delegates or a Cape Cod farmer like Todd! All these theories don't do a fellow any good; what he wants is to stick on a job and make good."

Though, in keeping with the general school-boyishness of the institution, the study-room supervisors tried to prevent conversation, there was always a current of whispering and low talk, and Sam Weintraub gave Una daily reports of the tennis, the dances, the dinners at the Prospect Athletic Club. Her evident awe of his urban amusements pleased him. He told his former idol, the slim, blond giggler, that she was altogether too fresh for a Bronx Kid, and he basked in Una's admiration. Through him she had a revelation of the New York in which people actually were born, which they took casually, as she did Panama.

She tried consciously to become a real New-Yorker herself. After lunch—her home-made lunch of sandwiches and an apple—which she ate in the buzzing, gossiping study-hall at noon-hour, she explored the city. Sometimes Sanford Hunt begged to go with her. Once Todd stalked along and embarrassed her by being indignant over an anti-socialist orator in Madison Square. Once, on Fifth Avenue, she met Sam Weintraub, and he nonchalantly pointed out, in a passing motor, a man whom he declared to be John D. Rockefeller.

Even at lunch-hour Una could not come to much understanding with the girls of the commercial college. They seemed alternately third-rate stenographers, and very haughty urbanites who knew all about "fellows" and "shows" and "glad rags." Except for good-natured, square-rigged Miss Moynihan, and the oldish, anxious, industrious Miss Ingalls, who, like Una, came from a small town, and the adorably pretty little Miss Moore, whom you couldn't help loving, Una saw the girls of the school only in a mass.

It was Sam Weintraub, J. J. Todd, and Sanford Hunt whom Una watched and liked, and of whom she thought when the school authorities pompously invited them all to a dance early in November.

§ 3

The excitement, the giggles, the discussions of girdles and slippers and hair-waving and men, which filled the study-hall at noon and the coat-room at closing hour, was like midnight silence compared with the tumult in Una's breast when she tried to make herself believe that either her blue satin evening dress or her white-and-pink frock of "novelty crêpe" was attractive enough for the occasion. The crêpe was the older, but she had worn the blue satin so much that now the crêpe suddenly seemed the newer, the less soiled. After discussions with her mother, which involved much holding up of the crêpe and the tracing of imaginary diagrams with a forefinger, she decided to put a new velvet girdle and new sleeve ruffles on the crêpe, and then she said, "It will have to do."

Very different is the dressing of the girl who isn't quite pretty, nor at all rich, from the luxurious joy which the beautiful woman takes in her new toilettes. Instead of the faint, shivery wonder as to whether men will realize how exquisitely the line of a new bodice accentuates the molding of her neck, the unpretty girl hopes that no one will observe how unevenly her dress hangs, how pointed and red and rough are her elbows, how clumsily waved her hair. "I don't think anybody will notice," she sighs, and is contemptuously conscious of her own stolid, straight, healthy waist, while her mother flutters about and pretends to believe that she is curved like a houri, like Helen of Troy, like Isolde at eighteen.

Una was touched by her mother's sincere eagerness in trying to make her pretty. Poor little mother. It had been hard on her to sit alone all day in a city flat, with no Panama neighbors to drop in on her, no meeting of the Panama Study Club, and with Una bringing home her books to work aloof all evening.

The day before the dance, J. J. Todd dourly asked her if he might call for her and take her home. Una accepted hesitatingly. As she did so, she unconsciously glanced at the decorative Sam Weintraub, who was rocking on his toes and flirting with Miss Moore, the kittenish belle of the school.

She must have worried for fifteen minutes over the question of whether she was going to wear a hat or a scarf, trying to remember the best social precedents of Panama as laid down by Mrs. Dr. Smith, trying to recall New York women as she had once or twice seen them in the evening on Broadway. Finally, she jerked a pale-blue chiffon scarf over her mildly pretty hair, pulled on her new long, white kid gloves, noted miserably that the gloves did not quite cover her pebbly elbows, and snapped at her fussing mother: "Oh, it doesn't matter. I'm a perfect sight, anyway, so what's the use of worrying!"

Her mother looked so hurt and bewildered that Una pulled her down into a chair, and, kneeling on the floor with her arms about her, crooned, "Oh, I'm just nervous, mumsie dear; working so hard and all. I'll have the *best* time, now you've made me so pretty for the dance." Clasped thus, an intense brooding affection holding them and seeming to fill the shabby sitting-room, they waited for the coming of her Tristan, her chevalier, the flat-footed J. J. Todd.

They heard Todd shamble along the hall. They wriggled with concealed laughter and held each other tighter when he stopped at the door of the flat and blew his nervous nose in a tremendous blast. . . . More vulgar possibly than the trumpetry which heralded the arrival of Lancelot at a château, but on the whole quite as effective.

She set out with him, observing his pitiful, home-cleaned, black sack-suit, and home-shined, expansive, black boots and ready-made tie, while he talked easily, and was merely rude about dances and clothes and the weather.

In the study-hall, which had been cleared of all seats except for a fringe along the walls, and was unevenly hung with school flags and patriotic bunting, Una found the empty-headed time-servers, the Little Folk, to whom she was so superior in the class-room. Brooklyn Jews used to side-street dance-halls, Bronx girls who went to the bartenders' ball, and the dinner and grand ball of the Clamchowder Twenty, they laughed and talked and danced—all three at once—with an ease which dismayed her.

To Una Golden, of Panama, the waltz and the two-step were solemn affairs. She could make her feet go in a one-two-three triangle with approximate accuracy, if she didn't take any liberties with them. She was relieved to find that Todd danced with a heavy accuracy which kept her from stumbling. . . . But their performance was solemn and joyless, while by her skipped Sam Weintraub, in evening clothes with black velvet collar and cuffs, swinging and making fantastic dips with the lovely Miss Moore, who cuddled into his arms and swayed to his swing.

"Let's cut out the next," said Todd, and she consented, though Sanford Hunt came boyishly, blushingly up to ask her for a dance. . . . She was intensely aware that she was a wall-flower, in a row with the anxious Miss Ingalls and the elderly frump, Miss Fisle. Sam Weintraub seemed to avoid her, and, though she tried to persuade herself that his greasy, curly, red hair and his pride of evening clothes and sharp face were blatantly Jewish, she knew that she admired his atmosphere of gorgeousness and was in despair at being shut out of it. She even feared that Sanford Hunt hadn't really wanted to dance with her, and she wilfully ignored his frequent glances of friendliness and his efforts to introduce her and his "lady friend." She was silent and hard, while poor Todd, trying not to be a radical and lecture on single-tax or municipal ownership, attempted to be airy about the theater, which meant the one show he had seen since he had come to New York.

From vague dissatisfaction she drifted into an active resentment at being shut out of the world of pretty things, of clinging gowns and graceful movement and fragrant rooms. While Todd was taking her home she was saying to herself over and over, "Nope; it's just as bad as parties at Panama. Never really enjoyed 'em. I'm out of it. I'll stick to my work. Oh, drat it!"

§ 4

Blindly, in a daily growing faith in her commercial future, she shut out the awkward gaieties of the school, ignored Todd and Sanford Hunt and Sam Weintraub, made no effort to cultivate the adorable Miss Moore's rather flattering friendliness for her. She was like a girl grind in a coeducational college who determines to head the class and to that devotes all of a sexless energy.

Only Una was not sexless. Though she hadn't the dancing-girl's oblivious delight in pleasure, though her energetic common sense and willingness to serve had turned into a durable plodding, Una was alive, normal, desirous of love, as the flower-faced girl grind of the college so often is not, to the vast confusion of numerous ardent young gentlemen.

She could not long forbid herself an interest in Sanford Hunt and Sam Weintraub; she even idealized Todd as a humble hero, a self-made and honest man, which he was, though Una considered herself highly charitable to him.

Sweet to her—even when he told her that he was engaged, even when it was evident that he regarded her as an older sister or as a very young and understanding aunt—was Sanford Hunt's liking. "Why do you like me —if you do?" she demanded one lunch-hour, when he had brought her a bar of milk-chocolate.

"Oh, I dun'no'; you're so darn honest, and you got so much more sense than this bunch of Bronx totties. Gee! they'll make bum stenogs. I know. I've worked in an office. They'll keep their gum and a looking-glass in the upper right-hand drawer of their typewriter desks, and the old man will call them down eleventy times a day, and they'll marry the shipping-clerk first time he sneaks out from behind a box. But you got sense, and somehow—gee! I never know how to express things— glad I'm taking this English composition stuff—oh, you just seem to understand a guy. I never liked that Yid Weintraub till you made me see how darn clever and nice he really is, even if he does wear spats."

Sanford told her often that he wished she was going

to come over to the Lowry Paint Company to work, when she finished. He had entered the college before her; he would be through somewhat earlier; he was going back to the paint company and would try to find an opening for her there. He wanted her to meet Mr. Julius Edward Schwirtz, the Manhattan salesman of the company.

When Mr. Schwirtz was in that part of town, interviewing the department-store buyers, he called up Sanford Hunt, and Sanford insisted that she come out to lunch with Schwirtz and himself and his girl. She went shyly.

Sanford's sweetheart proved to be as clean and sweet as himself, but mute, smiling instead of speaking, inclined to admire every one, without much discrimination. Sanford was very proud, very eager as host, and his boyish admiration of all his guests gave a certain charm to the corner of the crude German sausage-and-schnitzel restaurant where they lunched. Una worked at making the party as successful as possible, and was cordial to Mr. Julius Edward Schwirtz, the paint salesman.

Mr. Schwirtz was forty or forty-one, a red-faced, clipped - mustached, derby-hatted average citizen. He was ungrammatical and jocose; he panted a good deal and gurgled his soup; his nails were ragged-edged, his stupid brown tie uneven, and there were signs of a growing grossness and fatty unwieldiness about his neck, his shoulders, his waist. But he was affable. He quietly helped Sanford in ordering lunch, to the great economy of embarrassment. He was smilingly ready to explain to Una how a paint company office was run; what chances there were for a girl. He seemed to know his business, he didn't gossip, and his heavy, coarse-lipped smile was almost sweet when he said to Una, "Makes a hard-cased old widower like me pretty lonely to see this nice kid and girly here. Eh? Wish I had some children like them myself."

He wasn't vastly different from Henry Carson, this Mr. Schwirtz, but he had a mechanical city smartness in his manner and a jocular energy which the stringy-necked Henry quite lacked.

Because she liked to be with Sanford Hunt, hoped to get from Mr. Julius Edward Schwirtz still more of the feeling of how actual business men do business, she hoped for another lunch.

But a crisis unexpected and alarming came to interrupt her happy progress to a knowledge of herself and men.

§ 5

The Goldens had owned no property in Panama, Pennsylvania; they had rented their house. Captain Lew Golden, who was so urgent in advising others to purchase real estate—with a small, justifiable commission to himself—had never quite found time to decide on his own real-estate investments. When they had come to New York, Una and her mother had given up the house and sold the heavier furniture, the big beds, the stove. The rest of the furniture they had brought to the city and installed in a little flat way up on 148th Street.

Her mother was, Una declared, so absolutely the lady that it was a crying shame to think of her immured here in their elevatorless tenement; this new, clean, barren building of yellow brick, its face broken out with fire-escapes. It had narrow halls, stairs of slate treads and iron rails, and cheap wooden doorways which had begun to warp the minute the structure was finished—and sold. The bright-green burlap wall-covering in the hallways had faded in less than a year to the color of dry grass.

THE JOB

The janitor grew tired every now and then. He had been markedly diligent at first, but he was already giving up the task of keeping the building clean. It was one of, and typical of, a mile of yellow brick tenements; it was named after an African orchid of great loveliness, and it was filled with clerks, motormen, probationer policemen, and enormously prolific women in dressing-sacques.

The Goldens had three rooms and bath. A small linoleous gas-stove kitchen. A bedroom with standing wardrobe, iron bed, and just one graceful piece of furniture—Una's dressing-table; a room pervasively feminine in its scent and in the little piles of lingerie which Mrs. Golden affected more, not less, as she grew older. The living-room, with stiff, brown, woolen brocade chairs, transplanted from their Panama home, a red plush sofa, two large oak-framed Biblical pictures—"The Wedding-feast at Cana," and "Solomon in His Temple." This living-room had never been changed since the day of their moving in. Una repeatedly coveted the German color-prints she saw in shop windows, but she had to economize.

She planned that when she should succeed they would have such an apartment of white enamel and glass doors and mahogany as she saw described in the women's magazines. She realized mentally that her mother must be lonely in the long hours of waiting for her return, but she who was busy all day could never feel emotionally how great was that loneliness, and she expected her mother to be satisfied with the future.

Quite suddenly, a couple of weeks after the dance, when they were talking about the looming topic—what kind of work Una would be able to get when she should have completed school — her mother fell violently a-weeping; sobbed, "Oh, Una baby, I want to go home. I'm so lonely here—just nobody but you and the Sessionses. Can't we go back to Panama? You don't seem to really know what you *are* going to do."

"Why, mother—"

Una loved her mother, yet she felt a grim disgust, rather than pity. . . . Just when she had been working so hard! And for her mother as much as for herself. . . . She stalked over to the table, severely rearranged the magazines, slammed down a newspaper, and turned, angrily. "Why, can't you see? I *can't* give up my work now."

"Couldn't you get something to do in Panama, dearie?"

"You know perfectly well that I tried."

"But maybe now, with your college course and all— even if it took a little longer to get something there, we'd be right among the folks we know—"

"Mother, can't you understand that we have only a little over three hundred dollars now? If we moved again and everything, we wouldn't have two hundred dollars to live on. Haven't you *any* sense of finances?"

"You must not talk to me that way, my daughter!"

A slim, fine figure of hurt dignity, Mrs. Golden left the room, lay down in the bedroom, her face away from the door where Una stood in perplexity. Una ran to her, kissed her shoulder, begged for forgiveness. Her mother patted her cheek, and sobbed, "Oh, it doesn't matter," in a tone so forlorn and lonely that it did matter, terribly. The sadness of it tortured Una while she was realizing that her mother had lost all practical comprehension of the details of life, was become a child, trusting everything to her daughter, yet retaining a power of suffering such as no child can know.

It had been easy to bring her mother here, to start a career. Both of them had preconceived a life of gaiety and beauty, of charming people and pictures and concerts. But all those graces were behind a dusty wall of shorthand and typewriting. Una's struggle in coming to New York had just begun.

Gently arbitrary, dearer than ever to Una in her helpless longing for kindly neighbors and the familiar places, Mrs. Golden went on hoping that she could persuade Una to go back to Panama. She never seemed to realize that their capital wasn't increasing as time passed. Sometimes impatient at her obtuseness, sometimes passionate with comprehending tenderness, Una devoted herself to her, and Mr. Schwirtz and Sanford Hunt and Sam Weintraub and Todd faded. She treasured her mother's happiness at their Christmas dinner with the Sessionses. She encouraged the Sessionses to come up to the flat as often as they could, and she lulled her mother to a tolerable calm boredom. Before it was convenient to think of men again, her school-work was over.

The commercial college had a graduation once a month. On January 15, 1906, Una finished her course, regretfully said good-by to Sam Weintraub, and to Sanford Hunt, who had graduated in mid-December, but had come back for "class commencement"; and at the last moment she hesitated so long over J. J. Todd's hints about calling some day, that he was discouraged and turned away. Una glanced about the study-hall—the first place where she had ever been taken seriously as a worker—and marched off to her first battle in the war of business.

CHAPTER IV

SANFORD HUNT telephoned to Una that he and Mr. Julius Edward Schwirtz — whom he called "Eddie"—had done their best to find an "opening" for her in the office of the Lowry Paint Company, but that there was no chance.

The commercial college gave her the names of several possible employers, but they all wanted approximate perfection at approximately nothing a week. After ten days of panic-stricken waiting at the employment office of a typewriter company, and answering want advertisements, the typewriter people sent her to the office of the *Motor and Gas Gazette*, a weekly magazine for the trade. In this atmosphere of the literature of lubricating oil and drop forgings and body enamels, as an eight-dollar-a-week copyist, Una first beheld the drama and romance of the office world.

§ 2

There is plenty of romance in business. Fine, large, meaningless, general terms like romance and business can always be related. They take the place of thinking, and are highly useful to optimists and lecturers.

But in the world of business there is a bewildered new Muse of Romance, who is clad not in silvery tissue of dreams, but in a neat blue suit that won't grow too shiny under the sleeves.

Adventure now, with Una, in the world of business;

4 [41]

of offices and jobs and tired, ordinary people who know such reality of romance as your masquerading earl, your shoddy Broadway actress, or your rosily amorous dairy-maid could never imagine. The youths of poetry and of the modern motor-car fiction make a long diversion of love; while the sleezy-coated office-man who surprises a look of humanness in the weary eyes of the office-woman, knows that he must compress all the wonder of madness into five minutes, because the Chief is prowling about, glancing meaningly at the little signs that declare, "Your time is your employer's money; don't steal it."

A world is this whose noblest vista is composed of desks and typewriters, filing-cases and insurance calendars, telephones, and the bald heads of men who believe dreams to be idiotic. Here, no galleon breasts the sky-line; no explorer in evening clothes makes love to an heiress. Here ride no rollicking cowboys, nor heroes of the great European war. It is a world whose crises you cannot comprehend unless you have learned that the difference between a 2-A pencil and a 2-B pencil is at least equal to the contrast between London and Tibet; unless you understand why a normally self-controlled young woman may have a week of tragic discomfort because she is using a billing-machine instead of her ordinary correspondence typewriter. The shifting of the water-cooler from the front office to the packing-room may be an epochal event to a copyist who apparently has no human existence beyond bending over a clacking typewriter, who seems to have no home, no family, no loves; in whom all pride and wonder of life and all transforming drama seem to be satisfied by the possession of a new V-necked blouse. The moving of the water-coolor may mean that she must now pass the sentinel office-manager; that therefore she no longer dares break the incredible monotony by expeditions to get glasses of water. As a consequence she gives up the office and marries unhappily.

A vast, competent, largely useless cosmos of offices. It spends much energy in causing advertisements of beer and chewing-gum and union suits and pot-cleansers to spread over the whole landscape. It marches out ponderous battalions to sell a brass pin. It evokes shoes that are uncomfortable, hideous, and perishable, and touchingly hopes that all women will aid the cause of good business by wearing them. It turns noble valleys into fields for pickles. It compels men whom it has never seen to toil in distant factories and produce useless wares, which are never actually brought into the office, but which it nevertheless sells to the heathen in the Solomon Islands in exchange for commodities whose very names it does not know; and in order to perform this miracle of transmutation it keeps stenographers so busy that they change from dewy girls into tight-lipped spinsters before they discover life.

The reason for it all, nobody who is actually engaged in it can tell you, except the bosses, who believe that these sacred rites of composing dull letters and solemnly filing them away are observed in order that they may buy the large automobiles in which they do not have time to take the air. Efficiency of production they have learned; efficiency of life they still consider an effeminate hobby.

An unreasonable world, sacrificing bird-song and tranquil dusk and high golden noons to selling junk—yet it rules us. And life lives there. The office is filled with thrills of love and distrust and ambition. Each alley between desks quivers with secret romance as ceaselessly as a battle-trench, or a lane in Normandy.

THE JOB

§ 3

Una's first view of the *Motor and Gas Gazette* was of an overwhelming mass of desks and files and books, and a confusing, spying crowd of strange people, among whom the only safe, familiar persons were Miss Moynihan, the good-natured solid block of girl whom she had known at the commercial college, and Mr. S. Herbert Ross, the advertising-manager, who had hired her. Mr. Ross was a poet of business; a squat, nervous little man, whose hair was cut in a Dutch bang, straight across his forehead, and who always wore a black bow tie and semi-clerical black clothes. He had eyed Una amusedly, asked her what was her reaction to green and crimson posters, and given her a little book by himself, "R U A Time-clock, Mr. Man?" which, in large and tremendously black type, related two stories about the youth of Carnegie, and strongly advocated industry, correspondence schools, and expensive advertising. When Una entered the office, as a copyist, Mr. S. Herbert Ross turned her over to the office-manager, and thereafter ignored her; but whenever she saw him in pompous conference with editors and advertisers she felt proudly that she knew him.

The commercial college had trained her to work with a number of people, as she was now to do in the office; but in the seriousness and savage continuity of its toil, the office was very different. There was no let-up; she couldn't shirk for a day or two, as she had done at the commercial college. It was not so much that she was afraid of losing her job as that she came to see herself as part of a chain. The others, beyond, were waiting for her; she mustn't hold them up. That was her first impression of the office system, that and the insignificance of herself in the presence of the office-hierarchy—manager above manager and the Mysterious Owner beyond all. She was alone; once she transgressed they would crush her. They had no personal interest in her, none of them, except her classmate, Miss Moynihan, who smiled at her and went out to lunch with her.

They two did not dare to sit over parcels of lunch with the curious other girls. Before fifteen-cent lunches of baked apples, greasy Napoleons, and cups of coffee, at a cheap restaurant, Miss Moynihan and she talked about the office-manager, the editors, the strain of copying all day, and they united in lyric hatred of the lieutenant of the girls, a satiric young woman who was a wonderful hater. Una had regarded Miss Moynihan as thick and stupid, but not when she had thought of falling in love with Charlie Martindale at a dance at Panama, not in her most fervid hours of comforting her mother, had she been so closely in sympathy with any human being as she was with Miss Moynihan when they went over and over the problems of office politics, office favorites, office rules, office customs.

The customs were simple: Certain hours for arrival, for lunch, for leaving; women's retiring-room embarrassedly discovered to be on the right behind the big safe; water-cooler in the center of the stenographers' room. But the office prejudices, the taboos, could not be guessed. They offered you every possible chance of "queering yourself." Miss Moynihan, on her very first day, discovered, perspiringly, that you must never mention the *Gazette's* rival, the *Internal Combustion News*. The *Gazette's* attitude was that the *News* did not exist— except when the *Gazette* wanted the plate of an advertisement which the *News* was to forward. You mustn't chew gum in the office; you were to ask favors of the lieutenant, not of the office-manager; and you mustn't be friendly

with Mr. Bush of the circulation department, nor with
Miss Caldwell, the filing-clerk. Why they were taboo
Una never knew; it was an office convention; they seemed
pleasant and proper people enough.

She was initiated into the science of office supplies.
In the commercial college the authorities had provided
stenographers' note-books and pencils, and the representatives of typewriter companies had given lectures on
cleaning and oiling typewriters, putting in new ribbons,
adjusting tension-wheels. But Una had not realized how
many tools she had to know——

Desks, filing-cabinets, mimeographs, adding-machines,
card indexes, desk calendars, telephone-extensions, ad-
justable desk-lights. Wire correspondence-baskets, eras-
ers, carbon paper, type-brushes, dust-rags, waste-baskets.
Pencils, hard and soft, black and blue and red. Pens,
pen-points, backing-sheets, note-books, paper-clips. Muci-
lage, paste, stationery; the half-dozen sorts of envelopes
and letter-heads.

Tools were these, as important in her trade as the mast-
head and black flag, the cutlasses and crimson sashes, the
gold doubloons and damsels fair of pirate fiction; or the
cheese and cream, old horses and slumberous lanes of
rustic comedy. As important, and perhaps to be deemed
as romantic some day; witness the rhapsodic advertisements of filing-cabinets that are built like battle-ships;
of carbon-paper that is magic-inked and satin-smooth.

Not as priest or soldier or judge does youth seek honor
to-day, but as a man of offices. The business subaltern,
charming and gallant as the jungle-gallopers of Kipling,
drills files, not of troops, but of correspondence. The
artist plays the keys, not of pianos, but of typewriters.
Desks, not decks; courts of office-buildings, not of palaces—
these are the stuff of our latter-day drama. Not through

wolf-haunted forests nor purple cañons, but through tiled hallways and elevators move our heroes of to-day.

And our heroine is important not because she is an Amazon or a Ramona, but because she is representative of some millions of women in business, and because, in a vague but undiscouraged way, she keeps on inquiring what women in business can do to make human their existence of loveless routine.

§ 4

Una spent much of her time in copying over and over—a hundred times, two hundred times—form-letters soliciting advertising, letters too personal in appearance to be multigraphed. She had lists of manufacturers of motor-car accessories, of makers of lubricating oils, of distributors of ball-bearings and speedometers and springs and carburetors and compositions for water-proofing automobile tops.

Sometimes she was requisitioned by the editorial department to copy in form legible for the printer the rough items sent in by outsiders for publication in the *Gazette*. Una, like most people of Panama, had believed that there was something artistic about the office of any publication. One would see editors—wonderful men like grand dukes, prone to lunch with the President. But there was nothing artistic about the editorial office of the *Gazette*—several young men in shirt-sleeves and green celluloid eye-shades, very slangy and pipe-smelly, and an older man with unpressed trousers and ragged mustache. Nor was there anything literary in the things that Una copied for the editorial department; just painfully handwritten accounts of the meeting of the Southeastern Iowa Auto-dealers' Association; or boasts about the increased sales of Roadeater Tires, a page originally smartly typed, but cut and marked up by the editors.

Lists and letters and items, over and over; sitting at her typewriter till her shoulder-blades ached and she had to shut her eyes to the blur of the keys. The racket of office noises all day. The three-o'clock hour when she felt that she simply could not endure the mill till five o'clock. No interest in anything she wrote. Then the blessed hour of release, the stretching of cramped legs, and the blind creeping to the Subway, the crush in the train, and home to comfort the mother who had been lonely all day.

Such was Una's routine in these early months of 1906. After the novelty of the first week it was all rigidly the same, except that distinct personalities began to emerge from the mass.

Especially the personality of Walter Babson.

§ 5

Out of the mist of strange faces, blurred hordes of people who swaggered up the office aisle so knowingly, and grinned at her when she asked questions, individualities began to take form:

Miss Moynihan; the Jewish stenographer with the laughing lips and hot eyes; the four superior older girls in a corner, the still more superior girl lieutenant, and the office-manager, who was the least superior of all; the telephone-girl; the office-boys; Mr. S. Herbert Ross and his assistant; the managing editor; a motor magnate whose connection was mysterious; the owner, a courteous, silent, glancing man who was reported to be hard and "stingy."

Other people still remained unidentifiable to her, but the office appeared smaller and less formidable in a month.

THE JOB

Out of each nine square feet of floor space in the office a novel might have been made: the tale of the managing editor's neurotic wife; the tragedy of Chubby Hubbard, the stupid young editor who had been a college football star, then an automobile racer, then a failure. And indeed there was a whole novel, a story told and retold, in the girls' gossip about each of the men before whom they were so demure. But it was Walter Babson whom the girls most discussed and in whom Una found the most interest.

On her first day in the office she had been startled by an astounding young man who had come flying past her desk, with his coat off, his figured waistcoat half open, his red four-in-hand tie askew under a rolling soft collar. He had dashed up to the office-manager and demanded, "Say! Say! Nat! Got that Kokomobile description copied for me yet? Heh? Gawd! you're slow. Got a cigarette?" He went off, puffing out cigarette smoke, shaking his head and audibly muttering, "Slow bunch, werry." He seemed to be of Una's own age, or perhaps a year older—a slender young man with horn-rimmed eye-glasses, curly black hair, and a trickle of black mustache. His sleeves were rolled up to his elbow, and Una had a secret, shamed, shivering thrill in the contrast of the dead-white skin of his thin forearms with the long, thick, soft, black hairs matted over them. They seemed at once feminine and acidly male.

"Crazy idiot," she observed, apparently describing herself and the nervous young man together. But she knew that she wanted to see him again.

She discovered that he was prone to such violent appearances; that his name was Walter Babson; that he was one of the three desk editors under the managing editor; that the stenographers and office-boys alternately

disapproved of him, because he went on sprees and borrowed money from anybody in sight, and adored him
because he was democratically frank with them. He was
at once a hero, clown, prodigal son, and preacher of honesty. It was variously said that he was a socialist, an
anarchist, and a believer in an American monarchy, which
he was reported as declaring would "give some color to
this flat-faced province of a country." It was related that
he had been "fresh" even to the owner, and had escaped
discharge only by being the quickest worker in the office,
the best handy man at turning motor statistics into lively
news-stories. Una saw that he liked to stand about,
bawling to the quizzical S. Herbert Ross that "this is
a hell of a shop to work in—rotten pay and no *esprit de
corps.* I'd quit and free-lance if I could break in with
fiction, but a rotten bunch of log-rollers have got
the inside track with all the magazines and book-
publishers."

"Ever try to write any fiction?" Una once heard S.
Herbert retort.

"No, but Lord! any fool could write better stuff than
they publish. It's all a freeze-out game; editors just accept stuff by their friends."

In one week Una heard Walter Babson make approximately the same assertions to three different men, and to
whoever in the open office might care to listen and profit
thereby. Then, apparently, he ceased to hear the call of
literature, and he snorted at S. Herbert Ross's stodgy
assistant that he was a wage-slave, and a fool not to form
a clerks' union. In a week or two he was literary again.
He dashed down to the office-manager, poked a sheet of
copy-paper at him, and yelped: "Say, Nat. Read that
and tell me just what you think of it. I'm going to put
some literary flavor into the *Gas-bag* even if it does explode

it. Look—see. I've taken a boost for the Kells Karburetor—rotten lying boost it is, too—and turned it into
this running verse, read it like prose, pleasant and easy
to digest, especially beneficial to children and S. Herbert
Souse, Sherbert Souse, I mean." He rapidly read an
amazing lyric beginning, "Motorists, you hadn't better
monkey with the carburetor, all the racers, all the swells,
have equipped their cars with Kells. We are privileged
to announce what will give the trade a jounce, that the
floats have been improved like all motorists would have
loved."

He broke off and shouted, "Punk last line, but I'll fix
it up. Say, that 'll get 'em all going, eh? Say, I bet the
Kells people use it in bill-board ads. all over the country,
and maybe sign my name. Ads., why say, it takes a
literary guy to write ads., not a fat-headed commercialist
like S. Charlie Hoss."

Two days later Una heard Babson come out and lament
that the managing editor didn't like his masterpiece and
was going to use the Kells Karburetor Kompany's original
write-up. "That's what you get when you try to give the
Gas-bag some literary flavor—don't appreciate it!"

She would rather have despised him, except that he
stopped by the office-boys' bench to pull their hair and
tell them to read English dictionaries. And when Miss
Moynihan looked dejected, Babson demanded of her,
"What's trouble, girlie? Anybody I can lick for you?
Glad to fire the owner, or anything. Haven't met you
yet, but my name is Roosevelt, and I'm the new janitor,"
with a hundred other chuckling idiocies, till Miss Moynihan was happy again. Una warmed to his friendliness,
like that of a tail-wagging little yellow pup.

And always she craved the touch of his dark, blunt,
nervous hands. Whenever he lighted a cigarette she was

startled by his masculine way of putting out the match and jerking it away from him in one abrupt motion. . . . She had never studied male mannerisms before. To Miss Golden of Panama men had always been "the boys."

All this time Walter Babson had never spoken to her.

CHAPTER V

THE office-manager came casually up to Una's desk and said, "You haven't taken any dictation yet, have you?"

"No, but," with urgent eagerness, "I'd like— I'm quite fast in stenography."

"Well, Mr. Babson, in the editorial department, wants to give some dictation and you might try—"

Una was so excited that she called herself a silly little fool. She seized her untouched note-book, her pencils sharpened like lances, and tried to appear a very mouse of modesty as she marched down the office to take her first real dictation, to begin her triumphant career. . . . And to have Walter Babson, the beloved fool, speak to her.

It was a cold shock to have to stand waiting behind Babson while he rummaged in his roll-top desk and apparently tried to pull out his hair. He looked back at her and blurted, "Oh! You, Miss Golden? They said you'd take some dictation. Chase those blue-prints off that chair and sit down. Be ready in a sec."

While she sat on the edge of the chair Babson yanked out drawers, plunged his wriggling hands into folders, thrashed through a pile of papers and letters that overflowed a wire basket, and even hauled a dictionary down from the top of the desk and hopefully peered inside the front cover. All the time he kept up comment at which Una smiled doubtfully, not quite sure whether it was meant for her or not:

"Now what the doggone doggonishness did I ever do with those doggone notes, anyway? I ask you, in the— Here they— Nope—"

At last he found inside a book on motor fuels the wad of copy-paper on which he had scrawled notes with a broad, soft pencil, and he began to dictate a short article on air-cooling. Una was terrified lest she be unable to keep up, but she had read recent numbers of the *Gazette* thoroughly, she had practised the symbols for motor technologies, and she was not troubled by being watched. Indeed, Babson seemed to have enough to do in keeping his restless spirit from performing the dismaying feat of leaping straight out of his body. He leaned back in his revolving desk-chair with a complaining squawk from the spring, he closed his eyes, put his fingers together piously, then seized the chair-arms and held them, while he cocked one eye open and squinted at a large alarm-clock on the desk. He sighed profoundly, bent forward, gazed at his ankle, and reached forward to scratch it. All this time he was dictating, now rapidly, now gurgling and grunting while he paused to find a word.

"Don't be so *nervous!*" Una wanted to scream at him, and she wanted to add, "You didn't ask my permission!" when he absently fumbled in a cigarette-box.

She didn't like Walter Babson, after all!

But he stopped after a rhapsody on the divine merits of an air-cooling system, clawed his billowing black hair, and sighed, "Sounds improbable, don't it? Must be true, though; it's going to appear in the *Gazette*, and that's the motor-dealer's bible. If you don't believe it, read the blurbs we publish about ourselves!" Then he solemnly winked at her and went on dictating.

When he had finished he demanded, "Ever take any dictation in this office before?"

"No, sir."

"Ever take any motor dictation at all?"

"No, sir."

"Then you'd better read that back to me. Your immejit boss—the office-manager—is all right, but the secretary of the company is always pussy-footing around, and if you're ever having any trouble with your stuff when old plush-ears is in sight, keep on typing fast, no matter what you put down. Now read me the dope."

It was approximately correct. He nodded, and, "Good work, little girl," he said. "You'll get along all right. You get my dictation better than that agitated antelope Miss Harman does, right now. That's all."

§ 2

So far as anything connected with Walter Babson could be regular, Una became his regular stenographer, besides keeping up her copying. He was always rushing out, apologizing for troubling her, sitting on the edge of her desk, dictating a short letter, and advising her to try his latest brand of health food, which, this spring, was bran biscuits—probably combined with highballs and too much coffee. The other stenographers winked at him, and he teased them about their coiffures and imaginary sweethearts. . . . For three days the women's coat-room boiled with giggles over Babson's declaration that Miss Mac-Throstle was engaged to a burglar, and was taking a correspondence course in engraving in order to decorate her poor dear husband's tools with birds and poetic mottoes.

Babson was less jocular with Una than with the bouncing girls who were natives of Harlem. But he smiled at her, as though they were understanding friends, and once he said, but quietly, rather respectfully, "You have nice hair—soft." She lay awake to croon that to herself, though she denied that she was in love with this eccentric waster.

Always Babson kept up his ejaculations and fidgeting. He often accused himself of shiftlessness and begged her to make sure that he dictated certain matter before he escaped for the evening. "Come in and bother the life out of me. Come in every half-hour," he would say. When she did come in he would crow and chuckle, "Nope. I refuse to be tempted yet; I am a busy man. But maybe I'll give you those verbal jewels of great price on your next visitation, oh thou in the vocative—some Latin scholar, eh? Keep it up, kid; good work. Maybe you'll keep me from being fired."

Usually he gave her the dictation before he went. But not always. And once he disappeared for four days—on a drunk, everybody said, in excited office gossip.

During Babson's desertion the managing editor called Una in and demanded, "Did Mr. Babson give you some copy about the Manning Wind Shield? No? Will you take a look in his desk for his notes about it?"

While Una was fumbling for the notes she did not expect to find, she went through all the agony of the little shawled foreign wife for the husband who has been arrested.

"I've got to help you!" she said to *his* desk, to his bag of Bull Durham, to his alarm-clock—even to a rather shocking collection of pictures of chorus-girls and diaphanously-clad dancers which was pasted inside the double drawer on the right side of the desk. In her great surge of emotion, she noticed these posturing hussies far less than she did a little volume of Rosetti, or the overshoes whose worn toes suddenly revealed to her that Walter Babson, the editor, was not rich—was not, perhaps, so very much better paid than herself.

She did not find the notes. She had to go to the managing editor, trembling, all her good little heart wild with pain. The editor's brows made a V at her report, and he grunted, "Well—"

For two days, till Walter Babson returned, she never failed to look up when the outer door of the office opened.

She found herself immensely interested in trying to discover, from her low plane as copyist, just what sort of a position Walter Babson occupied up among the select souls. Nor was it very difficult. The editor's stenographer may not appreciate all the subtleties of his wit, and the refinements of his manner may leave her cold, but she does hear things, she hears the Big Chief's complaints.

Una discovered that the owner and the managing editor did not regard Walter Babson as a permanent prop of the institution; that they would keep him, at his present salary of twenty-five dollars a week, only till some one happened in who would do the same work for less money. His prose was clever but irregular; he wasn't always to be depended upon for grammar; in everything he was unstable; yet the owner's secretary reported the owner as saying that some day, if Babson married the right woman, he would "settle down and make good."

Una did not dare to make private reservations regarding what "the right woman" ought to mean in this case, but she burned at the thought of Walter Babson's marrying, and for an instant she saw quite clearly the film of soft dark hair that grew just below his sharp cheek-bone. But she forgot the sweetness of the vision in scorn of herself for even thinking of marriage with a weakling; scorn of herself for aspiring to marry a man who regarded her as only a dull stenographer; and a maternal anxiety over him that was untouched by passion.

5

THE JOB

Babson returned to the office, immaculate, a thin, fiery soul. But he was closeted with the secretary of the company for an hour, and when he came out his step was slow. He called for Una and dictated articles in a quiet voice, with no jesting. His hand was unsteady, he smoked cigarettes constantly, and his eye was an unwholesome yellow.

She said to him suddenly, a few days later, "Mr. Babson, I'd be glad if I could take care of any papers or anything for you."

"Thanks. You might stick these chassis sketches away some place right now."

So she was given the chance to keep his desk straight. He turned to her for everything.

He said to her, abruptly, one dreary late afternoon of April when she felt immensely languid and unambitious: "You're going to succeed—unless you marry some dub. But there's one rule for success—mind you, I don't follow it myself, I *can't*, but it's a grand old hunch: 'If you want to get on, always be ready to occupy the job just ahead of you.' Only—what the devil *is* the job just ahead of a stenog.? I've been thinking of you and wondering. What is it?"

"Honestly, Mr. Babson, I don't know. Here, anyway. Unless it's lieutenant of the girls."

"Well—oh, that's just miffle-business, that kind of a job. Well, you'd better learn to express yourself, anyway. Some time you women folks will come into your own with both feet. Whenever you get the chance, take my notes and try to write a better spiel from them than I do. . . . That won't be hard, I guess!"

"I don't know why you are so modest, Mr. Babson. Every girl in the office thinks you write better than any of the other editors."

"Yuh—but they don't know. They think that just because I chuck 'em under the chin. I can't do this technical stuff. . . . Oh, *Lord!* what an evening it 'll be! . . . I suppose I'll go to a show. Nice, lonely city, what? . . . You come from here?"

"From Pennsylvania."

"Got any folks?"

"My mother is here with me."

"That's nice. I'll take her and you to some bum two-bit vaudeville show some night, if you'd like. . . . Got to show my gratitude to you for standing my general slovenliness. . . . Lord! nice evening—dine at a rôtisserie with a newspaper for companion. Well—g' night and g' luck."

Una surprised her mother, when they were vivisecting the weather after dinner, by suddenly crying all over the sofa cushions.

She knew all of Walter Babson's life from those two or three sentences of his.

§ 3

François Villons America has a-plenty. An astonishing number of Americans with the literary itch do contrive to make a living out of that affliction. They write motion-picture scenarios and fiction for the magazines that still regard detective stories as the zenith of original art. They gather in woman-scented flats to discuss sex, or in hard-voiced groups to play poker. They seem to find in the creation of literature very little besides a way of evading regular office hours. Below this stratum of people so successful that one sometimes sees their names in print is the yearning band of young men who want to write. Just to write—not to write anything in particular; not to express any definite thought, but to be literary, to be Bohemian, to dance with slim young authoresses of easy morals, and be jolly dogs and free souls. Some of them are dramatists with unacted dramas; some of them do free verse which is just as free as the productions of regular licensed poets. Some of them do short stories—striking, rather biological, very destructive of conventions. Some of them are ever so handy at all forms; they are perennial candidates for any job as book-reviewer, dramatic critic, or manuscript-reader, since they have the naïve belief that these occupations require neither toil nor training, and enable one to "write on the side." Meanwhile they make their livings as sub-editors on trade journals, as charity-workers, or as assistants to illiterate literary agents.

To this slum of literature Walter Babson belonged. He felt that he was an author, though none of his poetry had ever been accepted, and though he had never got beyond the first chapter of any of his novels, nor the first act of any of his plays (which concerned authors who roughly resembled Walter Babson).

He was distinguished from his fellows by the fact that each year he grew more aware that he hadn't even a dim candle of talent; that he was ill-planned and unpurposed; that he would have to settle down to the ordinary gray limbo of jobs and offices—as soon as he could get control of his chaotic desires. Literally, he hated himself at times; hated his own egotism, his treacherous appetite for drink and women and sloth, his imitative attempts at literature. But no one knew how bitterly he despised himself, in lonely walks in the rain, in savage pacing about his furnished room. To others he seemed vigorously conceited, cock-sure, noisily ready to blame the world for his own failures.

Walter Babson was born in Kansas. His father was a

farmer and horse-doctor, a heavy drinker, an eccentric who joined every radical political movement. In a country school, just such a one as Una had taught, then in high school in a near-by town, Walter had won all the prizes for essays and debating, and had learned a good deal about Shakespeare and Cæsar and George Washington. Also he had learned a good deal about drinking beer, smoking manfully, and tempting the giggling girls who hung about the "deepot." He ran away from high school, and in the most glorious years of his life worked his way down the Mississippi and up the Rio Grande, up to Alaska and down to Costa Rica, a butt and jester for hoboes, sailors, longshoremen, miners, cow-punchers, lunch-room owners, and proprietors of small newspapers. He learned to stick type and run a press. He returned to Kansas and worked on a country newspaper, studying poetry and college-entrance requirements in the evening. He had, at this time, the not entirely novel idea that "he ought to be able to make a lot of good fiction out of all his experiences." Actually, he had no experiences, because he had no instinct for beauty. The proof is that he read quite solemnly and reverently a vile little periodical for would-be authors, which reduced authorship to a way of earning one's living by supplying editors with cheap but ingenious items to fill space. It put literature on a level with keeping a five-and-ten-cent store. But Walter conned its pompous trade journal discussions as to whether the name and address of the author should be typed on the left or the right side of the first page of a manuscript; its lively little symposia, by such successful market-gardeners of literature as Mamie Stuyvesant Blupp and Bill Brown and Dr. J. F. Fitzneff, on the inspiring subject of whether it paid better to do filler verse for cheap magazines, or long verse for the big magazines. At the end, this almost madly idealistic journal gave a list of wants of editors; the editor of *Lingerie and Laughter* wanted "short, snappy stuff with a kick in it; especially good yarns about models, grisettes, etc." *Wanderlust* was in the market for "stories with a punch that appealed to every red-blooded American; nothing about psychology, problems, Europe, or love wanted." *The Plymouth Rock Fancier* announced that it could use "a good, lively rural poem every week; must be clean and original."

Pathos there was in all of this; the infinitely little men and women daring to buy and sell "short, snappy stuff" in this somber and terribly beautiful world of Balzac and Wells and Turgenieff. And pathos there was in that wasted year when Walter Babson sought to climb from the gossiping little prairie town to the grandeur of great capitals by learning to be an efficient manufacturer of "good, lively rural poems." He neglected even his college-entrance books, the Ruskin whose clots of gilt might have trained him to look for real gold, and the stilted Burke who might have given him a vision of empires and races and social destinies. And for his pathetic treachery he wasn't even rewarded. His club-footed verses were always returned with printed rejection slips.

When at last he barely slid into Jonathan Edwards College, Iowa, Walter was already becoming discouraged; already getting the habit of blaming the gods, capitalists, editors, his father, the owner of the country newspaper on which he had been working, for everything that went wrong. He yammered destructive theories which would have been as obnoxious to a genuine fighting revolutionist as they were sacrilegious to his hard-fisted, earnest, rustic classmates in Jonathan Edwards. For Walter was not protesting against social injustice. The slavery of rubber-gatherers in the Putumayo and of sweatshop-workers in

New York did not exist for him. He was protesting because, at the age of twenty, his name was not appearing in large flattering capitals on the covers of magazines.

Yet he was rather amusing; he helped plodding classmates with their assignments, and he was an active participant in all worthy movements to raise hell—as they admirably described it. By the end of his Freshman year he had given up all attempts to be a poet and to extract nourishment from the college classes, which were as hard and unpalatable as dried codfish. He got drunk, he vented his energy in noisy meetings with itinerant *filles de joie*, who were as provincial and rustic, as bewildered and unfortunate as the wild country boys, who in them found their only outlet for youth's madness. Walter was abruptly expelled from college by the one man in the college whom he respected—the saintly president, who had dreams of a new Harvard on the prairies.

So Walter Babson found himself at twenty-one an outcast. He declaimed—though no one would believe him —that all the gentle souls he had ever encountered were weak; all the virile souls vicious or suspicious.

He drifted. He doubted himself, and all the more noisily asserted his talent and the injustice of the world. He looked clean and energetic and desirous, but he had nothing on which to focus. He became an active but careless reporter on newspapers in Wichita, Des Moines, Kansas City, St. Louis, Seattle, Los Angeles, San Francisco. Between times he sold real-estate and insurance and sets of travel books, for he had no pride of journalism; he wanted to keep going and keep interested and make money and spend it; he wanted to express himself without trying to find out what his self was.

It must be understood that, for all his vices, Walter was essentially clean and kindly. He rushed into everything, the bad with the good. He was not rotten with heavy hopelessness; though he was an outcast from his home, he was never a pariah. Not Walter, but the smug, devilish cities which took their revenues from saloon-keeping were to blame when he turned from the intolerable dullness of their streets to the excitement of alcohol in the saloons and brothels which they made so much more amusing than their churches and parlors.

Everywhere in the Western newspaper circles Walter heard stories of Californians who had gone East and become geniuses the minute they crossed the Hudson. . . . Walter also went East and crossed the Hudson, but he did not become a genius. If there had been an attic to starve in, he would have starved in one, but as New York has nothing so picturesque, he starved in furnished rooms instead, while he wrote "special stories" for Sunday news-papers, and collected jokes for a syndicated humorous column. He was glad to become managing editor (though he himself was the only editor he had to manage) of a magazine for stamp-collectors. He wrote some advertise-ments for a Broadway dealer in automobile accessories, read half a dozen books on motors, and brazenly demanded his present position on the *Motor and Gas Gazette*.

He was as far from the rarified air of Bohemia (he really believed that sort of thing) as he had been in Kansas, except that he knew one man who made five thousand dollars a year by writing stories about lumberjacks, miners, cow-punchers, and young ladies of quite astound-ing courage. He was twenty-seven years old when he met Una Golden. He still read Omar Khayyam. He had a vague plan of going into real estate. There ought, he felt, to be money in writing real-estate advertise-ments.

He kept falling in love with stenographers and waitresses, with actresses whom he never met. He was never satisfied. He didn't at all know what he wanted, but he wanted something stronger than himself.

He was desperately lonely—a humorous figure who had dared to aspire beyond the manure-piles of his father's farm; therefore a young man to be ridiculed. And in his tragic loneliness he waited for the day when he should find any love, any labor, that should want him enough to seek him and demand that he sacrifice himself.

§ 4

It was Una's first city spring.

Save in the squares, where the bourgeoning trees made green-lighted spaces for noon-time lovers, there was no change; no blossomy stir in asphalt and cement and brick and steel. Yet everything was changed. Between the cornices twenty stories above the pavement you could see a slit of softer sky, and there was a peculiar radiance in just the light itself, whether it lay along the park turf or made its way down an air-well to rest on a stolid wall of yellow brick. The river breeze, flowing so persuasively through streets which had been stormed by dusty gales, bore happiness. Grind-organs made music for ragged, dancing children, and old brick buildings smelled warm. Peanut-wagons came out with a long, shrill whine, locusts of the spring.

In the office even the most hustling of the great ones became human. They talked of suburban gardens and of motoring out to country clubs for tennis. They smiled more readily, and shamelessly said, "I certainly got the spring fever for fair to-day"; and twice did S. Herbert Ross go off to play golf all afternoon. The stenographer who commuted—always there is one girl in the office who commutes—brought spring in the form of pussy-willows and apple-blossoms, and was noisily envied.

The windows were open now, and usually some one was speculatively looking down to the life on the pavement, eight stories below. At noon-hour the younger girls of the office strolled along the sidewalk in threes and fours, bareheaded, their arms about one another, their spring-time lane an irregular course between boxes in front of loft-buildings; or they ate their box-and-paper-napkin lunches on the fire-escape that wound down into the court. They gigglingly drew their skirts about their ankles and flirted with young porters and packers who leaned from windows across the court. Una sat with them and wished that she could flirt like the daughters of New York. She listened eagerly to their talk of gathering violets in Van Cortlandt Park and tramping on the Palisades. She noted an increased number of excited confidences to the effect that, "He says to me—" and "I says to him—" and, "Say, gee! honest, Tess, he's a swell fellow." She caught herself wanting to tramp the Palisades with—with the Walter Babson who didn't even know her first name.

When she left the flat these mornings she forgot her lonely mother instantly in the treacherous magic of the tender sky, and wanted to run away, to steal the blue and silver day for her own. But it was gone when she reached the office—no silver and blue day was here; but, on golden-oak desk and oak-and-frosted-glass semi-partitions, the same light as in the winter. Sometimes, if she got out early, a stilly afterglow of amber and turquoise brought back the spring. But all day long she merely saw signs that otherwhere, for other people, spring did exist; and she wistfully trusted in it as she watched and helped Walter Babson.

THE JOB

She was conscious that she was working more intimately with him as a comrade now, not as clerk with executive. There had been no one illuminating moment of under-standing; he was impersonal with her; but each day their relationship was less of a mechanical routine, more of a personal friendship. She felt that he really depended on her steady carefulness; she knew that through the wild tangle of his impulsiveness she saw a desire to be noble.

§ 5

He came clattering down the aisle of desks to her one May afternoon, and begged, "Say, Miss Golden, I'm stuck. I got to get out some publicity on the Governor's good-roads article we're going to publish; want to send it out to forty papers in advance, and I can't get only a dozen proofs. And it's got to go off to-night. Can you make me some copies? You can use onion-skin paper and carbon 'em and make anyway five copies at a whack. But prob'ly you'd have to stay late. Got anything on to-night? Could you do it? Could you do it? Could you?"

"Surely."

"Well, here's the stuff. Just single-space that intro-ductory spiel at the top, will you?"

Una rudely turned out of her typewriter a form-letter which she was writing for S. Herbert Ross, and began to type Walter's publicity, her shoulders bent, her eyes in-tent, oblivious to the steady stream of gossip which flowed from stenographer to stenographer, no matter how busy they were. He needed her! She would have stayed till midnight. While the keys burred under her fingers she was unconsciously telling herself a story of how she would be working half the night, with the office still and shadowy, of how a dead-white face would peer through

the window near her desk (difficult of accomplishment, as
the window was eight stories up in air), of how she was
to be pursued by a man on the way home; and how,
when she got there, her mother would say, "I just don't
see how you could neglect me like this all evening." All
the while she felt herself in touch with large affairs—an
article by the Governor of the State; these very sheets
that she was typing to go to famous newspapers, to the
"thundering presses" of which she had read in fiction;
urgency, affairs, and—doing something for Walter Babson.

She was still typing swiftly at five-thirty, the closing
hour. The article was long; she had at least two hours of
work ahead. Miss Moynihan came stockily to say good-
night. The other stenographers fluttered out to the elevators. Their corner became oppressively quiet. The
office-manager gently puttered about, bade her good-night,
drifted away. S. Herbert Ross boomed out of his office,
explaining the theory of advertising to a gasoleny man
in a pin-checked suit as they waddled to the elevator.
The telephone-girl hurried back to connect up a last
call, frowned while she waited, yanked out the plug, and
scuttled away—a creamy, roe-eyed girl, pretty and unhappy at her harassing job of connecting nervous talkers
all day. Four men, editors and advertising-men, shouldered out, bawling over a rather feeble joke about Bill's
desire for a drink and their willingness to help him slay
the booze-evil. Una was conscious that they had gone,
that walls of silence were closing about her clacking typewriter. And that Walter Babson had not gone; that he
was sharing with her this whispering forsaken office.

Presently he came rambling out of the editorial-room.

He had taken off his grotesque, great horn-rimmed
glasses. His eyes were mutinous in his dark melancholy
face; he drew a hand over them and shook his head.

Una was aware of all this in one glance. "Poor, tired boy!" she thought.

He sat on the top of the nearest desk, hugged his knee, rocked back and forth, and said, "Much left, Miss Golden?"

"I think I'll be through in about two hours."

"Oh, Lord! I can't let you stay that late."

"It doesn't matter. Really! I'll be glad. I haven't had to stay late much."

For quite the first time he stared straight at her, saw her as a human being. She was desperately hoping that her hair was smooth and that there wasn't any blue from the typewriter ribbon daubed on her cheeks! . . . He ceased his rocking; appraised her. A part of her brain was wondering what he would do; a part longing to smile temptingly at him; a part coldly commanding, "You will not be a little fool—he isn't interested in you, and you won't try to make him be, either!"

"Why, you look as fagged as I feel," he said. "I suppose I'm as bad as the rest. I kick like a steer when the Old Man shoves some extra work on me, and then I pass the buck and make *you* stay late. Say! Tell you what we'll do." Very sweet to her was his "we," and his intimacy of tone. "I'll start copying, too. I'm quite considerable at machine-pounding myself, and we can get the thing done and mailed by six-thirty or so, and then I'll buy you a handsome dinner at Childs's. Gosh! I'll even blow you to a piece of pie; and I'll shoot you up home by quarter to eight. Great stuff! Gimme a copy of the drool. Meanwhile you'll have a whole hour for worried maiden thoughts over going out to eat with the bad, crazy Wally Babson!"

His smile was a caress. Her breath caught, she smiled back at him fearfully. Then he was gone. In the editorial office was heard the banging of his heavy old typewriter—it was an office joke, Walter's hammering of the "threshing-machine."

She began to type again, with mechanical rapidity, not consciously seeing the copy, so distraught was she as she murmured, "Oh, I oughtn't to go out with him. . . . But I will! . . . What nonsense! Why shouldn't I have dinner with him. . . . Oh, I mustn't—I'm a typist and he's a boss. . . . But I will!"

Glancing down the quiet stretches of the office, to the windows looking to westward, she saw that the sky was a delicate primrose. In a loft-building rearing out of the low structures between her and the North River, lights were springing out, and she—who ought to have known that they marked weary, late-staying people like herself, fancied that they were the lights of restaurants for gay lovers. She dismissed her problem, forgot the mother who was waiting with a demand for all of Una's youth, and settled down to a happy excitement in the prospect of going out with Walter; of knowing him, of feeling again that smile.

He came prancing out with his copies of the article before she had finished. "Some copyist, eh?" he cried. "Say, hustle and finish. Gee! I've been smoking cigarettes to-day till my mouth tastes like a fish-market. Want to eat and forget my troubles."

With her excitement dulled to a matter-of-fact hungriness, she trotted beside him to a restaurant, one of the string of Vance eating-places, a food-mill which tried to achieve originality by the use of imitation rafters, a plate-rack aligned with landscape plates, and varnished black tables for four instead of the long, marble tables which crowded the patrons together in most places of the sort. Walter verbosely called her attention to the mottoes painted on the wood, the individual table lights in pink shades. "Just forget the eats, Miss Golden, and you can imagine you're in a regular restaurant. Gosh! this place ought to reconcile you to dining with the crazy Babson. I can't imagine a liaison in a place where coffee costs five cents."

He sounded boisterous, but he took her coat so languidly, he slid so loosely into his chair, that she burned with desire to soothe away his office weariness. She forgot all reserve. She burst out: "Why do you call yourself 'crazy'? Just because you have more energy than anybody else in the office?"

"No," he said, grimly, snatching at the menu, "because I haven't any purpose in the scheme of things."

Una told herself that she was pleased to see how the scrawny waitress purred at Walter when he gave his order. Actually she was feeling resentfully that no sawvoiced, galumphing Amazon of a waitress could appreciate Walter's smile.

In a Vance eating-place, ordering a dinner, and getting approximately what you order, is not a delicate epicurean art, but a matter of business, and not till an enormous platter of "Vance's Special Ham and Eggs, Country Style," was slammed down between them, and catsup, Worcestershire sauce, napkins, more rolls, water, and another fork severally demanded of the darting waitress, did Walter seem to remember that this was a romantic dinner with a strange girl, not a deal in food-supplies.

His wavering black eyes searched her face. She was agitatedly aware that her skin was broken out in a small red spot beside her lips; but she hoped that he would find her forehead clear, her mouth a flower. He suddenly nodded, as though he had grown used to her and found her comfortable. While his wreathing hands picked fantastically at a roll and made crosses with lumps of sugar, his questions probed at that hidden soul which she herself had never found. It was the first time that any one had demanded her formula of life, and in her struggle to express herself she rose into a frankness which Panama circles of courtship did not regard as proper to young women.

"What's your ambition?" he blurted. "Going to just plug along and not get anywhere?"

"No, I'm not; but it's hard. Women aren't trusted in business, and you can't count without responsibility. All I can do is keep looking."

"Go out for suffrage, feminism, so on?"

"I don't know anything about them. Most women don't know anything about them—about anything!"

"Huh! Most *people* don't! Wouldn't have office-grinding if people did know anything. . . . How much training have you had?"

"Oh, public school, high school, commercial college."

"Where?"

"Panama, Pennsylvania."

"I know. About like my own school in Kansas—the high-school principal would have been an undertaker if he'd had more capital. . . . Gee! principal and capital—might make a real cunning pun out of that if I worked over it a little. I know. . . . Go to church?"

"Why—why, yes, of course."

"Which god do you favor at present—Unitarian or Catholic or Christian Science or Seventh-Day Advent?"

"Why, it's the same—"

"Now don't spring that 'it's the same God' stuff on me. It isn't the same God that simply hones for candles and music in an Episcopal Church and gives the Plymouth Brotherhood a private copyright revelation that organs and candles are wicked."

THE JOB

"You're terribly sacrilegious."

"You don't believe any such thing. Or else you'd lam me—same as they used to do in the crusades. You don't really care a hang."

"No, I really don't care!" she was amazed to hear herself admit.

"Of course, I'm terribly crude and vulgar, but then what else can you be in dealing with a bunch of churches that haven't half the size or beauty of farmers' red barns? And yet the dubs go on asserting that they believe the church is God's house. If I were God, I'd sure object to being worse housed than the cattle. But, gosh! let's pass that up. If I started in on what I think of almost anything—churches or schools, or this lying advertising game—I'd yelp all night, and you could always answer me that I'm merely a neurotic failure, while the big guns that I jump on own motor-cars." He stopped his rapid tirade, chucked a lump of sugar at an interrogative cat which was making the round of the tables, scowled, and suddenly fired at her:

"What do you think of me?"

"You're the kindest person I ever met."

"Huh? Kind? Good to my mother?"

"Perhaps. You've made the office happy for me. I really admire you. . . . I s'pose I'm terribly unladylike to tell you."

"Gee whiz!" he marveled. "Got an admirer! And I always thought you were an uncommonly level-headed girl. Shows how you can fool 'em."

He smiled at her, directly, rather forlornly, proud of her praise.

Regardless of other tables, he thrust his arm across, and with the side of his hand touched the side of hers for a second. Dejectedly he said: "But why do you like me?

6   [73]

I've good intentions; I'm willing to pinch Tolstoi's laurels right off his grave, and orate like William Jennings Bryan. And there's a million yearners like me. There ain't a hall-bedroom boy in New York that wouldn't like to be a genius."

"I like you because you have fire. Mr. Babson, do you—"

"Walter!"

"How premature you are!"

"Walter!"

"You'll be calling me 'Una' next, and think how shocked the girls will be."

"Oh no. I've quite decided to call you 'Goldie.' Sounds nice and sentimental. But for heaven's sake go on telling me why you like me. That isn't a hackneyed subject."

"Oh, I've never known anybody with *fire*, except maybe S. Herbert Ross, and he—he—"

"He blobs around."

"Yes, something like that. I don't know whether you are ever going to do anything with your fire, but you do have it, Mr. Babson!"

"I'll probably get fired with it. . . . Say, do you read Omar?"

In nothing do the inarticulate "million hall-room boys who want to be geniuses," the ordinary, unshaved, not over-bathed, ungrammatical young men of any American city, so nearly transcend provincialism as in an enthusiasm over their favorite minor cynic, Elbert Hubbard or John Kendrick Bangs, or, in Walter Babson's case, Mr. Fitzgerald's variations on Omar. Una had read Omar as a pretty poem about roses and murmurous courts, but read him she had; and such was Walter's delight in that fact that he immediately endowed her with his own ability to enjoy cynicism. He jabbed at the menu with a fork and glowed and shouted, "Say, isn't it great, that quatrain about 'Take the cash and let the credit go'?"

While Una beamed and enjoyed her boy's youthful enthusiasm. Mother of the race, ancient tribal woman, medieval chatelaine, she was just now; kin to all the women who, in any age, have clapped their hands to their men's boasting.

She agreed with him that "All these guys that pride themselves on being gentlemen—like in English novels—are jus' the same as the dubs you see in ordinary life."

And that it was not too severe an indictment to refer to the advertising-manager as "S. Herbert Louse."

And that "the woman feeding by herself over at that corner table looks mysterious, somehow. Gee! there must be a tragedy in her life."

But her gratification in being admitted to his enthusiasms was only a background for her flare when he boldly caught up her white paw and muttered, "Tired little hand that has to work so hard!"

She couldn't move; she was afraid to look at him. Clattering restaurant and smell of roast pork and people about her all dissolved in her agitation. She shook her head violently to awaken herself, heard herself say, calmly, "It's terribly late. Don't you think it is?" and knew that she was arising. But she moved beside him down the street in languor, wondering in every cell of her etherealized body whether he would touch her hand again; what he would do. Not till they neared the Subway station did she, woman, the protector, noting his slow step and dragging voice, rouse herself to say, "Oh, don't come up in the Subway; I'm used to it, really!"

"My dear Goldie, you aren't used to anything in real life. Gee! I said that snappily, and it don't mean a thing!"

he gleefully pointed out. He seized her arm, which prickled to the touch of his fingers, rushed her down the Subway steps, and while he bought their tickets they smiled at each other.

Several times on the way up he told her that it was a pleasure to have some one who could "appreciate his honest-t'-God opinions of the managing editor and S. Herbert Frost."

The Subway, plunging through unvaried darkness, leviated them from the district of dark loft-buildings and theater-bound taxicabs to a far-out Broadway, softened with trees and brightened with small apartment-houses and little shops. They could see a great feathery space of vernal darkness down over the Hudson at the end of a street. Steel-bound nature seemed reaching for them wherever in a vacant lot she could get free and send out quickening odors of fresh garden soil.

"Almost country," said Walter.

An urgent, daring look came into his eyes, under the light-cluster. He stopped, took her arm. There was an edge of spring madness in his voice as he demanded, "Wouldn't you like to run away with me to-night? Feel this breeze on your lips—it's simply plumb-full of mystery. Wouldn't you like to run away? and we'd tramp the Palisades till dawn and go to sleep with the May sun glaring down the Hudson. Wouldn't you like to, wouldn't you?"

She was conscious that, though his head was passionately thrown back, his faunlike eyes stared into hers, and that his thin lips arched. Terribly she wanted to say, "Yes!" Actually, Una Golden of Panama and the *Gazette* office speculated, for a tenth of a second, whether she couldn't go. Madness—river-flow and darkness and the stars! But she said, "No, I'm afraid we couldn't possibly!"

"No," he said, slowly. "Of course—of course I didn't mean we *could;* but—Goldie, little Goldie that wants to live and rule things, wouldn't you *like* to go? *Wouldn't* you?"

"Yes! . . . You hurt my arm so! . . . Oh, don't! We must—"

Her low cry was an appeal to him to save them from spring's scornful, lusty demand; every throbbing nerve in her seemed to appeal to him; and it was not relief, but gratitude, that she felt when he said, tenderly, "Poor kid! . . . Which way? Come." They walked soberly toward the Golden flat, and soberly he mused, "Poor kids, both of us trying to be good slaves in an office when we want to smash things. . . . You'll be a queen—you'll grab the throne same as you grab papers offn my desk. And maybe you'll let me be court jester."

"Why do you say I'll—oh, be a queen? Do you mean literally, in business, an executive?"

"Hadn't thought just what it did imply, but I suppose it's that."

"But why, *why?* I'm simply one of a million stenographers."

"Oh, well, you aren't satisfied to take things just as they're handed to you. Most people are, and they stick in a rut and wonder who put them there. All this success business is a mystery—listen to how successful men trip themselves up and fall all over their foolish faces when they try to explain to a bunch of nice, clean, young clerks how they stole their success. But I know you'll get it, because you aren't satisfied easily—you take my work and do it. And yet you're willing to work in one corner till it's time to jump. That's my failing—I ain't willing to stick."

"I—perhaps—— Here's the flat."

"Lord!" he cried; "we *got* to walk a block farther and back."

"Well—"

They were stealing onward toward the breeze from the river before she had finished her "Well."

"Think of wasting this hypnotizing evening talking of success—word that means a big house in Yonkers! When we've become friends, Goldie, little Goldie. Business of souls grabbing for each other! Friends—at least to-night! Haven't we, dear? haven't we?"

"Oh, I hope so!" she whispered.

He drew her hand into his pocket and clasped it there. She looked shyly down. Strange that her hand should not be visible when she could feel its palm flame against his. She let it snuggle there, secure. . . . Mr. Walter Babson was not a young man with "bad prospects," or "good prospects"; he was love incarnate in magic warm flesh, and his hand was the hand of love. She was conscious of his hard-starched cuff pressing against her bare arm—a man's cuff under the rough surface of his man's coat-sleeve.

He brought her back to the vestibule of the flat. For a moment he held both her arms at the elbow and looked at her, while with a panic fear she wondered why she could not move—wondered if he were going to kiss her.

He withdrew his hands, sighed, "Good-night, Goldie. I won't be lonely to-night!" and turned abruptly away.

Through all of Mrs. Golden's long, sobbing queries as to why Una had left her alone all evening Una was patient. For she knew that she had ahead of her a quiet moment when she would stand alone with the god of love and pray to him to keep her boy, her mad boy, Walter.

While she heard her voice crisply explaining, "Why, you see, mother dear, I simply had to get some work done for the office—" Una was telling herself, "Some day he *will* kiss me, and I'm *not* sorry he didn't to-night—not now any more I'm not. . . . It's so strange—I like to have him touch me, and I simply never could stand other men touching me! . . . I wonder if he's excited now, too? I wonder what he's doing. . . . Oh, I'm glad, glad I loved his hands!"

CHAPTER VI

" I NEVER thought a nice girl could be in love with a
man who is bad, and I s'pose Walter is bad. Kind of.
But maybe he'll become good."

So Una simple-heartedly reflected on her way to the
Subway next morning. She could not picture what he
would do, now that it was hard, dry day again, and all
the world panted through dusty streets. And she recklessly didn't care. For Walter was not hard and dry and
dusty; and she was going to see him again! Sometimes
she was timorous about seeing him, because he had read
the longing in her face, had known her soul with its garments thrown away. But, timorous or not, she had to
see him; she would never let him go, now that he had made
her care for him.

Walter was not in sight when she entered the offices,
and she was instantly swept into the routine. Not
clasping hands beguiled her, but lists to copy, typing
errors to erase, and the irritating adjustment of a shift-
key which fiendishly kept falling. For two hours she
did not see him.

About ten-thirty she was aware that he was prosaically
strolling toward her.

Hundreds of times, in secret maiden speculations about
love, the girl Una had surmised that it would be embarrassing to meet a man the morning after you had yielded
to his caress. It had been perplexing—one of those myste-

ries of love over which virgins brood between chapters of
novels, of which they diffidently whisper to other girls
when young married friends are amazingly going to have
a baby. But she found it natural to smile up at Walter. . . .
In this varnished, daytime office neither of them admitted
their madness of meeting hands.

He merely stooped over her desk and said, sketchily,
"Mornin', little Goldie."

Then for hours he seemed to avoid her. She was afraid.
Most of all, afraid of her own desire to go to him and
wail that he was avoiding her.

At three o'clock, when the office tribe accept with naïve
gratitude any excuse to talk, to stop and tell one another
a new joke, to rush to the window and critically view a
parade, Una saw that Walter was beginning to hover
near her. She was angry that he did not come straight
to her. He did not seem quite to know whether he wanted
her or not. But her face was calm above her typing while
she watched him peer at her over the shoulder of S. Herbert Ross, to whom he was talking. He drew nearer to
her. He examined a poster. She was oblivious of him.
She was conscious that he was trying to find an excuse
to say something without openly admitting to the ever-
spying row of stenographers that he was interested in her.
He wambled up to her at last and asked for a letter she
had filed for him. She knew from the casual-looking
drop of his eyes that he was peering at the triangle of her
clear-skinned throat, and for his peeping uneasiness she
rather despised him. She could fancy herself shouting at
him, "Oh, stop fidgeting! Make up your mind whether you
like me or not, and hurry up about it. I don't care now."

In which secret defiance she was able to luxuriate—since
he was still in the office, not gone from her forever!—
till five o'clock, when the detached young men of offices

are wont to face another evening of lonely irrelevancy, and desperately begin to reach for companionship.

At that hour Walter rushed up and begged, "Goldie, you *must* come out with me this evening."

"I'm sorry, but it's so late—"

"Oh, I know. Gee! if you knew how I've been thinking about you all day! I've been wondering if I ought to— I'm no good; blooming waster, I told myself; and I wondered if I had any right to try to make you care; but— Oh, you *must* come, Goldie!"

Una's pride steeled her. A woman can forgive any vice of man more readily than she can forgive his not loving her so unhesitatingly that he will demand her without stopping to think of his vices. Refusal to sacrifice the beloved is not a virtue in youth.

Una said, clearly, "I am sorry, but I can't possibly this evening."

"Well—wish you could," he sighed.

As he moved away Una reveled in having refused his half-hearted invitation, but already she was aware that she would regret it. She was shaken with woman's fiercely possessive clinging to love.

The light on one side of her desk was shut off by the bulky presence of Miss Moynihan. She whispered, huskily, "Say, Miss Golden, you want to watch out for that Babson fellow. He acts like he was stuck on you. Say, listen; everybody says he's a bad one. Say, listen, honest; they say he'd compromise a lady jus' soon as not."

"Why, I don't know what you mean."

"Oh no, like fun you don't—him rubbering at you all day and pussy-footing around!"

"Why, you're perfectly crazy! He was merely asking me about some papers—"

"Oh yes, sure! Lemme tell you, a lady can't be none

too careful about her reputation with one of them skinny, dark devils like a Dago snooping around."

"Why, you're absolutely ridiculous! Besides, how do you know Mr. Babson is bad? Has he ever hurt anybody in the office?"

"No, but they say—"

"'They say'!"

"Now don't you go and get peeved after you and me been such good friends, Miss Golden. I don't know that this Babson fellow ever done anything worse than eat cracker-jack at South Beach, but I was just telling you what they all say—how he drinks and goes with a lot of totties and all; but—but he's all right if you say so, and— honest t' Gawd, Miss Golden, listen, honest, I wouldn't knock him for nothing if I thought he was your fellow! And," in admiration, "and him an editor! Gee!"

Una tried to see herself as a princess forgiving her honest servitor. But, as a matter of fact, she was plain angry that her romance should be dragged into the nastiness of office gossip. She resented being a stenographer, one who couldn't withdraw into a place for dreams. And she fiercely defended Walter in her mind; throbbed with a big, sweet pity for her nervous, aspiring boy whose quest for splendor made him seem wild to the fools about them.

When, just at five-thirty, Walter charged up to her again, she met him with a smile of unrestrained intimacy.

"If you're going to be home at *all* this evening, let me come up just for fifteen minutes!" he demanded.

"Yes!" she said, breathlessly. "Oh, I oughtn't to, but —come up at nine."

§ 2

Una had always mechanically liked children; had ejaculated, "Oh, the pink little darling!" over each neighborhood infant; had pictured children of her own; but never till that night had the desire to feel her own baby's head against her breast been a passion. After dinner she sat on the stoop of her apartment-house, watching the children at play between motors on the street.

"Oh, it would be wonderful to have a baby—a boy like Walter must have been—to nurse and pet and cry over!" she declared, as she watched a baby of faint, brown ringlets—hair that would be black like Walter's. Later she chided herself for being so bold, so un-Panamanian; but she was proud to know that she could long for the pressure of a baby's lips. The brick-walled street echoed with jagged cries of children; tired women in mussed waists poked their red, steamy necks out of windows; the sky was a blur of gray; and, lest she forget the job, Una's left wrist ached from typing; yet she heard the rustle of spring, and her spirit swelled with thankfulness as she felt her life to be not a haphazard series of days, but a divine progress.

Walter was coming—to-night!

She was conscious of her mother, up-stairs. From her place of meditation she had to crawl up the many steps to the flat and answer at least twenty questions as to what she had been doing. Of Walter's coming she could say nothing; she could not admit her interest in a man she did not know.

At a quarter to nine she ventured to say, ever so casually: "I feel sort of headachy. I think I'll run down and sit on the steps again and get a little fresh air."

"Let's have a little walk. I'd like some fresh air, too," said Mrs. Golden, brightly.

"Why—oh—to tell the truth, I wanted to think over some office business."

"Oh, of course, my dear, if I am in the *way*—!" Mrs. Golden sighed, and trailed pitifully off into the bedroom.

Una followed her, and wanted to comfort her. But she could say nothing, because she was palpitating over Walter's coming. The fifteen minutes of his stay might hold any splendor.

She could not change her clothes. Her mother was in the bedroom, sobbing.

All the way down the four flights of stairs she wanted to flee back to her mother. It was with a cold impatience that she finally saw Walter approach the house, ten minutes late. He was so grotesque in his frantic, puffing hurry. He was no longer the brilliant Mr. Babson, but a moist young man who hemmed and sputtered, "Gee!—couldn't find clean collar—hustled m' head off—just missed Subway express—couldn't make it—whew, I'm hot!"

"It doesn't matter," she condescended.

He dropped on the step just below her and mopped his forehead. Neither of them could say anything. He took off his horn-rimmed eye-glasses, carefully inserted the point of a pencil through the loop, swung them in a buzzing circle, and started to put them on again.

"Oh, keep them *off!*" she snapped. "You look so high-brow with them!"

"Y-yuh; why, s-sure!"

She felt very superior.

He feverishly ran a finger along the upper rim of his left ear, sprang up, stooped to take her hand, glared into her eyes till she shrank—and then a nail-cleaner, a common, ten-cent file, fell out of his inner pocket and clinked on the stone step.

"Oh, damn!" he groaned.

"I really think it *is* going to rain," she said.

They both laughed.

He plumped down beside her, uncomfortably wedged between her and the rail. He caught her hand, intertwined their fingers so savagely that her knuckles hurt. "Look here," he commanded, "you don't really think it's going to rain any such a darn thing! I've come fourteen billion hot miles up here for just fifteen minutes—yes, and you wanted to see me yourself, too! And now you want to talk about the history of recent rains."

In the bitter-sweet spell of his clasp she was oblivious of street, children, sky. She tried to withdraw her hand, but he squeezed her fingers the more closely and their two hands dropped on her thin knee, which tingled to the impact.

"But—but what did you want to see me about?" Her superiority was burnt away.

He answered her hesitation with a trembling demand: "I can't talk to you here! Can't we go some place— Come walk toward the river."

"Oh, I daren't—really, Walter. My mother feels so— so fidgety to-night and I must go back to her. . . . By and by."

"But would you like to go with me?"

"Yes!"

"Then that's all that matters!"

"Perhaps—perhaps we could go up on the roof here for just a few minutes. Then I must send you home."

"Hooray! Come on."

He boldly lifted her to her feet, followed her up the stairs. On the last dark flight, near the roof, he threw both arms about her and kissed her. She was amazed that she did not want to kiss him back, that his abandon did not stir her. Even while she was shocked and afraid, he kissed again, and she gave way to his kiss; her cold mouth grew desirous.

She broke away, with shocked pride—shocked most of all at herself, that she let him kiss her thus.

"You quiver so to my kiss!" he whispered, in awe.

"I don't!" she denied. "It just doesn't mean anything."

"It does, and you know it does. I had to kiss you. Oh, sweetheart, sweetheart, we are both so lonely! Kiss me."

"No, no!" She held him away from her.

"Yes, I tell you!"

She encircled his neck with her arm, laid her cheek beside his chin, rejoiced boundlessly in the man roughness of his chin, of his coat-sleeve, the man scent of him—scent of tobacco and soap and hair. She opened her lips to his. Slowly she drew her arm from about his neck, his arm from about her waist.

"Walter!" she mourned, "I did want you. But you must be good to me—not kiss me like that—not now, anyway, when I'm lonely for you and can't resist you. . . . Oh, it wasn't wrong, was it, when we needed each other so? It wasn't wrong, was it?"

"Oh no—no!"

"But not—not again—not for a long while. I want you to respect me. Maybe it wasn't wrong, dear, but it was terribly dangerous. Come, let's stand out in the cool air on the roof for a while and then you must go home."

They came out on the flat, graveled roof, round which all the glory of the city was blazing, and hand in hand, in a confidence delicately happy now, stood worshiping the spring.

"Dear," he said, "I feel as though I were a robber who had gone crashing right through the hedge around your soul, and then after that come out in a garden—the sweetest, coolest garden. . . . I *will* try to be good to you—and for you." He kissed her finger-tips.

"Yes, you did break through. At first it was just *a* kiss and the—oh, it was *the* kiss, and there wasn't anything else. Oh, do let me live in the little garden still."

"Trust me, dear."

"I will trust you. Come. I must go down now."

"Can I come to see you?"

"Yes."

"Goldie, listen," he said, as they came down-stairs to her hallway. "Any time you'd like to marry me—I don't advise it, I guess I'd have good intentions, but be a darn poor hand at putting up shelves—but any time you'd like to marry me, or any of those nice conventional things, just lemme know, will you? Not that it matters much. What matters is, I want to kiss you good-night."

"No, what matters is, I'm not going to let you!....Not to-night. . . . Good-night, dear."

She scampered down the hall. She tiptoed into the living-room, and for an hour she brooded, felt faint and ashamed at her bold response to his kiss, yet wanted to feel his sharp-ridged lips again. Sometimes in a bitter frankness she told herself that Walter had never even thought of marriage till their kiss had fired him. She swore to herself that she would not give all her heart to love; that she would hold him off and make him value her precious little store of purity and tenderness. But passion and worry together were lost in a prayer for him. She knelt by the window till her own individuality was merged with that of the city's million lovers.

§ 3

Like sickness and war, the office grind absorbs all personal desires. Love and ambition and wisdom it turns to its own purposes. Every day Una and Walter saw each other. Their hands touched as he gave her papers to file; there was affection in his voice when he dictated, and once, outside the office door, he kissed her. Yet their love was kept suspended. They could not tease each other and flirt raucously, like the telephone-girl and the elevator-starter.

Every day he begged her to go to dinner with him, to let him call at the flat, and after a week she permitted him to come.

§ 4

At dinner, when Una told her mother that a young gentleman at the office—in fact, Mr. Babson, the editor whose dictation she took—was going to call that evening, Mrs. Golden looked pleased, and said: "Isn't that nice! Why, you never told mother he was interested in you!"

"Well, of course, we kind of work together—"

"I do hope he's a nice, respectful young man, not one of these city people that flirt and drink cocktails and heaven knows what all!"

"Why, uh—I'm sure you'll like him. Everybody says he's the cleverest fellow in the shop."

"Office, dear, not shop. . . . Is he— Does he get a big salary?"

"Why, mums, I'm sure I haven't the slightest idea! How should I know?"

"Well, I just asked. . . . Will you put on your pink-and-white crêpe?"

"Don't you think the brown silk would be better?"

"Why, Una, I want you to look your prettiest! You must make all the impression you can."

"Well, perhaps I'd better," Una said, demurely.

Despite her provincial training, Mrs. Golden had a much better instinct for dress than her sturdy daughter.

7 [89]

So long as she was not left at home alone, her mild selfishness did not make her want to interfere with Una's interests. She ah'd and oh'd over the torn border of Una's crêpe dress, and mended it with quick, pussy-like movements of her fingers. She tried to arrange Una's hair so that its pale golden texture would shine in broad, loose undulations, and she was as excited as Una when they heard Walter's bouncing steps in the hall, his nervous tap at the door, his fumbling for a push-button.

Una dashed wildly to the bedroom for a last nose-powdering, a last glance at her hair and nails, and slowly paraded to the door to let him in, while Mrs. Golden stood primly, with folded hands, like a cabinet photograph of 1885.

So the irregular Walter came into a decidedly regular atmosphere and had to act like a pure-minded young editor.

They conversed—Lord! how they conversed! Mrs. Golden respectably desired to know Mr. Babson's opinions on the weather, New-Yorkers, her little girl Una's work, fashionable city ministers, the practical value of motor-cars, and the dietetic value of beans—the large, white beans, not the small, brown ones—she had grown both varieties in her garden at home (Panama, Pennsylvania, when Mr. Golden, Captain Golden he was usually called, was alive)—and had Mr. Babson ever had a garden, or seen Panama? And was Una *really* attending to her duties?

All the while Mrs. Golden's canary trilled approval of the conversation.

Una listened, numbed, while Walter kept doing absurd things with his face—pinched his lips and tapped his teeth and rubbed his jaw as though he needed a shave. He took off his eye-glasses to wipe them and tied his thin legs in a knot, and all the while said, "Yes, there's certainly a great deal to that."

At a quarter to ten Mrs. Golden rose, indulged in a little kitten yawn behind her silvery hand, and said: "Well, I think I must be off to bed. . . . I find these May days so languid. Don't you, Mr. Babson? Spring fever. I just can't seem to get enough sleep. . . . Now you mustn't stay up *too* late, Una dear."

The bedroom door had not closed before Walter had darted from his chair, picked Una up, his hands pressing tight about her knees and shoulders, kissed her, and set her down beside him on the couch.

"Wasn't I good, huh? Wasn't I good, huh? Wasn't I? Now who says Wally Babson ain't a good parlor-pup, huh? Oh, you old darling, you were twice as agonized as me!"

And that was all he said—in words. Between them was a secret, a greater feeling of unfettered intimacy, because together they had been polite to mother—tragic, pitiful mother, who had been enjoying herself so much without knowing that she was in the way.. That intimacy needed no words to express it; hands and cheeks and lips spoke more truly. They were children of emotion, young and crude and ignorant, groping for life and love, all the world new to them, despite their sorrows and waiting. They were clerklings, not lords of love and life, but all the more easily did they yield to longing for happiness. Between them was the battle of desire and timidity—and not all the desire was his, not hers all the timidity. She fancied sometimes that he was as much afraid as was she of debasing their shy seeking into unveiled passion. Yet his was the initiative; always she panted and wondered what he would do next, feared and wondered and rebuked—and desired.

He abruptly drew her head to his shoulder, smoothed

her hair. She felt his fingers again communicate to her every nerve a tingling electric force. She felt his lips quest along her cheek and discover the soft little spot just behind her ear. She followed the restless course of his hands across her shoulders, down her arm, lingeringly over her hand. His hand seemed to her to have an existence quite apart from him, to have a mysterious existence of its own. In silence they rested there. She kept wondering if his shoulder had not been made just for her cheek. With little shivers she realized that this was his shoulder, Walter's, a man's, as the rough cloth prickled her skin. Silent they were, and for a time secure, but she kept speculating as to what he would dare to do next—and she fancied that he was speculating about precisely the same thing.

He drew a catching breath, and suddenly her lips were opening to his.

"Oh, you mustn't—you promised—" she moaned, when she was able to draw back her head.

Again he kissed her, quickly, then released her and began to talk rapidly of—nothing. Apropos of offices and theaters and the tides of spring, he was really telling her that, powerful though his restless curiosity was, greatly though their poor little city bodies craved each other, yet he did respect her. She scarce listened, for at first she was bemused by two thoughts. She was inquiring sorrowfully whether it was only her body that stirred him—whether he found any spark in her honest little mind. And, for her second thought, she was considering in an injured way that this was not love as she had read of it in novels. "I didn't know just what it would be—but I didn't think it would be like this," she declared.

Love, as depicted in such American novels by literary pastors and matrons of perfect purity as had sifted into

THE JOB

the Panama public library, was an affair of astounding rescues from extreme peril, of highly proper walks in lanes, of laudable industry on the part of the hero, and of not more than three kisses—one on the brow, one on the cheek, and, in the very last paragraph of the book, one daringly but reverently deposited upon the lips. These young heroes and heroines never thought about bodies at all, except when they had been deceived in a field of asterisks. So to Una there was the world-old shock at the earthiness of love—and the penetrating joy of that earthiness. If real love was so much more vulgar than she had supposed, yet also it was so much more overwhelming that she was glad to be a flesh-and-blood lover, bruised and bewildered and estranged from herself, instead of a polite murmurer.

Gradually she was drawn back into a real communion with him when he damned the human race for serfs fighting in a dungeon, warring for land, for flags, for titles, and calling themselves kings. Walter took the same theories of socialism, single-tax, unionism, which J. J. Todd, of Chatham, had hacked out in commercial-college days, and he made them bleed and yawp and be hotly human. For the first time—Walter was giving her so many of those First Times of life!—Una realized how strong is the demand of the undermen for a conscious and scientific justice. She denied that stenographers could ever form a union, but she could not answer his acerb, "Why not?"

It was not in the patiently marching Una to be a creative thinker, yet she did hunger for self-mastery, and ardently was she following the erratic gibes at civilization with which young Walter showed his delight in having an audience, when the brown, homely Golden family clock struck eleven.

"Heavens!" she cried. "You must run home at once. Good-night, dear."

He rose obediently, nor did their lips demand each other again.

Her mother awoke to yawn. "He is a very polite young man, but I don't think he is solid enough for you, dearie. If he comes again, do remind me to show him the kodaks of your father, like I promised."

Then Una began to ponder the problem which is so weighty to girls of the city—where she could see her lover, since the parks were impolite and her own home obtrusively dull to him.

Whether Walter was a peril or not, whether or not his love was angry and red and full of hurts, yet she knew that it was more to her than her mother or her conventions or her ambitious little job. Thus gladly confessing, she fell asleep, and a new office day began, for always the office claims one again the moment that the evening's freedom is over.

CHAPTER VII

THESE children of the city, where there is no place for love-making, for discovering and testing each other's hidden beings, ran off together in the scanted parties of the ambitious poor. Walter was extravagant financially as he was mentally, but he had many debts, some conscience, and a smallness of salary. She was pleased by the smallest diversions, however, and found luxury in a bowl of chop-suey. He took her to an Italian restaurant and pointed out supposititious artists. They had gallery seats for a Maude Adams play, at which she cried and laughed whole-heartedly and held his hand all through. Her first real tea was with him—in Panama one spoke of "ladies' afternoon tea," not of "tea." She was awed by his new walking-stick and the new knowledge of cinnamon toast which he displayed for her. She admired, too, the bored way he swung his stick as they sauntered into and out of the lobbies of the great hotels.

The first flowers from a real florist's which she had ever received, except for a bunch of carnations from Henry Carson at Panama high-school commencement, came from Walter—long-stemmed roses in damp paper and a florist's box, with Walter's card inside.

And perhaps the first time that she had ever really seen spring, felt the intense light of sky and cloud and fresh greenery as her own, was on a Sunday just before the fragrant first of June, when Walter and she slipped away from her mother and walked in Central Park, shabby but unconscious.

She explored with him, too; felt adventurous in quite respectable Japanese and Greek and Syrian restaurants.

But her mother waited for her at home, and the job, the office, the desk, demanded all her energy.

Had they seen each other less frequently, perhaps Walter would have let dreams serve for real kisses, and have been satisfied. But he saw her a hundred times a day—and yet their love progressed so little. The propinquity of the office tantalized them. And Mrs. Golden kept them apart.

§ 2

The woman who had aspired and been idle while Captain Golden had toiled for her, who had mourned and been idle while Una had planned for her, and who had always been a compound of selfishness and love, was more and more accustomed to taking her daughter's youth to feed her comfort and her canary—a bird of atrophied voice and uncleanly habit.

If this were the history of the people who wait at home, instead of the history of the warriors, rich credit would be given to Mrs. Golden for enduring the long, lonely days, listening for Una's step. A proud, patient woman with nothing to do all day but pick at a little housework, and read her eyes out, and wish that she could run in and be neighborly with the indifferent urbanites who formed about her a wall of ice. Yet so confused are human purposes that this good woman who adored her daughter also sapped her daughter's vigor. As the office loomed behind all of Una's desires, so behind the office, in turn, was ever the shadowy thought of the appealing figure there at home; and toward her mother Una was very compassionate.

Yes, and so was her mother!

Mrs. Golden liked to sit soft and read stories of young love. Partly by nature and partly because she had learned that thus she could best obtain her wishes, she was gentle as a well-filled cat and delicate as a tulle scarf. She was admiringly adhesive to Una as she had been to Captain Golden, and she managed the new master of the house just as she had managed the former one. She listened to dictates pleasantly, was perfectly charmed at suggestions that she do anything, and then gracefully forgot.

Mrs. Golden was a mistress of graceful forgetting. Almost never did she remember to do anything she didn't want to do. She did not lie about it; she really and quite beautifully did forget.

Una, hurrying off to the office every morning, agonized with the effort to be on time, always had to stop and prepare a written list of the things her mother was to do. Otherwise, bespelled by the magazine stories which she kept forgetting and innocently rereading, Mrs. Golden would forget the marketing, forget to put the potatoes on to boil, forget to scrub the bathroom. . . . And she often contrived to lose the written list, and searched for it, with trembling lips but no vast persistence.

Una, bringing home the palsying weariness of the day's drudgery, would find a cheery welcome — and the work not done; no vegetables for dinner, no fresh boric-acid solution prepared for washing her stinging eyes.

Nor could Una herself get the work immediately out of the way, because her mother was sure to be lonely, to need comforting before Una could devote herself to anything else or even wash away the sticky office grime. . . . Mrs. Golden would have been shocked into a stroke could she have known that while Una was greeting her, she was muttering within herself, "I do wish I could brush my teeth first!"

If Una was distraught, desirous of disappearing in order to get hold of herself, Mrs. Golden would sigh, "Dear, have I done something to make you angry?" In any case, whether Una was silent or vexed with her, the mother would manage to be hurt but brave; sweetly distressed, but never quite tearful. And Una would have to kiss her, pat her hair, before she could escape and begin to get dinner (with her mother helping, always ready to do anything that Una's doggedly tired mind might suggest, but never suggesting novelties herself).

After dinner, Mrs. Golden was always ready to do whatever Una wished—to play cribbage, or read aloud, or go for a walk—not a *long* walk; she was so delicate, you know, but a nice *little* walk with her dear, dear daughter. . . . For such amusements she was ready to give up all her own favorite evening diversions—namely, playing solitaire, and reading and taking nice little walks. . . . But she did not like to have Una go out and leave her, nor have naughty, naughty men like Walter take Una to the theater, as though they wanted to steal the dear daughter away. And she wore Una's few good frocks, and forgot to freshen them in time for Una to wear them. Otherwise, Mrs. Golden had the unselfishness of a saint on a marble pillar.

Una, it is true, sometimes voiced her irritation over her mother's forgetfulness and her subsequent pathos, but for that bitterness she always blamed herself, with horror remembered each cutting word she had said to the Little

Mother Saint (as, in still hours when they sat clasped like lovers, she tremblingly called her).

§ 3

Mrs. Golden's demand of Una for herself had never been obvious till it clashed with Walter's demand.

Una and Walter talked it over, but they seemed mutely to agree, after the evening of Mrs. Golden and conversation, that it was merely balking for him to call at the flat. Nor did Una and Mrs. Golden discuss why Mr. Babson did not come again, or whether Una was seeing him. Una was accustomed to say only that she would be "away this evening," but over the teapot she quoted Walter's opinions on Omar, agnosticism, motor magazines, pipe-smoking, Staten Island, and the Himalayas, and it was evident that she was often with him.

Mrs. Golden's method of opposition was very simple. Whenever Una announced that she was going out, her mother's bright, birdlike eyes filmed over; she sighed and hesitated, "Shall I be alone all evening—after all day, too?" Una felt like a brute. She tried to get her mother to go to the Sessionses' flat more often, to make new friends, but Mrs. Golden had lost all her adaptability. She clung to Una and to her old furniture as the only recognizable parts of her world. Often Una felt forced to refuse Walter's invitations; always she refused to walk with him on the long, splendid Saturday afternoons of freedom. Nor would she let him come and sit on the roof with her, lest her mother see them in the hall and be hurt.

So it came to pass that only in public did she meet Walter. He showed his resentment by inviting her out less and less, by telling her less and less frankly his ambitions and his daily dabs at becoming a great man.

Apparently he was rather interested in a flour-faced actress at his boarding-house.

Never, now, did he speak of marriage. The one time when he had spoken of it, Una had been so sure of their happiness that she had thought no more of that formality than had his reckless self. But now she yearned to have him "propose," in the most stupid, conventional, pink-romance fashion. "Why can't we be married?" she fancied herself saying to him, but she never dared say it aloud.

Often he was abstracted when he was with her, in the office or out. Always he was kindly, but the kindliness seemed artificial. She could not read his thoughts, now that she had no hand-clasp to guide her.

On a hot, quivering afternoon of early July, Walter came to her desk at closing-hour and said, abruptly: "Look. You've simply *got* to come out with me this evening. We'll dine at a little place at the foot of the Palisades. I can't stand seeing you so little. I won't ask you again! You aren't fair."

"Oh, I don't mean to be unfair—"

"Will you come? Will you?"

His voice glared. Regardless of the office folk about them, he put his hand over hers. She was sure that Miss Moynihan was bulkily watching them. She dared not take time to think.

"Yes," she said, "I will go."

§ 4

It was a beer-garden frequented by yachtless German yachtsmen in shirt-sleeves, boating-caps, and mustaches like muffs, but to Una it was Europe and the banks of the Rhine, that restaurant below the Palisades where she dined with Walter.

THE JOB

A placid hour it was, as dusk grew deeper and more fragrant, and they leaned over the terrace rail to meditate on the lights springing out like laughing jests incarnate—reflected lights of steamers paddling with singing excursionists up the Hudson to the storied hills of Rip Van Winkle; imperial sweeps of fire that outlined the mighty city across the river.

Walter was at peace. He spared her his swart intensity; he shyly quoted Tennyson, and bounced with cynicisms about "Sherbert Souse" and "the *Gas-bag*." He brought happiness to her, instead of the agitation of his kisses.

She was not an office machine now, but one with the village lovers of poetry, as her job-exhaustion found relief in the magic of the hour, in the ancient music of the river, in breezes which brought old tales down from the Catskills.

She would have been content to sit there for hours, listening to the twilight, absently pleating the coarse table-cloth, trying to sip the saline claret which he insisted on their drinking. She wanted nothing more. . . . And she had so manœuvered their chairs that the left side of her face, the better side, was toward him!

But Walter grew restless. He stared at the German yachtsmen, at their children who ate lumps of sugar dipped in claret, and their wives who drank beer. He commented needlessly on a cat which prowled along the terrace rail. He touched Una's foot with his, and suddenly condemned himself for not having been able to bring her to a better restaurant. He volubly pointed out that their roast chicken had been petrified—"vile restaurant, very vile food."

"Why, I love it here!" she protested. "I'm perfectly happy to be just like this."

As she turned to him with a smile that told all her

tenderness, she noted how his eyes kept stealing from the riverside to her, and back again, how his hands trembled as he clapped two thick glass salt-shakers together. A current of uneasiness darted between them.

He sprang up. "Oh, I can't sit still!" he said. "Come on. Let's walk down along the river."

"Oh, can't we just sit here and be quiet?" she pleaded, but he rubbed his chin and shook his head and sputtered: "Oh, rats, you can't see the river, now that they've turned on the electric lights here. Come on. Besides, it 'll be cooler right by the river."

She felt a menace; the darkness beyond them was no longer dreaming, but terror-filled. She wanted to refuse, but he was so fretfully demanding that she could only obey him.

Up on the crest of the Palisades is an "amusement park," and suburbs and crowded paths; and across the river is New York, in a solid mass of apartment-houses; but between Palisades and river, at the foot of the cliffs, is an unfrequented path which still keeps some of the wildness it had when it was a war-path of the Indians. It climbs ridges, twists among rocks, dips into damp hollows, widens out into tiny bowling-greens for Hendrik Hudson's fairy men. By night it is ghostly, and beside it the river whispers strange tragedies.

Along this path the city children crept, unspeaking, save when his two hands, clasping her waist to guide her down a rocky descent, were clamorous.

Where a bare sand jetty ran from the path out into the river's broad current, Walter stopped and whispered, "I wish we could go swimming."

"I wish we could—it's quite warm," she said, prosaically.

But river and dark woods and breeze overhead seemed

to whisper to her—whisper, whisper, all the shrouded night aquiver with low, eager whispers. She shivered to find herself imagining the unimaginable—that she might throw off her stodgy office clothes, her dull cloth skirt and neat blouse, and go swimming beside him, revel in giving herself up to the utter frankness of cool water laving her bare flesh.

She closed her mind. She did not condemn herself for wanting to bathe as Mother Eve had bathed, naked and unafraid. She did not condemn herself—but neither did she excuse. She was simply afraid. She dared not try to make new standards; she took refuge in the old standards of the good little Una. Though all about her called the enticing voices of night and the river, yet she listened for the tried counsel voices of the plain Panama streets and the busy office.

While she struggled, Walter stood with his arm fitted about her shoulder, letting the pregnant silence speak, till again he insisted: "Why couldn't we go swimming?" Then, with all the cruelly urgent lovers of the days of hungry poetry: "We're going to let youth go by and never dare to be mad. Time will get us—we'll be old—it will be too late to enjoy being mad." His lyric cry dropped to a small-boy excuse: "Besides, it wouldn't hurt. . . . Come on. Think of plunging in."

"No, no, no, no!" she cried, and ran from him up the jetty, back to the path. . . . She was not afraid of him, because she was so much more afraid of herself.

He followed sullenly as the path led them farther and farther. She stopped on a rise, and found herself able to say, calmly, "Don't you think we'd better go back now?"

"Maybe we ought to. But sit down here."

He hunched up his knees, rested his elbows on them,

and said, abstractedly, apparently talking to himself as much as to her:

"I'm sorry I've been so grouchy coming down the path. But I *don't* apologize for wanting us to go swimming. Civilization, the world's office-manager, tells us to work like fiends all day and be lonely and respectable all evening, and not even marry till we're thirty, because we can't afford to! That's all right for them as likes to become nice varnished desks, but not for me! I'm going to hunger and thirst and satisfy my appetites—even if it makes me selfish as the devil. I'd rather be that than be a bran-stuffed automaton that's never human enough to hunger. But of course you're naturally a Puritan and always will be one, no matter what you do. You're a good sort—I'd trust you to the limit—you're sincere and you want to grow. But me—my Wanderjahr isn't over yet. Maybe some time we'll again— I admire you, but—if I weren't a little mad I'd go literally mad. . . . Mad—mad!"

He suddenly undid the first button of her blouse and kissed her neck harshly, while she watched him, in a maze. He abruptly fastened the button again, sprang up, stared out at the wraith-filled darkness over the river, while his voice droned on, as though it were a third person speaking:

"I suppose there's a million cases a year in New York of crazy young chaps making violent love to decent girls and withdrawing because they have some hidden decency themselves. I'm ashamed that I'm one of them—me, I'm as bad as a nice little Y. M. C. A. boy—I bow to conventions, too. Lordy! the fact that I'm so old-fashioned as even to talk about 'conventions' in this age of Shaw and d'Annunzio shows that I'm still a small-town, district-school radical! I'm really as mid-Victorian as you are, in knowledge. Only I'm modern by instinct, and the

THE JOB

combination will always keep me half-baked, I suppose.
I don't know what I want from life, and if I did I wouldn't
know how to get it. I'm a Middle Western farmer, and
yet I regard myself about half the time as an Oxford man
with a training in Paris. You're lucky, girl. You have
a definite ambition—either to be married and have babies
or to boss an office. Whatever I did, I'd spoil you—at
least I would till I found myself—found out what I wanted.
... *Lord!* how I hope I do find myself some day!"

"Poor boy!" she suddenly interrupted; "it's all right.
Come, we'll go home and try to be good."

"Wonderful! There speaks the American woman, perfectly. You think I'm just chattering. You can't understand that I was never so desperately in earnest in my
life. Well, to come down to cases. Specification A—I
couldn't marry you, because we haven't either of us got
any money—aside from my not having found myself yet.
Ditto B—We can't play, just because you *are* a Puritan
and I'm a typical intellectual climber. Same C—I've
actually been offered a decent job in the advertising department of a motor-car company in Omaha, and now
I think I'll take it."

And that was all that he really had to say, just that
last sentence, though for more than an hour they discussed
themselves and their uncharted world, Walter trying to
be honest, yet to leave with her a better impression of
himself; Una trying to keep him with her. It was hard for
her to understand that Walter really meant all he said.

But, like him, she was frank.

There are times in any perplexed love when the lovers
revel in bringing out just those problems and demands
and complaints which they have most carefully concealed.
At such a time of mutual confession, if the lovers are
honest and tender, there is none of the abrasive hostility

8 [105]

of a vulgar quarrel. But the kindliness of the review need
not imply that it is profitable; often it ends, as it began,
with the wail, "What can we do?" But so much alike
are all the tribe of lovers, that the debaters never fail to
stop now and then to congratulate themselves on being
so frank!

Thus Una and Walter, after a careful survey of the
facts that he was too restless, that she was too Panaman-
ian and too much mothered, after much argument as to
what he had meant when he had said this, and what she
had thought he meant when he had said that, and whether
he could ever have been so inconsiderate as to have said
the other, and frequent admiration of themselves for
their open-mindedness, the questing lovers were of the
same purpose as at the beginning of their inquiry. He
still felt the urge to take up his pilgrimage again, to let
the "decent job" and Omaha carry him another stage in
his search for the shrouded gods of his nebulous faith.
And she still begged for a chance to love, to be needed;
still declared that he was merely running away from himself.

They had quite talked themselves out before he sighed:
"I don't dare to look and see what time it is. Come, we'll
have to go."

They swung arms together shyly as they stumbled back
over the path. She couldn't believe that he really would
go off to the West, of which she was so ignorant. But she
felt as though she were staggering into a darkness blinder
and ever more blind.

When she got home she found her mother awake, very
angry over Una's staying out till after midnight, and very
wordy about the fact that "that nice, clean young man,"
Mr. J. J. Todd, of Chatham and of the commercial college,
had come to call that evening. Una made little answer to

her. Through her still and sacred agony she could scarce hear her mother's petulant whining.

§ 5

Next morning at the office, Walter abruptly asked her to come out into the hall, told her that he was leaving without notice that afternoon. He could never bear to delay, once he had started out on the "Long Trail," he said, not looking at her. He hastily kissed her, and darted back into the office. She did not see him again till, at five-thirty, he gave noisy farewell to all the adoring stenographers and office-boys, and ironical congratulations to his disapproving chiefs. He stopped at her desk, hesitated noticeably, then said, "Good-by, Goldie," and passed on. She stared, hypnotized, as, for the last time, Walter went bouncing out of the office.

§ 6

A week later J. J. Todd called on her again. He was touching in his description of his faithful labor for the Charity Organization Society. But she felt dead; she could not get herself to show approval. It was his last call.

§ 7

Walter wrote to her on the train—a jumbled rhapsody on missing her honest companionship. Then a lively description of his new chief at Omaha. A lonely letter on a barren evening, saying that there was nothing to say. A note about a new project of going to Alaska. She did not hear from him again.

For weeks she missed him so tragically that she found herself muttering over and over, "Now I sha'n't ever have a baby that would be a little image of him."

When she thought of the shy games and silly love-words she had lavished, she was ashamed, and wondered if they had made her seem a fool to him.

But presently in the week's unchanging routine she found an untroubled peace; and in mastering her work she had more comfort than ever in his clamorous summons.

At home she tried not merely to keep her mother from being lonely, but actually to make her happy, to coax her to break into the formidable city. She arranged summer-evening picnics with the Sessionses.

She persuaded them to hold one of these picnics at the foot of the Palisades. During it she disappeared for nearly half an hour. She sat alone by the river. Suddenly, with a feverish wrench, she bared her breast, then shook her head angrily, rearranged her blouse, went back to the group, and was unusually gay, though all the while she kept her left hand on her breast, as though it pained her.

She had been with the *Gazette* for only a little over six months, and she was granted only a week's vacation. This she spent with her mother at Panama. In parties with old neighbors she found sweetness, and on a motor-trip with Henry Carson and his fiancée, a young widow, she let the fleeting sun-flecked land absorb her soul.

At the office Una was transferred to S. Herbert Ross's department, upon Walter's leaving. She sometimes took S. Herbert's majestic, flowing dictation. She tried not merely to obey his instructions, but also to discover his unvoiced wishes. Her wage was raised from eight dollars a week to ten. She again determined to be a real business woman. She read a small manual on advertising.

But no one in the *Gazette* office believed that a woman could bear responsibilities, not even S. Herbert Ross, with his aphorisms for stenographers, his prose poems about the ecstatic joy of running a typewriter nine hours a day, which appeared in large, juicy-looking type in business magazines.

She became bored, mechanical, somewhat hopeless. She planned to find a better job and resign. In which frame of mind she was rather contemptuous of the *Gazette* office; and it was an unforgetable shock suddenly to be discharged.

Ross called her in, on a winter afternoon, told her that he had orders from the owner to "reduce the force," because of a "change of policy," and that, though he was sorry, he would have to "let her go because she was one of the most recent additions." He assured her royally that he had been pleased by her work; that he would be glad to give her "the best kind of a recommend—and if the situation loosens up again, I'd be tickled to death to have you drop in and see me. Just between us, I think the owner will regret this tight-wad policy."

But Mr. S. Herbert Ross continued to go out to lunch with the owner, and Una went through all the agony of not being wanted even in the prison she hated. No matter what the reason, being discharged is the final insult in an office, and it made her timid as she began wildly to seek a new job.

CHAPTER VIII

IN novels and plays architects usually are delicate young men who wear silky Vandyke beards, play the piano, and do a good deal with pictures and rugs. They leap with desire to erect charming cottages for the poor, and to win prize contests for the Jackson County Courthouse. They always have good taste; they are perfectly mad about simplicity and gracefulness. But from the number of flat-faced houses and three-toned wooden churches still being erected, it may be deduced that somewhere there are architects who are not enervated by too much good taste.

Mr. Troy Wilkins, architect, with an office in the Septimus Building, was a commuter. He wore a derby and a clipped mustache, and took interest in cameras, player-pianos, phonographs, small motor-cars, speedometers, tires, patent nicotineless pipes, jolly tobacco for jimmy - pipes, tennis - rackets, correspondence courses, safety-razors, optimism, Theodore Roosevelt, pocket flashlights, rubber heels, and all other well-advertised wares. He was a conservative Republican and a Congregationalist, and on his desk he kept three silver-framed photographs—one of his wife and two children, one of his dog Rover, and one of his architectural masterpiece, the mansion of Peter B. Reardon, the copper king of Montana.

Mr. Troy Wilkins lamented the passing of the solid

and expensive stone residences of the nineties, but he kept "up to date," and he had added ideals about half-timbered villas, doorway settles, garages, and sleeping-porches to his repertoire. He didn't, however, as he often said, "believe in bungalows any more than he believed in these labor unions."

§ 2

Una Golden had been the chief of Mr. Troy Wilkins's two stenographers for seven months now—midsummer of 1907, when she was twenty-six. She had climbed to thirteen dollars a week. The few hundred dollars which she had received from Captain Golden's insurance were gone, and her mother and she had to make a science of saving—economize on milk, on bread, on laundry, on tooth-paste. But that didn't really matter, because Una never went out except for walks and moving-picture shows, with her mother. She had no need, no want of clothes to impress suitors. . . . She had four worn letters from Walter Babson which she re-read every week or two; she had her mother and, always, her job.

§ 3

Una, an errand-boy, and a young East-Side Jewish stenographer named Bessie Kraker made up the office force of Troy Wilkins. The office was on the eighth floor of the Septimus Building, which is a lean, jerry-built, flashingly pretentious cement structure with cracking walls and dirty, tiled hallways.

The smeary, red-gold paint which hides the imperfect ironwork of its elevators does not hide the fact that they groan like lost souls, and tremble and jerk and threaten to fall. The Septimus Building is typical of at least one half

of a large city. It was "run up" by a speculative builder
for a "quick turn-over." It is semi-fire-proof, but more semi
than fire-proof. It stands on Nassau Street, between two
portly stone buildings that try to squeeze this lanky im-
postor to death, but there is more cheerful whistling in its
hallways than in the halls of its disapproving neighbors.
Near it is City Hall Park and Newspaper Row, Wall
Street and the lordly Stock Exchange, but, aside from a
few dull and honest tenants like Mr. Troy Wilkins, the
Septimus Building is filled with offices of fly-by-night
companies—shifty promoters, mining-concerns, beauty-
parlors for petty brokers, sample-shoe shops, discreet
lawyers, and advertising dentists. Seven desks in one
large room make up the entire headquarters of eleven
international corporations, which possess, as capital,
eleven hundred and thirty dollars, much embossed stationery—and the seven desks. These modest capitalists
do not lease their quarters by the year. They are doing
very well if they pay rent for each of four successive
months. But also they do not complain about repairs;
they are not fussy about demanding a certificate of moral
perfection from the janitor. They speak cheerily to elevator-boys and slink off into saloons. Not all of them keep
Yom Kippur; they all talk of being "broad-minded."

Mr. Wilkins's office was small and agitated. It consisted of two rooms and an insignificant entry-hall, in
which last was a water-cooler, a postal scale, a pile of newspapers, and a morose office-boy who drew copies of Gibson
girls all day long on stray pieces of wrapping-paper, and
confided to Una, at least once a week, that he wanted to
take a correspondence course in window-dressing. In
one of the two rooms Mr. Wilkins cautiously made draw-
ings at a long table, or looked surprised over correspondence at a small old-fashioned desk, or puffed and scratched

as he planned form-letters to save his steadily waning business.

In the other room there were the correspondence-files, and the desks of Una, the chief stenographer, and of slangy East-Side Bessie Kraker, who conscientiously copied form-letters, including all errors in them, and couldn't, as Wilkins complainingly pointed out, be trusted with dictation which included any words more difficult than "sincerely."

From their window the two girls could see the windows of an office across the street. About once a month an interesting curly-haired youth leaned out of one of the windows opposite. Otherwise there was no view.

§ 4

Twelve o'clock, the hour at which most of the offices closed on Saturday in summer, was excitedly approaching. The office-women throughout the Septimus Building, who had been showing off their holiday frocks all morning, were hastily finishing letters, or rushing to the women's wash-rooms to discuss with one another the hang of new skirts. All morning Bessie Kraker had kept up a monologue, beginning, "Say, lis-ten, Miss Golden, say, gee! I was goin' down to South Beach with my gentleman friend this afternoon, and, say, what d' you think the piker had to go and get stuck for? He's got to work all afternoon. I don't care—I don't care! I'm going to Coney Island with Sadie, and I bet you we pick up some fellows and do the light fantastic till one G. M. Oh, you sad sea waves! I bet Sadie and me make 'em sad!"

"But we'll be straight," said Bessie, half an hour later, apropos of nothing. "But gee! it's fierce to not have any good times without you take a risk. But gee! my dad would kill me if I went wrong. He reads the Talmud all the time, and hates Goys. But gee! I can't stand it all the time being a mollycoddle. I wisht I was a boy! I'd be a' aviator."

Bessie had a proud new blouse with a deep V, the edges of which gaped a bit and suggested that by ingenuity one could see more than was evident at first. Troy Wilkins, while pretending to be absent-mindedly fussing about a correspondence-file that morning, had fogotten that he was much married and had peered at the V. Una knew it, and the sordidness of that curiosity so embarrassed her that she stopped typing to clutch at the throat of her own high-necked blouse, her heart throbbing. She wanted to run away. She had a vague desire to "help" Bessie, who purred at poor, good Mr. Wilkins and winked at Una and chewed gum enjoyably, who was brave and hardy and perfectly able to care for herself—an organism modified by the Ghetto to the life which still bewildered Una.

Mr. Wilkins went home at 11.17, after giving them enough work to last till noon. The office-boy chattily disappeared two minutes later, while Bessie went two minutes after that. Her delay was due to the adjustment of her huge straw hat, piled with pink roses and tufts of blue malines.

Una stayed till twelve. Her ambition had solidified into an unreasoning conscientiousness.

With Bessie gone, the office was so quiet that she hesitated to typewrite lest They sneak up on her—They who dwell in silent offices as They dwell beneath a small boy's bed at night. The hush was intimidating; her slightest movement echoed; she stopped the sharply tapping machine after every few words to listen.

At twelve she put on her hat with two jabs of the hatpins, and hastened to the elevator, exulting in freedom.

THE JOB

The elevator was crowded with girls in new white frocks, voluble about their afternoon's plans. One of them carried a wicker suit-case. She was, she announced, starting on her two weeks' vacation; there would be some boys, and she was going to have "a peach of a time."

Una and her mother had again spent a week of June in Panama, and she now recalled the bright, free mornings and lingering, wonderful twilights.

She had no place to go this holiday afternoon, and she longed to join a noisy, excited party. Of Walter Babson she did not think. She stubbornly determined to snatch this time of freedom. Why, of course, she asserted, she could play by herself quite happily! With a spurious gaiety she patted her small black hand-bag. She skipped across to the Sixth Avenue Elevated and went up to the department-store district. She made elaborate plans for the great adventure of shopping. Bessie Kraker had insisted, with the nonchalant shrillness of eighteen, that Una "had ought to wear more color"; and Una had found, in the fashion section of a woman's magazine, the suggestion for exactly the thing—"a modest, attractive frock of brown, with smart touches of orange" — and economical. She had the dress planned—ribbon-belt half brown and half orange, a collar edged with orange, cuffs slashed with it.

There were a score of mild matter-of-fact Unas on the same Elevated train with her, in their black hats and black jackets and black skirts and white waists, with one hint of coquetry in a white-lace jabot or a white-lace veil; faces slightly sallow or channeled with care, but eyes that longed to flare with love; women whom life didn't want except to type its letters about invoices of rubber heels; women who would have given their salvation for the chance to sacrifice themselves for love. . . . And there was one man on that Elevated train, a well-bathed man with cynical eyes, who read a little book with a florid gold cover, all about Clytemnestra, because he was certain that modern cities have no fine romance, no high tragedy; that you must go back to the Greeks for real feeling. He often aphorized, "Frightfully hackneyed to say, 'woman's place is in the home,' but really, you know, these women going to offices, vulgarizing all their fine womanliness, and this shrieking sisterhood going in for suffrage and Lord knows what. Give me the reticences of the harem rather than one of these office-women with gum-chewing vacuities. None of them clever enough to be tragic!" He was ever so whimsical about the way in which the suffrage movement had cheated him of the chance to find a "*grande amoureuse.*" He sat opposite Una in the train and solemnly read his golden book. He did not see Una watch with shy desire every movement of a baby that was talking to its mother in some unknown dialect of baby-land. He was feeling deep sensations about Clytemnestra's misfortunes—though he controlled his features in the most gentlemanly manner, and rose composedly at his station, letting a well-bred glance of pity fall upon the gum-chewers.

Una found a marvelously clean, new restaurant on Sixth Avenue, with lace curtains at the window and, between the curtains, a red geranium in a pot covered with red-crêpe paper tied with green ribbon. A new place! She was tired of the office, the Elevated, the flat on 148th Street, the restaurants where she tediously had her week-day lunches. She entered the new restaurant briskly, swinging her black bag. The place had Personality— the white enameled tables were set diagonally and clothed with strips of Japanese toweling. Una smiled at a lively photograph of two bunnies in a basket. With a sensation

THE JOB

of freedom and novelty she ordered coffee, chicken patty, and cocoanut layer-cake.

But the patty and the cake were very much like the hundreds of other patties and cakes which she had consumed during the past two years, and the people about her were of the horde of lonely workers who make up half of New York. The holiday enchantment dissolved. She might as well be going back to the office grind after lunch! She brooded, while outside, in that seething summer street, the pageant of life passed by and no voice summoned her. Men and girls and motors, people who laughed and waged commerce for the reward of love—they passed her by, life passed her by, a spectator untouched by joy or noble tragedy, a woman desperately hungry for life.

She began—but not bitterly, she was a good little thing, you know—to make the old familiar summary. She had no lover, no friend, no future. Walter—he might be dead, or married. Her mother and the office, between them, left her no time to seek lover or friend or success. She was a prisoner of affection and conscience.

She rose and paid her check. She did not glance at the picture of the bunnies in a basket. She passed out heavily, a woman of sterile sorrow.

§ 5

Una recovered her holiday by going shopping. An aisle-man in the dress-goods department, a magnificent creature in a braided morning-coat, directed her to the counter she asked for, spoke eloquently of woolen voiles, picked up her bag, and remarked, "Yes, we do manage to keep it cool here, even on the hottest days." A shopgirl laughed with her. She stole into one of the elevators, and, though she really should have gone home to her

THE JOB

mother, she went into the music department, where, among lattices wreathed with newly dusted roses, she listened to waltzes and two-steps played by a red-haired girl who was chewing gum and talking to a man while she played. The music roused Una to plan a wild dissipation. She would pretend that she had a sweetheart, that with him she was a-roving.

Una was not highly successful in her make-believe. She could not picture the imaginary man who walked beside her. She refused to permit him to resemble Walter Babson, and he refused to resemble anybody else. But she was throbbingly sure he was there as she entered a drug-store and bought a "Berline bonbon," a confection guaranteed to increase the chronic nervous indigestion from which stenographers suffer. Her shadow lover tried to hold her hand. She snatched it away and blushed. She fancied that a matron at the next tiny table was watching her silly play, reflected in the enormous mirror behind the marble soda-counter. The lover vanished. As she left the drug-store Una was pretending that she was still pretending, but found it difficult to feel so very exhilarated.

She permitted herself to go to a motion-picture show. She looked over all the posters in front of the theater, and a train-wreck, a seaside love-scene, a detective drama, all invited her.

A man in the seat in front of her in the theater nestled toward his sweetheart and harshly muttered, "Oh you old honey!" In the red light from the globe marking an exit she saw his huge red hand, with its thicket of little golden hairs, creep toward the hand of the girl.

Una longed for a love-scene on the motion-picture screen.

The old, slow familiar pain of congestion in the back of her neck came back. But she forgot the pain when the love-scene did appear, in a picture of a lake shore with a hotel porch, the flat sheen of photographed water, rushing boats, and a young hero with wavy black hair, who dived for the lady and bore her out when she fell out of a reasonably safe boat. The actor's wet, white flannels clung tight about his massive legs; he threw back his head with masculine arrogance, then kissed the lady. Una was dizzy with that kiss. She was shrinking before Walter's lips again. She could feel her respectable, type-writer-hardened fingers stroke the actor's swarthy, virile jaw. She gasped with the vividness of the feeling. She was shocked at herself; told herself she was not being "nice"; looked guiltily about; but passionately she called for the presence of her vague, imaginary lover.

"Oh, my dear, my dear, my dear!" she whispered, with a terrible cloistered sweetness—whispered to love itself.

Deliberately ignoring the mother who waited at home, she determined to spend a riotous evening going to a real theater, a real play. That is, if she could get a fifty-cent seat.

She could not.

"It's been exciting, running away, even if I can't go to the theater," Una comforted herself. "I'll go down to Lady Sessions's this evening. I'll pack mother off to bed. I'll take the Sessionses up some ice-cream, and we'll have a jolly time. . . . Mother won't care if I go. Or maybe she'll come with me" — knowing all the while that her mother would not come, and decidedly would care if Una deserted her.

However negligible her mother seemed from down-town, she loomed gigantic as Una approached their flat and assured herself that she was glad to be returning to the dear one.

The flat was on the fifth floor.

THE JOB

It was a dizzying climb—particularly on this hot afternoon.

§ 6

As Una began to trudge up the flat-sounding slate treads she discovered that her head was aching as though some one were pinching the top of her eyeballs. Each time she moved her head the pain came in a perceptible wave. The hallway reeked with that smell of onions and fried fish which had arrived with the first tenants. Children were dragging noisy objects about the halls. As the throb grew sharper during the centuries it took her to climb the first three flights of stairs, Una realized how hot she was, how the clammy coolness of the hall was penetrated by stabs of street heat which entered through the sun-haloed windows at the stair landings.

Una knocked at the door of her flat with that light, cheery tapping of her nails, like a fairy tattoo, which usually brought her mother running to let her in. She was conscious, almost with a physical sensation, of her mother; wanted to hold her close and, in the ecstasy of that caress, squeeze the office weariness from her soul. The Little Mother Saint—she was coming now—she was hurrying—

But the little mother was not hurrying. There was no response to Una's knock. As Una stooped in the dimness of the hallway to search in her bag for her latch-key, the pain pulsed through the top of her head again. She opened the door, and her longing for the embrace of her mother disappeared in healthy anger.

The living-room was in disorder. Her mother had not touched it all day—had gone off and left it.

"This is a little too much!" Una said, grimly.

The only signs of life were Mrs. Golden's pack of cards

THE JOB

for solitaire, her worn, brown Morris-chair, and accretions of the cheap magazines with pretty-girl covers which Mrs. Golden ransacked for love-stories. Mrs. Golden had been reading all the evening before, and pages of newspapers were crumpled in her chair, not one of them picked up. The couch, where Una had slept because it had been too hot for the two of them in a double bed, was still an eruption of bedclothes—the pillow wadded up, the sheets dragging out across the unswept floor. . . . The room represented discomfort, highly respectable poverty—and cleaning, which Una had to do before she could rest.

She sat down on the couch and groaned: "To have to come home to this! I simply can't trust mother. She hasn't done one—single—thing, not one single thing. And if it were only the first time—! But it's every day, pretty nearly. She's been asleep all day, and then gone for a walk. Oh yes, of course! She'll come back and say she'd forgotten this was Saturday and I'd be home early! Oh, of course!"

From the bedroom came a cough, then another. Una tried to keep her soft little heart in its temporary state of hardness long enough to have some effect on household discipline. "Huh!" she grunted. "Got a cold again. If she'd only stay outdoors a little—"

She stalked to the door of the bedroom. The blind was down, the window closed, the room stifling and filled with a yellow, unwholesome glimmer. From the bed her mother's voice, changed from its usual ring to a croak that was crepuscular as the creepy room, wheezed: "That —you—deary? I got—summer—cold—so sorry—leave work undone—"

"If you would only keep your windows *open*, my dear mother—"

9 [121]

Una marched to the window, snapped up the blind, banged up the sash, and left the room.

"I really can't see why!" was all she added. She did not look at her mother.

She slapped the living-room into order as though the disordered bedclothes and newspapers were bad children. She put the potatoes on to boil. She loosened her tight collar and sat down to read the "comic strips," the "Beauty Hints," and the daily instalment of the husband-and-wife serial in her evening paper. Una had nibbled at Shakespeare, Tennyson, Longfellow, and *Vanity Fair* in her high-school days, but none of these had satisfied her so deeply as did the serial's hint of sex and husband. She was absorbed by it. Yet all the while she was irritably conscious of her mother's cough—hacking, sore-sounding, throat-catching. Una was certain that this was merely one of the frequent imaginary ailments of her mother, who was capable of believing that she had cancer every time she was bitten by a mosquito. But this incessant crackling made Una jumpily anxious.

She reached these words in the serial: "I cannot forget, Amy, that whatever I am, my good old mother made me, with her untiring care and the gentle words she spoke to me when worried and harassed with doubt."

Una threw down the paper, rushed into the bedroom, crouched beside her mother, crying, "Oh, my mother sweetheart! You're just everything to me," and kissed her forehead.

The forehead was damp and cold, like a cellar wall. Una sat bolt up in horror. Her mother's face had a dusky flush, her lips were livid as clotted blood. Her arms were stiff, hard to the touch. Her breathing, rapid and agitated, like a frightened panting, was interrupted just then by a cough like the rattling of stiff, heavy paper, which left on her purple lips a little colorless liquid.

"Mother! Mother! My little mother—you're sick, you're really *sick*, and I didn't know and I spoke so harshly. Oh, what *is* it, what is it, mother dear?"

"Bad—cold," Mrs. Golden whispered. "I started coughing last night—I closed the door—you didn't hear me; you were in the other room—" Another cough wheezed dismally, shook her, gurgled in her yellow deep-lined neck. "C-could I have—window closed now?"

"No. I'm going to be your nurse. Just an awfully cranky old nurse, and so scientific. And you must have fresh air." Her voice broke. "Oh, and me sleeping away from you! I'll never do it again. I don't know what I *would* do if anything happened to you. . . . Do you feel any headache, dear?"

"No—not—not so much as— Side pains me—here."

Mrs. Golden's words labored like a steamer in heavy seas; the throbbing of her heart shook them like the throb of the engines. She put her hand to her right side, shakily, with effort. It lay there, yellow against the white muslin of her nightgown, then fell heavily to the bed, like a dead thing. Una trembled with fear as her mother continued, "My pulse—it's so fast—so hard breathing—side pain."

"I'll put on an ice compress and then I'll go and get a doctor."

Mrs. Golden tried to sit up. "Oh no, no, no! Not a doctor! Not a doctor!" she croaked. "Doctor Smyth will be busy."

"Well, I'll have him come when he's through."

"Oh no, no, can't afford—"

"Why—"

"And—they scare you so—he'd pretend I had pneu-

monia, like Sam's sister—he'd frighten me so—I just have
a summer cold. I—I'll be all right to-morrow, deary.
Oh no, no, *please* don't, please don't get a doctor.
Can't afford it—can't—"

Pneumonia! At the word, which brought the sterile
bitterness of winter into this fetid August room, Una was
in a rigor of fear, yet galvanized with belief in her mother's
bravery. "My brave, brave little mother!" she thought.

Not till Una had promised that she would not summon
the doctor was her mother quieted, though Una made the
promise with reservations. She relieved the pain in her
mother's side with ice compresses—the ice chipped from
the pitiful little cake in their tiny ice-box. She freshened
pillows, she smoothed sheets; she made hot broth and
bathed her mother's shoulders with tepid water and rubbed
her temples with menthol. But the fever increased, and
at times Mrs. Golden broke through her shallow slumber
with meaningless sentences, like the beginning of delirium.

At midnight she was panting more and more rapidly—
three times as fast as normal breathing. She was sunk
in a stupor. And Una, brooding by the bed, a crouched
figure of mute tragedy in the low light, grew more and
more apprehensive as her mother seemed to be borne
away from her. Una started up. She would risk her
mother's displeasure and bring the doctor. Just then,
even Doctor Smyth of the neighborhood practice and ob-
stetrical habits seemed a miracle-worker.

She had to go four blocks to the nearest drug-store
that would be open at this time of night, and there telephone the doctor.

She was aware that it was raining, for the fire-escape
outside shone wet in the light from a window across the
narrow court. She discovered she had left mackintosh
and umbrella at the office. Stopping only to set out a

clean towel, a spoon, and a glass on the chair by the bed, Una put on the old sweater which she secretly wore under her cheap thin jacket in winter. She lumbered wearily down-stairs. She prayed confusedly that God would give her back her headache and in reward make her mother well.

She was down-stairs at the heavy, grilled door. Rain was pouring. A light six stories up in the apartment-house across the street seemed infinitely distant and lonely, curtained from her by the rain. Water splashed in the street and gurgled in the gutters. It did not belong to the city as it would have belonged to brown woods or prairie. It was violent here, shocking and terrible. It took distinct effort for Una to wade out into it.

The modern city! Subway, asphalt, a wireless message winging overhead, and Una Golden, an office-woman in eye-glasses. Yet sickness and rain and night were abroad; and it was a clumsily wrapped peasant woman, bent-shouldered and heavily breathing, who trudged unprotected through the dark side-streets as though she were creeping along moorland paths. Her thought was dulled to everything but physical discomfort and the illness which menaced the beloved. Woman's eternal agony for the sick of her family had transformed the trim smoothness of the office-woman's face into wrinkles that were tragic and ruggedly beautiful.

§ 7

Again Una climbed the endless stairs to her flat. She unconsciously counted the beat of the weary, regular rhythm which her feet made on the slate treads and the landings—one, two, three, four, five, six, seven, landing, turn and—one, two, three, four, five, six, seven—over and over. At the foot of the last flight she suddenly believed that her mother needed her this instant. She broke the regular thumping rhythm of her climb, dashed up, cried out at the seconds wasted in unlocking the door. She tiptoed into the bedroom—and found her mother just as she had left her. In Una's low groan of gladness there was all the world's self-sacrifice, all the fidelity to a cause or to a love. But as she sat unmoving she came to feel that her mother was not there; her being was not in this wreck upon the bed.

In an hour the doctor soothed his way into the flat. He "was afraid there might be just a little touch of pneumonia." With breezy fatherliness which inspirited Una, he spoke of the possible presence of pneumococcus, of doing magic things with Romer's serum, of trusting in God, of the rain, of cold baths and digitalin. He patted Una's head and cheerily promised to return at dawn. He yawned and smiled at himself. He looked as roundly, fuzzily sleepy as a bunny rabbit, but in the quiet, forlorn room of night and illness he radiated trust in himself. Una said to herself, "He certainly must know what he is talking about."

She was sure that the danger was over. She did not go to bed, however. She sat stiffly in the bedroom and planned amusements for her mother. She would work harder, earn more money. They would move to a cottage in the suburbs, where they would have chickens and roses and a kitten, and her mother would find neighborly people again.

Five days after, late on a bright, cool afternoon, when all the flats about them were thinking of dinner, her mother died.

§ 8

There was a certain madness in Una's grief. Her agony was a big, simple, uncontrollable emotion, like the fanaticism of a crusader—alarming, it was, not to be reckoned with, and beautiful as a storm. Yet it was no more morbid than the little fits of rage with which a school-teacher relieves her cramped spirit. For the first time she had the excuse to exercise her full power of emotion.

Una evoked an image of her mother as one who had been altogether good, understanding, clever, and unfortunate. She regretted every moment she had spent away from her—remembered with scorn that she had planned to go to the theater the preceding Saturday, instead of sanctifying the time in the Nirvana of the beloved's presence; repented with writhing agony having spoken harshly about neglected household duties.

She even contrived to find it a virtue in her mother that she had so often forgotten the daily tasks—her mind had been too fine for such things. . . . Una retraced their life. But she remembered everything only as one remembers under the sway of music.

"If I could just have another hour, just one hour with her, and feel her hands on my eyes again—"

On the night before the funeral she refused to let even Mrs. Sessions stay with her. She did not want to share her mother's shadowy presence with any one.

She lay on the floor beside the bed where her mother was stately in death. It was her last chance to talk to her:

"Mother . . . Mother . . . Don't you hear me? It's Una calling. Can't you answer me this one last time? Oh, mother, think, mother dear, I can't ever hear your voice again if you don't speak to me now. . . . Don't you remember how we went home to Panama, our last vacation? Don't you remember how happy we were down at the lake? Little mother, you haven't forgotten, have you? Even if you don't answer, you know I'm watching by you, don't you? See, I'm kissing your hand. Oh, you did

want me to sleep near you again, this last night— Oh,
my God! oh, my God! the last night I shall ever spend
with her, the very last, last night."

All night long the thin voice came from the little white-
clad figure so insignificant in the dimness, now lying mo-
tionless on the comforter she had spread beside the bed,
and talking in a tone of ordinary conversation that was
uncanny in this room of invisible whisperers; now leaping
up to kiss the dead hand in a panic, lest it should already
be gone.

The funeral filled the house with intruders. The drive
to the cemetery was irritating. She wanted to leap out
of the carriage. At first she concentrated on the cushion
beside her till she thought of nothing in the world but
the faded bottle-green upholstery, and a ridiculous drift
of dust in the tufting. But some one was talking to her.
(It was awkward Mr. Sessions, for shrewd Mrs. Sessions
had the genius to keep still.) He kept stammering the
most absurd platitudes about how happy her mother
must be in a heaven regarding which he did not seem to
have very recent or definite knowledge. She was annoyed, not comforted. She wanted to break away, to
find her mother's presence again in that sacred place
where she had so recently lived and spoken.

Yet, when Una returned to the flat, something was gone.
She tried to concentrate on thought about immortality.
She found that she had absolutely no facts upon which
to base her thought. The hundreds of good, sound,
orthodox sermons she had heard gave her nothing but
vague pictures of an eternal church supper somewhere in
the clouds—nothing, blankly and terribly nothing, that
answered her bewildered wonder as to what had become
of the spirit which had been there and now was gone.

In the midst of her mingling of longing and doubt she

realized that she was hungry, and she rather regretted
having refused Mrs. Sessions's invitation to dinner. She
moved slowly about the kitchen.

The rheumatic old canary hobbled along the floor of
his cage and tried to sing. At that Una wept, "She never
will hear poor Dickie sing again."

Instantly she remembered—as clearly as though she
were actually listening to the voice and words—that her
mother had burst out, "Drat that bird, it does seem as if
every time I try to take a nap he just tries to wake me up."
Una laughed grimly. Hastily she reproved herself, "Oh,
but mother didn't mean—"

But in memory of that healthily vexed voice, it seemed
less wicked to take notice of food, and after a reasonable
dinner she put on her kimono and bedroom slippers,
carefully arranged the pillows on the couch, and lay among
them, meditating on her future.

For half an hour she was afire with an eager thought:
"Why can't I really make a success of business, now that
I can entirely devote myself to it? There's women—in
real estate, and lawyers and magazine editors—some of
them make ten thousand a year."

So Una Golden ceased to live a small-town life in New
York; so she became a genuine part of the world of
offices; took thought and tried to conquer this new way
of city-dwelling.

"Maybe I can find out if there's anything in life—now
—besides working for T. W. till I'm scrapped like an old
machine," she pondered. "How I hate letters about two-
family houses in Flatbush!"

She dug her knuckles into her forehead in the effort
to visualize the problem of the hopeless women in industry.

She was an Average Young Woman on a Job; she

thought in terms of money and offices; yet she was one with all the men and women, young and old, who were creating a new age. She was nothing in herself, yet as the molecule of water belongs to the ocean, so Una Golden humbly belonged to the leaven who, however confusedly, were beginning to demand, "Why, since we have machinery, science, courage, need we go on tolerating war and poverty and caste and uncouthness, and all that sheer clumsiness?"

Part II
THE OFFICE

CHAPTER IX

THE effect of grief is commonly reputed to be noble. But mostly it is a sterile nobility. Witness the widows who drape their musty weeds over all the living; witness the mother of a son killed in war who urges her son's comrades to bring mourning to the mothers of all the sons on the other side.

Grief is a paralyzing poison. It broke down Una's resistance to the cares of the office. Hers was no wholesome labor in which she could find sacred forgetfulness. It was the round of unessentials which all office-women know so desperately well. She bruised herself by shrinking from those hourly insults to her intelligence; and outside the office her most absorbing comfort was in the luxury of mourning—passion in black, even to the black-edged face-veil. . . . Though she was human enough to realize that with her fair hair she looked rather well in mourning, and shrewd enough to get it on credit at excellent terms.

She was in the office all day, being as curtly exact as she could. But in the evening she sat alone in her flat and feared the city.

Sometimes she rushed down to the Sessionses' flat, but the good people bored her with their assumption that she was panting to know all the news from Panama. She had drifted so far away from the town that the sixth assertion that "it was a great pity Kitty Wilson was going to marry that worthless Clark boy" aroused no interest in her. She was still more bored by their phonograph, on which they played over and over the same twenty records. She would make quick, unconvincing excuses about having to hurry away. Their slippered stupidity was a desecration of her mother's memory.

Her half-hysterical fear of the city's power was increased by her daily encounter with the clamorous streets, crowded elevators, frantic lunch-rooms, and, most of all, the experience of the Subway.

Amazing, incredible, the Subway, and the fact that human beings could become used to it, consent to spend an hour in it daily. There was a heroic side to this spectacle of steel trains clanging at forty miles an hour beneath twenty-story buildings. The engineers had done their work well, made a great thought in steel and cement. And then the business men and bureaucrats had made the great thought a curse. There was in the Subway all the romance which story-telling youth goes seeking: trains crammed with an inconceivable complexity of people— marquises of the Holy Roman Empire, Jewish factory hands, speculators from Wyoming, Iowa dairymen, quarreling Italian lovers, with their dramatic tales, their flux of every human emotion, under the city mask. But however striking these dramatic characters may be to the occasional spectator, they figure merely as an odor, a confusion, to the permanent serf of the Subway. . . . A long underground station, a catacomb with a cement platform, this was the chief feature of the city vista to the tired girl who waited there each morning. A clean space, but damp, stale, like the corridor to a prison—as indeed it was, since through it each morning Una entered the day's business life.

Then, the train approaching, filling the tunnel, like a

piston smashing into a cylinder; the shoving rush to get aboard. A crush that was ruffling and fatiguing to a man, but to a woman was horror.

Una stood with a hulking man pressing as close to her side as he dared, and a dapper clerkling squeezed against her breast. Above her head, to represent the city's culture and graciousness, there were advertisements of soap, stockings, and collars. At curves the wheels ground with a long, savage whine, the train heeled, and she was flung into the arms of the grinning clerk, who held her tight. She, who must never be so unladylike as to enter a polling-place, had breathed into her very mouth the clerkling's virile electoral odor of cigarettes and onions and decayed teeth.

A very good thing, the Subway. It did make Una quiver with the beginnings of rebellious thought as no suave preacher could ever have done. Almost hysterically she resented this daily indignity, which smeared her clean, cool womanhood with a grease of noise and smell and human contact.

As was the Subway, so were her noons of elbowing to get impure food in restaurants.

For reward she was permitted to work all day with Troy Wilkins. And for heavens and green earth, she had a chair and a desk.

But the human organism, which can modify itself to arctic cold and Indian heat, to incessant labor or the long enervation of luxury, learns to endure. Unwilling dressing, lonely breakfast, the Subway, dull work, lunch, sleepiness after lunch, the hopelessness of three o'clock, the boss's ill-tempers, then the Subway again, and a lonely flat, with no love, no creative work; and at last a long sleep so that she might be fresh for such another round of delight. So went the days. Yet all through them she found amuse-

ment, laughed now and then, and proved the heroism as
well as the unthinking servility of the human race.

§ 2

The need of feeling that there were people near to her
urged Una to sell her furniture and move from the flat
to a boarding-house.

She avoided Mrs. Sessions's advice. She was sure that
Mrs. Sessions would bustle about and find her a respectable place where she would have to be cheery. She didn't
want to be cheery. She wanted to think. She even bought
a serious magazine with articles. Not that she read it.

But she was afraid to be alone any more. Anyway, she
would explore the city.

Of the many New Yorks, she had found only Morning-
side Park, Central Park, Riverside Drive, the shopping
district, the restaurants and theaters which Walter had
discovered to her, a few down-town office streets, and her
own arid region of flats. She did not know the proliferating
East Side, the factories, the endless semi-suburban stretches
—nor Fifth Avenue. Her mother and Mrs. Sessions had
inculcated in her the earnest idea that most parts of New
York weren't quite nice. In over two years in the city she
had never seen a millionaire nor a criminal; she knew the
picturesqueness neither of wealth nor of pariah poverty.

She did not look like an adventurer when, at a Saturday
noon of October, she left the office—slight, kindly, rather
timid, with her pale hair and school-teacher eye-glasses,
and clear cheeks set off by comely mourning. But she
was seizing New York. She said over and over, "Why, I
can go and live any place I want to, and maybe I'll meet
some folks who are simply fascinating." She wasn't very
definite about these fascinating folks, but they implied

girls to play with and—she hesitated—and decidedly men, men different from Walter, who would touch her hand in courtly reverence.

She poked through strange streets. She carried an assortment of "Rooms and Board" clippings from the "want-ad" page of a newspaper, and obediently followed their hints about finding the perfect place. She resolutely did not stop at places not advertised in the paper, though nearly every house, in some quarters, had a sign, "Room to Rent." Una still had faith in the veracity of whatever appeared in the public prints, as compared with what she dared see for herself.

The advertisements led her into a dozen parts of the city frequented by roomers, the lonely, gray, detached people who dwell in other people's houses.

It was not so splendid a quest as she had hoped; it was too sharp a revelation of the cannon-food of the city, the people who had never been trained, and who had lost heart. It was scarcely possible to tell one street from another; to remember whether she was on Sixteenth Street or Twenty-sixth. Always the same rows of red-brick or brownstone houses, all alike, the monotony broken only by infrequent warehouses or loft-buildings; always the same doubtful mounting of stone steps, the same searching for a bell, the same waiting, the same slatternly, suspicious landlady, the same evil hallway with a brown hat-rack, a steel-engraving with one corner stained with yellow, a carpet worn through to the flooring in a large oval hole just in front of the stairs, a smell of cabbage, a lack of ventilation. Always the same desire to escape, though she waited politely while the landlady in the same familiar harsh voice went through the same formula.

Then, before she could flee to the comparatively fresh air of the streets, Una would politely have to follow the

10

panting landlady to a room that was a horror of dirty carpet, lumpy mattress, and furniture with everything worn off that could wear off. And at last, always the same phrases by which Una meant to spare the woman: "Well, I'll think it over. Thank you so much for showing me the rooms, but before I decide— Want to look around—"

Phrases which the landlady heard ten times a day.

She conceived a great-hearted pity for landladies. They were so patient, in face of her evident distaste. Even their suspiciousness was but the growling of a beaten dog. They sighed and closed their doors on her without much attempt to persuade her to stay. Her heart ached with their lack of imagination. They had no more imagination than those landladies of the insect world, the spiders, with their unchanging, instinctive, ancestral types of webs.

Her depression was increased by the desperate physical weariness of the hunt. Not that afternoon, not till two weeks later, did she find a room in a large, long, somber railroad flat on Lexington Avenue, conducted by a curly-haired young bookkeeper and his pretty wife, who provided their clients with sympathy, with extensive and scientific data regarding the motion-picture houses in the neighborhood, and board which was neither scientific nor very extensive.

It was time for Una to sacrifice the last material contact with her mother; to sell the furniture which she had known ever since, as a baby in Panama, she had crawled from this horsehair chair, all the long and perilous way across this same brown carpet, to this red-plush couch.

§ 3

It was not so hard to sell the furniture; she could even read and burn her father's letters with an unhappy reso-

luteness. Despite her tenderness, Una had something of
youth's joy in getting rid of old things, as preparation
for acquiring the new. She did sob when she found her
mother's straw hat, just as Mrs. Golden had left it, on the
high shelf of the wardrobe—as though her mother might
come in at any minute, put it on, and start for a walk.
She sobbed again when she encountered the tiny tear in the
bottom of the couch, which her own baby fingers had made
in trying to enlarge a pirate's cave. That brought the
days when her parents were immortal and all-wise; when
the home sitting-room, where her father read the paper
aloud, was a security against all the formidable world
outside.

But to these recollections Una could shut her heart.
To one absurd thing, because it was living, Una could not
shut her heart—to the senile canary.

Possibly she could have taken it with her, but she felt
confusedly that Dickie would not be appreciated in other
people's houses. She evaded asking the Sessionses to
shelter the bird, because every favor that she permitted
from that smug family was a bond that tied her to their
life of married spinsterhood.

"Oh, Dickie, Dickie, what am I going to do with you?"
she cried, slipping a finger through the wires of the cage.

The canary hopped toward her and tried to chirp his
greeting.

"Even when you were sick you tried to sing to me, and
mother did love you," she sighed. "I just can't kill you
—trusting me like that."

She turned her back, seeking to solve the problem by
ignoring it. While she was sorting dresses—some trace
of her mother in every fold, every wrinkle of the waists
and lace collars—she was listening to the bird in the cage.

"I'll think of some way—I'll find somebody who will

want you, Dickie dear," she murmured, desperately, now and then.

After dinner and nightfall, with her nerves twanging all the more because it seemed silly to worry over one dissolute old bird when all her life was breaking up, she hysterically sprang up, snatched Dickie from the cage, and trotted down-stairs to the street.

"I'll leave you somewhere. Somebody will find you," she declared.

Concealing the bird by holding it against her breast with a hand supersensitive to its warm little feathers, she walked till she found a deserted tenement doorway. She hastily set the bird down on a stone balustrade beside the entrance steps. Dickie chirped more cheerily, more sweetly than for many days, and confidingly hopped back to her hand.

"Oh, I can't leave him for boys to torture and I can't take him, I can't—"

In a sudden spasm she threw the bird into the air, and ran back to the flat, sobbing, "I can't kill it—I can't—there's so much death." Longing to hear the quavering affection of its song once more, but keeping herself from even going to the window to look for it, with bitter haste she completed her work of getting rid of things—things—things—the things which were stones of an imprisoning past.

§ 4

Shyness was over Una when at last she was in the house of strangers. She sat marveling that this square, white cubby-hole of a room was hers permanently, that she hadn't just come here for an hour or two. She couldn't get it to resemble her first impression of it. Now the hallway was actually a part of her life—every morning she would face the picture of a magazine-cover girl when she came out of her room.

Her agitation was increased by the problem of keeping up the maiden modesty appropriate to a Golden, a young female friend of the Sessionses', in a small flat with gentlemen lodgers and just one bathroom. Una was saved by not having a spinster friend with whom to share her shrinking modesty. She simply had to take waiting for her turn at the bathroom as a matter of course, and insensibly she was impressed by the decency with which these dull, ordinary people solved the complexities of their enforced intimacy. When she wildly clutched her virgin bathrobe about her and passed a man in the hall, he stalked calmly by without any of the teetering apologies which broad-beamed Mr. Sessions had learned from his genteel spouse.

She could not at first distinguish among her companions. Gradually they came to be distinct, important. They held numberless surprises for her. She would not have supposed that a bookkeeper in a fish-market would be likely to possess charm. Particularly if he combined that amorphous occupation with being a boarding-house proprietor. Yet her landlord, Herbert Gray, with his look of a track-athlete, his confessions of ignorance and his naïve enthusiasms about whatever in the motion pictures seemed to him heroic, large, colorful, was as admirable as the several youngsters of her town who had plodded through Princeton or Pennsylvania and come back to practise law or medicine or gentlemanly inheritance of business. And his wife, round and comely, laughing easily, wearing her clothes with an untutored grace which made her cheap waists smart, was so thoroughly her husband's comrade in everything, that these struggling nobodies had all the riches of the earth.

THE JOB

The Grays took Una in as though she were their guest, but they did not bother her. They were city-born, taught by the city to let other people live their own lives.

The Grays had taken a flat twice too large for their own use. The other lodgers, who lived, like monks on a bare corridor, along the narrow "railroad" hall, were three besides Una:

A city failure, one with a hundred thousand failures, a gray-haired, neat man, who had been everything and done nothing, and who now said evasively that he was "in the collection business." He read Dickens and played a masterful game of chess. He liked to have it thought that his past was brave with mysterious splendors. He spoke hintingly of great lawyers. But he had been near to them only as a clerk for a large law firm. He was grateful to any one for noticing him. Like most of the failures, he had learned the art of doing nothing at all. All Sunday, except for a two hours' walk in Central Park, and one game of chess with Herbert Gray, he dawdled in his room, slept, regarded his stocking-feet with an appearance of profound meditation, yawned, picked at the Sunday newspaper. Una once saw him napping on a radiant autumn Sunday afternoon, and detested him. But he was politely interested in her work for Troy Wilkins, carefully exact in saying, "Good-morning, miss," and he became as familiar to her as the gas-heater in her cubicle.

Second fellow-lodger was a busy, reserved woman, originally from Kansas City, who had something to do with some branch library. She had solved the problems of woman's lack of place in this city scheme by closing tight her emotions, her sense of adventure, her hope of friendship. She never talked to Una, after discovering that Una had no interesting opinions on the best reading for children nine to eleven.

THE JOB

These gentle, inconsequential city waifs, the Grays, the failure, the library-woman, meant no more to Una than the crowds who were near, yet so detached, in the streets. But the remaining boarder annoyed her by his noisy whine. He was an underbred maverick, with sharp eyes of watery blue, a thin mustache, large teeth, and no chin worth noticing. He would bounce in of an evening, when the others were being decorous and dull in the musty dining-room, and yelp: "How do we all find our seskpadalian selves this bright and balmy evenin'? How does your perspegacity discipulate, Herby? What's the good word, Miss Golden? Well, well, well, if here ain't our good old friend, the Rev. J. Pilkington Corned Beef; how 'r' you, Pilky? Old Mrs. Cabbage feelin' well, too? Well, well, still discussing the movies, Herby? Got any new opinions about Mary Pickford? Well, well. Say, I met another guy that's as nutty as you, Herby; he thinks that Wilhelm Jenkins Bryan is a great statesman. Let's hear some more about the Sage of Free Silver, Herby."

The little man was never content till he had drawn them into so bitter an argument that some one would rise, throw down a napkin, growl, "Well, if that's all you know about it—if you're all as ignorant as that, you simply ain't worth arguing with," and stalk out. When general topics failed, the disturber would catechize the library-woman about Louisa M. Alcott, or the failure about his desultory inquiries into Christian Science, or Mrs. Gray about the pictures plastering the dining-room —a dozen spiritual revelations of apples and oranges, which she had bought at a department-store sale.

The maverick's name was Fillmore J. Benson. Strangers called him Benny, but his more intimate acquaintances, those to whom he had talked for at least an hour, were requested to call him Phil. He made a number of pretty puns about his first name. He was, surprisingly, a doctor—not the sort that studies science, but the sort that studies the gullibility of human nature—a "Doctor of Manipulative Osteology." He had earned a diploma by a correspondence course, and had scrabbled together a small practice among retired shopkeepers. He was one of the strange, impudent race of fakers who prey upon the clever city. He didn't expect any one at the Grays' to call him a "doctor."

He drank whisky and gambled for pennies, was immoral in his relations with women and as thick-skinned as he was blatant. He had been a newsboy, a contractor's clerk, and climbed up by the application of his wits. He read enormously—newspapers, cheap magazines, medical books; he had an opinion about everything, and usually worsted every one at the Grays' in arguments. And he did his patients good by giving them sympathy and massage. He would have been an excellent citizen had the city not preferred to train him, as a child in its reeling streets, to a sharp unscrupulousness.

Una was at first disgusted by Phil Benson, then perplexed. He would address her in stately Shakespearean phrases which, as a boy, he had heard from the gallery of the Academy of Music. He would quote poetry at her. She was impressed when he almost silenced the library-woman, in an argument as to whether Longfellow or Whittier was the better poet, by parroting the whole of "Snow Bound."

She fancied that Phil's general pea-weevil aspect concealed the soul of a poet. But she was shocked out of her pleasant fabling when Phil roared at Mrs. Gray: "Say, what did the baker use this pie for? A bureau or a trunk? I've found three pairs of socks and a safety-pin in my slab, so far."

THE JOB

Pretty Mrs. Gray was hurt and indignant, while her husband growled: "Aw, don't pay any attention to that human phonograph, Amy. He's got bats in his belfry."

Una had acquired a hesitating fondness for the mute gentleness of the others, and it infuriated her that this insect should spoil their picnic. But after dinner Phil Benson dallied over to her, sat on the arm of her chair, and said: "I'm awfully sorry that I make such a bum hit with you, Miss Golden. Oh, I can see I do, all right. You're the only one here that can understand. Somehow it seems to me—you aren't like other women I know. There's something—somehow it's different. A—a temperament. You dream about higher things than just food and clothes. Oh," he held up a deprecating hand, "don't deny it. I'm mighty serious about it, Miss Golden. I can see it, even if you haven't waked up to it as yet."

The absurd part of it was that, at least while he was talking, Mr. Phil Benson did believe what he was saying, though he had borrowed all of his sentiments from a magazine story about hobohemians which he had read the night before.

He also spoke of reading good books, seeing good plays, and the lack of good influences in this wicked city.

He didn't overdo it. He took leave in ten minutes— to find good influences in a Kelly pool-parlor on Third Avenue. He returned to his room at ten, and, sitting with his shoeless feet cocked up on his bed, read a story in *Racy Yarns*. While beyond the partition, about four feet from him, Una Golden lay in bed, her smooth arms behind her aching head, and worried about Phil's lack of opportunity.

She was finding in his loud impudence a twisted resemblance to Walter Babson's erratic excitability, and that won her, for love goes seeking new images of the god that is dead.

Next evening Phil varied his tactics by coming to dinner early, just touching Una's hand as she was going into the dining-room, and murmuring in a small voice, "I've been thinking so much of the helpful things you said last evening, Miss Golden."

Later, Phil talked to her about his longing to be a great surgeon—in which he had the tremendous advantage of being almost sincere. He walked down the hall to her room, and said good-night lingeringly, holding her hand.

Una went into her room, closed the door, and for full five minutes stood amazed. "Why!" she gasped, "the little man is trying to make love to me!"

She laughed over the absurdity of it. Heavens! She had her Ideal. The Right Man. He would probably be like Walter Babson—though more dependable. But whatever the nature of the paragon, he would in every respect be just the opposite of the creature who had been saying good-night to her.

She sat down, tried to read the paper, tried to put Phil out of her mind. But he kept returning. She fancied that she could hear his voice in the hall. She dropped the paper to listen.

"I'm actually interested in him!" she marveled. "Oh, that's ridiculous!"

§ 5

Now that Walter had made a man's presence natural to her, Una needed a man, the excitation of his touch, the solace of his voice. She could not patiently endure a cloistered vacuousness.

Even while she was vigorously representing to herself that he was preposterous, she was uneasily aware that

Phil was masculine. His talons were strong; she could feel their clutch on her hands. "He's a rat. And I do wish he wouldn't—spit!" she shuddered. But under her scorn was a surge of emotion. . . . A man, not much of a man, yet a man, had wanted the contact of her hand, been eager to be with her. Sensations vast as night or the ocean whirled in her small, white room. Desire, and curiosity even more, made her restless as a wave.

She caught herself speculating as she plucked at the sleeve of her black mourning waist: "I wonder would I be more interesting if I had the orange-and-brown dress I was going to make when mother died? . . . Oh, shame!"

Yet she sprang up from the white-enameled rocker, tucked in her graceless cotton corset-cover, stared at her image in the mirror, smoothed her neck till the skin reddened.

§ 6

Phil talked to her for an hour after their Sunday-noon dinner. She had been to church; had confessed indeterminate sins to a formless and unresponsive deity. She felt righteous, and showed it. Phil caught the cue. He sacrificed all the witty things he was prepared to say about Mrs. Gray's dumplings; he gazed silently out of the window till she wondered what he was thinking about, then he stumblingly began to review a sermon which he said he had heard the previous Sunday—though he must have been mistaken, as he shot several games of Kelly pool every Sunday morning, or slept till noon.

"The preacher spoke of woman's influence. You don't know what it is to lack a woman's influence in a fellow's life, Miss Golden. I can see the awful consequences among my patients. I tell you, when I sat there in church and saw the colored windows—" He sighed portentously.

His hand fell across hers—his lean paw, strong and warm-blooded from massaging puffy old men. "I tell you I just got sentimental, I did, thinking of all I lacked."

Phil melted mournfully away—to indulge in a highly cheerful walk on upper Broadway with Miss Becky Rosenthal, sewer for the Sans Peur Pants and Overalls Company—while in her room Una grieved over his forlorn desire to be good.

§ 7

Two evenings later, when November warmed to a passing Indian summer of golden skies that were pitifully far away from the little folk in city streets, Una was so restless that she set off for a walk by herself.

Phil had been silent, glancing at her and away, as though he were embarrassed.

"I wish I could do something to help him," she thought, as she poked down-stairs to the entrance of the apartment-house.

Phil was on the steps, smoking a cigarette-sized cigar, scratching his chin, and chattering with his kinsmen, the gutter sparrows.

He doffed his derby. He spun his cigar from him with a deft flip of his fingers which somehow agitated her. She called herself a little fool for being agitated, but she couldn't get rid of the thought that only men snapped their fingers like that.

"Goin' to the movies, Miss Golden?"

"No, I was just going for a little walk."

"Well, say, walks, that's where I live. Why don't you invite Uncle Phil to come along and show you the town? Why, I knew this burg when they went picnicking at the reservoir in Bryant Park."

He swaggered beside her without an invitation. He

did not give her a chance to decline his company—and soon she did not want to. He led her down to Gramercy Park, loveliest memory of village days, houses of a demure red and white ringing a fenced garden. He pointed out to her the Princeton Club, the Columbia Club, the National Arts, and the Players', and declared that two men leaving the last were John Drew and the most famous editor in America. He guided her over to Stuyvesant Park, a barren square out of old London, with a Quaker school on one side, and the voluble Ghetto on the other. He conducted her through East Side streets, where Jewish lovers parade past miles of push-carts and venerable Rabbis read the Talmud between sales of cotton socks, and showed her a little café which was a hang-out for thieves. She was excited by this contact with the underworld.

He took her to a Lithuanian restaurant, on a street which was a débâcle. One half of the restaurant was filled with shaggy Lithuanians playing cards at filthy tables; the other half was a clean haunt for tourists who came to see the slums, and here, in the heart of these "slums," saw only one another.

"Wait a while," Phil said, "and a bunch of Seeing-New-Yorkers will land here and think we're crooks."

In ten minutes a van-load of sheepish trippers from the Middle West filed into the restaurant and tried to act as though they were used to cocktails. Una was delighted when she saw them secretly peering at Phil and herself; she put one hand on her thigh and one on the table, leaned forward and tried to look tough, while Phil pretended to be quarreling with her, and the trippers' simple souls were enthralled by this glimpse of two criminals. Una really enjoyed the acting; for a moment Phil was her companion in play; and when the trippers had gone rustling out to view other haunts of vice she smiled at Phil unrestrainedly.

Instantly he took advantage of her smile, of their companionship.

He was really as simple-hearted as the trippers in his tactics.

She had been drinking ginger-ale. He urged her now to "have a real drink." He muttered confidentially: "Have a nip of sherry or a New Orleans fizz or a Bronx. That 'll put heart into you. Not enough to affect you a-tall, but just enough to cheer up on. Then we'll go to a dance and really have a time. Gee! poor kid, you don't get any fun."

"No, no, I *never* touch it," she said, and she believed it, forgetting the claret she had drunk with Walter Babson.

She felt unsafe.

He laughed at her; assured her from his medical experience that "lots of women need a little tonic," and boisterously ordered a glass of sherry for her.

She merely sipped it. She wanted to escape. All their momentary frankness of association was gone. She feared him; she hated the complaisant waiter who brought her the drink; the fat proprietor who would take his pieces of silver, though they were the price of her soul; the policeman on the pavement, who would never think of protecting her; and the whole hideous city which benignly profited by saloons. She watched another couple down at the end of the room—an obese man and a young, pretty girl, who was hysterically drunk. Not because she had attended the Women's Christian Temperance Union at Panama and heard them condemn "the demon rum," but because the sickish smell of the alcohol was all about her now, she suddenly turned into a crusader. She sprang up, seized her gloves, snapped, "I will not touch the stuff."

She marched down the room, out of the restaurant and away, not once looking back at Phil.

In about fifteen seconds she had a humorous picture of Phil trying to rush after her, but stopped by the waiter to pay his check. She began to wonder if she hadn't been slightly ridiculous in attempting to slay Demon Rum by careering down the restaurant. But "I don't care!" she said, stoutly. "I'm glad I took a stand instead of just rambling along and wondering what it was all about, the way I did with Walter."

Phil caught up to her and instantly began to complain. "Say, you certainly made a sight out of yourself—and out of me—leaving me sitting there with the waiter laughing his boob head off at me. Lord! I'll never dare go near the place again."

"Your own fault." This problem was so clear, so unconfused to her.

"It wasn't all my fault," he said. "You didn't have to take a drink." His voice fell to a pathetic whimper. "I was showing you hospitality the best way I knew how. You won't never know how you hurt my feelin's."

The problem instantly became complicated again. Perhaps she *had* hurt his rudimentary sense of courtesy. Perhaps Walter Babson would have sympathized with Phil, not with her. She peeped at Phil. He trailed along with a forlorn baby look which did not change.

She was very uncomfortable as she said a brief goodnight at the flat. She half wished that he would give her a chance to recant. She saw him and his injured feelings as enormously important.

She undressed in a tremor of misgiving. She put her thin, pretty kimono over her nightgown, braided her hair, and curled on the bed, condemning herself for having been so supercilious to the rat who had never had a chance.

It was late—long after eleven—when there was a tapping on the door.

She started, listened rigidly.

Phil's voice whispered from the hall: "Open your door just half an inch, Miss Golden. Something I wanted to say."

Her pity for him made his pleading request like a command. She drew her kimono close and peeped out at him.

"I knew you were up," he whispered; "saw the light under your door. I been so worried. I *didn't* mean to shock you, or nothing, but if you feel I *did* mean to, I want to apologize. Gee! me, I couldn't sleep one wink if I thought you was offended."

"It's all right—" she began.

"Say, come into the dining-room. Everybody gone to bed. I want to explain—gee! you gotta give me a chance to be good. If *you* don't use no good influence over me, nobody never will, I guess."

His whisper was full of masculine urgency, husky, bold. She shivered. She hesitated, did not answer.

"All right," he mourned. "I don't blame you none, but it's pretty hard—"

"I'll come just for a moment," she said, and shut the door.

She was excited, flushed. She wrapped her braids around her head, gentle braids of pale gold, and her undistinguished face, thus framed, was young and sweet.

She hastened out to the dining-room.

What was the "parlor" by day the Grays used for their own bedroom, but the dining-room had a big, ugly, leather settee and two rockers, and it served as a secondary living-room.

Here Phil waited, at the end of the settee. She headed

for a rocker, but he piled sofa-cushions for her at the other end of the settee, and she obediently sank down there.

"Listen," he said, in a tone of lofty lamentation, "I don't know as I can ever, *ever* make you understand I just wanted to give you a good time. I seen you was in mourning, and I thinks, 'Maybe you could brighten her up a little—'"

"I am sorry I didn't understand."

"Una, Una! Do you suppose you could ever stoop to helping a bad egg like me?" he demanded.

His hand fell on hers. It comforted her chilly hand. She let it lie there. Speech became difficult for her.

"Why, why yes—" she stammered.

In reaction to her scorn of him, she was all accepting faith.

"Oh, if you could—and if I could make you less lonely sometimes—"

In his voice was a perilous tenderness; for the rat, trained to beguile neurotic patients in his absurd practice, could croon like the very mother of pity.

"Yes, I am lonely sometimes," she heard herself admitting—far-off, dreaming, needing the close affection that her mother and Walter had once given her.

"Poor little girl—you're so much better raised and educated than me, but you got to have friendship jus' same."

His arm was about her shoulder. For a second she leaned against him.

All her scorn of him suddenly gathered in one impulse. She sprang up—just in time to catch a grin on his face.

"You gutter-rat!" she said. "You aren't worth my telling you what you are. You wouldn't understand. You can't see anything but the gutter."

He was perfectly unperturbed: "Poor stuff, kid. Weak

11　　　　　　　　[153]

come-back. Sounds like a drayma. But, say, listen, honest, kid, you got me wrong. What's the harm in a little hugging—"

She fled. She was safe in her room. She stood with both arms outstretched. She did not feel soiled by this dirty thing. She was triumphant. In the silhouette of a water-tank, atop the next-door apartment-house, she saw a strong tower of faith.

"Now I don't have to worry about him. I don't have to make any more decisions. I know! I'm through! No one can get me just because of curiosity about sex again. I'm free. I can fight my way through in business and still keep clean. I can! I was hungry for—for even that rat. I--Una Golden! Yes, I was. But I don't want to go back to him. I've won!

"Oh, Walter, Walter, I do want you, dear, but I'll get along without you, and I'll keep a little sacred image of you."

CHAPTER X

THE three-fourths of Una employed in the office of
Mr. Troy Wilkins was going through one of those
periods of unchanging routine when all past drama seems
unreal, when nothing novel happens nor apparently ever
will happen—such a time of dull peacefulness as makes up
the major part of our lives.

Her only definite impressions were the details of daily
work, the physical aspects of the office, and the presence
of the "Boss."

§ 2

Day after day the same details of the job: letters
arriving, assorted, opened, answered by dictation, the
answers sealed and stamped (and almost every day the
same panting crisis of getting off some cosmically important letter). . . . The reception of callers; welcome to
clients; considerate but firm assurances to persons looking
for positions that there was "no opening just at *present—*"
The suave answering of irritating telephone calls. . . . The
filing of letters and plans; the clipping of real-estate-
transfer items from newspapers. . . . The supervision of
Bessie Kraker and the office-boy.

Equally fixed were the details of the grubby office itself. Like many men who have pride in the smartest
suburban homes available, Mr. Wilkins was content with

an office shabby and inconvenient. He regarded beautiful offices as in some way effeminate. . . . His wasn't effeminate; it was undecorative as a filled ash-tray, despite Una's daily following up of the careless scrubwomen with dust-cloth and whisk. She knew every inch of it, as a gardener knows his plot. She could never keep from noticing and running her finger along the pebbled glass of the oak-and-glass partition about Mr. Wilkins's private office, each of the hundreds of times a day she passed it; and when she lay awake at midnight, her finger-tips would recall precisely the feeling of that rough surface, even to the sharp edges of a tiny flaw in the glass over the bookcase.

Or she would recall the floor-rag—symbol of the hard realness of the office grind. . . .

It always hung over the twisted, bulbous lead pipes below the stationary basin in the women's wash-room provided by the Septimus Building for the women on three floors. It was a rag ancient and slate-gray, grotesquely stiff and grotesquely hairy at its frayed edges—a corpse of a scrub-rag in *rigor mortis*. Una was annoyed with herself for ever observing so unlovely an object, but in the moment of relaxation when she went to wash her hands she was unduly sensitive to that eternal rag, and to the griminess of the wash-room—the cracked and yellow-stained wash-bowl, the cold water that stung in winter, the roller-towel which she spun round and round in the effort to find a dry, clean, square space, till, in a spasm of revulsion, she would bolt out of the wash-room with her face and hands half dried.

Woman's place is in the home. Una was doubtless purely perverse in competing with men for the commercial triumphs of running that gray, wet towel round and round on its clattering roller, and of wondering whether for the entire remainder of her life she would see that dead scrub-rag.

It was no less annoying a fact that Bessie and she had only one waste-basket, which was invariably at Bessie's desk when Una reached for it.

Or that the door of the supply-cupboard always shivered and stuck.

Or that on Thursday, which is the three P.M. of the week, it seemed impossible to endure the tedium till Saturday noon; and that, invariably, her money was gone by Friday, so that Friday lunch was always a mere insult to her hunger, and she could never get her gloves from the cleaner till after Saturday pay-day.

Una knew the office to a point where it offered few beautiful surprises.

And she knew the tactics of Mr. Troy Wilkins.

All managers—"bosses"—"chiefs"—have tactics for keeping discipline; tricks which they conceive as profoundly hidden from their underlings, and which are intimately known and discussed by those underlings. . . . There are the bosses who "bluff," those who lie, those who give good-fellowship or grave courtesy in lieu of wages. None of these was Mr. Wilkins. He was dully honest and clumsily paternal. But he was a roarer, a grumbler; he bawled and ordained, in order to encourage industry and keep his lambs from asking for "raises." Thus also he tried to conceal his own mistakes; when a missing letter for which everybody had been anxiously searching was found on his own desk, instead of in the files, he would blare, "Well, why didn't you tell me you put it on my desk, heh?" He was a delayer also and, in poker patois, a passer of the buck. He would feebly hold up a decision for weeks, then make a whole campaign of getting his office to rush through the task in order to catch up; have a form of masculine-commuter hysterics because Una and Bessie didn't do the typing in a miraculously short time. . . . He never cursed; he was an ecclesiastical believer that one of the chief aims of man is to keep from saying those mystic words "hell" and "damn"; but he could make "darn it" and "why in tunket" sound as profane as a gambling-den. . . . There was included in Una's duties the pretense of believing that Mr. Wilkins was the greatest single-handed villa architect in Greater New York. Some-times it nauseated her. But often he was rather pathetic in his shaky desire to go on having faith in his super-seded ability, and she would willingly assure him that his rivals, the boisterous young firm of Soule, Smith & Fiss-leben, were frauds.

All these faults and devices of Mr. Troy Wilkins Una knew. Doubtless he would have been astonished to hear that fact, on evenings in his plate-racked, much-raftered, highly built - in suburban dining - room, when he discoursed to the admiring Mrs. Wilkins and the mouse-like little Wilkinses on the art of office discipline; or mornings in the second smoker of the 8.16 train, when he told the other lords of the world that "these stenographers are all alike—you simply can't get 'em to learn system."

It is not recorded whether Mr. Wilkins also knew Una's faults—her habit of falling a-dreaming at 3.30 and trying to make it up by working furiously at 4.30; her habit of awing the good-hearted Bessie Kraker by posing as a nun who had never been kissed nor ever wanted to be; her graft of sending the office-boy out for ten-cent boxes of cocoanut candy; and a certain resentful touchiness and ladylikeness which made it hard to give her necessary orders. Mr. Wilkins has never given testimony, but he is not the villain of the tale, and some authorities have a suspicion that he did not find Una altogether perfect.

§ 3

It must not be supposed that Una or her million sisters in business were constantly and actively bored by office routine.

Save once or twice a week, when he roared, and once or twice a month, when she felt that thirteen dollars a week was too little, she rather liked Mr. Wilkins—his honesty, his desire to make comfortable homes for people, his cheerful "Good-morning!" his way of interrupting dictation to tell her antiquated but jolly stories, his stolid, dependable-looking face.

She had real satisfaction in the game of work—in winning points and tricks—in doing her work briskly and well, in helping Mr. Wilkins to capture clients. She was eager when she popped in to announce to him that a wary, long-pursued "prospect" had actually called. She was rather more interested in her day's work than are the average of meaningless humanity who sell gingham and teach algebra and cure boils and repair lawn-mowers, because she was daily more able to approximate perfection, to look forward to something better—to some splendid position at twenty or even twenty-five dollars a week. She was certainly in no worse plight than perhaps ninety-five million of her free and notoriously red-blooded fellow-citizens.

But she was in no better plight. There was no drama, no glory in affection, nor, so long as she should be tied to Troy Wilkins's dwindling business, no immediate increase in power. And the sameness, the unceasing discussions with Bessie regarding Mr. Wilkins—Mr. Wilkins's hat,

Mr. Wilkins's latest command, Mr. Wilkins's lost fountain-pen, Mr. Wilkins's rudeness to the salesman for the Sky-line Roofing Company, Mr. Wilkins's idiotic friendship for Muldoon, the contractor, Mr. Wilkins's pronounced unfairness to the office-boy in regard to a certain lateness in arrival—

At best, Una got through day after day; at worst, she was as profoundly bored as an explorer in the arctic night.

§ 4

Una, the initiate New-Yorker, continued her study of city ways and city currents during her lunch-hours. She went down to Broad Street to see the curb market; marveled at the men with telephones in little coops behind opened windows; stared at the great newspaper offices on Park Row, the old City Hall, the mingling on lower Broadway of sky-challenging buildings with the history of pre-Revolutionary days. She got a momentary prejudice in favor of socialism from listening to an attack upon it by a noon-time orator—a spotted, badly dressed man whose favorite slur regarding socialists was that they were spotted and badly dressed. She heard a negro shouting dithyrambics about some religion she could never make out.

Sometimes she lunched at a newspaper-covered desk, with Bessie and the office-boy, on cold ham and beans and small, bright-colored cakes which the boy brought in from a bakery. Sometimes she had boiled eggs and cocoa at a Childs restaurant with stenographers who ate baked apples, rich Napoleons, and, always, coffee. Sometimes at a cafeteria, carrying a tray, she helped herself to crackers and milk and sandwiches. Sometimes at the Arden Tea Room, for women only, she encountered charity-workers and virulently curious literary ladies, whom she endured for the marked excellence of the Arden chicken croquettes. Sometimes Bessie tempted her to a Chinese restaurant, where Bessie, who came from the East Side and knew a trick or two, did not order chop-suey, like a tourist, but noodles and eggs foo-young.

In any case, the lunch-hour and the catalogue of what she was so vulgar as to eat were of importance in Una's history, because that hour broke the routine, gave her for an hour a deceptive freedom of will, of choice between Boston beans and—New York beans. And her triumphant common sense was demonstrated, for she chose light, digestible food, and kept her head clear for the afternoon, while her overlord, Mr. Troy Wilkins, like vast numbers of his fellow business men, crammed himself with beefsteak-and-kidney pudding, drugged himself with cigar smoke and pots of strong coffee and shop-talk, spoke earnestly of the wickedness of drunkenness, and then, drunk with food and tobacco and coffee and talk, came back dizzy, blur-eyed, slow-nerved; and for two hours tried to get down to work.

After hours of trudging through routine, Una went home.

She took the Elevated now instead of the Subway. That was important in her life. It meant an entire change of scenery.

On the Elevated, beside her all evening, hovering over her bed at night, was Worry.

"Oh, I ought to have got all that Norris correspondence copied to-day. I *must* get at it first thing in the morning. . . . I wonder if Mr. Wilkins was sore because I stayed out so long for lunch? . . . What would I do if I were fired?"

So would she worry as she left the office. In the evening she wouldn't so much criticize herself as suddenly and

without reason remember office settings and incidents
—startle at a picture of the T-square at which she had
stared while Mr. Wilkins was telephoning. . . . She wasn't
weary because she worried; she worried because she was
weary from the airless, unnatural, straining life. She
worried about everything available, from her soul to her
finger-nails; but the office offered the largest number of
good opportunities.

"After all," say the syndicated philosophers, "the office
takes only eight or nine hours a day. The other fifteen or
sixteen, you are free to do as you wish—loaf, study, become an athlete." This illuminative suggestion is usually
reinforced by allusions to Lincoln and Edison.

Only—you aren't a Lincoln or an Edison, for the most
part, and you don't do any of those improving things.
You have the office with you, in you, every hour of the
twenty-four, unless you sleep dreamlessly and forget—
which you don't. Probably, like Una, you do not take
any exercise to drive work-thoughts away.

She often planned to take exercise regularly; read of it
in women's magazines. But she could never get herself
to keep up the earnest clowning of bedroom calisthenics;
gymnasiums were either reekingly crowded or too expensive—and even to think of undressing and dressing
for a gymnasium demanded more initiative than was left
in her fagged organism. There was walking—but city
streets become tiresomely familiar. Of sports she was
consistently ignorant.

So all the week she was in the smell and sound of the
battle, until Saturday evening with its blessed rest—the
clean, relaxed time which every woman on the job knows.

Saturday evening! No work to-morrow! A prospect
of thirty-six hours of freedom. A leisurely dinner, a
languorous slowness in undressing, a hot bath, a clean

nightgown, and fresh, smooth bed-linen. Una went to
bed early to enjoy the contemplation of these luxuries.
She even put on a lace bed-cap adorned with pink silk
roses. The pleasure of relaxing in bed, of looking lazily
at the pictures in a new magazine, of drifting into slumber
—not of stepping into a necessary sleep that was only the
anteroom of another day's labor. . . .

Such was her greatest joy in this period of unevent-
fulness.

§ 5

Una was, she hoped, "trying to think about things."
Naturally, one who used that boarding-house phrase
could not think transformingly.

She wasn't illuminative about Romain Rolland or
Rodin or village welfare. She was still trying to decide
whether the suffrage movement was ladylike and whether
Dickens or Thackeray was the better novelist. But she
really was trying to decide.

She compiled little lists of books to read, "movements"
to investigate. She made a somewhat incoherent written
statement of what she was trying to do, and this she kept
in her top bureau drawer, among the ribbons, collars, imitation pearl necklaces, handkerchiefs, letters from Walter,
and photographs of Panama and her mother.

She took it out sometimes, and relieved the day's ac-
cumulated suffering by adding such notes as:

"Be nice & human w. employes if ever have any of
own; office wretched hole anyway bec. of econ. system;
W. used to say, why make worse by being cranky."

Or:

"Study music, it brings country and W. and poetry
and everything; take piano les. when get time."

So Una tramped, weary always at dusk, but always re-created at dawn, through one of those periods of timeless, unmarked months, when all drama seems past and unreal and apparently nothing will ever happen again.

Then, in one week, everything became startling—she found melodrama and a place of friendship.

CHAPTER XI

"I'M tired of the Grays. They're very nice people, but they can't talk," said Una to Bessie Kraker, at lunch in the office, on a February day.

"How do yuh mean 'can't talk'? Are they dummies?" inquired Bessie.

"Dummies?"

"Yuh, sure, deef and dumb."

"Why, no, I mean they don't talk my language—they don't, oh, they don't, I suppose you'd say 'conversationalize.' Do you see?"

"Oh yes," said Bessie, doubtfully. "Say, listen, Miss Golden. Say, I don't want to butt in, and maybe you wouldn't be stuck on it much, but they say it's a dead-swell place to live—Miss Kitson, the boss's secretary where I was before, lived there—"

"Say, for the love o' Mike, *say* it: *Where?*" interrupted the office-boy.

"You shut your nasty trap. I was just coming to it. The Temperance and Protection Home, on Madison Avenue just above Thirty-fourth. They say it's kind of strict, but, gee! there's a' *ausgezeichnet* bunch of dames there, artists and everything, and they say they feed you swell, and it only costs eight bucks a week."

"Well, maybe I'll look at it," said Una, dubiously.

Neither the forbidding name nor Bessie's moral recommendation made the Home for Girls sound tempting, but

Una was hungry for companionship; she was cold now toward the unvarying, unimaginative desires of men. Among the women "artists and everything" she might find the friends she needed.

The Temperance and Protection Home Club for Girls was in a solemn, five-story, white sandstone structure with a severe doorway of iron grill, solid and capable-looking as a national bank. Una rang the bell diffidently. She waited in a hall that, despite its mission settee and red-tiled floor, was barrenly clean as a convent. She was admitted to the business-like office of Mrs. Harriet Fike, the matron of the Home.

Mrs. Fike had a brown, stringy neck and tan bangs. She wore a mannish coat and skirt, flat shoes of the kind called "sensible" by everybody except pretty women, and a large silver-mounted crucifix.

"Well?" she snarled.

"Some one— I'd like to find out about coming here to live—to see the place, and so on. Can you have somebody show me one of the rooms?"

"My dear young lady, the first consideration isn't to 'have somebody show you' or anybody else a room, but to ascertain if you are a fit person to come here."

Mrs. Fike jabbed at a compartment of her desk, yanked out a corduroy-bound book, boxed its ears, slammed it open, glared at Una in a Christian and Homelike way, and began to shoot questions:

"Whatcha name?"

"Una Golden."

"Miss uh Miss?"

"I didn't quite—"

"Miss or Mrs., I *said*. Can't you understand English?"

"See here, I'm not being sent to jail that I know of!" Una rose, tremblingly.

Mrs. Fike merely waited and snapped: "Sit down. You look as though you had enough sense to understand that we can't let people we don't know anything about enter a decent place like this. . . . Miss or Mrs., I said?"

"Miss," Una murmured, feebly sitting down again.

"What's your denomination? . . . No agnostics or Catholics allowed!"

Una heard herself meekly declaring, "Methodist."

"Smoke? Swear? Drink liquor? Got any bad habits?"

"No!"

"Got a lover, sweetheart, gentleman friend? If so, what name or names?"

"No."

"That's what they all say. Let me tell you that later, when you expect to have all these male cousins visit you, we'll reserve the privilege to ask questions. . . . Ever served a jail sentence?"

"Now really—! Do I look it?"

"My dear miss, wouldn't you feel foolish if I said 'yes'? *Have* you? I warn you we look these things up!"

"No, I have *not*."

"Well, that's comforting. . . . Age?"

"Twenty-six."

"Parents living? Name nearest relatives? Nearest friends? Present occupation?"

Even as she answered this last simple question and Mrs. Fike's suspicious query about her salary, Una felt as though she were perjuring herself, as though there were no such place as Troy Wilkins's office—and Mrs. Fike knew it; as though a large policeman were secreted behind the desk and would at any moment pop out and drag her off to jail. She answered with tremorous carefulness. By now, the one thing that she wanted to do was to escape from that Christian and strictly supervised Napoleon, Mrs. Fike, and flee back to the Grays.

"Previous history?" Mrs. Fike was grimly continuing, and she followed this question by ascertaining Una's ambitions, health, record for insanity, and references.

Mrs. Fike closed the query-book, and observed:

"Well, you are rather fresh, but you seem to be acceptable—and now you may look us over and see whether we are acceptable to you. Don't think for one moment that this institution needs you, or is trying to lift you out of a life of sin, or that we suppose this to be the only place in New York to live. We know what we want—we run things on a scientific basis—but we aren't so conceited as to think that everybody likes us. Now, for example, I can see that you don't like me and my ways one bit. But Lord love you, that isn't necessary. The one thing necessary is for me to run this Home according to the book, and if you're fool enough to prefer a slap-dash boarding-house to this hygienic Home, why, you'll make your bed—or rather some slattern of a landlady will make it—and you can lie in it. Come with me. No; first read the rules."

Una obediently read that the young ladies of the Temperance Home were forbidden to smoke, make loud noises, cook, or do laundry in their rooms, sit up after midnight, entertain visitors "of any sort except mothers and sisters" in any place in the Home, "except in the parlors for that purpose provided." They were not permitted to be out after ten unless their names were specifically entered in the "Out-late Book" before their going. And they were "requested to answer all reasonable questions of matron, or board of visitors, or duly qualified inspectors, regarding moral, mental, physical, and commercial well-being and progress."

THE JOB

Una couldn't resist asking, "I suppose it isn't forbidden to sleep in our rooms, is it?"

Mrs. Fike looked over her, through her, about her, and remarked: "I'd advise you to drop all impudence. You see, you don't do it well. We admit East Side Jews here and they are so much quicker and wittier than you country girls from Pennsylvania and Oklahoma, and Heaven knows where, that you might just as well give up and try to be ladies instead of humorists. Come, we will take a look at the Home."

By now Una was resolved not to let Mrs. Fike drive her away. She would "show her"; she would "come and live here just for spite."

What Mrs. Fike thought has not been handed down.

She led Una past a series of closets, each furnished with two straight chairs on either side of a table, a carbon print of a chilly-looking cathedral, and a slice of carpet on which one was rather disappointed not to find the label, "Bath Mat."

"These are the reception-rooms where the girls are allowed to receive callers. *Any* time—up to a quarter to ten," Mrs. Fike said.

Una decided that they were better fitted for a hair-dressing establishment.

The living-room was her first revelation of the Temperance Home as something besides a prison—as an abiding-place for living, eager, sensitive girls. It was not luxurious, but it had been arranged by some one who made allowance for a weakness for pretty things, even on the part of young females observing the rules in a Christian home. There was a broad fireplace, built-in book-shelves, a long table; and, in wicker chairs with chintz cushions, were half a dozen curious girls. Una was sure that one of them, a fizzy-haired, laughing girl, secretly nodded to her, and she was comforted.

12

THE JOB

Up the stairs to a marvelous bathroom with tempting shower-baths, a small gymnasium, and, on the roof, a garden and loggia and basket-ball court. It was cool and fresh up here, on even the hottest summer evenings, and here the girls were permitted to lounge in negligées till after ten, Mrs. Fike remarked, with a half-smile.

Una smiled back.

As they went through the bedroom floors, with Mrs. Fike stalking ahead, a graceful girl in lace cap and negligeé came bouncing out of a door between them, drew herself up and saluted Mrs. Fike's back, winked at Una amicably, and for five steps imitated Mrs. Fike's aggressive stride.

"Yes, I would be glad to come here!" Una said, cheerfully, to Mrs. Fike, who looked at her suspiciously, but granted: "Well, we'll look up your references. Meantime, if you like—or don't like, I suppose—you might talk to a Mrs. Esther Lawrence, who wants a room-mate."

"Oh, I don't think I'd like a room-mate."

"My dear young lady, this place is simply full of young persons who would like and they wouldn't like—and forsooth we must change every plan to suit their high and mighty convenience! I'm not at all sure that we shall have a single room vacant for at least six months, and of course—"

"Well, could I talk to Mrs.—Lawrence, was it?"

"Most assuredly. I *expect* you to talk to her! Come with me."

Una followed abjectly, and the matron seemed well pleased with her reformation of this wayward young woman. Her voice was curiously anemic, however, as she rapped on a bedroom door and called, "Oh, Mrs. Lawrence!"

A husky, capable voice within, "Yeah, what is 't?"

"It's Mrs. Fike, deary. I think I have a room-mate for you."

"Well, you wait 'll I get something on, will you!"

Mrs. Fike waited. She waited two minutes. She looked at a wrist-watch in a leather band while she tapped her sensibly clad foot. She tried again: "We're *waiting*, deary!"

There was no answer from within, and it was two minutes more before the door was opened.

Una was conscious of a room pleasant with white-enameled woodwork; a denim-covered couch and a narrow, prim brass bed, a litter of lingerie and sheets of newspaper; and, as the dominating center of it all, a woman of thirty, tall, high-breasted, full-faced, with a nose that was large but pleasant, black eyes that were cool and direct and domineering—Mrs. Esther Lawrence.

"You kept us waiting so long," complained Mrs. Fike.

Mrs. Lawrence stared at her as though she were an impudent servant. She revolved on Una, and with a self-confident kindliness in her voice, inquired, "What's your name, child?"

"Una Golden."

"We'll talk this over. . . . Thank you, Mrs. Fike."

"Well, now," Mrs. Fike endeavored, "be sure you both are satisfied—"

"Don't you worry! We will, all right!"

Mrs. Fike glared at her and retired.

Mrs. Lawrence grinned, stretched herself on the couch, mysteriously produced a cigarette, and asked, "Smoke?"

"No, thanks."

"Sit down, child, and be comfy. Oh, would you mind opening that window? Not supposed to smoke. . . . Poor Ma Fike—I just can't help deviling her. Please don't think I'm usually as nasty as I am with her. She has to be kept in her place or she'll worry you to death. . . . Thanks. . . . Do sit down—woggle up the pillow on the bed and be comfy. . . . You look like a nice kid—me, I'm a lazy, slatternly, good-natured old hex, with all the bad habits there are and a profound belief that the world is a hell of a place, but I'm fine to get along with, and so let's take a shot at rooming together. If we scrap, we can quit instanter, and no bad feelings. . . . I'd really like to have you come in, because you look as though you were on, even if you are rather meek and kitteny; and I'm scared to death they'll wish some tough little Mick on to me, or some pious sister who hasn't been married and believes in pussy-footing around and taking it all to God in prayer every time I tell her the truth. . . . What do you think, kiddy?"

Una was by this cock-sure, disillusioned, large person more delighted than by all the wisdom of Mr. Wilkins or the soothing of Mrs. Sessions. She felt that, except for Walter, it was the first time since she had come to New York that she had found an entertaining person.

"Yes," she said, "do let's try it."

"Good! Now let me warn you first off, that I may be diverting at times, but I'm no good. To-morrow I'll pretend to be a misused and unfortunate victim, but your young and almost trusting eyes make me feel candid for about fifteen minutes. I certainly got a raw deal from my beloved husband—that's all you'll hear from me about him. By the way, I'm typical of about ten thousand married women in business about whose noble spouses nothing is ever said. But I suppose I ought to have bucked up and made good in business (I'm a bum stenog. for Pitcairn, McClure & Stockley, the bond house). But I can't. I'm too lazy, and it doesn't seem worth while. . . . And, oh, we *are* exploited, women who are on jobs. The bosses give us a lot of taffy and raise their hats—but they don't raise our wages, and they think that if they keep us till two G.M. taking dictation they make it all right by apologizing. Women are a lot more conscientious on jobs than men are—but that's because we're fools; you don't catch the men staying till six-thirty because the boss has shystered all afternoon and wants to catch up on his correspondence. But we—of course we don't dare to make dates for dinner, lest we have to stay late. We don't *dare!*"

"I bet *you* do!"

"Yes—well, I'm not so much of a fool as some of the rest—or else more of a one. There's Mamie Magen— she's living here; she's with Pitcairn, too. You'll meet her and be crazy about her. She's a lame Jewess, and awfully plain, except she's got lovely eyes, but she's got a mind like a tack. Well, she's the little angel-pie about staying late, and some day she'll probably make four thousand bucks a year. She'll be mayor of New York, or executive secretary of the Young Women's Atheist Association or something. But still, she doesn't stay late and plug hard because she's scared, but because she's got ambition. But most of the women—Lord! they're just cowed sheep."

"Yes," said Una.

A million discussions of Women in Business going on— a thousand of them at just that moment, perhaps—men employers declaring that they couldn't depend on women in their offices, women asserting that women were the more conscientious. Una listened and was content; she had found some one with whom to play, with whom to talk and hate the powers. . . . She felt an impulse to tell Mrs. Lawrence all about Troy Wilkins and her mother and —and perhaps even about Walter Babson. But she merely treasured up the thought that she could do that some day, and politely asked:

"What about Mrs. Fike? Is she as bad as she seems?"

"Why, that's the best little skeleton of contention around here. There's three factions. Some girls say she's just plain devil—mean as a floor-walker. That's what I think—she's a rotter and a four-flusher. You notice the way she crawls when I stand up to her. Why, they won't have Catholics here, and I'm one of those wicked people, and she knows it! When she asked my religion I told her I was a 'Romanist Episcopalian,' and she sniffed and put me down as an Episcopalian—I saw her! . . . Then some of the girls think she's really good-hearted—just gruff—bark worse than her bite. But you ought to see how she barks at some of the younger girls—scares 'em stiff—and keeps picking on them about regulations—makes their lives miserable. Then there's a third section that thinks she's merely institutionalized—training makes her as hard as any other kind of a machine. You'll find lots like her in this town—in all the charities."

"But the girls—they do have a good time here?"

"Yes, they do. It's sort of fun to fight Ma Fike and all the fool rules. I enjoy smoking here twice as much as I would anywhere else. And Fike isn't half as bad as the board of visitors—bunch of fat, rich, old Upper-West-Siders with passementeried bosoms, doing tea-table charity, and asking us impertinent questions, and telling a bunch of hard-worked slaves to be virtuous and wash behind their ears—the soft, ignorant, conceited, impractical parasites! But still, it's all sort of like a cranky boarding-school for girls—and you know what fun the girls have there, with midnight fudge parties and a teacher pussy-footing down the hall trying to catch them."

"I don't know. I've never been to one."

"Well—doesn't matter. . . . Another thing—some day, when you come to know more men— Know many?"

"Very few."

"Well, you'll find this town is full of bright young men seeking an economical solution of the sex problem—to speak politely—and you'll find it a relief not to have them on your door-step. 'S safe here. . . . Come in with me, kid. Give me an audience to talk to."

"Yes," said Una.

§ 2

It was hard to leave the kindly Herbert Grays of the flat, but Una made the break and arranged all her silver toilet-articles—which consisted of a plated-silver hair-brush, a German-silver nail-file, and a good, plain, honest rubber comb—on the bureau in Mrs. Lawrence's room.

With the shyness of a girl on her first night in boarding-school, Una stuck to Mrs. Lawrence's side in the noisy flow of strange girls down to the dining-room. She was used to being self-absorbed in the noisiest restaurants, but she was trembly about the knees as she crossed the room among curious upward glances; she found it very hard to use a fork without clattering it on the plate when she sat with Mrs. Lawrence and four strangers, at a table for six.

They all were splendidly casual and wise and good-looking. With no men about to intimidate them—or to attract them—they made a solid phalanx of bland, satis-fied femininity, and Una felt more barred out than in an office. She longed for a man who would be curious about her, or cross with her, or perform some other easy, cus-tomary, simple-hearted masculine trick.

But she was taken into the friendship of the table when Mrs. Lawrence had finished a harangue on the cardinal sin of serving bean soup four times in two weeks.

"Oh, shut up, Lawrence, and introduce the new kid!" said one girl.

"You wait till I get through with my introductory remarks, Cassavant. I'm inspired to-night. I'm going to take a plate of bean soup and fit it over Ma Fike's head—upside down."

"Oh, give Ma Fike a rest!"

Una was uneasy. She wasn't sure whether this repartee was friendly good spirits or a nagging feud. Like all the ungrateful human race, she considered whether she ought to have identified herself with the noisy Esther Lawrence on entering the Home. So might a freshman wonder, or the guest of a club; always the amiable and vulgar Lawrences are most doubted when they are best-intentioned.

Una was relieved when she was welcomed by the four:

Mamie Magen, the lame Jewess, in whose big brown eyes was an eternal prayer for all of harassed humanity.

Jennie Cassavant, in whose eyes was chiefly a prayer that life would keep on being interesting—she, the dark, slender, loquacious, observant child who had requested Mrs. Lawrence to shut up.

Rose Larsen, like a pretty, curly-haired boy, though her shoulders were little and adorable in a white-silk waist.

Mrs. Amesbury, a nun of business, pale and silent; her thin throat shrouded in white net; her voice low and self-conscious; her very blood seeming white—a woman with an almost morbid air of guarded purity, whom you could never associate with the frank crudities of marriage. Her movements were nervous and small; she never smiled; you couldn't be boisterous with her. Yet, Mrs. Lawrence whispered she was one of the chief operators of the telephone company, and, next to the thoughtful and suffering Mamie Magen, the most capable woman she knew.

"How do you like the Tempest and Protest, Miss Golden?" the lively Cassavant said, airily.

"I don't—"

"Why! The Temperance and Protection Home."

"Well, I like Mrs. Fike's shoes. I should think they'd be fine to throw at cats."

"Good work, Golden. You're admitted!"

"Say, Magen," said Mrs. Lawrence, "Golden agrees with me about offices—no chance for women—"

Mamie Magen sighed, and "Esther," she said, in a voice which must naturally have been rasping, but which she had apparently learned to control like a violin— "Esther dear, if you could ever understand what offices have done for me! On the East Side—always it was work and work and watch all the pretty girls in our block get T. B. in garment-factories, or marry fellows that weren't any good and have a baby every year, and get so thin and worn out; and the garment-workers' strikes and picketing on cold nights. And now I am in an office—all the fellows are dandy and polite—not like the floor superintendent where I worked in a department store; he would call down a cash-girl for making change slow—! I have a chance to do anything a man can do. The boss is just crazy to find women that will take an *interest* in the work, like it was their own—you know, he told you so himself—"

"Sure, I know the line of guff," said Mrs. Lawrence. "And you take an interest, and get eighteen plunks per for doing statistics that they couldn't get a real college male in trousers to do for less than thirty-five."

"Or put it like this, Lawrence," said Jennie Cassavant. "Magen admits that the world in general is a muddle, and she thinks offices are heaven because by comparison with sweat-shops they are half-way decent."

The universal discussion was on. Everybody but Una and the nun of business threw everything from facts to bread pills about the table, and they enjoyed themselves in as unfeminized and brutal a manner as men in a café. Una had found some one with whom to talk her own shop —and shop is the only reasonable topic of conversation in the world; witness authors being intellectual about editors and romanticism; lovers absorbed in the technique of holding hands; or mothers interested in babies, recipes, and household ailments.

After dinner they sprawled all over the room of Una and Mrs. Lawrence, and talked about theaters, young men, and Mrs. Fike for four solid hours—all but the pretty, boyish Rose Larsen, who had a young man coming to call at eight. Even the new-comer, Una, was privileged to take part in giving Rose extensive, highly detailed, and not entirely proper advice—advice of a completeness which would doubtless have astonished the suitor, then dressing somewhere in a furnished room and unconscious of the publicity of his call. Una also lent Miss Larsen a pair of silk stockings, helped three other girls to coerce her curly hair, and formed part of the solemn procession that escorted her to the top of the stairs when the still unconscious young man was announced from below. And it was Una who was able to see the young man without herself being seen, and to win notoriety by being able to report that he had smooth black hair, a small mustache, and carried a stick.

Una was living her boarding-school days now, at twenty-six. The presence of so many possible friends gave her self-confidence and self-expression. She went to bed happy that night, home among her own people, among the women who, noisy or reticent, slack or aspiring, were joined to make possible a life of work in a world still heavy-scented with the ideals of the harem.

CHAPTER XII

THAT same oasis of a week gave to Una her first taste of business responsibility, of being in charge and generally comporting herself as do males. But in order to rouse her thus, Chance broke the inoffensive limb of unfortunate Mr. Troy Wilkins as he was stepping from his small bronchial motor-car to an icy cement block, on seven o'clock of Friday evening.

When Una arrived at the office on Saturday morning she received a telephone message from Mr. Wilkins, directing her to take charge of the office, of Bessie Kraker, and the office-boy, and the negotiations with the Comfy Coast Building and Development Company regarding the planning of three rows of semi-detached villas.

For three weeks the office was as different from the treadmill that it familiarly had been, as the Home Club and Lawrence's controversial room were different from the Grays' flat. She was glad to work late, to arrive not at eight-thirty, but at a quarter to eight, to gallop down to a cafeteria for coffee and a sandwich at noon, to be patient with callers, and to try to develop some knowledge of spelling in that child of nature, Bessie Kraker. She walked about the office quickly, glancing proudly at its neatness. Daily, with an operator's headgear, borrowed from the telephone company, over her head, she spent half an hour talking with Mr. Wilkins, taking his dictation, receiving his cautions and suggestions, reassuring him that in his absence the Subway ran and Tammany still ruled. After an agitated conference with the vice-president of the Comfy Coast Company, during which she was eloquent as an automobile advertisement regarding Mr. Wilkins's former masterpieces with their "every modern improvement, parquet floors, beam ceilings, plate-rack, hardwood trim throughout, natty and novel decorations," Una reached the zenith of salesman's virtues—she "closed the deal."

Mr. Wilkins came back and hemmed and hawed a good deal; he praised the work she hadn't considered well done, and pointed out faults in what she considered particularly clever achievements, and was laudatory but dissatisfying in general. In a few days he, in turn, reached the zenith of virtue on the part of boss—he raised her salary. To fifteen dollars a week. She was again merely his secretary, however, and the office trudged through another normal period when all past drama seemed incredible and all the future drab.

But Una was certain now that she could manage business, could wheedle Bessies and face pompous vice-présidents and satisfy querulous Mr. Wilkinses. She looked forward; she picked at architecture as portrayed in Mr. Wilkins's big books; she learned the reason and manner of the rows of semi-detached, semi-suburban, semi-comfortable, semi-cheap, and somewhat less than semi-attractive houses.

She was not afraid of the office world now; she had a part in the city and a home.

§ 2

She thought of Walter Babson. Sometimes, when Mrs. Lawrence was petulant or the office had been unusually exhausting, she fancied that she missed him. But instead of sitting and brooding over folded hands, in woman's ancient fashion, she took a man's unfair advantage—she went up to the gymnasium of the Home Club and worked with the chest-weights and flying-rings—a solemn, happy, busy little figure. She laughed more deeply, and she felt the enormous rhythm of the city, not as a menacing roar, but as a hymn of triumph.

She could never be intimate with Mamie Magen as she was with the frankly disillusioned Mrs. Lawrence; she never knew whether Miss Magen really liked her or not; her smile, which transfigured her sallow face, was equally bright for Una, for Mrs. Fike, and for beggars. Yet it was Miss Magen whose faith in the purpose of the struggling world inspired Una. Una walked with her up Madison Avenue, past huge old brownstone mansions, and she was unconscious of suiting her own quick step to Miss Magen's jerky lameness as the Jewess talked of her ideals of a business world which should have generosity and chivalry and the accuracy of a biological laboratory; in which there would be no need of charity to employee. . . . Or to employer.

Mamie Magen was the most highly evolved person Una had ever known. Una had, from books and newspapers and Walter Babson, learned that there were such things as socialists and earnest pessimists, and the race sketchily called "Bohemians"—writers and artists and social workers, who drank claret and made love and talked about the free theater, all on behalf of the brotherhood of man. Una pictured the socialists as always attacking capitalists; the pessimists as always being bitter and egotistic; Bohemians as always being dissipated, but as handsome and noisy and gay.

But Mamie Magen was a socialist who believed that

the capitalists with their profit-sharing and search for improved methods of production were as sincere in desiring the scientific era as were the most burning socialists; who loved and understood the most oratorical of the young socialists with their hair in their eyes, but also loved and understood the clean little college boys who came into business with a desire to make it not a war, but a crusade. She was a socialist who was determined to control and glorify business; a pessimist who was, in her gentle reticent way, as scornful of half-churches, half-governments, half-educations, as the cynical Mrs. Lawrence. Finally, she who was not handsome or dissipated or gay, but sallow and lame and Spartan, knew "Bohemia" better than most of the professional Hobohemians. As an East Side child she had grown up in the classes and parties of the University Settlement; she had been held upon the then juvenile knees of half the distinguished writers and fighters for reform, who had begun their careers as settlement workers; she, who was still unknown, a clerk and a nobody, and who wasn't always syntactical, was accustomed to people whose names had been made large and sonorous by newspaper publicity; and at the age when ambitious lady artists and derailed Walter Babsons came to New York and determinedly seized on Bohemia, Mamie Magen had outgrown Bohemia and become a worker.

To Una she explained the city, made it comprehensible, made art and economics and philosophy human and tangible. Una could not always follow her, but from her she caught the knowledge that the world and all its wisdom is but a booby, blundering school-boy that needs management and could be managed, if men and women would be human beings instead of just business men, or plumbers, or army officers, or commuters, or educators, or authors, or clubwomen, or traveling salesmen, or Socialists, or Republicans, or Salvation Army leaders, or wearers of clothes. She preached to Una a personal kinghood, an education in brotherhood and responsible nobility, which took in Una's job as much as it did government ownership or reading poetry.

§ 3

Not always was Una breathlessly trying to fly after the lame but broad-winged Mamie Magen. She attended High Mass at the Spanish church on Washington Heights with Mrs. Lawrence; felt the beauty of the ceremony; admired the simple, classic church; adored the padre; and for about one day planned to scorn Panama Method-ism and become a Catholic, after which day she forgot about Methodism and Catholicism. She also accom-panied Mrs. Lawrence to a ceremony much less impressive and much less easily forgotten—to a meeting with a man.

Mrs. Lawrence never talked about her husband, but in this reticence she was not joined by Rose Larsen or Jennie Cassavant. Jennie maintained that the misfitted Mr. Lawrence was alive, very much so; that Esther and he weren't even divorced, but merely separated. The only sanction Mrs. Lawrence ever gave to this report was to blurt out one night: "Keep up your belief in the mysticism of love and all that kind of sentimental sex stuff as long as you can. You'll lose it some day fast enough. Me, I know that a woman needs a man just the same as a man needs a woman—and just as darned unpoetically. Being brought up a Puritan, I never can quite get over the feel-ing that I oughtn't to have anything to do with men— me as I am—but believe me it isn't any romantic ideal. I sure want 'em."

Mrs. Lawrence continually went to dinners and theaters with men; she told Una all the details, as women do, from the first highly proper handshake down in the pure-minded hall of the Home Club at eight, to the less proper good-night kiss on the dark door-step of the Home Club at midnight. But she was careful to make clear that one kiss was all she ever allowed, though she grew dithyrambic over the charming, lonely men with whom she played— a young doctor whose wife was in a madhouse; a clever, restrained, unhappy old broker.

Once she broke out: "Hang it! I want love, and that's all there is to it—that's crudely all there ever is to it with any woman, no matter how much she pretends to be satisfied with mourning the dead or caring for children, or swatting a job or being religious or anything else. I'm a low-brow; I can't give you the economics of it and the spiritual brotherhood and all that stuff, like Mamie Magen. But I know women want a man and love—all of it."

Next evening she took Una to dinner at a German res-taurant, as chaperon to herself and a quiet, insistent, staring, good-looking man of forty. While Mrs. Lawrence and the man talked about the opera, their eyes seemed to be defying each other. Una felt that she was not wanted. When the man spoke hesitatingly of a cabaret, Una made excuse to go home.

Mrs. Lawrence did not return till two. She moved about the room quietly, but Una awoke.

"I'm *glad* I went with him," Mrs. Lawrence said, an-grily, as though she were defending herself.

Una asked no questions, but her good little heart was afraid. Though she retained her joy in Mrs. Lawrence's willingness to take her and her job seriously, Una was dismayed by Mrs. Lawrence's fiercely uneasy interest in men. . . . She resented the insinuation that the sharp, unexpected longing to feel Walter's arms about her might be only a crude physical need for a man, instead of a mystic fidelity to her lost love.

Being a lame marcher, a mind which was admittedly "shocked at each discovery of the aliveness of theory," Una's observation of the stalking specter of sex did not lead her to make any very lucid conclusions about the matter. But she did wonder a little if this whole business of marriages and marriage ceremonies and legal bonds which any clerkly pastor can gild with religiosity was so sacred as she had been informed in Panama. She wondered a little if Mrs. Lawrence's obvious requirement of man's companionship ought to be turned into a sneaking theft of love. Una Golden was not a philosopher; she was a workaday woman. But into her workaday mind came a low light from the fire which was kindling the world; the dual belief that life is too sacred to be taken in war and filthy industries and dull education; and that most forms and organizations and inherited castes are not sacred at all.

§ 4

The aspirations of Mamie Magen and the alarming frankness of Mrs. Lawrence were not all her life at the Home Club. With pretty Rose Larsen and half a dozen others she played. They went in fluttering, beribboned parties to the theater; they saw visions at symphony concerts, and slipped into exhibits of contemporary artists at private galleries on Fifth Avenue. When spring came they had walking parties in Central Park, in Van Cortlandt Park, on the Palisades, across Staten Island, and picnicked by themselves or with neat, trim-minded, polite men clerks from the various offices and stores where the girls worked. They had a perpetual joy in annoying Mrs. Fike by parties on fire-escapes, by lobster Newburgh suppers at midnight. They were discursively excited for a week when Rose Larsen was followed from the surface-car to the door by an unknown man; and they were un-happily excited when, without explanations, slim, daring Jennie Cassavant was suddenly asked to leave the Home Club; and they had a rose-lighted dinner when Livy Hedger announced her engagement to a Newark lawyer.

Various were the Home Club women in training and work and ways; they were awkward stenographers and dependable secretaries; fashion artists and department-store clerks; telephone girls and clever college-bred per-sons who actually read manuscripts and proof, and wrote captions or household-department squibs for women's magazines—real editors, or at least real assistant edi-tors; persons who knew authors and illustrators, as did the great Magen. They were attendants in dentists' offices and teachers in night-schools and filing-girls and manicurists and cashiers and blue-linen-gowned super-waitresses in artistic tea-rooms. And cliques, caste, they did have. Yet their comradeship was very sweet, quite real; the factional lines were not drawn according to salary or education or family, but according to gaiety or sobriety or propriety.

Una was finding not only her lost boarding-school days, but her second youth—perhaps her first real youth.

Though the questions inspired by the exceptional Miss Magen and the defiant Mrs. Lawrence kept her restless, her association with the play-girls, her growing acquaint-anceship with women who were easy-minded, who had friends and relatives and a place in the city, who did not agonize about their jobs or their loves, who received young men casually and looked forward to marriage and a com-fortable flat in Harlem, made Una feel the city as her own proper dwelling. Now she no longer plodded along the streets wonderingly, a detached little stranger; she walked briskly and contentedly, heedless of crowds, returning to her own home in her own city. Most workers of the city remain strangers to it always. But chance had made Una an insider.

It was another chapter in the making of a business woman, that spring of happiness and new stirrings in the Home Club; it was another term in the unplanned, uninstructed, muddling, chance-governed college which civilization unwittingly keeps for the training of men and women who will carry on the work of the world.

It passed swiftly, and July and vacation-time came to Una.

CHAPTER XIII

IT was hard enough to get Mr. Wilkins to set a definite date for her summer vacation; the time was delayed and juggled till Mrs. Lawrence, who was to have gone with Una, had to set off alone. But it was even harder for Una to decide where to go for her vacation.

There was no accumulation of places which she had fervently been planning to see. Indeed, Una wasn't much interested in any place besides New York and Panama; and of the questions and stale reminiscences of Panama she was weary. She decided to go to a farm in the Berkshires largely because she had overheard a girl in the Subway say that it was a good place.

When she took the train she was brave with a new blue suit, a new suit-case, a two-pound box of candy, copies of the *Saturday Evening Post* and the *Woman's Home Companion*, and Jack London's *People of the Abyss*, which Mamie Magen had given her. All the way to Pittsfield, all the way out to the farm by stage, she sat still and looked politely at every large detached elm, every cow or barefoot boy.

She had set her methodical mind in order; had told herself that she would have time to think and observe. Yet if a census had been taken of her thoughts, not sex nor economics, not improving observations of the flora and fauna of western Massachusetts, would have been found, but a half-glad, half-hysterical acknowledgment

that she had not known how tired and office-soaked she
was till now, when she had relaxed, and a dull, recurrent
wonder if two weeks would be enough to get the office
poison out of her body. Now that she gave up to it, she
was so nearly sick that she couldn't see the magic of the
sheer green hillsides and unexpected ponds, the elm-shrined
winding road, towns demure and white. She did not notice the huge, inn-like farm-house, nor her bare room, nor
the noisy dining-room. She sat on the porch, exhausted,
telling herself that she was enjoying the hill's slope down
to a pond that was yet bright as a silver shield, though
its woody shores had blurred into soft darkness, the enchantment of frog choruses, the cooing pigeons in the barn-
yard.

"Listen. A cow mooing. Thank the Lord I'm away
from New York—clean forgotten it—might be a million
miles away!" she assured herself.

Yet all the while she continued to picture the office—
Bessie's desk, Mr. Wilkins's inkwell, the sinister gray
scrub-rag in the wash-room, and she knew that she needed
some one to lure her mind from the office.

She was conscious that some man had left the chattering
rocking-chair group at the other end of the long porch
and had taken the chair beside her.

"Miss Golden!" a thick voice hesitated.

"Yes."

"Say, I thought it was you. Well, well, the world's
pretty small, after all. Say, I bet you don't remember me."

In the porch light Una beheld a heavy-shouldered,
typical American business man, in derby hat and
clipped mustache, his jowls shining with a recent shave;
an alert, solid man of about forty-five. She remembered
him as a man she had been glad to meet; she felt guiltily
that she ought to know him—perhaps he was a Wilkins

client, and she was making future difficulty in the office. But place him she could not.

"Oh yes, yes, of course, though I can't just remember your name. I always can remember faces, but I never can remember names," she achieved.

"Sure, I know how it is. I've often said, I never forget a face, but I never can remember names. Well, sir, you remember Sanford Hunt that went to the commercial college—"

"Oh, *now* I know—you're Mr. Schwirtz of the Lowry Paint Company, who had lunch with us and told me about the paint company—Mr. Julius Schwirtz."

"You got me. . . . Though the fellows usually call me 'Eddie'—Julius Edward Schwirtz is my full name—my father was named Julius, and my mother's oldest brother was named Edward—my old dad used to say it wasn't respectful to him because I always preferred 'Eddie'— old codger used to get quite het up about it. Julius sounds like you was an old Roman or something, and in the business you got to have a good easy name. Say, speaking of that, I ain't with Lowry any more; I'm chief salesman for the Ætna Automobile Varnish and Wax Company. I certainly got a swell territory—New York, Philly, Bean-Town, Washi'nun, Balt'more, Cleveland, Columbus, Akron, and so on, and of course most especially Detroit. Sell right direct to the jobbers and the big auto companies. Good bunch of live wires. Some class! I'm rolling in my little old four thousand bucks a year now, where before I didn't hardly make more 'n twenty-six or twenty-eight hundred. Keeps me on the jump alrightee. Fact. I got so tired and run-down— I hadn't planned to take any vacation at all, but the boss himself says to me, 'Eddie, we can't afford to let you get sick; you're the best man we've got,' he says, 'and you got to take a good

vacation now and forget all about business for a couple
weeks.' 'Well,' I says, 'I was just wondering if you was
smart enough to get along without me if I was to sneak
out and rubber at some scenery and maybe get up a flir-
tation with a pretty summer girl'—and I guess that must
be you, Miss Golden!—and he laughs and says, 'Oh yes,
I guess the business wouldn't go bust for a few days,' and
so I goes down and gets a shave and a hair-cut and a singe
and a shampoo—there ain't as much to cut as there used
to be, though—ha, ha!—and here I am."

"Yes!" said Una affably. . . .

Miss Una Golden, of Panama and the office, did not
in the least feel superior to Mr. Eddie Schwirtz's robust
commonness. The men she knew, except for pariahs like
Walter Babson, talked thus. She could admire Mamie
Magen's verbal symphonies, but with Mr. Schwirtz she
was able to forget her little private stock of worries and
settle down to her holiday.

Mr. Schwirtz hitched forward in his rocker, took off
his derby, stroked his damp forehead, laid his derby and
both his hands on his stomach, rocked luxuriously, and
took a fresh hold on the conversation:

"But say! Here I am gassing all about myself, and
you'll want to be hearing about Sandy Hunt. Seen him
lately?"

"No, I've lost track of him—you *do* know how it is in
such a big city."

"Sure, I know how it is. I was saying to a fellow just
the other day, 'Why, gosh all fish-hooks!' I was saying,
'it seems like it's harder to keep in touch with a fellow
here in New York than if he lived in Chicago—time you
go from the Bronx to Flatbush or Weehawken, it's time
to turn round again and go home!' Well, Hunt's married
—you know, to that same girl that was with us at lunch

THE JOB

that day—and he's got a nice little house in Secaucus. He's still with Lowry. Good job, too, assistant bookkeeper, pulling down his little twenty-seven-fifty regular, and they got a baby, and let me tell you she makes him a mighty fine wife, mighty bright little woman. Well, now, say! How are *you* getting along, Miss Golden? Everything going bright and cheery?"

"Yes—kind of."

"Well, that's good. You'll do fine, and pick up some good live wire of a husband, too—"

"I'm never going to marry. I'm going—"

"Why, sure you are! Nice, bright woman like you sticking in an office! Office is no place for a woman. Takes a man to stand the racket. Home's the place for a woman, except maybe some hatchet-faced old battle-ax like the cashier at our shop. Shame to spoil a nice home with her. Why, she tried to hold up my vacation money, because she said I'd overdrawn—"

"Oh, but Mr. *Schwirtz*, what can a poor girl do, if you high and mighty men don't want to marry her?"

"Pshaw. There ain't no trouble like that in your case, I'll gamble!"

"Oh, but there is. If I were pretty, like Rose Larsen —she's a girl that stays where I live—oh! I could just eat her up, she's so pretty, curly hair and big brown eyes and a round face like a boy in one of those medieval pictures—"

"That's all right about pretty squabs. They're all right for a bunch of young boys that like a cute nose and a good figger better than they do sense— Well, you notice I remembered you, all right, when you went and forgot poor old Eddie Schwirtz. Yessir, by golly! teetotally plumb forgot me. I guess I won't get over *that* slam for a while."

"Now that isn't fair, Mr. Schwirtz; you know it isn't
—it's almost dark here on the porch, even with the lamps.
I couldn't really see you. And, besides, I *did* recognize
you—I just couldn't think of your name for the moment."

"Yuh, that listens fine, but poor old Eddie's heart is
clean busted just the same—me thinking of you and your
nice complexion and goldie hair and the cute way you
talked at our lunch—whenever Hunt shut up and gave
you a chance—honest, I haven't forgot yet the way you
took off old man—what was it?—the old stiff that ran the
commercial college, what was his name?"

"Mr. Whiteside?" Una was enormously pleased and
interested. Far off and dim were Miss Magen and the
distressing Mrs. Lawrence; and the office of Mr. Troy
Wilkins was fading.

"Yuh, I guess that was it. Do you remember how you
gave us an imitation of him telling the class that if they'd
work like sixty they might get to be little tin gods on
wheels like himself, and how he'd always keep dropping
his eye-glasses and fishing 'em up on a cord while he was
talking—don't you remember how you took him off?
Why, I thought Mrs. Hunt-that-is—I've forgotten what
her name was before Sandy married her—why, I thought
she'd split, laughing. She admired you a whole pile,
lemme tell you; I could see that."

Not unwelcome to the ears of Una was this praise, but
she was properly deprecatory: "Why, she probably
thought I was just a stuffy, stupid, ugly old thing, as old
as—"

"As old as Eddie Schwirtz, heh? Go on, insult me!
I can stand it! Lemme tell you I ain't forty-three till
next October. Look here now, little sister, I know when
a woman admires another. Lemme tell you, if you'd
ever traveled for dry-goods like I did, out of St. Paul

once, for a couple of months—nev-er again; paint and
varnish is good enough for Eddie any day—and if you'd
sold a bunch of women buyers, you'd know how they
looked when they liked a thing, alrightee! Not that I
want to knock The Sex, y' understand, but you know
yourself, bein' a shemale, that there's an awful lot of
cats among the ladies—God bless 'em—that wouldn't admit another lady was beautiful, not if she was as good-
looking as Lillian Russell, corking figger and the swellest
dresser in town."

"Yes, perhaps—sometimes," said Una.

She did not find Mr. Schwirtz dull.

"But I was saying: It was a cinch to see that Sandy's
girl thought you was ace high, alrightee. She kept her
eyes glommed onto you all the time."

"But what would she find to admire?"

"Uh-huh, fishing for compliments!"

"No, I am *not*, so there!" Una's cheeks burned de-
lightfully. She was back in Panama again—in Panama,
where for endless hours on dark porches young men tease
young women and tell them that they are beautiful. . . .
Mr. Schwirtz was direct and "jolly," like Panama people;
but he was so much more active and forceful than Henry
Carson; so much more hearty than Charlie Martindale;
so distinguished by that knowledge of New York streets
and cafés and local heroes which, to Una, the recent con-
vert to New York, seemed the one great science.

Their rockers creaked in complete sympathy.

The perfect summer man took up his shepherd's tale:

"There's a whole lot of things she'd certainly oughta
have admired in you, lemme tell you. I suppose probably
Maxine Elliott is better-looking than what you are, maybe,
but I always was crazy over your kind of girl—blond
hair and nice, clear eyes and just shoulder-high—kind of a

girl that could snuggle down beside a fireplace and look like she grew there—not one of these domineerin' sufferin' cats females. No, nor one of these overdressed New-York chickens, neither, but cute and bright—"

"Oh, you're just flattering me, Mr. Schwirtz. Mr. Hunt told me I should watch out for you."

"No, no; you got me wrong there. 'I dwell on what-is-it mountain, and my name is Truthful James,' like the poet says! Believe me, I may be a rough-neck drummer, but I notice these things."

"Oh! . . . Oh, do you like poetry?"

Without knowing precisely what she was trying to do, Una was testing Mr. Schwirtz according to the somewhat contradictory standards of culture which she had acquired from Walter Babson, Mamie Magen, Esther Lawrence, Mr. Wilkins's books on architecture, and stray copies of *The Outlook*, *The Literary Digest*, *Current Opinion*, *The Nation*, *The Independent*, *The Review of Reviews*, *The World's Work*, *Collier's*, and *The Atlantic Monthly*, which she had been glancing over in the Home Club library. She hadn't learned much of the technique of the arts, but she had acquired an uneasy conscience of the sort which rather discredits any book or music or picture which it easily enjoys. She was, for a moment, apologetic to these insistent new standards, because she had given herself up to Mr. Schwirtz's low conversation. . . . She was not vastly different from a young lady just back in Panama from a term in the normal school, with new lights derived from a gentlemanly young English teacher with poetic interests and a curly mustache.

"Sure," affirmed Mr. Schwirtz, "I like poetry fine. Used to read it myself when I was traveling out of St. Paul and got kind of stuck on a waitress at Eau Claire." This did not perfectly satisfy Una, but she was more satisfied that he had heard the gospel of culture after he had described, with much detail, his enjoyment of a "fella from Boston, perfessional reciter; they say he writes swell poetry himself; gave us a program of Kipling and Ella Wheeler Wilcox before the Elks—real poetic fella."

"Do you go to concerts, symphonies, and so on, much?" Una next catechized.

"Well, no; that's where I fall down. Just between you and I, I never did have much time for these high-brows that try to make out they're so darn much better than common folks by talking about motifs and symphony poems and all that long-haired stuff. Fellow that's in music goods took me to a Philharmonic concert once, and I couldn't make head or tail of the stuff—conductor batting a poor musician over the ear with his swagger-stick (and him a union man, oughta kicked to his union about the way the conductor treated him) and him coming back with a yawp on the fiddle and getting two laps ahead of the brass band, and they all blowing their stuffings out trying to catch up. Music they call that! And once I went to grand opera—lot of fat Dutchmen all singing together like they was selling old rags. Aw nix, give me one of the good old songs like 'The Last Rose of Summer.' . . . I bet *you* could sing that so that even a sporting-goods drummer would cry and think about the sweetheart he had when he was a kid."

"No, I couldn't—I can't sing a note," Una said, delightedly. . . . She had laughed very much at Mr. Schwirtz's humor. She slid down in her chair and felt more expansively peaceful than she ever had been in the stress of Walter Babson.

"Straight, now, little sister. Own up. Don't you get more fun out of hearing Raymond Hitchcock sing than you do out of a bunch of fiddles and flutes fighting out a piece by Vaugner like they was Kilkenny cats? 'Fess up, now; don't you get more downright amusement?"

"Well, maybe I do, sometimes; but that doesn't mean that all this cheap musical comedy music is as good as opera, and so on, if we had our—had musical educations—"

"Oh yes; that's what they all say! But I notice that Hitchcock and George M. Cohan go on drawing big audiences every night—yes, and the swellest, best-dressed, smartest people in New York and Brooklyn, too—it's in the gallery at the opera that you find all these Wops and Swedes and Lord knows what-all. And when a bunch of people are out at a lake, say, you don't ever catch 'em singing Vaugner or Lits or Gryge or any of them guys. If they don't sing, 'In the Good Old Summer-Time,' it's 'Old Black Joe,' or 'Nelly Was a Lady,' or something that's really got some *melody* to it."

The neophyte was lured from her new-won altar. Cold to her knees was the barren stone of the shrine; and she feebly recanted, "Yes, that's so."

Mr. Schwirtz cheerfully took out a cigar, smelled it, bit it, luxuriously removed the band, requested permission to smoke, lighted the cigar without waiting for an answer to that request, sighed happily, and dived again:

"Not that I'm knocking the high-brows, y' understand. This dress-suit music is all right for them that likes it. But what I object to is their trying to stuff it down *my* throat! I let 'em alone, and if I want to be a poor old low-brow and like reg'lar music, I don't see where they get off to be telling me I got to go to concerts. Honest now, ain't that the truth?"

"Oh yes, *that* way—"

"All these here critics telling what low-brows us American business men are! Just between you and I, I bet I knock down more good, big, round, iron men every week than nine-tenths of these high-brow fiddlers—yes, and college professors and authors, too!"

"Yes, but you shouldn't make money your standard," said Una, in company with the invisible chorus of Mamie Magen and Walter Babson.

"Well, then, what *are* you going to make a standard?" asked Mr. Schwirtz, triumphantly.

"Well—" said Una.

"Understan' me; I'm a high-brow myself some ways. I never could stand these cheap magazines. I'd stop the circulation of every last one of them; pass an act of Congress to make every voter read some A-1, high-class, intellectual stuff. I read Rev. Henry van Dyke and Newell Dwight Hillis and Herbert Kaufman and Billy Sunday, and all these brainy, inspirational fellows, and let me tell you I get a lot of talking-points for selling my trade out of their spiels, too. I don't *believe* in all this cheap fiction—these nasty realistic stories (like all the author could see in life was just the bad side of things— I tell you life's bad enough without emphasizing the rotten side, all these unhappy marriages and poverty and everything—I believe if you can't write bright, optimistic, *cheerful* things, better not write at all). And all these sex stories! Don't believe in 'em! Sensational! Don't believe in cheap literature of *no* sort. . . . Oh, of course it's all right to read a coupla detective stories or a nice, bright, clean love-story just to pass the time away. But me, I like real, classy, high-grade writers, with none of this slangy dialogue or vulgar stuff. 'Specially I like essays on strenuous, modern American life, about not being in a rut, but putting a punch in life. Yes, *sir!*"

"I'm glad," said Una. "I do like improving books."

"You've said it, little sister. . . . Say, gee! you don't know what a luxury it is for me to talk about books and literature with an educated, cultured girl like you. Now take the rest of these people here at the farm—nice folks, you understand, mighty well-traveled, broad-gauged, intelligent folks, and all that. There's a Mr. and Mrs. Cannon; he's some kind of an executive in the Chicago stock-yards—nice, fat, responsible job. And he was saying to me, 'Mr. Schwirtz,' he says, 'Mrs. C. and I had never been to New England till this summer, but we'd toured every other part of the country, and we've done Europe thoroughly and put in a month doing Florida, and now,' he says, 'I think we can say we've seen every point of interest that's worth an American's time.' They're good American people like that, well-traveled and nice folks. But *books*—Lord! they can't talk about books no more than a Jersey City bartender. So you can imagine how pleased I was to find you here. .... World's pretty small, all right. Say, I just got here yesterday, so I suppose we'll be here about the same length o' time. If you wouldn't think I was presumptuous, I'd like mighty well to show you some of the country around here. We could get up a picnic party, ten or a dozen of us, and go up on Bald Knob and see the scenery and have a real jolly time. And I'd be glad to take you down to Lesterhampton—there's a real old-fashioned inn down there, they say, where Paul Revere stayed one time; they say you can get the best kind of fried chicken and corn on cob and real old-fashioned New England blueberry pie. Would you like to?"

"Why, I should be very pleased to," said Una.

§ 2

Mr. Schwirtz seemed to know everybody at the farm. He had been there only thirty-six hours, but already he called Mr. Cannon "Sam," and knew that Miss Vincent's married sister's youngest child had recently passed away with a severe and quite unexpected attack of cholera morbus. Mr. Schwirtz introduced Una to the others so fulsomely that she was immediately taken into the inner political ring. He gave her a first lesson in auction pinochle also. They had music and recitations at ten, and Una's shyness was so warmed away that she found herself reciting, "I'm Only Mammy's Pickaninny Coon."

She went candle-lighted up to a four-poster bed. As she lay awake, her job-branded mind could not keep entirely away from the office, the work she would have to do when she returned, the familiar series of indefinite worries and disconnected office pictures. But mostly she let the rustle of the breathing land inspirit her while she thought of Mr. Julius Edward Schwirtz.

She knew that he was ungrammatical, but she denied that he was uncouth. His deep voice had been very kindly; his clipped mustache was trim; his nails, which had been ragged at that commercial-college lunch, were manicured now; he was sure of himself, while Walter Babson doubted and thrashed about. All of which meant that the tired office-woman was touchily defensive of the man who liked her.

She couldn't remember just where she had learned it, but she knew that Mr. Schwirtz was a widower.

§ 3

The fact that she did not have to get up and go to the office was Una's chief impression at awakening, but she was not entirely obtuse to the morning, to the chirp of a robin, the cluck of the hens, the creak of a hay-wagon, and the sweet smell of cattle. When she arose she looked down a slope of fields so far away that they seemed smooth as a lawn. Solitary, majestic trees cast long shadows over a hilly pasture of crisp grass worn to inviting paths by the cropping cattle. Beyond the valley was a range of the Berkshires with every tree distinct.

Una was tired, but the morning's radiance inspired her. "My America—so beautiful! Why do we turn you into stuffy offices and ugly towns?" she marveled while she was dressing.

But as breakfast was not ready, her sudden wish to do something magnificent for America turned into what she called a "before-coffee grouch," and she sat on the porch waiting for the bell, and hoping that the conversational Mr. Schwirtz wouldn't come and converse. It was to his glory that he didn't. He appeared in masterful white-flannel trousers and a pressed blue coat and a new Panama, which looked well on his fleshy but trim head. He said, "Mornin'," cheerfully, and went to prowl about the farm.

All through the breakfast Una caught the effulgence of Mr. Schwirtz's prosperous-looking solidness, and almost persuaded herself that his jowls and the slabs of fat along his neck were powerful muscles.

He asked her to play croquet. Una played a game which had been respected in the smartest croqueting circles of Panama; she defeated him; and while she blushed and insisted that he ought to have won, Mr. Schwirtz chuckled about his defeat and boasted of it to the group on the porch.

"I was afraid," he told her, "I was going to find this farm kinda tame. Usually expect a few more good fellows and highballs in mine, but thanks to you, little sister, looks like I'll have a bigger time than a high-line poker party."

14 [201]

He seemed deeply to respect her, and Una, who had never had the débutante's privilege of ordering men about, who had avoided Henry Carson and responded to Walter Babson and obeyed chiefs in offices, was now at last demanding that privilege. She developed feminine whims and desires. She asked Mr. Schwirtz to look for her handkerchief, and bring her magazine, and arrange her chair cushions, and take her for a walk to "the Glade."

He obeyed breathlessly.

Following an old and rutted woodland road to the Glade, they passed a Berkshire abandoned farm—a solid house of stone and red timbers, softened by the long grasses that made the orchard a pleasant place. They passed berry-bushes—raspberry and blackberry and currant, now turned wild; green-gold bushes that were a net for sunbeams. They saw yellow warblers flicker away, a kingbird swoop, a scarlet tanager glisten in flight.

"Wonder what that red bird is?" He admiringly looked to her to know.

"Why, I think that's a cardinal."

"Golly! I wish I knew about nature."

"So do I! I don't really know a thing—"

"Huh! I bet you do!"

"—though I ought to, living in a small town so long. I'd planned to buy me a bird-book," she rambled on, giddy with sunshine, "and a flower-book and bring them along, but I was so busy getting away from the office that I came off without them. Don't you just love to know about birds and things?"

"Yuh, I cer'nly do; I cer'nly do. Say, this beats New York, eh? I don't care if I never see another show or a cocktail. Cer'nly do beat New York. Cer'nly does! I was saying to Sam Cannon, 'Lord,' I says, 'I wonder what a fellow ever stays in the city for; never catch me there

if I could rake in the coin out in the country, no, *sir!*"
And he laughed and said he guessed it was the same way
with him. No, sir; my idea of perfect happiness is to be
hiking along here with you, Miss Golden."

He gazed down upon her with a mixture of amorousness
and awe. The leaves of scrub-oaks along the road crin-
kled and shone in the sun. She was lulled to slumberous
content. She lazily beamed her pleasure back at him,
though a tiny hope that he would be circumspect, not be
too ardent, stirred in her. He was touching in his desire
to express his interest without ruffling her. He began to
talk about Miss Vincent's affair with Mr. Starr, the
wealthy old boarder at the farm. In that topic they passed
safely through the torrid wilderness of summer shine and
tangled blooms.

The thwarted boyish soul that persisted in Mr.
Schwirtz's barbered, unexercised, coffee-soaked, tobacco-
filled, whisky-rotted, fattily degenerated city body shone
through his red-veined eyes. He was having a *fête cham-
pêtre.* He gathered berries and sang all that he remembered of "Nut Brown Ale," and chased a cow and pantingly
stopped under a tree and smoked a cigar as though he enjoyed it. In his simple pleasure Una was glad. She admired him when he showed his trained, professional side
and explained (with rather confusing details) why the
Ætna Automobile Varnish Company was a success. But
she fluttered up to her feet, became the wilful débutante
again, and commanded, "Come *on*, Mr. Slow! We'll
never reach the Glade." He promptly struggled up to his
feet. There was lordly devotion in the way he threw
away his half-smoked cigar. It indicated perfect chivalry. . . . Even though he did light another in about
three minutes.

The Glade was filled with a pale-green light;   arching

trees shut off the heat of the summer afternoon, and the leaves shone translucent. Ferns were in wild abundance. They sat on a fallen tree, thick upholstered with moss, and listened to the trickle of a brook. Una was utterly happy. In her very weariness there was a voluptuous feeling that the air was dissolving the stains of the office.

He urged a compliment upon her only once more that day; but she gratefully took it to bed with her: "You're just like this glade—make a fellow feel kinda calm and want to be good," he said. "I'm going to cut out—all this boozing and stuff— Course you understand I never make a *habit* of them things, but still a fellow on the road—"

"Yes," said Una.

All evening they discussed croquet, Lenox, Florida, Miss Vincent and Mr. Starr, the presidential campaign, and the food at the farm-house. Boarders from the next farm-house came a-calling, and the enlarged company discussed the food at both of the farm-houses, the presidential campaign, Florida, and Lenox. The men and women gradually separated; relieved of the strain of general and polite conversation, the men gratefully talked about business conditions and the presidential campaign and food and motoring, and told sly stories about Mike and Pat, or about Ikey and Jakey; while the women listened to Mrs. Cannon's stories about her youngest son, and compared notes on cooking, village improvement societies, and what Mrs. Taft would do in Washington society if Judge Taft was elected President. Miss Vincent had once shaken hands with Judge Taft, and she occasionally referred to the incident. Mrs. Cannon took Una aside and told her that she thought Mr. Starr and Miss Vincent must have walked down to the village together that afternoon, as she had distinctly seen them coming back up the road.

Yet Una did not feel Panama-ized.

She was a grown-up person, accepted as one, not as Mrs. Golden's daughter; and her own gossip now passed at par.

And all evening she was certain that Mr. Schwirtz was watching her.

§ 4

The boarders from the two farm-houses organized a tremendous picnic on Bald Knob, with sandwiches and chicken salad and cake and thermos bottles of coffee and a whole pail of beans and a phonograph with seven records; with recitations and pastoral merriment and kodaks snapping every two or three minutes; with groups sitting about on blankets, and once in a while some one explaining why the scenery was so scenic. Una had been anxious lest Mr. Schwirtz "pay her too marked attentions; make them as conspicuous as Mr. Starr and Miss Vincent"; for in the morning he had hung about, waiting for a game of croquet with her. But Mr. Schwirtz was equally pleasant to her, to Miss Vincent, and to Mrs. Cannon; and he was attractively ardent regarding the scenery. "This cer'nly beats New York, eh? Especially you being here," he said to her, aside.

They sang ballads about the fire at dusk, and trailed home along dark paths that smelled of pungent leaf-mold. Mr. Schwirtz lumbered beside her, heaped with blankets and pails and baskets till he resembled a camel in a caravan, and encouraged her to tell how stupid and unenterprising Mr. Troy Wilkins was. When they reached the farm-house the young moon and the great evening star were low in a wash of turquoise above misty meadows; frogs sang; Una promised herself a long and unworried sleep; and the night tingled with an indefinable **magic.**

She was absolutely, immaculately happy, for the first time since she had been ordered to take Walter Babson's dictation.

§ 5

Mr. Schwirtz was generous; he invited all the boarders to a hay-ride picnic at Hawkins's Pond, followed by a barn dance. He took Una and the Cannons for a motor ride, and insisted on buying—not giving, but buying—dinner for them, at the Lesterhampton Inn.

When the débutante Una bounced and said she *did* wish she had some candy, he trudged down to the village and bought for her a two-pound box of exciting chocolates. And when she longed to know how to play tennis, he rented balls and two rackets, tried to remember what he had learned in two or three games of ten years before, and gave her elaborate explanations. Lest the farm-house experts (Mr. Cannon was said by Mrs. Cannon to be one of the very best players at the Winnetka Country Club) see them, Una and Mr. Schwirtz sneaked out before breakfast. Their tennis costumes consisted of new canvas shoes. They galloped through the dew and swatted at balls ferociously—two happy dubs who proudly used all the tennis terms they knew.

§ 6

Mr. Schwirtz was always there when she wanted him, but he never intruded, he never was urgent. She kept him away for a week; but in their second week Mr. and Mrs. Cannon, Mr. Starr, Miss Vincent, and the pleasant couple from Gloversville all went away, and Una and Mr. Schwirtz became the elder generation, the seniors, of the boarders. They rather looked down upon the new boarders who came in—tenderfeet, people who didn't know about Bald Knob or the Glade or Hawkins's Pond, people who weren't half so witty or comfy as the giants of those golden, olden days when Mr. Cannon had ruled. Una and Mr. Schwirtz deigned to accompany them on picnics, even grew interested in their new conceptions of the presidential campaign and croquet and food, yet held rather aloof, as became the *ancien régime;* took confidential walks together, and in secret laughed enormously when the green generation gossiped about them as though they were "interested in each other," as Mr. Starr and Miss Vincent had been in the far-forgotten time. Una blushed a little when she discovered that every one thought they were engaged, but she laughed at the rumor, and she laughed again, a nervous young laugh, as she repeated it to Mr. Schwirtz.

"Isn't it a shame the way people gossip! Silly billies," she said. "We never talked that way about Mr. Starr and Miss Vincent—though in their case we would have been justified."

"Yes, bet they *were* engaged. Oh, say, did I tell you about the first day I came here, and Starr took me aside, and says he—"

In their hour-long talks Mr. Schwirtz had not told much about himself, though of his business he had talked often. But on an afternoon when they took a book and a lunch and tramped off to a round-topped, grassy hill, he finally confided in her, and her mild interest in him as an amiable companion deepened to sympathy.

The book was *The People of the Abyss,* by Jack London, which Mamie Magen had given to Una as an introduction to a knowledge of social conditions. Una had planned to absorb it; to learn how the shockingly poor live. Now she read the first four pages to Mr. Schwirtz. After each page he said that he was interested. At the end of the fourth page, when Una stopped for breath, he commented: "Fine writer, that fella London. And they say he's quite a fella; been a sailor and a miner and all kinds of things; ver' intimate friend of mine knows him quite well—met him in 'Frisco—and he says he's been a sailor and all kinds of things. But he's a socialist. Tell you, I ain't got much time for these socialists. Course I'm kind of a socialist myself lots-a ways, but these here fellas that go around making folks discontented—! Agitators—! Don't suppose it's that way with this London— he must be pretty well fixed, and so of course he's prob'ly growing conservative and sensible. But *most* of these socialists are just a lazy bunch of bums that try and see how much trouble they can stir up. They think that just because they're too lazy to find an opening, that they got the right to take the money away from the fellas that hustle around and make good. Trouble with all these socialist guys is that they don't stop to realize that you can't change human nature. They want to take away all the rewards for initiative and enterprise, just as Sam Cannon was saying. Do you s'pose I'd work my head off putting a proposition through if there wasn't anything in it for me? Then, 'nother thing, about all this submerged tenth—these 'People of the Abyss,' and all the rest: I don't feel a darn bit sorry for them. They stick in London or New York or wherever they are, and live on charity, and if you offered 'em a good job they wouldn't take it. Why, look here! all through the Middle West the farmers are just looking for men at three dollars a day, and for hired girls, they'd give hired girls three and four dollars a week and a good home. But do all these people go out and get the jobs? Not a bit of it! They'd rather stay home and yelp about socialism and anarchism and Lord knows what-all. 'Nother thing: I never could figger out what all these socialists and I. W. W.'s, these 'I Won't Work's,' would do if we *did* divide up and hand all the industries over to them. I bet they'd be the very first ones to kick for a return to the old conditions! I tell you, it surprises me when a good, bright man like Jack London or this fella, Upton Sinclair—they say he's a well-educated fella, too—don't stop and realize these things."

"But—" said Una.

Then she stopped.

Her entire knowledge of socialism was comprised in the fact that Mamie Magen believed in it, and that Walter Babson alternated between socialism, anarchism, and a desire to own a large house in Westchester and write poetry and be superior to the illiterate mass. So to the economic spokesman for the Great American Business Man her answer was:

"But—"

"Then look here," said Mr. Schwirtz. "Take yourself. S'pose you like to work eight hours a day? Course you don't. Neither do I. I always thought I'd like to be a gentleman farmer and take it easy. But the good Lord saw fit to stick us into these jobs, that's all we know about it; and we do our work and don't howl about it like all these socialists and radicals and other wind-jammers that know more than the Constitution and Congress and a convention of Philadelphia lawyers put together. You don't want to work as hard as you do and then have to divide up every Saturday with some lazy bum of a socialist that's too lazy to support himself—yes, or to take a bath!—now do you?"

"Well, no," Una admitted, in face of this triumphant exposure of liberal fallacies.

The book slipped into her lap.

THE JOB

"How wonderful that line of big woolly clouds is, there between the two mountains!" she said. "I'd just like to fly through them. . . . I *am* tired. The clouds rest me so."

"Course you're tired, little sister. You just forget about all those guys in the abyss. Tell you a person on the job's got enough to do looking out for himself."

"Well—" said Una.

Suddenly she lay back, her hands behind her head, her fingers outstretched among the long, cool grasses. A hum of insects surrounded her. The grasses towering above her eyes were a forest. She turned her head to watch a lady-bug industriously ascend one side of a blade of grass, and with equal enterprise immediately descend the other side. With the office always in her mind as material for metaphors, Una compared the lady-bug's method to Troy Wilkins's habit of having his correspondence filed and immediately calling for it again. She turned her face to the sky. She was uplifted by the bold contrast of cumulus clouds and the radiant blue sky.

Here she could give herself up to rest; she was so secure now, with the affable Mr. Schwirtz to guard her against outsiders—more secure and satisfied, she reflected, than she could ever have been with Walter Babson. . . . A hawk soared above her, a perfect thing of sun-brightened grace, the grasses smelled warm and pleasant, and under her beat the happy heart of the summer land.

"I'm a poor old rough-neck," said Mr. Schwirtz, "but to-day, up here with you, I feel so darn good that I almost think I'm a decent citizen. Honest, little sister, I haven't felt so bully for a blue moon."

"Yes, and I—" she said.

He smoked, while she almost drowsed into slumber to the lullaby of the afternoon.

When a blackbird chased a crow above her, and she

sat up to watch the aerial privateering, Mr. Schwirtz began to talk.

He spoke of the flight of the Wright brothers in France and Virginia, which were just then—in the summer of 1908—arousing the world to a belief in aviation. He had as positive information regarding aeroplanes as he had regarding socialism. It seemed that a man who was tremendously on the inside of aviation—who was, in fact, going to use whole tons of aeroplane varnish on aeroplane bodies, next month or next season—had given Mr. Schwirtz secret advices that within five years, by 1913, aeroplanes would be crossing the Atlantic daily, and conveying passengers and mail on regular routes between New York and Chicago.... "Though," said Mr. Schwirtz, in a sophisticated way, "I don't agree with these crazy enthusiasts that believe aeroplanes will be used in war. Too easy to shoot 'em down." His information was so sound that he had bought a hundred shares of stock in his customer's company. In on the ground floor. Stock at three dollars a share. Would be worth two hundred a share the minute they started regular passenger-carrying.

"But at that, I only took a hundred shares. I don't believe in all this stock-gambling. What I want is sound, conservative investments," said Mr. Schwirtz.

"Yes, I should think you'd be awfully practical," mused Una. "My! three dollars to two hundred! You'll make an awful lot out of it."

"Well, now, I'm not saying anything. I don't pretend to be a Wisenheimer. May be nine or ten years—nineteen seventeen or nineteen eighteen—before we are doing a regular business. And at that, the shares may never go above par. But still, I guess I'm middlin' practical—not like these socialists, ha, ha!"

"How did you ever get your commercial training?"

THE JOB

The question encouraged him to tell the story of his life.

Mostly it was a story of dates and towns and jobs—jobs he had held and jobs from which he had resigned, and all the crushing things he had said to the wicked bosses during those victorious resignings. . . . Clerk in a general store, in a clothing-store, in a hardware-store—all these in Ohio. A quite excusable, almost laudable, failure in his own hardware-store in a tiny Wisconsin town. Half a dozen clerkships. Collector for a harvester company in Nebraska, going from farm to farm by buggy. Traveling salesman for a St. Paul wholesaler, for a Chicago clothing-house. Married. Partner with his brother-in-law in a drug, paint, and stationery store. Traveling for a Boston paint-house. For the Lowry Paint Company of Jersey City. Now with the automobile wax company. A typical American business career, he remarked, though somehow distinctive, *different*— A guiding star—

Una listened murmuringly, and he was encouraged to try to express the inner life behind his jobs. Hesitatingly he sought to make vivid his small-boy life in the hills of West Virginia: carving initials, mowing lawns, smoking corn silk, being arrested on Hallowe'en, his father's death, a certain Irving who was his friend, "carrying a paper route" during two years of high school. His determination to "make something of himself." His arrival in Columbus, Ohio, with just seventy-eight cents—he emphasized it: "just seventy-eight cents, that's every red cent I had, when I started out to look for a job, and I didn't know a single guy in town." His reading of books during the evenings of his first years in Ohio; he didn't "remember their titles, exactly," he said, but he was sure that "he read a lot of them." . . . At last he spoke of his wife, of their buggy-riding, of their neat frame house with the lawn and the porch swing. Of their quarrels—he made it clear that his wife had been "finicky," and had "fool notions," but he praised her for having "come around and learned that a man is a man, and sometimes he means a lot better than it looks like; prob'ly he loves her a lot better than a lot of these plush-soled, soft-tongued fellows that give 'em a lot of guff and lovey-dovey stuff and don't shell out the cash. She was a good sport—one of the best."

Of the death of their baby boy.

"He was the brightest little kid—everybody loved him. When I came home tired at night he would grab my finger —see, this first finger—and hold it, and want me to show him the bunny-book. . . . And then he died."

Mr. Schwirtz told it simply, looking at clouds spread on the blue sky like a thrown handful of white paint.

Una had hated the word "widower"; it had suggested Henry Carson and the Panama undertaker and funerals and tired men trying to wash children and looking for a new wife to take over that work; all the smell and grease of disordered side-street kitchens. To her, now, Julius Edward Schwirtz was not a flabby-necked widower, but a man who mourned, who felt as despairingly as could Walter Babson the loss of the baby who had crowed over the bunny-book. She, the motherless, almost loved him as she stood with him in the same depth of human grief. And she cried a little, secretly, and thought of her longing for the dead mother, as he gently went on:

"My wife died a year later. I couldn't get over it; seemed like I could have killed myself when I thought of any mean thing I might have said to her—not meaning anything, but hasty-like, as a man will. Couldn't seem to get over it. Evenings were just hell; they were so— empty. Even when I was out on the road, there wasn't anybody to write to, anybody that *cared*. Just sit in a hotel room and think about her. And I just couldn't realize that she was gone. Do you know, Miss Golden, for months, whenever I was coming back to Boston from a trip, it was *her* I was coming back to, seemed like, even though I *knew* she wasn't there—yes, and evenings at home when I'd be sitting there reading, I'd think I heard her step, and I'd look up and smile—and she wouldn't be there; she wouldn't *ever* be there again. . . . She was a lot like you—same cute, bright sort of a little woman, with light hair—yes, even the same eye-glasses. I think maybe that's why I noticed you particular when I first met you at that lunch and remembered you so well afterward. . . . Though you're really a lot brighter and better educated than what she was—I can see it now. I don't mean no disrespect to her; she was a good sport; they don't make 'em any better or finer or truer; but she hadn't never had much chance; she wasn't educated or a live wire, like you are. . . . You don't mind my saying that, do you? How you mean to me what she meant—"

"No, I'm glad—" she whispered.

Unlike the nimble Walter Babson, Mr. Schwirtz did not make the revelation of his tragedy an excuse for trying to stir her to passion. But he had taken and he held her hand among the long grasses, and she permitted it.

That was all.

He did not arouse her; still was it Walter's dark head and the head of Walter's baby that she wanted to cradle on her breast. But for Mr. Schwirtz she felt a good will that was broad as the summer afternoon.

"I am very glad you told me. I *do* understand. I lost my mother just a year ago," she said, softly.

He squeezed her hand and sighed, "Thank you, little sister." Then he rose and more briskly announced, "Getting late—better be hiking, I guess."

Not again did he even touch her hand. But on his last night at the farm-house he begged, "May I come to call on you in New York?" and she said, "Yes, please do."

She stayed for a day after his departure, a long and lonely Sunday. She walked five miles by herself. She thought of the momently more horrible fact that vacation was over, that the office would engulf her again. She declared to herself that two weeks were just long enough holiday to rest her, to free her from the office; not long enough to begin to find positive joy.

Between shudders before the swiftly approaching office she thought of Mr. Schwirtz. (She still called him that to herself. She couldn't fit "Eddie" to his trim bulkiness, his maturity.)

She decided that he was wrong about socialism; she feebly tried to see wherein, and determined to consult her teacher in ideals, Mamie Magen, regarding the proper answers to him. She was sure that he was rather crude in manners and speech, rather boastful, somewhat loquacious.

"But I do like him!" she cried to the hillsides and the free sky. "He would take care of me. He's kind; and he would learn. We'll go to concerts and things like that in New York—dear me, I guess I don't know any too much about art things myself. I don't know why, but even if he isn't interesting, like Mamie Magen, I *like* him—I think!"

§ 7

On the train back to New York, early Monday morning, she felt so fresh and fit, with morning vigorous in her and about her, that she relished the thought of attacking the job. Why, she rejoiced, every fiber of her was simply soaked with holiday; she was so much stronger and happier; New York and the business world simply couldn't be the same old routine, because she herself was different.

But the train became hot and dusty; the Italians began to take off their collars and hand-painted ties.

And hot and dusty, perspiring and dizzily rushing, were the streets of New York when she ventured from the Grand Central station out into them once more.

It was late. She went to the office at once. She tried to push away her feeling that the Berkshires, where she had arisen to a cool green dawn just that morning, were leagues and years away. Tired she was, but sunburnt and easy-breathing. She exploded into the office, set down her suit-case, found herself glad to shake Mr. Wilkins's hand and to answer his cordial, "Well, well, you're brown as a berry. Have a good time?"

The office *was* different, she cried—cried to that other earlier self who had sat in a train and hoped that the office would be different.

She kissed Bessie Kraker, and by an error of enthusiasm nearly kissed the office-boy, and told them about the farm-house, the view from her room, the Glade, Bald Knob, Hawkins's Pond; about chickens and fresh milk and pigeons aflutter; she showed them the kodak pictures taken by Mrs. Cannon and indicated Mr. Starr and Miss Vincent and laughed about them till—

"Oh, Miss Golden, could you take a little dictation now?" Mr. Wilkins called.

There was also a pile of correspondence unfiled, and the office supplies were low, and Bessie was behind with her copying, and the office-boy had let the place get as dusty as a hay-loft—and the stiff, old, gray floor-rag was grimly at its post in the wash-room.

"The office *isn't* changed," she said; and when she went out at three for belated lunch, she added, "and New

York isn't, either. Oh, Lord! I really am back here. Same old hot streets. Don't believe there *are* any Berkshires; just seems now as though I hadn't been away at all."

She sat in negligée on the roof of the Home Club and learned that Rose Larsen and Mamie Magen and a dozen others had just gone on vacation.

"Lord! it's over for me," she thought. "Fifty more weeks of the job before I can get away again—a whole year. Vacation is farther from me now than ever. And the same old grind. . . . Let's see, I've got to get in touch with the Adine Company for Mr. Wilkins before I even do any filing in the morning—"

She awoke, after midnight, and worried: "I *mustn't* forget to get after the Adine Company, the very first thing in the morning. And Mr. Wilkins has *got* to get Bessie and me a waste-basket apiece. Oh, Lord! I wish Eddie Schwirtz were going to take me out for a walk to-morrow, the old darling that he is— I'd walk *anywhere* rather than ask Mr. Wilkins for those blame waste-baskets!"

15

MRS. ESTHER LAWRENCE was, she said, bored by the general atmosphere of innocent and bounding girlhood at the Temperance Home Club, and she persuaded Una to join her in taking a flat—three small rooms —which they made attractive with Japanese toweling and Russian, or at least Russian-Jew, brassware. Here Mrs. Lawrence's men came calling, and sometimes Mr. Julius Edward Schwirtz, and all of them, except Una herself, had cigarettes and highballs, and Una confusedly felt that she was getting to be an Independent Woman.

Then, in January, 1909, she left the stiff, gray scrubrag which symbolized the routine of Mr. Troy Wilkins's office.

In a magazine devoted to advertising she had read that Mr. S. Herbert Ross, whom she had known as advertising-manager of the *Gas and Motor Gazette*, had been appointed advertising-manager for Pemberton's—the greatest manufactory of drugs and toilet articles in the world. Una had just been informed by Mr. Wilkins that, while he had an almost paternal desire to see her successful financially and otherwise, he could never pay her more than fifteen dollars a week. He used a favorite phrase of commuting captains of commerce: "Personally, I'd be glad to pay you more, but fifteen is all the position is worth." She tried to persuade him that there is no position which cannot be made "worth more." He promised to "think it over." He was still taking a few months to think it over

THE JOB

—while her Saturday pay-envelope remained as thin as ever—when Bessie Kraker resigned, to marry a mattress-renovator, and in Bessie's place Mr. Wilkins engaged a tall, beautiful blonde, who was too much of a lady to take orders from Una. This wrecked Una's little office home, and she was inspired to write to Mr. S. Herbert Ross at Pemberton's, telling him what a wise, good, noble, efficient man he was, and how much of a privilege it would be to become his secretary. She felt that Walter Babson must have been inexact in ever referring to Mr. Ross as "Sherbet Souse."

Mr. Ross disregarded her letter for ten days, then so urgently telephoned her to come and see him that she took a taxicab clear to the Pemberton Building in Long Island City. After paying a week's lunch money for the taxicab, it was rather hard to discover why Mr. Ross had been quite so urgent. He rolled about his magnificent mahogany and tapestry office, looked out of the window at the Long Island Railroad tracks, and told her (in confidence) what fools all the *Gas Gazette* chiefs had been, and all his employers since then. She smiled appreciatively, and tried to get in a tactful remark about a position. She did discover that Mr. Ross had not as yet chosen his secretary at Pemberton's, but beyond this Una could find no evidence that he supposed her to have come for any reason other than to hear his mellow wisdom and even mellower stories.

After more than a month, during which Mr. Ross diverted himself by making appointments, postponing them, forgetting them, telephoning, telegraphing, sending special-delivery letters, being paged at hotels, and doing all the useless melodramatic things he could think of, except using an aeroplane or a submarine, he decided to make her his secretary at twenty dollars a week. Two

[219]

THE JOB

days later it occurred to him to test her in regard to speed
in dictation and typing, and a few other minor things of
the sort which her ability as a long-distance listener had
made him overlook.   Fortunately, she also passed this test.

When she told Mr. Wilkins that she was going to leave,
he used another set of phrases which all side-street office
potentates know—they must learn these *clichés* out of a
little red-leather manual. . . . He tightened his lips and
tapped on his desk-pad with a blue pencil; he looked
grieved and said, touchingly: "I think you're making a
mistake.   I was making plans for you; in fact, I had just
about decided to offer you eighteen dollars a week, and
to advance you just as fast as the business will warrant.
I, uh, well, I think you're making a mistake in leaving a
sure thing, a good, sound, conservative place, for something
you don't know anything about.   I'm not in any way
urging you to stay, you understand, but I don't like to
see you making a mistake."

But he had also told Bessie Kraker that she was "making a mistake" when she had resigned to be married, and
he had been so very certain that Una could never be
"worth more" than fifteen.   Una was rather tart about
it.   Though Mr. Ross didn't want her at Pemberton's
for two weeks more, she told Mr. Wilkins that she was
going to leave on the following Saturday.

It did not occur to her till Mr. Wilkins developed nervous indigestion by trying to "break in" a new secretary
who couldn't tell a blue-print from a set of specifications,
that he had his side in the perpetual struggle between ill-
paid failure employers and ill-paid ambitious employees.
She was sorry for him as she watched him putter, and
she helped him; stayed late, and powerfully exhorted her
successor.   Mr. Wilkins revived and hoped that she would
stay another week, but stay she could not.   Once she

knew that she was able to break away from the scrub-rag, that specter of the wash-room, and the bleak, frosted glass on the semi-partition in front of her desk, no wage could have helped her. Every moment here was an edged agony.

In this refusal there may have been a trace of aspiration. Otherwise the whole affair was a hodge-podge of petty people and ignoble motives—of Una and Wilkins and S. Herbert Ross and Bessie Kraker, who married a mattress-renovator, and Bessie's successor; of fifteen dollars a week, and everybody trying to deceive everybody else; of vague reasons for going, and vaguer reasons for letting Una go, and no reason at all for her remaining; in all, an ascent from a scrub-rag to a glorified soap-factory designed to provide Mr. Pemberton's daughters-in-law with motors.

So long as her world was ruled by chance, half-training, and lack of clear purpose, how could it be other than a hodge-podge?

§ 2

She could not take as a holiday the two weeks intervening between the Wilkins office and Pemberton's. When she left Wilkins's, exulting, "This is the last time I'll ever go down in one of these rickety elevators," she had, besides her fifteen dollars in salary, one dollar and seventeen cents in the savings-bank.

Mamie Magen gave her the opportunity to spend the two weeks installing a modern filing-system at Herzfeld & Cohn's.

So Una had a glimpse of the almost beautiful thing business can be.

Herzfeld and Cohn were Jews, old, white-bearded, orthodox Jews; their unpoetic business was the jobbing of

iron beds; and Una was typical of that New York which
the Jews are conquering, in having nebulous prejudices
against the race; in calling them "mean" and "grasping"
and "un-American," and wanting to see them shut out of
offices and hotels.

Yet, with their merry eyes, their quick little foreign
cries and gestures of sympathy, their laughter that
rumbled in their tremendous beards, their habit of having
coffee and pinochle in the office every Friday afternoon,
their sincere belief that, as the bosses, they were not
omniscient rulers, but merely elder fellow-workers—with
these un-American, eccentric, patriarchal ways, Herzfeld
and Cohn had made their office a joyous adventure.
Other people "in the trade" sniffed at Herzfeld and Cohn
for their Quixotic notions of discipline, but they made it
pay in dividends as well as in affection. At breakfast
Una would find herself eager to get back to work, though
Herzfeld and Cohn had but a plain office in an ugly building of brownstone and iron Corinthian columns, resem-
bling an old-fashioned post-office, and typical of all that
block on Church Street. There was such gentleness here
as Una was not to find in the modern, glazed-brick palace
of Pemberton's.

§ 3

Above railroad yards and mean tenements in Long
Island City, just across the East River from New York,
the shining milky walls of Pemberton's bulk up like a
castle overtowering a thatched village. It is magnifi-
cently the new-fashioned, scientific, efficient business
institution. . . . Except, perhaps, in one tiny detail.
King Pemberton and his princely sons do not believe in
all this nonsense about profit-sharing, or a minimum
wage, or an eight-hour day, or pensions, or any of the
[222]

other fads by which dangerous persons like Mr. Ford, the motor manufacturer, encourage the lazier workmen to think that they have just as much right to rise to the top as the men who have had nerve and foresight. And indeed Mr. Pemberton may be sound. He says that he bases wages on the economic law of supply and demand, instead of on sentiment; and how shrewdly successful are he and his sons is indicated by the fact that Pemberton's is one of the largest sources of drugs and proprietary medicines in the world; the second largest manufactory of soda-fountain syrups; of rubber, celluloid, and leather goods of the kind seen in corner drug-stores; and the third largest manufactory of soaps and toilet articles. It has been calculated that ninety-three million women in all parts of the world have ruined their complexions, and, therefore, their souls, by Pemberton's creams and lotions for saving the same; and that nearly three-tenths of the alcohol consumed in prohibition counties is obtained in Pemberton's tonics and blood-builders and women's specifics, the last being regarded by large farmers with beards as especially tasty and stimulating. Mr. Pemberton is the Napoleon of patent medicine, and also the Napoleon of drugs used by physicians to cure the effects of patent medicine. He is the Shakespeare of ice-cream sodas, and the Edison of hot-water bags. He rules more than five thousand employees, and his name is glorious on cartons in drug-stores, from Sandy Hook to San Diego, and chemists' shops from Hong-Kong to the Scilly Isles. He is a modern Allah, and Mr. S. Herbert Ross is his prophet.

§ 4

Una discovered that Mr. Ross, who had been negligible as advertising-manager of the *Gas and Motor Gazette*, had, in two or three years, become a light domestic great man, because he so completely believed in his own genius, and because advertising is the romance, the faith, the mystery of business.   Mr. Pemberton, though he knew well enough that soap-making was a perfectly natural phenomenon, could never get over marveling at the supernatural manner in which advertising seemed to create something out of nothing.   It took a cherry fountain syrup which was merely a chemical imitation that under an old name was familiar to everybody; it gave the syrup a new name, and made twenty million children clamor for it.   Mr. Pemberton could never quite understand that advertising was merely a matter of salesmanship by paper and ink, nor that Mr. Ross's assistants, who wrote the copy and drew the pictures and selected the mediums and got the "mats" over to the agency on time, were real advertising men.   No, the trusting old pirate believed it was also necessary to have an ordained advertising-manager like Mr. Ross, a real initiate, who could pull a long face and talk about "the psychology of the utilitarian appeal" and "pulling power" and all the rest of the theology.   So he, who paid packing-girls as little as four dollars a week, paid Mr. Ross fifteen thousand dollars a year, and let him have competent assistants, and invited him out to the big, lonely, unhappy Pemberton house in the country, and listened to his sacerdotal discourses, and let him keep four or five jobs at once.   For, besides being advertising-manager for Pemberton's, Mr. Ross went off to deliver Lyceum lectures and Chautauqua addresses and club chit-chats on the blessings of selling more soap or underwear; and for the magazines he wrote prose poems about stars, and sympathy, and punch, and early rising, and roadside flowers, and argosies, and farming, and saving money.

THE JOB

All this doge-like splendor Una discovered, but could scarcely believe, for in his own office Mr. Ross seemed but as the rest of us—a small round man, with a clown-like little face and hair cut Dutch-wise across his forehead. When he smoked a big cigar he appeared naughty. One expected to see his mother come and judiciously smack him. But more and more Una felt the force of his attitude that he was a genius incomparable. She could not believe that he knew what a gorgeous fraud he was. On the same day, he received an advance in salary, discharged an assistant for requesting an advance in salary, and dictated a magazine filler to the effect that the chief duty of executives was to advance salaries. She could not chart him. . . . Thus for thousands of years have servants been amazed at the difference between pontiffs in the pulpit and pontiffs in the pantry.

Doubtless it helped Mr. Ross in maintaining his sublimity to dress like a cleric—black, modest suits of straight lines, white shirts, small, black ties. But he also wore silk socks, which he reflectively scratched while he was dictating. He was of an elegance in linen handkerchiefs, in a chased-gold cigarette-case, in cigarettes with a monogram. Indeed, he often stopped during dictation to lean across the enormous mahogany desk and explain to Una how much of a connoisseur he was in tennis, fly-casting, the ordering of small, smart dinners at the Plaza.

He was fond of the word "smart."

"Rather smart poster, eh?" he would say, holding up the latest creation of his genius—that is to say, of his genius in hiring the men who had planned and prepared the creation.

Mr. Ross was as full of ideas as of elegance. He gave birth to ideas at lunch, at "conferences," while motoring, while being refreshed with a manicure and a violet-ray

[225]

treatment at a barber-shop in the middle of one of his arduous afternoons. He would gallop back to the office with notes on these ideas, pant at Una in a controlled voice, "Quick—your book—got a' idea," and dictate the outline of such schemes as the Tranquillity Lunch Room —a place of silence and expensive food; the Grand Arcade —a ten-block-long rival to Broadway, all under glass; the Barber-Shop Syndicate, with engagement cards sent out every third week to notify customers that the time for a hair-cut had come again. None of these ideas ever had anything to do with assisting Mr. Pemberton in the sale of soap, and none of them ever went any farther than being outlined. Whenever he had dictated one of them, Mr. Ross would assume that he had already made a million out of it, and in his quiet, hypnotizing voice he would permit Una to learn what a great man he was. Hitching his chair an inch nearer to her at each sentence, looking straight into her eyes, in a manner as unboastful as though he were giving the market price of eggs, he would tell her how J. Pierpont Morgan, Burbank, or William Randoph Hearst had praised him; or how much more he knew about electricity or toxicology or frogs or Java than anybody else in the world.

Not only a priest, but a virtuoso of business was he, and Una's chief task was to keep assuring him that he was a great man, a very great man—in fact, as great as he thought he was. This task was, to the uneasily sincere Una, the hardest she had ever attempted. It was worth five dollars more a week than she had received from Troy Wilkins—it was worth a million more!

She got confidence in herself from the ease with which she satisfied Mr. Ross by her cold, canned compliments. And though she was often dizzied by the whirling dynamo of Pemberton's, she was not bored by the routine of valeting Mr. Ross in his actual work. . . . For Mr. Ross actually did work now and then, though his chief duty was to make an impression on old Mr. Pemberton, his sons, and the other big chiefs. Still, he did condescend to "put his O. K." on pictures, on copy and proof for magazine advertisements, car cards, window-display "cut-outs," and he dictated highly ethical reading matter for the house organ, which was distributed to ten thousand drug-stores, and which spoke well of honesty, feminine beauty, gardening, and Pemberton's. Occasionally he had a really useful idea, like the celebrated slogan, "*Pemberton's* Means PURE," which you see in every street-car, on every fourth or fifth bill-board. It is frequent as the "In God We Trust" on our coins, and at least as accurate. This slogan, he told Una, surpassed "A train every hour on the hour," or "The watch that made the dollar famous," or, "The ham what am," or any of the other masterpieces of lyric advertising. He had created it after going into a sibyllic trance of five days, during which he had drunk champagne and black coffee, and ridden about in hansoms, delicately brushing his nose with a genuine California poppy from the Monterey garden of R. L. S.

If Mr. Ross was somewhat agitating, he was calm as the desert compared with the rest of Pemberton's.

His office, which was like a million-dollar hotel lobby, and Una's own den, which was like the baggage-porter's den adjoining the same, were the only spots at Pemberton's where Una felt secure. Outside of them, fourteen stories up in the titanic factory, was an enormous office-floor, which was a wilderness of desks, toilet-rooms, elevators, waiting-rooms, filing-cabinets. Her own personality was absorbed in the cosmic (though soapy) personality of Pemberton's. Instead of longing for a change, she clung to her own corner, its desk and spring-back chair, and the insurance calendar with a high-colored picture of Washington's farewell. She preferred to rest here rather than in the "club-room and rest-room for women employees," on which Mr. Pemberton so prided himself.

Una heard rumors of rest-rooms which were really beautiful, really restful; but at Pemberton's the room resembled a Far Rockaway cottage rented by the week to feeble-minded bookkeepers. Musty it was, with curtains awry, and it must have been of use to all the branches of the Pemberton family in cleaning out their attics. Here was the old stuffed chair in which Pemberton I. had died, and the cot which had been in the cook's room till she had protested. The superstition among the chiefs was that all the women employees were very grateful for this charity. The room was always shown to exclamatory visitors, who told Mr. Pemberton that he was almost too good. But in secret conclaves at lunch the girls called the room "the junk-shop," and said that they would rather go out and sit on the curb.

Una herself took one look—and one smell—at the room, and never went near it again.

But even had it been enticing, she would not have frequented it. Her caste as secretary forbade. For Pemberton's was as full of caste and politics as a Republican national convention; caste and politics, cliques and factions, plots and secrets, and dynasties that passed and were forgotten.

Plots and secrets Una saw as secretary to Mr. Ross. She remembered a day on which Mr. Ross, in her presence, assured old Pemberton that he hoped to be with the firm for the rest of his life, and immediately afterward dictated a letter to the president of a rival firm in the effort to secure a new position. He destroyed the carbon copy of that letter and looked at Una as serenely as ever.

THE JOB

Una saw him read letters on the desks of other chiefs while he was talking to them; saw him "listen in" on telephone calls, and casually thrust his foot into doors, in order to have a glimpse of the visitors in offices. She saw one of the younger Pembertons hide behind a book-case while his father was talking to his brother. She knew that this Pemberton and Mr. Ross were plotting to oust the brother, and that the young, alert purchasing agent was trying to undermine them both. She knew that one of the girls in the private telephone exchange was the mistress and spy of old Pemberton. All of the chiefs tried to emulate the *moyen-age* Italians in the arts of smiling poisoning—but they did it so badly; they were as fussily ineffectual as a group of school-boys who hate their teacher. Not "big deals" and vast grim power did they achieve, but merely a constant current of worried insecurity, and they all tended to prove Mrs. Lawrence's assertion that the office-world is a method of giving the largest possible number of people the largest possible amount of nervous discomfort, to the end of producing the largest possible quantity of totally useless articles. . . . The struggle extended from the chiefs to the clerks; they who tramped up and down a corridor, waiting till a chief was alone, glaring at others who were also manœuvering to see him; they who studied the lightest remark of any chief and rushed to allies with the problem of, "Now, what did he mean by that, do you think?" . . . A thousand questions of making an impression on the overlords, and of "House Policy"—that malicious little spirit which stalks through the business house and encourages people to refuse favors.

Una's share in the actual work at Pemberton's would have been only a morning's pastime, but her contact with the high-voltage current of politics exhausted her—and taught her that commercial rewards come to those who demand and take.

The office politics bred caste. Caste at Pemberton's was as clearly defined as ranks in an army.

At the top were the big chiefs, the officers of the company, and the heads of departments—Mr. Pemberton and his sons, the treasurer, the general manager, the purchasing-agent, the superintendents of the soda-fountain-syrup factory, of the soap-works, of the drug-laboratories, of the toilet-accessories shops, the sales-manager, and Mr. S. Herbert Ross. The Olympian council were they; divinities to whom the lesser clerks had never dared to speak. When there were rumors of "a change," of "a cut-down in the force," every person on the office floor watched the chiefs as they assembled to go out to lunch together—big, florid, shaven, large-chinned men, talking easily, healthy from motoring and golf, able in a moment's conference at lunch to "shift the policy" and to bring instant poverty to the families of forty clerks or four hundred workmen in the shops. When they jovially entered the elevator together, some high-strung stenographer would rush over to one of the older women to weep and be comforted. . . . An hour from now her tiny job might be gone.

Even the chiefs' outside associates were tremendous, buyers and diplomatic representatives; big-chested men with watch-chains across their beautiful tight waistcoats. And like envoys extraordinary were the efficiency experts whom Mr. Pemberton occasionally had in to speed up the work a bit more beyond the point of human endurance. . . . One of these experts, a smiling and pale-haired young man who talked to Mr. Ross about the new poetry, arranged to have office-boys go about with trays of water-glasses at ten, twelve, two, and four. Thitherto, the stenographers had wasted a great deal of time in trotting to the battery of water-coolers, in actually being human and relaxed and gossipy for ten minutes a day. After the visitation of the expert the girls were so efficient that they never for a second stopped their work —except when one of them would explode in hysteria and be hurried off to the rest-room. But no expert was able to keep them from jumping at the chance to marry any one who would condescend to take them out of this efficient atmosphere.

Just beneath the chiefs was the caste of bright young men who would some day have the chance to be beatified into chiefs. They believed enormously in the virtue of spreading the blessings of Pemberton's patent medicines; they worshiped the house policy. Once a month they met at what they called "punch lunches," and listened to electrifying addresses by Mr. S. Herbert Ross or some other inspirer, and turned fresh, excited eyes on one another, and vowed to adhere to the true faith of Pemberton's, and not waste their evenings in making love, or reading fiction, or hearing music, but to read diligently about soap and syrups and window displays, and to keep firmly before them the vision of fifteen thousand dollars a year. They had quite the best time of any one at Pemberton's, the bright young men. They sat, in silk shirts and new ties, at shiny, flat-topped desks in rows; they answered the telephone with an air; they talked about tennis and business conditions, and were never, never bored.

Intermingled with this caste were the petty chiefs, the office-managers and bookkeepers, who were velvety to those placed in power over them, but twangily nagging to the girls and young men under them. Failures themselves, they eyed sourly the stenographers who desired two dollars more a week, and assured them that while *personally* they would be *very* glad to obtain the advance for them, it would be "unfair to the other girls." They were very strong on the subject of not being unfair to the other girls, and their own salaries were based on "keeping down overhead." Oldish men they were, wearing last-year hats and smoking Virginia cigarettes at lunch; always gossiping about the big chiefs, and at night disappearing to homes and families in New Jersey or Harlem. Awe-encircled as the very chiefs they appeared when they lectured stenographers, but they cowered when the chiefs spoke to them, and tremblingly fingered their frayed cuffs.

Such were the castes above the buzzer-line.

Una's caste, made up of private secretaries to the chiefs, was not above the buzzer. She had to leap to the rattle-snake tattoo, when Mr. Ross summoned her, as quickly as did the newest Jewish stenographer. But hers was a staff corps, small and exclusive and out of the regular line. On the one hand she could not associate with the chiefs; on the other, it was expected of her in her capacity as daily confidante to one of the gods, that she should not be friendly, in coat-room or rest-room or elevator, with the unrecognized horde of girls who merely copied or took the bright young men's dictation of letters to drug-stores. These girls of the common herd were expected to call the secretaries, "Miss," no matter what street-corner impertinences they used to one another.

There was no caste, though there was much factional rivalry, among the slaves beneath—the stenographers, copyists, clerks, waiting-room attendants, office-boys, elevator-boys. They were expected to keep clean and be quick-moving; beyond that they were as unimportant to the larger phases of office politics as frogs to a summer hotel. Only the cashier's card index could remember their names. . . . Though they were not deprived of the chief human satisfaction and vice—feeling superior. The most snuffle-nosed little mailing-girl on the office floor felt superior to all of the factory workers, even the foremen, quite as negro house-servants look down on poor white trash.

Jealousy of position, cattishness, envy of social standing —these were as evident among the office-women as they are in a woman's club; and Una had to admit that woman's cruelty to woman often justified the prejudices of executives against the employment of women in business; that women were the worst foes of Woman.

To Una's sympathies, the office proletarians were her own poor relations. She sighed over the cheap jackets, with silesia linings and raveled buttonholes, which nameless copyists tried to make attractive by the clean embroidered linen collars which they themselves laundered in wash-bowls in the evening. She discovered that even after years of experience with actual office-boys and elevator-boys, Mr. Ross still saw them only as slangy, comic-paper devils. Then, in the elevator, she ascertained that the runners made about two hundred trips up and down the dark chutes every day, and wondered if they always found it comic to do so. She saw the office-boys, just growing into the age of interest in sex and acquiring husky male voices and shambling sense of shame, yearn at the shrines of pasty-faced stenographers. She saw the humanity of all this mass—none the less that they envied her position and spoke privily of "those snippy private secretaries that think they're so much sweller than the rest of us."

She watched with peculiar interest one stratum: the old ladies, the white-haired, fair-handed women of fifty

16   [233]

and sixty and even seventy, spinsters and widows, for whom life was nothing but a desk and a job of petty pickings—mailing circulars or assorting letters or checking up lists. She watched them so closely because she speculated always, "Will I ever be like that?"

They seemed comfortable; gossipy they were, and fond of mothering the girls. But now and then one of them would start to weep, cry for an hour together, with her white head on a spotty desk-blotter, till she forgot her homelessness and uselessness. Epidemics of hysteria would spring up sometimes, and women of thirty-five or forty—normally well content—would join the old ladies in sobbing. Una would wonder if she would be crying like that at thirty-five—and at sixty-five, with thirty barren, weeping years between. Always she saw the girls of twenty-two getting tired, the women of twenty-eight getting dry and stringy, the women of thirty-five in a solid maturity of large-bosomed and widowed spinsterhood, the old women purring and catty and tragic. . . . She herself was twenty-eight now, and she knew that she was growing sallow, that the back of her neck ached more often, and that she had no release in sight save the affably dull Mr. Julius Edward Schwirtz.

Machines were the Pemberton force, and their greatest rivals were the machines of steel and wood, at least one of which each new efficiency expert left behind him: Machines for opening letters and sealing them, automatic typewriters, dictation phonographs, pneumatic chutes. But none of the other machines was so tyrannical as the time-clock. Una admitted to herself that she didn't see how it was possible to get so many employees together promptly without it, and she was duly edified by the fact that the big chiefs punched it, too. . . . But she noticed that after punching it promptly at nine, in an unctuous manner which said to all beholders, "You see that even I subject myself to this delightful humility," Mr. S. Herbert Ross frequently sneaked out and had breakfast. . . .

She knew that the machines were supposed to save work. But she was aware that the girls worked just as hard and long and hopelessly after their introduction as before; and she suspected that there was something wrong with a social system in which time-saving devices didn't save time for anybody but the owners. She was not big enough nor small enough to have a patent cure-all solution ready. She could not imagine any future for these women in business except the accidents of marriage or death—or a revolution in the attitude toward them. She saw that the comfortable average men of the office sooner or later, if they were but faithful and lived long enough, had opportunities, responsibility, forced upon them. No such force was used upon the comfortable average women!

She endeavored to picture a future in which women, the ordinary, philoprogenitive, unambitious women, would have some way out besides being married off or killed off. She envisioned a complete change in the fundamental purpose of organized business from the increased production of soap—or books or munitions—to the increased production of happiness. How this revolution was to be accomplished she had but little more notion than the other average women in business. She blindly adopted from Mamie Magen a half-comprehended faith in a Fabian socialism, a socializing that would crawl slowly through practical education and the preaching of kinship, through profit-sharing and old-age pensions, through scientific mosquito-slaying and cancer-curing and food reform and the abolition of anarchistic business competition, to a goal of tolerable and beautiful life. Of one thing she was sure: This age, which should adjudge happiness to be as valuable as soap or munitions, would never come so long as the workers accepted the testimony of paid spokesmen like S. Herbert Ross to the effect that they were contented and happy, rather than the evidence of their own wincing nerves to the effect that they lived in a polite version of hell. . . . She was more and more certain that the workers weren't discontented enough; that they were too patient with lives insecure and tedious. But she refused to believe that the age of comparative happiness would always be a dream; for already, at Herzfeld & Cohn's she had tasted of an environment where no one considered himself a divinely ruling chief, and where it was not a crime to laugh easily. But certainly she did not expect to see this age during her own life. She and her fellows were doomed, unless they met by chance with marriage or death; or unless they crawled to the top of the heap. And this last she was determined to do. Though she did hope to get to the top without unduly kicking the shrieking mass of slaves beneath her, as the bright young men learned to do.

Whenever she faced Mr. Ross's imperturbable belief that things-as-they-are were going pretty well, that "you can't change human nature," Una would become meek and puzzled, lose her small store of revolutionary economics, and wonder, grope, doubt her millennial faith. Then she would again see the dead eyes of young girls as they entered the elevators at five-thirty, and she would rage at all chiefs and bright young men. . . . A gold-eye-glassed, kitten-stepping, good little thing she was, and competent to assist Mr. Ross in his mighty labors, yet at heart she was a shawled Irish peasant, or a muzhik lost in the vastness of the steppes; a creature elemental and despairing, facing mysterious powers of nature—human nature.

CHAPTER XV

M R. JULIUS EDWARD SCHWIRTZ was a regular visitant at the flat of Mrs. Lawrence and Una. Mrs. Lawrence liked him; in his presence she abandoned her pretense of being interested in Mamie Magen's arid intellectualism, and Una's quivering anxieties. Mr. Schwirtz was ready for any party, whenever he was "in off the road."

Una began to depend on him for amusements. Mrs. Lawrence encouraged her to appear at her best before him. When he or one of Mrs. Lawrence's men was coming the two women had an early and quick dinner of cold ham and canned soup, and hastily got out the electric iron to press a frock; produced Pemberton's Flesh-Tinted Vanisho Powder, and the lip-stick whose use Una hated, but which she needed more and more as she came back from the office bloodless and cold. They studied together the feminine art of using a new veil, a flower, or fresh white-kid gloves, to change one's appearance.

Poor Una! She was thinking now, secretly and shame-facedly, of the "beautifying methods" which she saw advertised in every newspaper and cheap magazine. She rubbed her red, desk-calloused elbows with Pemberton's cold-cream. She cold-creamed and massaged her face every night, standing wearily before a milky mirror in the rather close and lingerie-scattered bedroom, solemnly rotating her fingers about her cheeks and forehead, stopping to conjecture that the pores in her nose were getting enlarged. She rubbed her hair with Pemberton's "Olivine and Petrol" to keep it from growing thin, and her neck with cocoanut oil to make it more full. She sent for a bottle of "Mme. LeGrand's Bust-Developer," and spent several Saturday afternoons at the beauty parlors of Mme. Isoldi, where in a little booth shut off by a white-rubber curtain, she received electrical massages, applications of a magic N-ray hair-brush, vigorous cold-creaming and warm-compressing, and enormous amounts of advice about caring for the hair follicles, from a young woman who spoke French with a Jewish accent.

By a twist of psychology, though she had not been particularly fond of Mr. Schwirtz, but had anointed herself for his coming because he was a representative of men, yet after months of thus dignifying his attentions, the very effort made her suppose that she must be fond of him. Not Mr. Schwirtz, but her own self did she befool with Pemberton's "Preparations de Paris."

Sometimes with him alone, sometimes with him and Mrs. Lawrence and one of Mrs. Lawrence's young business-man attendants, Una went to theaters and dinners and heterogeneous dances.

She was dazzled and excited when Mr. Schwirtz took her to the opening of the Champs du Pom-Pom, the latest potpourri of amusements on Broadway. All under one roof were a super-vaudeville show, a smart musical comedy, and the fireworks of one-act plays; a Chinese restaurant, and a Louis Quinze restaurant and a Syrian desert-caravan restaurant; a ballroom and an ice-skating rink; a summer garden that, in midwinter, luxuriated in real trees and real grass, and a real brook crossed by Japanese bridges. Mr. Schwirtz was tireless and extravagant and hearty at the Champs du Pom-Pom. He made

THE JOB

Una dance and skate; he had a box for the vaudeville;
he gave her caviar canapé and lobster *à la Rue des Trois
Sœurs* in the Louis Quinze room; and sparkling Bur-
gundy in the summer garden, where mocking-birds sang
in the wavering branches above their table. Una took
away an impressionistic picture of the evening—

Scarlet and shadowy green, sequins of gold, slim shoulders veiled in costly mist. The glitter of spangles, the hiss-
ing of silk, low laughter, and continual music quieter than
a dream. Crowds that were not harsh busy folk of the
streets, but a nodding procession of gallant men and
women. A kindly cleverness which inspirited her, and
a dusky perfume in which she could meditate forever,
like an Egyptian goddess throned at the end of incense-
curtained aisles. Great tapestries of velvet and jeweled
lights; swift, smiling servants; and the languorous well-
being of eating strange, delicious foods. Orchids and the
scent of poppies and spell of the lotos-flower, the bead of
wine and lips that yearned; ecstasy in the Oriental pride
of a superb Jewess who was singing to the demure enchantment of little violins. Her restlessness satisfied, a
momentary pang of distrust healed by the brotherly
talk of the broad-shouldered man who cared for her and
nimbly fulfilled her every whim. An unvoiced desire to
keep him from drinking so many highballs; an enduring
thankfulness to him when she was back at the flat; a
defiant joy that he had kissed her good-night—just once,
and so tenderly; a determination to "be good for him,"
and a fear that he had "spent too much money on her
to-night," and a plan to reason with him about whisky
and extravagance. A sudden hatred of the office to which
she would have to return in the morning, and a stronger,
more sardonic hatred of hearing Mr. S. Herbert Ross
pluck out his vest-pocket harp and hymn his own praise

in a one-man choir, cherubic, but slightly fat. A descent from high gardens of moonlight to the reality of the flat, where Lawrence was breathing loudly in her sleep; the oily smell of hairs tangled in her old hair-brush; the sight of the alarm-clock which in just six hours would be flogging her off to the mill. A sudden, frightened query as to what scornful disdain Walter Babson would fling at her if he saw her glorying in this Broadway circus with the heavy Mr. Schwirtz. A ghostly night-born feeling that she still belonged to Walter, living or dead, and a wonder as to where in all the world he might be. A defiant protest that she idealized Walter, that he wasn't so awfully superior to the Champs du Pom-Pom as this astral body of his was pretending, and a still more defiant gratitude to Mr. Schwirtz as she crawled into the tousled bed and Mrs. Lawrence half woke to yawn, "Oh, that—you—Gold'n? *Gawd!* I'm sleepy. Wha' time is 't?"

§ 2

Una was sorry. She hated herself as what she called a "quitter," but now, in January, 1910, she was at an *impasse*. She could just stagger through each day of S. Herbert Ross and office diplomacies. She had been at Pemberton's for a year and a third, and longer than that with Mrs. Lawrence at the flat. The summer vacation of 1909 she had spent with Mrs. Lawrence at a Jersey coast resort. They had been jealous, had quarreled, and made it up every day, like lovers. They had picked up two summer men, and Mrs. Lawrence had so often gone off on picnics with her man that Una had become uneasy, felt soiled, and come back to the city early. For this Mrs. Lawrence had never forgiven her. She had recently become engaged to a doctor who was going to Akron, Ohio, and she exasperated Una by giving her bland advice about trying to get married. Una never knew whether she was divorced, or whether the mysterious Mr. Lawrence had died.

But even the difficile Lawrence was preferable to the strain at the office. Una was tired clean through and through. She felt as though her very soul had been drained out by a million blood-sucker details—constant adjustments to Ross's demands for admiration of his filthiest office political deals, and the need of keeping friendly with both sides when Ross was engaged in one of his frequent altercations with an assistant.

Often she could not eat in the evening. She would sit on the edge of the bed and cry hopelessly, with a long, feeble, peculiarly feminine sobbing, till Mrs. Lawrence slammed the door and went off to the motion pictures. Una kept repeating a little litany she had made regarding the things she wished people would stop doing—praying to be delivered from Ross's buoyant egotism, from Mrs. Lawrence's wearing of Una's best veils, from Mr. Schwirtz's acting as though he wanted to kiss her whenever he had a whisky breath, from the office-manager who came in to chat with her just when she was busiest, from the office-boy who always snapped his fingers as he went down the corridor outside her door, and from the elevator-boy who sucked his teeth.

She was sorry. She wanted to climb. She didn't want to be a quitter. But she was at an *impasse.*

On a January day the Pemberton office beheld that most terrifying crisis that can come to a hard, slave-driving office. As the office put it, "The Old Man was on a rampage."

Mr. Pemberton, senior, most hoarily awful of all the big chiefs, had indigestion or a poor balance-sheet. He decided that everything was going wrong. He raged from room to room. He denounced the new poster, the new top for the talcum-powder container, the arrangement of the files, and the whispering in the amen corner of veteran stenographers. He sent out flocks of "office memoes." Everybody trembled. Mr. Pemberton's sons actually did some work; and, as the fire spread and the minor bosses in turn raged among their subordinates, the girls who packed soap down in the works expected to be "fired." After a visitation from Mr. Pemberton and three raging memoes within fifteen minutes, Mr. S. Herbert Ross retreated toward the Lafayette Café, and Una was left to face Mr. Pemberton's bear-like growls on his next appearance.

When he did appear he seemed to hold her responsible for all the world's long sadness. Meanwhile the printer was telephoning for Mr. Ross's O.K. on copy, the engravers wanted to know where the devil was that color-proof, the advertising agency sarcastically indicated that it was difficult for them to insert an advertisement before they received the order, and a girl from the cashier's office came nagging in about a bill for India ink.

The memoes began to get the range of her desk again, and Mr. Pemberton's voice could be heard in a distant part of the office, approaching, menacing, all-pervading.

Una fled. She ran to a wash-room, locked the door, leaned panting against it, as though detectives were pursuing her. She was safe for a moment. They might miss her, but she was insulated from demands of, "Where's Ross, Miss Golden? Well, why *don't* you know where he is?" from telephone calls, and from memoes whose polite "please" was a gloved threat.

But even to this refuge the familiar sound of the office penetrated—the whirr which usually sounded as a homogeneoûs murmur, but which, in her acute sensitiveness, she now analyzed into the voices of different typewriters—one flat, rapid, staccato; one a steady, dull rattle. The "zzzzz" of typewriter-carriages being shoved back. The roll of closing elevator doors, and the rumble of the ascending elevator. The long burr of an unanswered telephone at a desk, again and again; and at last an angry "Well! Hello? Yes, yes; this 's Mr. Jones. What-duh-yuh want?" Voices mingled; a shout for Mr. Brown; the hall-attendant yelping: "Miss Golden! Where's Miss Golden? Anything for Sanford? Mr. Smith, d'you know if there's anything for Sanford?" Always, over and through all, the enveloping clatter of typewriters, and the city roar behind that, breaking through the barrier of the door.

The individual, analyzed sounds again blended in one insistent noise of hurry which assailed Una's conscience, summoned her back to her work.

She sighed, washed her stinging eyes, opened the door, and trailed back toward her den.

In the corridor she passed three young stenographers and heard one of them cry: "Yes, but I don't care if old Alfalfa goes on a rampage twenty-five hours a day. I'm through. Listen, May, say, what d'you know about me? I'm engaged! No, honest, straight I am! Look at me ring! Aw, it is not; it's a regular engagement-ring. I'm going to be out of this hell-hole in two weeks, and Papa Pemberton can work off his temper on somebody else. Me, I'm going to do a slumber marathon till noon every day."

"Gee!"

"Engaged!"

—said the other girls, and—

"Engaged! Going to sleep till noon every day. And

not see Mr. Ross or Mr. Pemberton! That's my idea of heaven!" thought Una.

There was a pile of inquiring memoes from Mr. Pemberton and the several department heads on her desk. As she looked at them Una reached the point of active protest.

"S. Herbert runs for shelter when the storm breaks, and leaves me here to stand it. Why isn't *he* supposed to be here on the job just as much as I am?" she declaimed. "Why haven't I the nerve to jump up and go out for a cup of tea the way he would? By jiminy! I will!"

She was afraid of the indefinite menace concealed in all the Pemberton system as she signaled an elevator. But she did not answer a word when the hall-attendant said, "You are going out, Miss Golden?"

She went to a German-Jewish bakery and lunch-room, and reflectively got down thin coffee served in a thick cup, a sugar-warted *Kaffeekuche*, and two crullers. She was less willing to go back to work than she had been in her refuge in the wash-room. She felt that she would rather be dead than return and subject herself to the strain. She was "through," like the little engaged girl. She was a "quitter."

For half an hour she remained in the office, but she left promptly at five-thirty, though her desk was choked with work and though Mr. Ross telephoned that he would be back before six, which was his chivalrous way of demanding that she stay till seven.

Mr. Schwirtz was coming to see her that evening. He had suggested vaudeville.

She dressed very carefully. She did her hair in a new way.

When Mr. Schwirtz came she cried that she *couldn't* go to a show. She was "clean played out." She didn't know what she could do. Pemberton's was too big a threshing-machine for her. She was tired—"absolutely all in."

"Poor little sister!" he said, and smoothed her hair.

She rested her face on his shoulder. It seemed broad and strong and protective.

She was glad when he put his arm about her.

She was married to Mr. Schwirtz about two weeks later.

§ 3

She had got herself to call him "Ed." . . . "Eddie" she could not encompass, even in that fortnight of rushing change and bewilderment.

She asked for a honeymoon trip to Savannah. She wanted to rest; she had to rest or she would break, she said.

They went to Savannah, to the live-oaks and palmettoes and quiet old squares.

But she did not rest. Always she brooded about the unleashed brutality of their first night on the steamer, the strong, inescapable man-smell of his neck and shoulders, the boisterous jokes he kept telling her.

He insisted on their staying at a commercial hotel at Savannah. Whenever she went to lie down, which was frequently, he played poker and drank highballs. He tried in his sincerest way to amuse her. He took her to theaters, restaurants, road-houses. He arranged a three days' hunting-trip, with a darky cook. He hired motor-boats and motor-cars and told her every "here's a new one," that he heard. But she dreaded his casual-seeming suggestions that she drink plenty of champagne; dreaded his complaints, whiney as a small boy, "Come now, Unie, show a little fire. I tell you a fellow's got a right to expect it at this time." She dreaded his frankness of undressing, of shaving; dreaded his occasional irritated protests of "Don't be a finicking, romantic school-miss. I may not wear silk underclo' and perfume myself like some bum actor, but I'm a regular guy"; dreaded being alone with him; dreaded always the memory of that first cataclysmic night of their marriage; and mourned, as in secret, for year on year, thousands of women do mourn. "Oh, I wouldn't care now if he had just been gentle, been considerate. . . . Oh, Ed *is* good; he *does* mean to care for me and give me a good time, but—"

When they returned to New York, Mr. Schwirtz said, robustly: "Well, little old trip made consid'able hole in my wad. I'm clean busted. Down to one hundred bucks in the bank."

"Why, I thought you were several thousand ahead!"

"Oh—oh! I lost most of that in a little flyer on stocks —thought I'd make a killing, and got turned into lamb-chops; tried to recoup my losses on that damn flying-machine, passenger-carrying game that that —— —— —— —— let me in for. Never mind, little sister; we'll start saving now. And it was worth it. Some trip, eh? You enjoyed it, didn't you—after the first couple days, while you were seasick? You'll get over all your fool, girly-girly notions now. Women always are like that. I remember the first missus was, too. . . . And maybe a few other skirts, though I guess I hadn't better tell no tales outa school on little old Eddie Schwirtz, eh? Ha, ha! . . . Course you high-strung virgin kind of shemales take some time to learn to get over your choosey, finicky ways. But, Lord love you! I don't mind that much. Never could stand for these rough-necks that claim they'd rather have a good, healthy walloping country wench than a nice, refined city lady. Why, I *like* refinement! Yes, sir, I sure do! . . . Well, it sure was some trip. Guess we won't forget it in a hurry, eh? Sure is nice to rub up against some Southern swells like we did that night at the Avocado Club. And that live bunch of salesmen. Gosh! Say, I'll never forget that Jock Sanderson. He was a comical cuss, eh? That story of his—"

"No," said Una, "I'll never forget the trip."

But she tried to keep the frenzy out of her voice. The frenzy was dying, as so much of her was dying. She hadn't realized a woman can die so many times and still live. Dead had her heart been at Pemberton's, yet it had secreted enough life to suffer horribly now, when it was again being mauled to death.

And she wanted to spare this man.

She realized that poor Ed Schwirtz, puttering about their temporary room in a side-street family hotel, yawning and scratching his head, and presumably comfortable in suspenders over a woolen undershirt—she realized that he treasured a joyous memory of their Savannah diversions.

She didn't want to take joy away from anybody who actually had it, she reflected, as she went over to the coarse-lace hotel curtains, parted them, stared down on the truck-filled street, and murmured, "No, I can't ever forget."

Part III
MAN AND WOMAN

CHAPTER XVI

FOR two years Una Golden Schwirtz moved amid the blank procession of phantoms who haunt cheap family hotels, the apparitions of the corridors, to whom there is no home, nor purpose, nor permanence. Mere lodgers for the night, though for score on score of tasteless years they use the same alien hotel room as a place in which to take naps and store their trunks and comb their hair and sit waiting—for nothing. The men are mysterious. They are away for hours or months, or they sit in the smoking-room, glancing up expectant of fortunes that never come. But the men do have friends; they are permitted familiarities by the bartender in the café. It is the women and children who are most dehumanized. The children play in the corridors; they become bold and sophisticated; they expect attention from strangers. At fourteen the girls have long dresses and mature admirers, and the boys ape the manners of their shallow elders and discuss brands of cigarettes. The women sit and rock, empty-hearted and barren of hands. When they try to make individual homes out of their fixed molds of rooms—the hard walls, the brass bedsteads, the inevitable bureaus, the small rockers, and the transoms that always let in too much light from the hall at night—then they are only the more pathetic. For the small pictures of pulpy babies photographed as cupids, the tin souvenirs and the pseudo-Turkish scarves draped over trunks rob the rooms of the simplicity which is their only merit.

THE JOB

For two years—two years snatched out of her life and traded for somnambulatory peace, Una lived this spectral life of one room in a family hotel on a side street near Sixth Avenue. The only other dwelling-places she saw were the flats of friends of her husband.

He often said, with a sound of pride: "We don't care a darn for all these would-be social climbers. The wife and I lead a regular Bohemian life. We know a swell little bunch of live ones, and we have some pretty nifty parties, lemme tell you, with plenty poker and hard liquor. And one-two of the bunch have got their own cars—I tell you they make a whole lot more coin than a lot of these society-column guys, even if they don't throw on the agony; and we all pile in and go up to some road-house, and sing, and play the piano, and have a real time."

Conceive Una—if through the fumes of cheap cigarettes you can make out the low lights of her fading hair—sitting there, trying patiently to play a "good, canny fist of poker"—which, as her husband often and irritably assured her, she would never learn to do. He didn't, he said, mind her losing his "good, hard-earned money," but he "hated to see Eddie Schwirtz's own wife more of a boob than Mrs. Jock Sanderson, who's a regular guy; plays poker like a man."

Mrs. Sanderson was a black-haired, big-bosomed woman with a face as hard and smooth and expressionless as a dinner-plate, with cackling laughter and a tendency to say, "Oh, hell, boys!" apropos of nothing. She was a "good sport" and a "good mixer," Mr. Schwirtz averred; and more and more, as the satisfaction of having for his new married mistress a "refined lady" grew dull, he adjured the refined lady to imitate Mrs. Sanderson.

Fortunately, Mr. Schwirtz was out of town two-thirds

of the time. But one-third of the time was a good deal, since for weeks before his coming she dreaded him; and for weeks after his going she remembered him with chill shame; since she hadn't even the whole-hearted enthusiasm of hating him, but always told herself that she was a prude, an abnormal, thin-blooded creature, and that she ought to appreciate "Ed's" desire to have her share his good times, be coarse and jolly and natural.

His extravagance was constant. He was always planning to rent an expensive apartment and furnish it, but the money due him after each trip he spent immediately and they were never able to move away from the family hotel. He had to have taxicabs when they went to theaters. He would carol, "Oh, don't let's be pikers, little sister—nothing too good for Eddie Schwirtz, that's my motto." And he would order champagne, the one sort of good wine that he knew. He always overtipped waiters and enjoyed his own generosity. Generous he really was, in a clumsy way. He gave to Una all he had over from his diversions; urged her to buy clothes and go to matinées while he was away, and told it as a good joke that he "blew himself" so extensively on their parties that he often had to take day-coaches instead of sleepers for a week after he left New York. . . . Una had no notion of how much money he made, but she knew that he never saved it. She would beg: "Why don't you do like so many of the other traveling-men? Your Mr. Sanderson is saving money and buying real estate, even though he does have a good time. Let's cut out some of the unnecessary parties and things—"

"Rats! My Mr. Sanderson is a leet-le tight, like all them Scotch laddies. I'm going to start saving one of these days. But what can you do when the firm screws you down on expense allowances and don't hardly allow you one red cent of bonus on new business? There's no chance for a man to-day—these damn capitalists got everything lashed down. I tell you I'm getting to be a socialist."

He did not seem to be a socialist of the same type as Mamie Magen, but he was interested in socialism to this extent—he always referred to it at length whenever Una mentioned saving money.

She had not supposed that he drank so much. Always he smelled of whisky, and she found quart bottles of it in his luggage when he returned from a trip.

But he never showed signs of drunkenness, except in his urgent attentions to her after one of their "jolly Bohemian parties."

More abhorrent to her was the growing slackness in his personal habits. . . . He had addressed her with great volubility and earnestness upon his belief that now they were married, she must get rid of all her virginal book-learned notions about reticence between husband and wife. Such feminine "hanky-panky tricks," he assured her, were the cause of "all these finicky, unhappy marriages and these rotten divorces—lot of fool clubwomen and suffragettes and highbrows expecting a man to be like a nun. A man's a man, and the sooner a female gets on to that fact and doesn't nag, nag, nag him, and let's him go round being comfortable and natural, the kinder he'll be to her, and the better it 'll be for all parties concerned. Every time! Don't forget that, old lady. Why, there's J. J. Vance at our shop. Married one of these up-dee-dee, poetry-reading, finicky women. Why, he did *everything* for that woman. Got a swell little house in Yonkers, and a vacuum cleaner, and a hired girl, and everything. Then, my God! she said she was *lonely!* Didn't have enough housework, that was the trouble

with her; and darned if she doesn't kick when J. J. comes
in all played out at night because he makes himself comfortable and sits around in his shirt-sleeves and slippers.
Tell you, the first thing these women have gotta learn is
that a man's a man, and if they learn that they won't
need a vote!"

Mr. Schwirtz's notion of being a man was to perform
all hygienic processes as publicly as the law permitted.
Apparently he was proud of his God-given body—though
it had been slightly bloated since God had given it to
him—and wanted to inspire her not only with the artistic
vision of it, but with his care for it. . . . His thick woolen
undergarments were so uncompromisingly wooleny.

Nor had Mr. Schwirtz any false modesty in his speech.
If Una had made out a list of all the things she considered
the most banal or nauseatingly vulgar, she would have
included most of the honest fellow's favorite subjects.
And at least once a day he mentioned his former wife.
At a restaurant dinner he gave a full account of her death,
embalming, and funeral.

Una identified him with vulgarity so completely that
she must often have been unjust to him. At least she
was surprised now and then by a reassertion that he was
a "highbrow," and that he decidedly disapproved of any
sort of vulgarity. Several times this came out when he
found her reading novels which were so coarsely realistic
as to admit the sex and sweat of the world.

"Even if they *are* true to life," he said, "I don't see
why it's necessary to drag in unpleasant subjects. I tell
you a fella gets too much of bad things in this world
without reading about 'em in books. Trouble with all
these 'realists' as you call 'em, is that they're such dirty-
minded hounds themselves that all they can see in life
is the bad side."

THE JOB

Una surmised that the writers of such novels might, perhaps, desire to show the bad side in the hope that life might be made more beautiful. But she wasn't quite sure of it, and she suffered herself to be overborne, when he snorted: "Nonsense! These fellas are just trying to show how sensational they can be, t' say nothing of talking like they was so damn superior to the rest of us. Don't read 'em. Read pure authors like Howard Bancock Binch, where, whenever any lady gets seduced or anything like that, the author shows it's because the villain is an atheist or something, and he treats all those things in a nice, fine, decent manner. Good Gawd! sometimes a fella 'd think, to see you scrooge up your nose when I'm shaving, that I'm common as dirt, but lemme tell you, right now, miss, I'm a darn sight too refined to read any of these nasty novels where they go to the trouble of describing homes that ain't any better than pig-pens. Oh, and another thing! I heard you telling Mrs. Sanderson you thought all kids oughta have sex education. My *Gawd!* I don't know where you get those rotten ideas! Certainly not from me. Lemme tell you, no kid of mine is going to be made nasty-minded by having a lot of stuff like that taught her. Yes, sir, actually taught her right out in school."

Una was sufficiently desirous of avoiding contention to keep to novels which portrayed life—offices and family hotels and perspiratory husbands—as all for the best. But now and then she doubted, and looked up from the pile of her husband's white-footed black-cotton socks to question whether life need be confined to Panama and Pemberton and Schwirtz.

In deference to Mr. Schwirtz's demands on the novelists, one could scarce even suggest the most dreadful scene in Una's life, lest it be supposed that other women really are subject to such horror, or that the statistics regarding immoral diseases really mean anything in households such as we ourselves know. . . . She had reason to suppose that her husband was damaged goods. She crept to an old family doctor and had a fainting joy to find that she had escaped contamination.

"Though," said the doctor, "I doubt if it would be wise to have a child of his."

"I won't!" she said, grimly.

She knew the ways of not having children. The practical Mr. Schwirtz had seen to that. Strangely enough, he did not object to birth-control, even though it was discussed by just the sort of people who wrote these sensational realistic novels.

There were periods of reaction when she blamed herself for having become so set in antipathy that she always looked for faults; saw as a fault even the love for amusements which had once seemed a virtue in him.

She tried, wistfully and honestly, to be just. She reminded herself constantly that she had enjoyed some of the parties with him—theater and a late supper, with a couple just back from South America.

But—there were so many "buts"! Life was all one obliterating But.

Her worst moments were when she discovered that she had grown careless about appearing before him in that drabbest, most ignoble of feminine attire—a pair of old corsets; that she was falling into his own indelicacies.

Such marionette tragedies mingled ever with the grander passion of seeing life as a ruined thing; her birthright to aspiring cleanness sold for a mess of quick-lunch pottage. And as she walked in a mist of agony, a dumb, blind creature heroically distraught, she could scarce distinguish between sordidness and the great betrayals, so chill and thick was the fog about her.

She thought of suicide, often, but too slow and sullen was her protest for the climax of suicide. And the common sense which she still had urged her that some day, incredibly, there might again be hope. Oftener she thought of a divorce. Of that she had begun to think even on the second day of her married life. She suspected that it would not be hard to get a divorce on statutory grounds. Whenever Mr. Schwirtz came back from a trip he would visibly remove from his suit-case bunches of letters in cheaply pretentious envelopes of pink and lavender. She scorned to try to read them, but she fancied that they would prove interesting to the judges.

§ 2

When Mr. Schwirtz was away Una was happy by contrast. Indeed she found a more halcyon rest than at any other period since her girlhood; and in long hours of thinking and reading and trying to believe in life, the insignificant good little thing became a calm-browed woman.

Mrs. Lawrence had married the doctor and gone off to Ohio. They motored much, she wrote, and read aloud, and expected a baby. Una tried to be happy in them.

Una had completely got out of touch with Mr. and Mrs. Sessions, but after her marriage she had gone to call on Mamie Magen, now prosperous and more earnest than ever, in a Greenwich Village flat; on Jennie Cassavant, sometime of the Home Club, now obscurely on the stage; on curly-haired Rose Larsen, who had married a young lawyer. But Una had fancied that they were suspiciously kind to her, and in angry pride she avoided them. She often wondered what they had heard about Mr. Schwirtz from the talkative Mrs. Lawrence. She conceived scenes in which she was haughtily rhapsodic in defending her good, sensible husband before them. Then she would long for them and admit that doubtless she had merely imagined their supercilious pity. But she could not go back to them as a beggar for friendship.

Also, though she never admitted this motive to herself, she was always afraid that some day, if she kept in touch with them, her husband would demand: "Why don't you trot out these fussy lady friends of yours? Ashamed of me, eh?"

So she drifted away from them, and at times when she could not endure solitariness she depended upon the women of the family hotel, whom she met in the corridors and café and "parlor."

The aristocrats among them, she found, were the wives of traveling salesmen, good husbands and well loved, most of them, writing to their wives daily and longing for the time when they could have places in the suburbs, with room for chickens and children and love. These aristocrats mingled only with the sound middle-class of the hotel women, whose husbands were clerks and book-keepers resident in the city, or traveling machinery experts who went about installing small power-plants. They gossiped with Una about the husbands of the *déclassé* women—men suspected to be itinerant quack doctors, sellers of dubious mining or motor stock, or even crooks and gamblers.

There was a group of three or four cheery, buxom, much-bediamonded, much-massaged women, whose occasionally appearing husbands were sleek and overdressed. To Una these women were cordial. They invited her to go shopping, to matinées. But they stopped so often for cocktails, they told so many intimate stories of their relations with their husbands, that Una was timid before them, and edged away from their invitations except when she was desperately lonely. Doubtless she learned more about the mastery of people from them, however, than from the sighing, country-bred hotel women of whom she was more fond; for the cheerful hussies had learned to make the most of their shoddy lives.

Only one woman in the hotel did Una accept as an actual friend—Mrs. Wade, a solid, slangy, contented woman with a child to whom she was devoted. She had, she told Una, "been stuck with a lemon of a husband. He was making five thousand a year when I married him, and then he went to pieces. Good-looking, but regular poor white trash. So I cleaned house—kicked him out. He's in Boston now. Touches me for a ten-spot now and then. I support myself and the kid by working for a department store. I'm a wiz. at bossing dressmakers—make a Lucile gown out of the rind of an Edam cheese. Take nothing off nobody—especially you don't see me taking any more husbands off nobody."

Mostly, Una was able to make out an existence by herself.

She read everything—from the lacy sentimentalism of Myrtle Read to Samuel Butler and translations of Gorky and Flaubert. She nibbled at histories of art, and was confirmed in her economic theology by shallow but earnest manuals of popular radicalism. She got books from a branch public library, or picked them up at second-hand stalls. At first she was determined to be "serious" in her reading, but more and more she took light fiction as a drug to numb her nerves—and forgot the tales as soon as she had read them.

THE JOB

In ten years of such hypnotic reading Mrs. Una Golden Schwirtz would not be very different from that Mrs. Captain Golden who, alone in a flat, had read all day, and forgotten what she had read, and let life dream into death.

But now Una was still fighting to keep in life.

She began to work out her first definite philosophy of existence. In essence it was not so very different from the blatant optimism of Mr. S. Herbert Ross—except that it was sincere.

"Life is hard and astonishingly complicated," she concluded. "No one great reform will make it easy. Most of us who work—or want to work—will always have trouble or discontent. So we must learn to be calm, and train all our faculties, and make others happy."

No more original than this was her formulated philosophy—the commonplace creed of a commonplace woman in a rather less than commonplace family hotel. The important thing was not the form of it, but her resolve not to sink into nothingness. . . . She hoped that some day she would get a job again. She sometimes borrowed a typewriter from the manager of the hotel, and she took down in shorthand the miscellaneous sermons—by Baptists, Catholics, Reformed rabbis, Christian Scientists, theosophists, High Church Episcopalians, Hindu yogis, or any one else handy—with which she filled up her dull Sundays. . . . Except as practice in stenography she found their conflicting religions of little value to lighten her life. The ministers seemed so much vaguer than the hard-driving business men with whom she had worked; and the question of what Joshua had done seemed to have little relation to what Julius Schwirtz was likely to do. The city had come between her and the Panama belief that somehow, mysteriously, one acquired virtue by enduring dull sermons.

She depended more on her own struggle to make a philosophy.

That philosophy, that determination not to sink into paralyzed despair, often broke down when her husband was in town, but she never gave up trying to make it vital to her.

So, through month on month, she read, rocking slowly in the small, wooden rocker, or lying on the coarse-coverleted bed, while round her the hotel room was still and stale-smelling and fixed, and outside the window passed the procession of life—trucks laden with crates of garments consigned to Kansas City and Bangor and Seattle and Bemidji; taxicabs with passengers for the mammoth hotels; office-girls and policemen and sales-men and all the lusty crew that had conquered the city or were well content to be conquered by it.

CHAPTER XVII

LATE in the summer of 1912, at a time when Una did not expect the return of her husband for at least three weeks, she was in their room in the afternoon, reading "Salesmanship for Women," and ruminatively eating lemon-drops from a small bag.

As though he were a betrayed husband dramatically surprising her, Mr. Schwirtz opened the door, dropped a large suit-case, and stood, glaring.

"Well!" he said, with no preliminary, "so here you are! For once you could—"

"Why, Ed! I didn't expect to see you for—"

He closed the door and gesticulated. "No! Of course you didn't. Why ain't you out with some of your swell friends that I ain't good enough to meet, shopping, and buying dresses, and God knows what—"

"Why, Ed!"

"Oh, don't 'why-Ed' me! Well, ain't you going to come and kiss me? Nice reception when a man's come home tired from a hard trip—wife so busy reading a book that she don't even get up from her chair and make him welcome in his own room that he pays for Yes, by—"

"Why, you didn't—you don't act as though—"

"Yes, sure, that's right; lay it all on—"

"—you wanted me to kiss you."

"Well, neither would anybody if they'd had all the worries I've had, sitting there worrying on a slow, hot train that stopped at every pig-pen—yes, and on a day-coach, too, by golly! *Somebody* in this family has got to economize!—while you sit here cool and comfortable; not a thing on your mind but your hair; not a thing to worry about except thinking how damn superior you are to your husband! Oh, sure! But I made up my mind—I thought it all out for once, and I made up my mind to one thing, you can help me out by economizing, anyway."

"Oh, Ed, I don't know what you're driving at. I *haven't* been extravagant, ever. Why, I've asked you any number of times not to spend so much money for suppers and so forth—"

"Yes, sure, lay it all onto me. I'm fair game for everybody that's looking for a nice, soft, easy, safe boob to kick! Why, look there!"

While she still sat marveling he pounced on the meek little five-cent bag of lemon-drops, shook it as though it were a **very** small kitten, and whined: "Look at this! Candy or something all the while! You never have a single cent left when I come home—candy and ice-cream sodas, and matinées, and dresses, and everything you can think of. If it ain't one thing, it's another. Well, you'll either save from now on—"

"Look here! What do you mean, working off your grouch on—"

"—or else you won't *have* anything to spend, un'er-stand? And when it comes down to talking about grouches I suppose you'll be real *pleased* to know—this will be sweet news, probably, to *you*—I've been fired!"

"Fired? Oh, Ed!"

"Yes, fired-oh-Ed. Canned. Got the gate. Thrown out. Got the razzle-dazzle. Got the hook thrown into me. Bounced. Kiyudeled. That is, at least, I will be, as soon as I let the old man get at me, judging from the

THE JOB

love-letters he's been sending me, inviting me to cut a switch and come out to the wood-shed with him."

"Oh, Ed dear, what was the trouble?"

She walked up to him, laid her hand on his shoulder. Her voice was earnest, her eyes full of pity. He patted her hand, seemed from her gentle nearness to draw comfort—not passion. He slouched over to the bed, and sat with his thick legs stuck out in front of him, his hands in his trousers pockets, while he mused:

"Oh, I don't hardly know what it *is* all about. My sales have been falling off, all rightee. But, good Lord! that's no fault of mine. I work my territory jus' as hard as I ever did, but I can't meet the competition of the floor-wax people. They're making an auto polish now— better article at a lower price—and what can I do? They got a full line, varnish, cleaner, polish, swell window displays, national advertising, swell discounts—everything; and I can't buck competition like that. And then a lot of the salesmen at our shop are jealous of me, and one thing and another. Well, now I'll go down and spit the old man in the eye couple o' times, and get canned, unless I can talk him out of his bad acting. Oh, I'll throw a big bluff. I'll be the little misunderstood boy, but I don't honestly think I can put anything across on him. I'm— Oh, hell, I guess I'm getting old. I ain't got the pep I used to have. Not but what J. Eddie Schwirtz can still sell goods, but I can't talk up to the boss like I could once. I gotta feel some sympathy at the home office. And I by God deserve it—way I've worked and slaved for that bunch of cutthroats, and now— Sure, that's the way it goes in this world. I tell you, I'm gonna turn socialist!"

"Ed—listen, Ed. Please, oh, *please* don't be offended now; but don't you think perhaps the boss thinks you drink too much?"

"How could he? I don't drink very much, and you know it. I don't hardly touch a drop, except maybe just for sociability. God! this temperance wave gets my goat! Lot of hot-air females telling me what I can do and what I can't do—fella that knows when to drink and when to stop. Drink? Why, you ought to see some of the boys! There's Burke McCullough. Say, I bet he puts away forty drinks a day, if he does one, and I don't know that it hurts him any; but me—"

"Yes, I know, dear. I was just thinking—maybe your boss is one of the temperance cranks," Una interrupted. Mr. Schwirtz's arguments regarding the privileges of a manly man sounded very familiar. This did not seem to be a moment for letting her husband get into the full swing of them. She begged: "What will you do if they let you out? I wish there was something I could do to help."

"Dun'no'. There's a pretty close agreement between a lot of the leading paint-and-varnish people—gentleman's agreement—and it's pretty hard to get in any place if you're in Dutch with any of the others. Well, I'm going down now and watch 'em gwillotine me. You better not wait to have dinner with me. I'll be there late, thrashing all over the carpet with the old man, and then I gotta see some fellas and start something. Come here, Una."

He stood up. She came to him, and when he put his two hands on her shoulders she tried to keep her aversion to his touch out of her look.

He shook his big, bald head. He was unhappy and his eyes were old. "Nope," he said; "nope. Can't be done. You mean well, but you haven't got any fire in you. Kid, can't you understand that there are wives who've got so much passion in 'em that if their husbands came home clean-licked, like I am, they'd—oh, their husbands woufd just naturally completely forget their troubles in love—real love, with fire in it. Women that aren't ashamed of having bodies. . . . But, oh, Lord! it ain't your fault. I shouldn't have said anything. There's lots of wives like you. More 'n one man's admitted his wife was like that, when he's had a couple drinks under his belt to loosen his tongue. You're not to blame, but— I'm sorry. . . . Don't mind my grouch when I came in. I was so hot, and I'd been worrying and wanted to blame things onto somebody. . . . Don't wait for me at dinner. If I ain't here by seven, go ahead and feed. Good-by."

§ 2

All she knew was that at six a woman's purring voice on the telephone asked if Mr. Eddie Schwirtz had re- turned to town yet. That he did not reappear till after midnight. That his return was heralded by wafting breezes with whisky laden. That, in the morning, there was a smear of rice powder on his right shoulder and that he was not so urgent in his attentions to her as or- dinarily. So her sympathy for him was lost. But she discovered that she was neither jealous nor indignant— merely indifferent.

He told her at breakfast that, with his usual discern- ment, he had guessed right. When he had gone to the office he had been discharged.

"Went out with some business acquaintances in the evening—got to pull all the wires I can now," he said.

She said nothing.

§ 3

They had less than two hundred dollars ahead. But Mr. Schwirtz borrowed a hundred from his friend, Burke

McCullough, and did not visibly have to suffer from want of highballs, cigars, and Turkish baths. From the window of their room Una used to see him cross the street to the café entrance of the huge Saffron Hotel—and once she saw him emerge from it with a fluffy blonde. But she did not attack him. She was spellbound in a strange apathy, as in a dream of swimming on forever in a warm and slate-hued sea. She was confident that he would soon have another position. He had over-ridden her own opinions about business—the opinions of the underling who never sees the great work as a rounded whole—till she had come to have a timorous respect for his commercial ability.

Apparently her wifely respect was not generally shared in the paint business. At least Mr. Schwirtz did not soon get his new position.

The manager of the hotel came to the room with his bill and pressed for payment. And after three weeks— after a night when he had stayed out very late and come home reeking with perfume—Mr. Schwirtz began to hang about the room all day long and to soak himself in the luxury of complaining despair.

Then came the black days.

There were several scenes (during which she felt like a beggar about to be arrested) between Mr. Schwirtz and the landlord, before her husband paid part of a bill whose size astounded her.

Mr. Schwirtz said that he was "expecting something to turn up—nothin' he could do but wait for some telephone calls." He sat about with his stockinged feet cocked up on the bed, reading detective stories till he fell asleep in his chair. He drank from unlabeled pint flasks of whisky all day. Once, when she opened a bureau drawer of his by mistake, she saw half a dozen whisky-flasks mixed with grimy collars, and the sour smell nauseated her. But on food—they had to economize on that! He took her to a restaurant of fifteen-cent breakfasts and twenty-five-cent dinners. It was the "parlor floor" of an old brownstone house — two rooms, with eggy table-cloths, and moldings of dusty stucco.

She avoided his presence as much as possible. Mrs. Wade, the practical dressmaker, who was her refuge among the women of the hotel, seemed to understand what was going on, and gave Una a key to her room. Here Una sat for hours. When she went back to their room quarrels would spring up apropos of anything or nothing.

The fault was hers as much as his. She was no longer trying to conceal her distaste, while he, who had a marital conscience of a sort, was almost pathetic in his apologies for being unable to "show her a good time." And he wanted her soothing. He was more and more afraid of her as the despair of the jobless man in the hard city settled down on him. He wanted her to agree with him that there was a conspiracy against him.

She listened to him and said nothing, till he would burst out in abuse:

"You women that have been in business simply ain't fit to be married. You think you're too good to help a man. Yes, even when you haven't been anything but dub stenographers. I never noticed that you were such a whale of a success! I don't suppose you remember how you used to yawp to me about the job being too much for you! And yet when I want a little sympathy you sit there and hand me the frozen stare like you were the president of the Standard Oil Company and I was a bum office-boy. Yes, sir, I tell you business simply unfits a skirt for marriage."

"No," she said, "not for marriage that has any love and comradeship in it. But I admit a business woman doesn't care to put up with being a cow in a stable."

"What the devil do you mean—"

"Maybe," she went on, "the business women will bring about a new kind of marriage in which men will *have* to keep up respect and courtesy. . . . I wonder—I wonder how many millions of women in what are supposed to be happy homes are sick over being chambermaids and mistresses till they get dulled and used to it. Nobody will ever know. All these books about women being emancipated—you'd think marriage had changed entirely. Yet, right now, in 1912, in Panama and this hotel—not changed a bit. The business women must simply *compel* men to—oh, to shave!"

She went out (perhaps she slammed the door a little, in an unemancipated way) to Mrs. Wade's room.

That discussion was far more gentle and coherent than most of their quarrels.

It may have been rather to tne credit of Mr. Schwirtz —it may have been a remnant of the clean pride which the boy Eddie Schwirtz must once have had, that, whenever she hinted that she would like to go back to work—he raged: "So you think I can't support you, eh? My God! I can stand insults from all my old friends—the fellas that used to be tickled to death to have me buy 'em a drink, but now they dodge around the corner as though they thought I was going to try to borrow four bits from 'em—I can stand their insults, but, by God! it *is* pretty hard on a man when his own wife lets him know that she don't think he can support her!"

And he meant it.

She saw that, felt his resentment. But she more and more often invited an ambition to go back to work, to be independent and busy, no matter how weary she might become. To die, if need be, in the struggle. Certainly that death would be better than being choked in muck. . . . One of them would have to go to work, anyway.

She discovered that an old acquaintance of his had offered him an eighteen-dollar-a-week job as a clerk in a retail paint-shop, till he should find something better. Mr. Schwirtz was scornful about it, and his scorn, which had once intimidated Una, became grotesquely absurd to her.

Then the hotel-manager came with a curt ultimatum: "Pay up or get out," he said.

Mr. Schwirtz spent an hour telephoning to various acquaintances, trying to raise another hundred dollars. He got the promise of fifty. He shaved, put on a collar that for all practical purposes was quite clean, and went out to collect his fifty as proudly as though he had earned it.

Una stared at herself in the mirror over the bureau, and said, aloud: "I don't believe it! It isn't you, Una Golden, that worked, and paid your debts. You can't, dear, you simply *can't* be the wife of a man who lives by begging— a dirty, useless, stupid beggar. Oh, no, no! You wouldn't do that—you *couldn't* marry a man like that simply because the job had exhausted you. Why, you'd die at work first. Why, if you married him for board and keep, you'd be a prostitute—you'd be marrying him just because he was a 'good provider.' And probably, when he didn't provide any more, you'd be quitter enough to leave him—maybe for another man. You couldn't do that. I don't believe life could bully you into doing that. . . . Oh, I'm hysterical; I'm mad. I can't believe I am what I am—and yet I am! . . . Now he's getting that fifty and buying a drink—"

§ 4

Mr. Schwirtz actually came home with forty-five out of the fifty intact. That was because he wanted to be able to pay the hotel-manager and insultingly inform him that they were going to leave. . . . The manager bore up under the blow. . . . They did move to a "furnished housekeeping-room" on West Nineteenth Street—in the very district of gray rooms and pathetic landladies where Una had sought a boarding-house after the death of her mother.

As furnished housekeeping-rooms go, theirs was highly superior. Most of them are carpetless, rusty and small of coal-stove, and filled with cockroaches and the smell of carbolic acid. But the *maison* Schwirtz was almost clean. It had an impassioned green carpet, a bedspring which scarcely sagged at all, a gas-range, and at least a dozen vases with rococo handles and blobs of gilt.

"Gee! this ain't so bad," declared Mr. Schwirtz. "We can cook all our eats here, and live on next to nothing per, till the big job busts loose."

With which he prepared to settle down to a life of leisure. He went out and bought a pint of whisky, a pound of steak, a pound of cheese, a loaf of bread, six cigars, and for her a bar of fudge.

So far as Una could calculate, he had less than forty dollars. She burst out on him. She seemed to be speaking with the brusque voice of an accomplishing man. In that voice was all she had ever heard from executives; all the subconsciously remembered man-driving force of the office world. She ordered him to go and take the job in the paint-shop—at eighteen dollars a week, or eight dollars a week. She briefly, but thoroughly, depicted him as alcohol-soaked, poor white trash. She drove him out, and when he was gone she started to make their rooms presentable, with an energy she had not shown for months. She began to dust, to plan curtains for the room, to plan to hide the bric-à-brac, to plan to rent a typewriter and get commercial copying to do.

If any one moment of life is more important than the others, this may have been her crisis, when her husband had become a begging pauper and she took charge; began not only to think earnest, commonplace, little Una thoughts about "mastering life," but actually to master it.

CHAPTER XVIII

SO long as Mr. Schwirtz contrived to keep his position in the retail paint-store, Una was busy at home, copying documents and specifications and form-letters for a stenographic agency and trying to make a science of quick and careful housework.

She suspected that, now he had a little money again, Mr. Schwirtz was being riotous with other women—as riotous as one can be in New York on eighteen dollars a week, with debts and a wife to interfere with his manly pleasures. But she did not care; she was getting ready to break the cocoon, and its grubbiness didn't much matter.

Sex meant nothing between them now. She did not believe that she would ever be in love again, in any phase, noble or crude. While she aspired and worked she lived like a nun in a cell. And now that she had something to do, she could be sorry for him. She made the best possible dinners for him on their gas-range. She realized —sometimes, not often, for she was not a contemplative seer, but a battered woman—that their marriage had been as unfair to him as it was to her. In small-town boy-gang talks behind barns, in clerkly confidences as a young man, in the chatter of smoking-cars and provincial hotel offices, he had been trained to know only two kinds of women, both very complaisant to smart live-wires: The bouncing lassies who laughed and kissed and would

share with a man his pleasures, such as poker and cocktails, and rapid motoring to no place in particular; and
the meek, attentive, "refined" kind, the wives and mothers who cared for a man and admired him and believed
whatever he told them about his business.

Una was of neither sort for him, though for Walter
Babson she might have been quite of the latter kind.
Mr. Schwirtz could not understand her, and she was as
sorry for him as was compatible with a decided desire to
divorce him and wash off the stain of his damp, pulpy
fingers with the water of life.

But she stayed home, and washed and cooked, and
earned money for him—till he lost his retail-store position
by getting drunk and being haughty to a customer.

Then the chrysalis burst and Una was free again. Free
to labor, to endeavor—to die, perhaps, but to die clean.
To quest and meet whatever surprises life might hold.

§ 2

She couldn't go back to Troy Wilkins's, nor to Mr. S.
Herbert Ross and the little Pemberton stenographers
who had enviously seen her go off to be married. But she
made a real business of looking for a job. While Mr.
Schwirtz stayed home and slept and got mental bed-sores
and drank himself to death—rather too slowly—on another fifty dollars which he had borrowed after a Verdun
campaign, Una was joyous to be out early, looking over
advertisements, visiting typewriter companies' employment agencies.

She was slow in getting work because she wanted twenty
dollars a week. She knew that any firm taking her at
this wage would respect her far more than if she was an
easy purchase.

THE JOB

Work was slow to come, and she, who had always been so securely above the rank of paupers who submit to the dreadful surgery of charity, became afraid. She went at last to Mamie Magen.

Mamie was now the executive secretary of the Hebrew Young Women's Professional Union. She seemed to be a personage. In her office she had a secretary who spoke of her with adoring awe, and when Una said that she was a personal friend of Miss Magen the secretary cried: "Oh, then perhaps you'd like to go to her apartment, at —— Washington Place. She's almost always home for tea at five."

The small, tired-looking Una, a business woman again, in her old tailor-made and a new, small hat, walked longingly toward Washington Place and tea.

In her seven years in New York she had never known anybody except S. Herbert Ross who took tea as a regular function. It meant to her the gentlest of all forms of distinction, more appealing than riding in motors or going to the opera. That Mamie Magen had, during Una's own experience, evolved from a Home Club girl to an executive who had tea at her apartment every afternoon was inspiriting; meeting her an adventure.

An apartment of buff-colored walls and not bad prints was Mamie's, small, but smooth; and taking tea in a manner which seemed to Una impressively suave were the insiders of the young charity-workers' circle. But Mamie's uncouth face and eyes of molten heroism stood out among them all, and she hobbled over to Una and kissed her. When the cluster had thinned, she got Una aside and invited her to the "Southern Kitchen," on Washington Square.

Una did not speak of her husband. "I want to get on the job again, and I wish you'd help me. I want something

at twenty a week (I'm more than worth it) and a chance
to really climb," was all she said, and Mamie nodded.

And so they talked of Mrs. Harriet Fike of the Home
Club, of dreams and work and the fight for suffrage.
Una's marriage slipped away—she was ardent and un-
stained again.

Mamie's nod was worth months of Mr. Schwirtz's pro-
fuse masculine boasts. Within ten days, Mamie's friend,
Mr. Fein, of Truax & Fein, the real-estate people, sent for
Una and introduced her to Mr. Daniel T. Truax. She
was told to come to work on the following Monday as
Mr. Truax's secretary, at twenty-one dollars a week.

She went home defiant, determined to force her husband to let her take the job. . . . She didn't need to use
force. He—slippered and drowsy by the window—said:
"That's fine; that 'll keep us going till my big job breaks.
I'll hear about it by next week, *anyway*. Then, in three-
four weeks you can kick Truax & Fein in the face and beat
it. Say, girlie, that's fine! Say, tell you what I'll do.
Let's have a little party to celebrate. I'll chase out and
rush a growler of beer and some wienies—"

"No! I've got to go out again."

"Can't you stop just long enough to have a little cele-
bration? I—I been kind of lonely last few days, little
sister. You been away so much, and I'm too broke to go
out and look up the boys now."

He was peering at her with a real wistfulness, but in
the memory of Mamie Magen, the lame woman of the
golden heart, Una could not endure his cackling enthusiasm
about the job he would probably never get.

"No, I'm sorry—" she said, and closed the door. From
the walk she saw him puzzled and anxious at the window.
His face was becoming so ruddy and fatuous and babyish.
She was sorry for him—but she was not big enough to do

anything about it. Her sorrow was like sympathy for a mangy alley cat which she could not take home.

She had no place to go. She walked for hours, planlessly, and dined at a bakery and lunch-room in Harlem. Sometimes she felt homeless, and always she was prosaically footsore, but now and then came the understanding that she again had a chance.

CHAPTER XIX

SO, toward the end of 1912, when she was thirty-one years old, Mrs. Una Golden Schwirtz began her business career, as confidential secretary to Mr. Truax, of Truax & Fein.

Her old enemy, routine, was constantly in the field. Routine of taking dictation, of getting out the letters, prompting Mr. Truax's memory as to who Mrs. A was, and what Mr. B had telephoned, keeping plats and plans and memoes in order, making out cards regarding the negotiations with possible sellers of suburban estates. She did not, as she had hoped, always find this routine one jolly round of surprises. She was often weary, sometimes bored.

But in the splendor of being independent again and of having something to do that seemed worth while she was able to get through the details that never changed from day to day. And she was rewarded, for the whole job was made fascinating by human contact. She found herself enthusiastic about most of the people she met at Truax & Fein's; she was glad to talk with them, to work with them, to be taken seriously as a brain, a loyalty, a woman.

By contrast with two years of hours either empty or filled with Schwirtz, the office-world was of the loftiest dignity. It may have been that some of the men she met were Schwirtzes to their wives, but to her they had to be fellow-workers. She did not believe that the long hours,

the jealousies, the worry, or Mr. Truax's belief that he
was several planes above ordinary humanity, were desirable or necessary parts of the life at Truax & Fein's.
Here, too, she saw nine hours of daily strain aging slim
girls into skinny females. But now her whole point of
view was changed. Instead of looking for the evils of the
business world, she was desirous of seeing in it all the blessings she could; and, without ever losing her belief that
it could be made more friendly, she was, nevertheless,
able to rise above her own personal weariness and see
that the world of jobs, offices, business, had made itself
creditably superior to those other muddled worlds of
politics and amusement and amorous Schwirtzes. She
believed again, as in commercial college she had callowly
believed, that business was beginning to see itself as communal, world-ruling, and beginning to be inspired to
communal, kingly virtues and responsibility.

Looking for the good (sometimes, in her joy of escape,
looking for it almost with the joy of an S. Herbert Ross in
picking little lucrative flowers of sentiment along the roadside) she was able to behold more daily happiness about her.

Fortunately, Traux & Fein's was a good office, not too
hard, not too strained and factional like Pemberton's;
not wavering like Troy Wilkins's. Despite Mr. Truax's
tendency to courteous whining, it was doing its work
squarely and quietly. That was fortunate. Offices differ
as much as office-managers, and had chance condemned
Una to another nerve-twanging Pemberton's her slight
strength might have broken. She might have fallen
back to Schwirtz and the gutter.

Peaceful as reapers singing on their homeward path
now seemed the teasing voices of men and girls as, in a
group, they waited for the elevator at five-thirty-five.
The cheerful, "Good-night, Mrs. Schwirtz!" was a vesper

benediction, altogether sweet with its earnest of rest and friendship.

Tranquillity she found when she stayed late in the deserted office. Here no Schwirtz could reach her. Here her toil counted for something in the world's work—in the making of suburban homes for men and women and children. She sighed, and her breast felt barren, as she thought of the children. But tranquillity there was, and a brilliant beauty of the city as across dark spaces of evening were strung the jewels of light, as in small, French restaurants sounded desirous violins. On warm evenings of autumn Una would lean out of the window and be absorbed in the afterglow above the North River: smoke-clouds from Jersey factories drifting across the long, carmine stain, air sweet and cool, and the yellow-lighted windows of other skyscrapers giving distant companionship. She fancied sometimes that she was watching the afterglow over a far northern lake, among the pines; and with a sigh more of content than of restlessness she turned back to her work. . . . Time ceased to exist when she worked alone. Of time and of the office she was manager. What if she didn't go out to dinner till eight? She could dine whenever she wanted to. If a clumsy man called Eddie Schwirtz got hungry he could get his own dinner. What if she did work slowly? There were no telephone messages, no Mr. Truax to annoy her. She could be leisurely and do the work as it should be done. . . . She was no longer afraid of the rustling silence about her, as Una Golden had been at Troy Wilkins's. She was a woman now, and trained to fill the blank spaces of the deserted office with her own colored thoughts.

Hours of bustling life in the daytime office had their human joys as well. Una went out of her way to be friendly with the ordinary stenographers, and, as there was no vast Pembertonian system of caste, she succeeded, and had all the warmth of their little confidences. Nor after her extensive experience with Messrs. Schwirtz, Sanderson, and McCullough, did even the noisiest of the salesmen offend her. She laughed at the small signs they were always bringing in and displaying: "Oh, forget it! I've got troubles of my own!" or, "Is that you again? Another half hour gone to hell!" The sales-manager brought this latter back from Philadelphia and hung it on his desk, and when the admiring citizenry surrounded it, Una joined them. . . . As a married woman she was not expected to be shocked by the word, "hell!" . . .

But most beautiful was Christmas Eve, when all distinctions were suspended for an hour before the office closed, when Mr. Truax distributed gold pieces and handshakes, when "Chas.," the hat-tilted sales-manager, stood on a chair and sang a solo. Mr. Fein hung holly on all their desks, and for an hour stenographers and salesmen and clerks and chiefs all were friends.

When she went home to Schwirtz she tried to take some of the holiday friendship. She sought to forget that he was still looking for the hypothetical job, while he subsisted on her wages and was increasingly apologetic. She boasted to herself that her husband hated to ask her for money, that he was large and strong and masculine.

She took him to dinner at the Pequoit, in a room of gold and tapestry. But he got drunk, and wept into his sherbet that he was a drag on her; and she was glad to be back in the office after Christmas.

§ 2

The mist of newness had passed, that confusion of the recent arrival in office or summer hotel or revengeful reception; and she now saw the office inhabitants as separate people. She wondered how she could ever have thought that the sales-manager and Mr. Fein were confusingly alike, or have been unable to get the salesmen's names right.

There was the chief, Mr. Daniel T. Truax, usually known as "D. T.," a fussily courteous whiner with a rabbity face (his pink nose actually quivered), a little yellow mustache, and a little round stomach. Himself and his business he took very seriously, though he was far less tricky than Mr. Pemberton. The Real Estate Board of Trade was impressed by his unsmiling insistence on the Dignity of the Profession, and always asked him to serve on committees. It was Mr. Truax who bought the property for sub-development, and though he had less abstract intelligence than Mr. Fein, he was a better judge of "what the people want"; of just how high to make restrictions on property, and what whim would turn the commuters north or south in their quest for homes.

There was the super-chief, the one person related to the firm whom Una hated—Mrs. D. T. Truax. She was not officially connected with the establishment, and her office habits were irregular. Mostly they consisted in appearing at the most inconvenient hours and asking maddening questions. She was fat, massaged, glittering, wheezy-voiced, nagging. Una peculiarly hated Mrs. Truax's nails. Una's own finger-tips were hard with typing; her manicuring was a domestic matter of clipping and hypocritical filing. But to Mrs. Truax manicuring was a life-work. Because of much clipping of the cuticle, the flesh at the base of each nail had become a noticeably raised cushion of pink flesh. Her nails were too pink, too shiny, too shapely, and sometimes they were an unearthly white at the ends, because of nail-paste left under them. At that startling whiteness Una stared all the while Mrs. Truax was tapping her fingers and prying into the private morals of the pretty hall-girl, and enfilading Una with the lorgnon that so perfectly suited her Upper West Side jowls.

Collating Mrs. Truax and the matrons of the Visiting Board of the Temperance Home Club, Una concluded that women trained in egotism, but untrained in business, ought to be legally enjoined from giving their views to young women on the job.

The most interesting figure in the office was Mr. Fein, the junior partner, a Harvard Jew, who was perfectly the new type of business man. Serious, tall, spectacled, clean-shaven, lean-faced, taking business as a profession, and kindly justice as a religion, studying efficiency, but hating the metamorphosis of clerks into machines, he was the distinction and the power of Truax & Fein. At first Una had thought him humorless and negligible, but she discovered that it was he who pulled Mr. Truax out of his ruts, his pious trickeries, his cramping economies. She found that Mr. Fein loved books and the opera, and that he could be boyish after hours.

Then the sales-manager, that driving but festive soul, Mr. Charles Salmond, whom everybody called "Chas." —pronounced "Chaaz"—a good soul who was a little tiresome because he was so consistently an anthology of New York. He believed in Broadway, the Follies, good clothes, a motor-car, Palm Beach, and the value of the Salvation Army among the lower classes. When Mr. Fein fought for real beauty in their suburban developments it was Chas. who echoed all of New York by rebelling, "We aren't in business for our health—this idealistic game is O. K. for the guys that have the cash, but you can't expect my salesmen to sell this Simplicity and High-Thinking stuff to prospects that are interested in nothing but a sound investment with room for a garage and two kids."

Sixty or seventy salesmen, clerks, girls—these Una was beginning to know.

Finally, there was a keen, wide-awake woman, willing to do anything for anybody, not forward, but not to be overridden—a woman with a slight knowledge of architecture and a larger knowledge of the way of promotion; a woman whom Una took seriously; and the name of this paragon was Mrs. Una Golden Schwirtz

Round these human islands flowed a sea of others. She had a sense of flux, and change, and energy; of hundreds of thousands of people rushing about her always —crowds on Broadway and Fifth Avenue and Sixth, and on Thirty-fourth Street, where stood the Zodiac Building in which was the office. Crowds in the hall of the Zodiac Building, examining the black-and-white directory board with its list of two hundred offices, or waiting to surge into one of the twelve elevators—those packed vertical railroads. A whole village life in the hallway of the Zodiac Building: the imperial elevator-starter in a uniform of blue and gold, and merely regal elevator-runners with less gold and more faded blue; the oldest of the elevator-boys, Harry, the Greek, who knew everybody in the building; the cigar-stand, with piles of cigarettes, cans of advertised tobacco, maple fudge wrapped in tinfoil, stamps, and even a few cigars, also the keeper thereof, an Italian with an air of swounding romance. More romantic Italians in the glass-inclosed barber-shop—Desperate Desmond devils, with white coats like undress uniforms, and mustaches that recalled the Riviera and baccarat and a secret-service count; the two manicure-girls of the barber-shop, princesses reigning among admirers from the offices up-stairs; janitors, with brooms, and charwomen with pails, and a red, sarcastic man, the engineer, and a meek puppet who was merely the superintendent of the whole thing. . . . Una watched these village people, to whom the Zodiac hall was Main Street, and in their satisfied conformation to a life of marble floors and artificial light she found such settled existence as made her feel at home in this town, with its eighteen strata called floors. She, too, at least during the best hours of the day, lived in the Zodiac Building's microcosm.

And to her office penetrated the ever flowing crowds— salesmen, buyers of real estate, inquirers, persons who seemed to have as a hobby the collection of real-estate folders. Indeed, her most important task was the strategy of "handling callers"—the callers who came to see Mr. Truax himself, and were passed on to Una by the hall-girl. To the clever secretary the management of callers becomes a question of scientific tactics, and Una was clever at it because she liked people.

She had to recognize the type of awkward shabby visitor who looks like a beggar, but has in his pocket the cash for investment in lots. And the insinuating caller, with tailor-made garments and a smart tie, who presents himself as one who yearns to do a good turn to his dear, dear personal friend, Mr. D. T. Truax, but proves to be an insurance-agent or a salesman of adding-machines. She had to send away the women with high-pitched voices and purely imaginary business, who came in for nothing whatever, and were willing to spend all of their own time and Mr. Truax's in obtaining the same; women with unsalable houses to sell or improbable lots to buy, dissatisfied clients, or mere cranks—old, shattered, unhappy women, to whom Una could give sympathy, but no time.

. . . She was expert at standing filially listening to them at the elevator, while all the time her thumb steadily pressed the elevator signal.

Una had been trained, perhaps as much by enduring Mr. Schwirtz as by pleasing Mr. S. Herbert Ross, to be firm, to say no, to keep Mr. Truax's sacred rites undisturbed. She did not conventionally murmur, "Mr. Truax is in a conference just now, and if you will tell me the nature of your business—" Instead, she had surprising, delightful, convincing things for Mr. Truax to be doing, just at that particular *moment*—

From Mr. Truax himself she learned new ways of delicately getting rid of people. He did not merely rise to indicate that an interview was over, but also arranged a system of counterfeit telephone-calls, with Una calling up from the outside office, and Mr. Truax answering, "Yes, I'll be through now in just a moment," as a hint for the visitor. He even practised such play-acting as putting on his hat and coat and rushing out to greet an important but unwelcome caller with, "Oh, I'm so sorry I'm just going out—late f' important engagement—given m' secretary full instructions, and I know she'll take care of you jus' as well as I could personally," and returning to his private office by a rear door.

Mr. Truax, like Mr. S. Herbert Ross, gave Una maxims. But his had very little to do with stars and argosies, and the road to success, and vivisection, and the abstract virtues. They concerned getting to the office on time, and never letting a customer bother him if an office salesman could take care of the matter.

So round Una flowed all the energy of life; and she of the listening and desolate hotel room and the overshadowing storm-clouds was happy again.

She began to make friendships. "Chas.," the office-manager, stopped often at her desk to ridicule—and Mr. Fein to praise—the plans she liked to make for garden-suburbs which should be filled with poets, thatched roofs, excellent plumbing, artistic conversation, fireplaces, incinerators, books, and convenient trains.

"Some day," said Mr. Fein to her, "we'll do that sort of thing, just as the Sage Foundation is doing it at Forest Hills." And he smiled encouragingly.

"Some day," said Mr. Truax, "when you're head of a women's real-estate firm, after you women get the vote, and rusty, old-fashioned people like me are out of the way, perhaps you can do that sort of thing." And he smiled encouragingly.

"Rot," said Chas., and amiably chucked her under the chin.

CHAPTER XX

TRUAX & FEIN was the first firm toward which Una was able to feel such loyalty as is supposed to distinguish all young aspirants—loyalty which is so well spoken of by bosses, and which is so generally lacking among the bossed. Partly, this was her virtue, partly it was the firm's, and partly it was merely the accident of her settling down.

She watched the biological growth of Truax & Fein with fascination; was excited when they opened a new subdivision, and proudly read the half-page advertisements thereof in the Sunday newspapers.

That loyalty made her study real estate, not merely stenography; for to most stenographers their work is the same whether they take dictation regarding real estate, or book-publishing, or felt slippers, or the removal of taconite. They understand transcription, but not what they transcribe. She read magazines—*System*, *Printer's Ink*, *Real Estate Record* (solemnly studying "Recorded Conveyances," and "Plans Filed for New Construction Work," and "Mechanics' Liens"). She got ideas for houses from architectural magazines, garden magazines, women's magazines. But what most indicated that she was a real devotee was the fact that, after glancing at the front-page headlines, the society news, and the joke column in her morning paper, she would resolutely turn to "The Real Estate Field."

On Sundays she often led Mr. Schwirtz for a walk among the new suburban developments. . . . For always, no matter what she did at the office, no matter how much Mr. Truax depended on her or Mr. Fein praised her, she went home to the same cabbage-rose-carpeted house-keeping-room, and to a Mr. Schwirtz who had seemingly not stirred an inch since she had left him in the morning. . . . Mr. Schwirtz was of a harem type, and not much adapted to rustic jaunting, but he obediently followed his master and tried to tell stories of the days when he had known all about real estate, while she studied model houses, the lay of the land, the lines of sewers and walks.

That was loyalty to Truax & Fein as much as desire for advancement.

And that same loyalty made her accept as fellow-workers even the noisiest of the salesmen—and even Beatrice Joline.

Though Mr. Truax didn't "believe in" women salesmen, one woman briskly overrode his beliefs: Miss Beatrice Joline, of the Gramercy Park Jolines, who cheerfully called herself "one of the *nouveau pauvre*," and conde-scended to mere Upper West Side millionaires, and had to earn her frocks and tea money. She earned them, too; but she declined to be interested in office regulations or office hours. She sold suburban homes as a free lance, and only to the very best people. She darted into the office now and then, slender, tall, shoulder-swinging, an exclamation-point of a girl, in a smart, check suit and a Bendel hat. She ignored Una with a coolness which re-duced her to the status of a new stenographer. All the office watched Miss Joline with hypnotized envy. Always in offices those who have social position outside are ob-served with secret awe by those who have not.

Once, when Mr. Truax was in the act of persuading an

unfortunate property-owner to part with a Long Island estate for approximately enough to buy one lot after the estate should be subdivided into six hundred lots, Miss Joline had to wait. She perched on Una's desk, outside Mr. Truax's door, swung her heels, inspected the finger-ends of her chamois gloves, and issued a command to Una to perform conversationally.

Una was thinking, "I'd like to spank you—and then I'd adore you. You're what story-writers call a thorough-bred."

While unconscious that a secretary in a tabby - gray dress and gold eye-glasses was venturing to appraise her, Miss Joline remarked, in a high, clear voice: "Beastly bore to have to wait, isn't it! I suppose you can rush right in to see Mr. Truax any time you want to, Mrs. Ummmmm."

"Schwirtz. Rotten name, isn't it?" Una smiled up condescendingly.

Miss Joline stopped kicking her heels and stared at Una as though she might prove to be human, after all.

"Oh no, it's a very nice name," she said. "Fancy being called Joline. Now Schwirtz sounds rather like Schenck, and that's one of the smartest of the old names. . . . Uh, *would* it be too much trouble to see if Mr. Truax is still engaged?"

"He is. . . . Miss Joline, I feel like doing something I've wanted to do for some time. Of course we both know you think of me as 'that poor little dub, Mrs. What's-her-name, D. T.'s secretary—"

"Why, really—"

"—or perhaps you hadn't thought of me at all. I'm naturally quite a silent little dub, but I've been learning that it's silly to be silent in business. So I've been planning to get hold of you and ask you where and how you get those suits of yours, and what I ought to wear. You see, after you marry I'll still be earning my living, and perhaps if I could dress anything like you I could fool some business man into thinking I was clever."

"As I do, you mean," said Miss Joline, cheerfully.

"Well—"

"Oh, I don't mind. But, my dear, good woman—oh, I suppose I oughtn't to call you that."

"I don't care what you call me, if you can tell me how to make a seventeen-fifty suit look like *Vogue*. Isn't it awful, Miss Joline, that us lower classes are interested in clothes, too?"

"My dear girl, even the beautiful, the accomplished Beatrice Joline—I'll admit it—knows when she is being teased. I went to boarding-school, and if you think I haven't ever been properly and thoroughly, and oh, most painstakingly told what a disgusting, natural snob I am, you ought to have heard Tomlinson, or any other of my dear friends, taking me down. I rather fancy you're kinder-hearted than they are; but, anyway, you don't insult me half so scientifically."

"I'm so sorry. I tried hard— I'm a well-meaning insulter, but I haven't the practice."

"My dear, I adore you. Isn't it lovely to be frank? When us females get into Mr. Truax's place we'll have the most wonderful time insulting each other, don't you think? But, really, please don't think I like to be rude. But you see we Jolines are so poor that if I stopped it all my business acquaintances would think I was admitting how poor we are, so I'm practically forced to be horrid. Now that we've been amiable to each other, what can I do for you? . . . Does that sound business-like enough?"

"I want to make you give me some hints about clothes. I used to like terribly crude colors, but I've settled down to tessie things that are safe—this gray dress, and brown, and black."

"Well, my dear, I'm the best little dressmaker you ever saw, and I do love to lay down the law about clothes. With your hair and complexion, you ought to wear clear blues. Order a well-made—be sure it's well-made, no matter what it costs. Get some clever little Jew socialist tailor off in the outskirts of Brooklyn, or some heathenish place, and stand over him. A well-made tailored suit of not too dark navy blue, with matching blue crêpe de Chine blouses with nice, soft, white collars, and cuffs of crêpe or chiffon—and change 'em often."

"What about a party dress? Ought I to have satin, or chiffon, or blue net, or what?"

"Well, satin is too dignified, and chiffon too perishable, and blue net is too tessie. Why don't you try black net over black satin? You know there's really lots of color in black satin if you know how to use it. Get good materials, and then you can use them over and over again—perhaps white chiffon over the black satin."

"White over black?"

Though Miss Joline stared down with one of the quick, secretive smiles which Una hated, the smile which reduced her to the rank of a novice, her eyes held Miss Joline, made her continue her oracles.

"Yes," said Miss Joline, "and it isn't very expensive. Try it with the black net first, and have soft little folds of white tulle along the edge of the décolletage—it's scarcely noticeable, but it does soften the neck-line. And wear a string of pearls. Get these Artifico pearls, a dollar-ninety a string. . . . Now you see how useful a snob is to the world! I'd never give you all this god-like advice if I didn't want to advertise what an authority I am on 'Smart Fashions for Limited Incomes.'"

THE JOB

"You're a darling," said Una.

"Come to tea," said Miss Joline.

They did go to tea. But before it, while Miss Joline was being voluble with Mr. Truax, Una methodically made notes on the art of dress and filed them for future reference. Despite the fact that, with the support of Mr. Schwirtz as her chief luxury, she had only sixteen dollars in the world, she had faith that she would sometime take a woman's delight in dress, and a business woman's interest in it. . . . This had been an important hour for her, though it cannot be authoritatively stated which was the more important—learning to dress, or learning not to be in awe of a Joline of Gramercy Park.

They went to tea several times in the five months before the sudden announcement of Miss Joline's engagement to Wally Castle, of the Tennis and Racquet Club. And at tea they bantered and were not markedly different in their use of forks or choice of pastry. But never were they really friends. Una, of Panama, daughter of Captain Golden, and wife of Eddie Schwirtz, could comprehend Walter Babson and follow Mamie Magen, and even rather despised that Diogenes of an enameled tub, Mr. S. Herbert Ross; but it seemed probable that she would never be able to do more than ask for bread and railway tickets in the language of Beatrice Joline, whose dead father had been ambassador to Portugal and friend to Henry James and John Hay.

§ 2

It hurt a little, but Una had to accept the fact that Beatrice Joline was no more likely to invite her to the famous and shabby old house of the Jolines than was Mrs. Truax to ask her advice about manicuring. They did, however, have dinner together on an evening when

THE JOB

Miss Joline actually seemed to be working late at the office.

"Let's go to a Café des Enfants," said Miss Joline. "Such a party! And, honestly, I do like their coffee and the nice, shiny, bathroom walls."

"Yes," said Una, "it's almost as much of a party to me as running a typewriter. . . . Let's go Dutch to the Martha Washington."

"Verra well. Though I did want buckwheats and little sausages. Exciting!"

"Huh!" said Una, who was unable to see any adventurous qualities in a viand which she consumed about twice a week.

Miss Joline's clean litheness, her gaiety that had never been made timorous or grateful by defeat or sordidness, her whirlwind of nonsense, blended in a cocktail for Una at dinner. Schwirtz, money difficulties, weariness, did not exist. Her only trouble in the entire universe was the reconciliation of her admiration for Miss Joline's amiable superiority to everybody, her gibes at the salesmen, and even at Mr. Truax, with Mamie Magen's philanthropic socialism. (So far as this history can trace, she never did reconcile them.)

She left Miss Joline with a laugh, and started home with a song—then stopped. She foresaw the musty room to which she was going, the slatternly incubus of a man. Saw—with just such distinctness as had once dangled the stiff, gray scrub-rag before her eyes—Schwirtz's every detail: bushy chin, stained and collarless shirt, trousers like old chair-covers. Probably he would always be like this. Probably he would never have another job. But she couldn't cast him out. She had married him, in his own words, as a "good provider." She had lost the bet; she would be a good loser—and a good provider for

THE JOB

him. . . . Always, perhaps. . . . Always that mass of spoiled babyhood waiting at home for her. . . . Always apologetic and humble—she would rather have the old, grumbling, dominant male. . . .

She tried to push back the moment of seeing him again. Her steps dragged, but at last, inevitably, grimly, the house came toward her. She crept along the moldy hall, opened the door of their room, saw him—

She thought it was a stranger, an intruder. But it was veritably her husband, in a new suit that was fiercely pressed and shaped, in new, gleaming, ox-blood shoes, with a hair-cut and a barber shave. He was bending over the bed, which was piled with new shirts, Afro-American ties, new toilet articles, and he was packing a new suit-case.

He turned slowly, enjoying her amazement. He finished packing a shirt. She said nothing, standing at the door. Teetering on his toes and watching the effect of it all on her, he lighted a large cigar.

"Some class, eh?" he said.

"Well—"

"Nifty suit, eh? And how are those for swell ties?"

"Very nice. . . . From whom did you borrow the money?"

"Now that cer'nly is a nice, sweet way to congratulate friend hubby. Oh, *sure!* Man lands a job, works his head off getting it, gets an advance for some new clothes he's simply got to have, and of course everybody else congratulates him—everybody but his own wife. She sniffs at him—not a word about the new job, of course. First crack outa the box, she gets busy suspecting him, and says, 'Who you been borrowing of now?' And this after always acting as though she was an abused little innocent that nobody appreciated—".

He was in mid-current, swimming strong, and waving

his cigar above the foaming waters, but she pulled him out of it with, "I *am* sorry. I ought to have known. I'm a beast. I am glad, awfully glad you've got a new job. What is it?"

"New company handling a new kind of motor for row-boats—converts 'em to motor-boats in a jiffy—outboard motors they call 'em. Got a swell territory and plenty bonus on new business."

"Oh, isn't that fine! It's such a fine surprise—and it's cute of you to keep it to surprise me with all this while—"

"Well, 's a matter of fact, I just got on to it to-day. Ran into Burke McCullough on Sixth Avenue, and he gave me the tip."

"Oh!" A forlorn little "Oh!" it was. She had pictured him proudly planning to surprise her. And she longed to have the best possible impression of him, because of a certain plan which was hotly being hammered out in her brain. She went on, as brightly as possible:

"And they gave you an advance? That's fine."

"Well, no, *they* didn't, exactly, but Burke introduced me to his clothier, and I got a swell line of credit."

"Oh!"

"Now for the love of Pete, don't go oh-ing and ah-ing like that. You've handed me the pickled visage since I got the rowdy-dow on my last job—good Lord! you acted like you thought I *liked* to sponge on you. Now let me tell you I've kept account of every red cent you've spent on me, and I expect to pay it back."

She tried to resist her impulse, but she couldn't keep from saying, as nastily as possible: "How nice. When?"

"Oh, I'll pay it back, all right, trust you for that! You won't fail to keep wising me up on the fact that you think I'm a drunken bum. You'll sit around all day in a hotel

and take it easy and have plenty time to figger out all
the things you can roast me for, and then spring them on
me the minute I get back from a trip all tired out. Like
you always used to."

"Oh, I did not!" she wailed.

"Sure you did."

"And what do you mean by my sitting around, from
now on—"

"Well, what the hell else are you going to do? You can't
play the piano or maybe run an aeroplane, can you?"

"Why, I'm going to stay on my job, of course, Ed."

"You are not going-to-of-course-stay-on-your-job-Ed,
any such a thing. Lemme tell you that right here and now,
my lady. I've stood just about all I'm going to stand of
your top-lofty independence and business airs—as though
you weren't a wife at all, but just as 'be-damned-to-you'
independent as though you were as much of a business man
as I am! No, sir, you'll do what *I* say from now on.
I've been tied to your apron strings long enough, and now
I'm the boss—see? Me!" He tapped his florid bosom.
"You used to be plenty glad to go to poker parties and
leg-shows with me, when I wanted to, but since you've
taken to earning your living again you've become so
ip-de-dee and independent that when I even suggest
rushing a growler of beer you scowl at me, and as good as
say you're too damn almighty good for Eddie Schwirtz's
low-brow amusements. And you've taken to staying out
all hours—course it didn't matter whether I stayed here
without a piece of change, or supper, or anything else, or
any amusements, while you were out whoop-de-doodling
around— You *said* it was with women!"

She closed her eyes tight; then, wearily: "You mean,
I suppose, that you think I was out with men."

"Well, I ain't insinuating anything about what you

been doing. You been your own boss, and of course I had to take anything off anybody as long as I was broke. But lemme tell you, from now on, no pasty-faced female is going to rub it in any more. You're going to try some of your own medicine. You're going to give up your rotten stenographer's job, and you're going to stay home where I put you, and when I invite you to come on a spree you're going to be glad—"

Her face tightened with rage. She leaped at him, shook him by the shoulder, and her voice came in a shriek:

"Now that's enough. I'm through. You did mean to insinuate I was out with men. I wasn't—but that was just accident. I'd have been glad to, if there'd been one I could have loved even a little. I'd have gone anywhere with him—done anything! And now we're through. I stood you as long as it was my job to do it. *God!* what jobs we women have in this chivalrous world that honors women so much!—but now that you can take care of yourself, I'll do the same."

"What d' yuh mean?"

"I mean this."

She darted at the bed, yanked from beneath it her suit-case, and into it began to throw her toilet articles.

Mr. Schwirtz sat upon the bed and laughed enormously.

"You women cer'nly are a sketch!" he caroled. "Going back to mamma, are you? Sure! That's what the first Mrs. Schwirtz was always doing. Let's see. Once she got as far as the depot before she came back and admitted that she was a chump. I doubt if you get that far. You'll stop on the step. You're too tightwad to hire a taxi, even to try to scare me and make it unpleasant for me."

Una stopped packing, stood listening. Now, her voice unmelodramatic again, she replied:

"You're right about several things. I probably was

thoughtless about leaving you alone evenings—though it is *not* true that I ever left you without provision for supper. And of course you've often left me alone back there in the hotel while you were off with other women—"

"Now who's insinuating?" He performed another char- acteristic peroration. She did not listen, but stood with warning hand up, a small but plucky-looking traffic police- man, till he ceased, then went on:

"But I can't really blame you. Even in this day when people like my friend Mamie Magen think that feminism has won everything, I suppose there must still be a ma- jority of men like you—men who've never even heard of feminism, who think that their women are breed cattle. I judge that from the conversations I overhear in res- taurants and street-cars, and these pretty vaudeville jokes about marriage that you love so, and from movie pictures of wives beating husbands, and from the fact that women even yet haven't the vote. I suppose that you don't really know many men besides the mucky cattle- drover sort, and I can't blame you for thinking like them—"

"Say, what is all this cattle business about? I don't seem to recall we were discussing stockyards. Are you trying to change the conversation, so you won't even have to pack your grip before you call your own bluff about leaving me? Don't get it at all, at all!"

"You will get it, my friend! . . . As I say, I can see— now it's too late—how mean I must have been to you often. I've probably hurt your feelings lots of times—"

"You have, all right."

"—but I still don't see how I could have avoided it. I don't blame myself, either. We two simply never could get together—you're two-thirds the old-fashioned brute, and I'm at least one-third the new, independent woman.

THE JOB

We wouldn't understand each other, not if we talked a thousand years. Heavens alive! just see all these silly discussions of suffrage that men like you carry on, when the whole thing is really so simple: simply that women are intelligent human beings, and have the right—"

"Now who mentioned suffrage? If you'll kindly let me know what you're trying to get *at*, then—"

"You see? We two never could understand each other! So I'm just going to clean house. Get rid of things that clutter it up. I'm going, to-night, and I don't think I shall ever see you again, so do try to be pleasant while I'm packing. This last time. . . . Oh, I'm free again. And so are you, you poor, decent man. Let's congratulate each other."

§ 3

Despite the constant hammering of Mr. Schwirtz, who changed swiftly from a tyrant to a bewildered orphan, Una methodically finished her packing, went to a hotel, and within a week found in Brooklyn, near the Heights, a pleasant white-and-green third-floor-front.

Her salary had been increased to twenty-five dollars a week.

She bought the blue suit and the crêpe de Chine blouse recommended by Miss Beatrice Joline. She was still sorry for Mr. Schwirtz; she thought of him now and then, and wondered where he had gone. But that did not prevent her enjoying the mirror's reflection of the new blouse.

§ 4

While he was dictating to Una, Mr. Truax monologized: "I don't see why we can't sell that Boutell family a lot. We wouldn't make any profit out of it, now, anyway—

that's nearly eaten up by the overhead we've wasted on them. But I hate to give them up, and your friend Mr. Fein says that we aren't scientific salesmen if we give up the office problems that everybody takes a whack at and seems to fail on."

More and more Mr. Truax had been recognizing Una as an intelligence, and often he teased her regarding her admiration for Mr. Fein's efficiency. Now he seemed almost to be looking to her for advice as he plaintively rambled on:

"Every salesman on the staff has tried to sell this asinine Boutell family and failed. We've got the lots—give 'em anything from a fifteen-thousand-dollar-restriction, water-front, high-class development to an odd lot behind an Italian truck-farm. They've been considering a lot at Villa Estates for a month, now, and they aren't—"

"Let me try them."

"Let you try them?"

"Try to sell them."

"Of course, if you want to—in your own time outside. This is a matter that the selling department ought to have disposed of. But if you want to try—"

"I will. I'll try them on a Saturday afternoon—next Saturday."

"But what do you know about Villa Estates?"

"I walked all over it, just last Sunday. Talked to the resident salesman for an hour."

"That's good. I wish all our salesmen would do something like that."

All week Una planned to attack the redoubtable Boutells. She telephoned (sounding as well-bred and clever as she could) and made an appointment for Saturday afternoon. The Boutells were going to a matinée, Mrs. Boutell's grating voice informed her, but they would be pleased t' see Mrs. Schwirtz after the show. All week Una asked advice of "Chas.," the sales-manager, who, between extensive exhortations to keep away from selling —"because it's the hardest part of the game, and, believe me, it gets the least gratitude"—gave her instructions in the tactics of "presenting a proposition to a client," "convincing a prospect of the salesman's expert knowledge of values," "clinching the deal," "talking points," and "desirability of location."

Wednesday evening Una went out to Villa Estates to look it over again, and she conducted a long, imaginary conversation with the Boutells regarding the nearness of the best school in Nassau County.

But on Saturday morning she felt ill. At the office she wailed on the shoulder of a friendly stenographer that she would never be able to follow up this, her first chance to advance.

She went home at noon and slept till four. She arrived at the Boutells' flat looking like a dead leaf. She tried to skip into the presence of Mrs. Boutell—a dragon with a frizz—and was heavily informed that Mr. Boutell wouldn't be back till six, and that, anyway, they had "talked over the Villa Estates proposition, and decided it wasn't quite time to come to a decision—be better to wait till the weather cleared up, so a body can move about."

"Oh, Mrs. Boutell, I just can't argue it out with you," Una howled. "I *do* know Villa Estates and its desirability for you, but this is my very first experience in direct selling, and as luck *would* have it, I feel perfectly terrible to-day."

"You poor lamb!" soothed Mrs. Boutell. "You do look terrible sick. You come right in and lie down and I'll have my Lithuanian make you a cup of hot beef-tea."

While Mrs. Boutell held her hand and fed her beef-tea,

THE JOB

Una showed photographs of Villa Estates and became
feebly oratorical in its praises, and when Mr. Boutell
came home at six-thirty they all had a light dinner together, and went to the moving-pictures, and through them
talked about real estate, and at eleven Mr. Boutell uneasily took the fountain-pen which Una resolutely held
out to him, and signed a contract to purchase two lots at
Villa Estates, and a check for the first payment.

Una had climbed above the rank of assistant to the
rank of people who do things.

CHAPTER XXI

TO Una and to Mr. Fein it seemed obvious that, since women have at least half of the family decision regarding the purchase of suburban homes, women salesmen of suburban property should be at least as successful as men. But Mr. Truax had a number of "good, sound, conservative" reasons why this should not be so, and therefore declined to credit the evidence of Una, Beatrice Joline, and saleswomen of other firms that it really was so.

Yet, after solving the Boutell office problem, Una was frequently requisitioned by "Chas." to talk to women about the advantages of sites for themselves and their children, while regular and intelligent (that is, male) salesmen worked their hypnotic arts on the equally regular and intelligent men of the families. Where formerly it had seemed an awesome miracle, like chemistry or poetry, to "close a deal" and bring thousands of dollars into the office, now Una found it quite normal. Responsibility gave her more poise and willingness to take initiative. Her salary was raised to thirty dollars a week. She banked two hundred dollars of commissions, and bought a Japanese-blue silk negligée, a wrist-watch, and the gown of black satin and net recommended by Miss Joline. Yet officially she was still Mr. Truax's secretary; she took his dictation and his moods.

THE JOB

Her greatest reward was in the friendship of the careful, diligent Mr. Fein.

She never forgot a dinner with Mr. Fein, at which, for the first time, she heard a complete defense of the employer's position—saw the office world from the standpoint of the "bosses."

"I never believed I'd be friendly with one of the capitalists," Una was saying at their dinner, "but I must admit that you don't seem to want to grind the faces of the poor."

"I don't. I want to wash 'em."

"I'm serious."

"My dear child, so am I," declared Mr. Fein. Then, apparently addressing his mixed grill, he considered: "It's nonsense to say that it's just the capitalists that ail the world. It's the slackers. Show me a man that we can depend on to do the necessary thing at the necessary moment without being nudged, and we'll keep raising him before he has a chance to ask us, even."

"No, you don't—that is, I really think you do, Mr. Fein, personally, but most bosses are so afraid of a big pay-roll that they deliberately discourage their people till they lose all initiative. I don't know; perhaps they're victims along with their employees. Just now I adore my work, and I do think that business can be made as glorious a profession as medicine, or exploring, or anything, but in most offices, it seems to me, the biggest ideal the clerks have is *safety*—a two-family house on a stupid street in Flatbush as a reward for being industrious. Doesn't matter whether they *enjoy* living there, if they're just secure. And you do know—Mr. Truax doesn't, but you do know—that the whole office system makes pale, timid, nervous people out of all the clerks—"

"But, good heavens! child, the employers have just as hard a time. Talk about being nervous! Take it in our game. The salesman does the missionary work, but the employer is the one who has to worry. Take some big deal that seems just about to get across—and then falls through just when you reach for the contract and draw a breath of relief. Or say you've swung a deal and have to pay your rent and office force, and you can't get the commission that's due you on an accomplished sale. And your clerks dash in and want a raise, under threat of quitting, just at the moment when you're wondering how you'll raise the money to pay them their *present* salaries on time! Those are the things that make an employer a nervous wreck. He's got to keep it going. I tell you there's advantages in being a wage-slave and having the wages coming—"

"But, Mr. Fein, if it's just as hard on the employers as it is on the employees, then the whole system is bad."

"Good Lord! of course it's bad. But do you know anything in this world that isn't bad—that's anywhere near perfect? Except maybe Bach fugues? Religion, education, medicine, war, agriculture, art, pleasure, *anything*— all systems are choked with clumsy, outworn methods and ignorance—the whole human race works and plays at about ten-per-cent. efficiency. The only possible ground for optimism about the human race that I can see is that in most all lines experts are at work showing up the deficiencies—proving that alcohol and war are bad, and consumption and Greek unnecessary—and making a beginning. You don't do justice to the big offices and mills where they have real efficiency tests, and if a man doesn't make good in one place, they shift him to another."

THE JOB

"There aren't very many of them. In all the offices I've ever seen, the boss's indigestion is the only test of employees."

"Yes, yes, I know, but that isn't the point. The point is that they are making such tests—beginning to. Take the schools where they actually teach future housewives to cook and sew as well as to read aloud. But, of course, I admit the very fact that there can be and are such schools and offices is a terrible indictment of the slatternly schools and bad-tempered offices we usually do have, and if you can show up this system of shutting people up in tread-mills, why go to it, and good luck. The longer people are stupidly optimistic, the longer we'll have to wait for improvements. But, believe me, my dear girl, for every ardent radical who says the whole thing is rotten there's ten clever advertising-men who think it's virtue to sell new brands of soap-powder that are no better than the old brands, and a hundred old codgers who are so broken into the office system that they think they are perfectly happy—don't know how much fun in life they miss. Still, they're no worse than the adherents to any other paralyzed system. Look at the comparatively intelligent people who fall for any freak religious system and let it make their lives miserable. I suppose that when the world has no more war or tuberculosis, then offices will be exciting places to work in—but not till then. And meantime, if the typical business man with a taste for fishing heard even so mild a radical as I am, he'd sniff, 'The fellow don't know what he's talking about; everybody in all the offices I know is perfectly satisfied.'"

"Yes, changes will be slow, I suppose, but that doesn't excuse bosses of to-day for thinking they are little tin gods."

"No, of course it doesn't. But people in authority always do that. The only thing we can do about it is for us, personally, to make our offices as clean and amusing as we can, instead of trying to buy yachts. But don't ever think either that capitalists are a peculiar race of fiends, different from anarchists or scrubwomen, or that we'll have a millennium about next election. We've got to be anthropological in our view. It's taken the human race about five hundred thousand years to get where it is, and presumably it will take quite a few thousand more to become scientific or even to understand the need of scientific conduct of everything. I'm not at all sure that there's any higher wisdom than doing a day's work, and hoping the Subway will be a little less crowded next year, and in voting for the best possible man, and then forgeting all the *Weltschmertz*, and going to an opera. It sounds pretty raw and crude, doesn't it? But living in a world that's raw and crude, all you can do is to be honest and not worry."

"Yes," said Una.

She grieved for the sunset-colored ideals of Mamie Magen, for the fine, strained, hysterical enthusiasms of Walter Babson, as an enchantment of thought which she was dispelling in her effort to become a "good, sound, practical business woman." Mr. Fein's drab opportunist philosophy disappointed her. Yet, in contrast to Mr. Schwirtz, Mr. Truax, and Chas., he was hyperbolic; and after their dinner she was gushingly happy to be hearing the opportunist melodies of "Il Trovatore" beside him.

§ 3

The Merryton Realty Company had failed, and Truax & Fein were offered the small development property of Crosshampton Hill Gardens at so convenient a price that they could not refuse it, though they were already "carrying" as many properties as they could easily handle. In a characteristic monologue Mr. Truax asked a select audience, consisting of himself, his inkwell, and Una, what he was to do.

"Shall I try to exploit it and close it out quick? I've got half a mind to go back to the old tent-and-brass-band method and auction it off. The salesmen have all they can get away with. I haven't even a good, realiable resident salesman I could trust to handle it on the grounds."

"Let me try it!" said Una. "Give me a month's trial as salesman on the ground, and see what I can do. Just run some double-leaded classified ads. and forget it. You can trust me; you know you can. Why, I'll write my own ads., even: 'View of Long Island Sound, and beautiful rolling hills. Near to family yacht club, with swimming and sailing.' I know I could manage it."

Mr. Truax pretended not to hear, but she rose, leaned over his desk, stared urgently at him, till he weakly promised: "Well, I'll talk it over with Mr. Fein. But you know it wouldn't be worth a bit more salary than you're getting now. And what would I do for a secretary?"

"I don't worry about salary. Think of being out on Long Island, now that spring is coming! And I'll find a successor and train her."

"Well—" said Mr. Truax, while Una took her pencil and awaited dictation with a heart so blithe that she could scarcely remember the symbols for "Yours of sixteenth instant received."

CHAPTER XXII

OF the year and a half from March, 1914, to the autumn of 1915, which Una spent on Long Island, as the resident salesman and director of Crosshampton Hill Gardens, this history has little to say, for it is a treatise regarding a commonplace woman on a job, and at the Gardens there was no job at all, but one long summer day of flushed laughter. It is true that "values were down on the North Shore" at this period, and sales slow; it is true that Una (in high tan boots and a tweed suit from a sporting-goods house) supervised carpenters in constructing a bungalow as local office and dwelling-place for herself. It is true that she quarreled with the engineer planning the walks and sewers, usurped authority and discharged him, and had to argue with Mr. Truax for three hours before he sustained her decision. Also, she spent an average of nine hours a day in waiting for people or in showing them about, and serving tea and biscuits to dusty female villa-hunters. And she herself sometimes ran a lawn-mower and cooked her own meals. But she had respect, achievement, and she ranged the open hills from the stirring time when dogwood blossoms filled the ravines with a fragrant mist, round the calendar, and on till the elms were gorgeous with a second autumn, and sunsets marched in naked glory of archangels over the Connecticut hills beyond the flaming waters of Long Island Sound. Slow-moving, but gentle, were the winter months, for she became a part of the commuting town of Crosshampton Harbor, not as the negligible daughter of a Panama Captain Golden, but as a woman with the glamour of independence, executive position, city knowledge, and a certain marital mystery. She was invited to parties at which she obediently played bridge, to dances at the Harbor Yacht Club, to meetings of the Village Friendly Society. A gay, easy-going group, with cocktail-mixers on their sideboards, and motors in their galvanized-iron garages, but also with savings-bank books in the drawers beneath their unit bookcases, took her up as a woman who had learned to listen and smile. And she went with them to friendly, unexacting dances at the Year-Round Inn, conducted by Charley Duquesne, in the impoverished Duquesne mansion on Smiley Point. She liked Charley, and gave him advice about bedroom chintzes for the inn, and learned how a hotel is provisioned and served. Charley did not know that her knowledge of chintzes was about two weeks old and derived from a buyer at Wanamacy's. He only knew that it solved his difficulties.

She went into the city about once in two weeks, just often enough to keep in touch with Truax, Fein, Chas., and Mamie Magen, the last of whom had fallen in love with a socialistic Gentile charities secretary, fallen out again, and was quietly dedicating all her life to Hebrew charities.

Una closed the last sale at Crosshampton Hill Gardens in the autumn of 1915, and returned to town, to the office-world and the job. Her record had been so clean and promising that she was able to demand a newly-created position—woman sales-manager, at twenty-five hundred dollars a year, selling direct and controlling five other women salesmen.

Mr. Truax still "didn't believe in" women salesmen,

and his lack of faith was more evident now that Una was back in the office. Una grew more pessimistic as she realized that his idea of women salesmen was a pure, high, aloof thing which wasn't to be affected by anything happening in his office right under his nose. But she was too busy selling lots, instructing her women aides, and furnishing a four-room flat near Stuyvesant Park, to worry much about Mr. Truax. And she was sure that Mr. Fein would uphold her. She had the best of reasons for that assurance, namely, that Mr. Fein had hesitatingly made a formal proposal for her hand in marriage.

She had refused him for two reasons—that she already had one husband somewhere or other, and the more cogent reason that though she admired Mr. Fein, found him as cooling and pleasant as lemonade on a July evening, she did not love him, did not want to mother him, as she had always wanted to mother Walter Babson, and as, now and then, when he had turned to her, she had wanted to mother even Mr. Schwirtz.

The incident brought Mr. Schwirtz to her mind for a day or two. But he was as clean gone from her life as was Mr. Henry Carson, of Panama. She did not know, and did not often speculate, whether he lived or continued to die. If the world is very small, after all, it is also very large, and life and the world swallow up those whom we have known best, and they never come back to us.

§ 2

Una had, like a Freshman envying the Seniors, like a lieutenant in awe of the council of generals, always fancied that when she became a real executive with a salary of several thousands, and people coming to her for orders, she would somehow be a different person from the good

21 [313]

THE JOB

little secretary. She was astonished to find that in her private office and her new flat, and in her new velvet suit she was precisely the same yearning, meek, efficient woman as before. But she was happier. Despite her memories of Schwirtz and the fear that some time, some place, she would encounter him and be claimed as his wife, and despite a less frequent fear that America would be involved in the great European war, Una had solid joy in her office achievements, in her flat, in taking part in the vast suffrage parade of the autumn of 1915, and feeling comradeship with thousands of women.

Despite Mr. Fein's picture of the woes of executives, Una found that her new power and responsibility were inspiring as her little stenographer's wage had never been. Nor, though she did have trouble with the women responsible to her at times, though she found it difficult to secure employees on whom she could depend, did Una become a female Troy Wilkins.

She was able to work out some of the aspirations she had cloudily conceived when she had herself been a slave. She did find it possible to be friendly with her aides, to be on tea and luncheon and gossip terms of intimacy with them, to confide in them instead of tricking them, to use frank explanations instead of arbitrary rules; and she was rewarded by their love and loyalty. Her chief quarrels were with Mr. Truax in regard to raising the salaries and commissions of her assistant saleswomen.

Behind all these discoveries regarding the state of being an executive, behind her day's work and the evenings at her flat when Mamie Magen and Mr. Fein came to dinner, there were two tremendous secrets:

For her personal life, her life outside the office, she had found a way out such as might, perhaps, solve the question of loneliness for the thousands of other empty-hearted, fruitlessly aging office-women. Not love of a man. She would rather die than have Schwirtz's clumsy feet trampling her reserve again. And the pleasant men who came to her flat were—just pleasant. No, she told herself, she did not need a man or man's love. But a child's love and presence she did need.

She was going to adopt a child. That was her way out.

She was thirty-four now, but by six of an afternoon she felt forty. Youth she would find—youth of a child's laughter, and the healing of its downy sleep.

She took counsel with Mamie Magen (who immediately decided to adopt a child also, and praised Una as a discoverer) and with the good housekeeping women she knew at Crosshampton Harbor. She was going to be very careful. She would inspect a dozen different orphan-asylums.

Meanwhile her second secret was making life pregnant with interest:

She was going to change her job again—for the last time she hoped. She was going to be a creator, a real manager, unhampered by Mr. Truax's unwillingness to accept women as independent workers and by the growing animosity of Mrs. Truax.

§ 3

Una's interest in the Year-Round Inn at Crosshampton Harbor, the results obtained by reasonably good meals and a little chintz, and her memory of the family hotel, had led her attention to the commercial possibilities of inn-keeping.

She was convinced that, despite the ingenuity and care displayed by the managers of the great urban hotels and the clever resorts, no calling included more unimaginative slackers than did innkeeping. She had heard traveling-men at Pemberton's and at Truax & Fein's complain of sour coffee and lumpy beds in the hotels of the smaller towns; of knives and forks that had to be wiped on the napkins before using; of shirt-sleeved proprietors who loafed within reach of the cuspidors while their wives tried to get the work done.

She began to read the *Hotel News* and the *Hotel Bulletin*, and she called on the manager of a supply-house for hotels.

She read in the *Bulletin* of Bob Sidney, an ex-traveling-man, who, in partnership with a small capitalist, had started a syndicate of inns. He advertised: "The White Line Hotels. Fellow-drummers, when you see the White Line sign hung out, you know you're in for good beds and good coffee."

The idea seemed good to her. She fancied that traveling-men would go from one White Line Hotel to another. The hotels had been established in a dozen towns along the Pennsylvania Railroad, in Norristown, Reading, Will-iamsport, and others, and now Bob Sidney was promising to invade Ohio and Indiana. The blazed White Line across the continent caught Una's growing commercial imagination. And she liked several of Mr. Sidney's ideas: The hotels would wire ahead to others of the Line for accommodations for the traveler; and a man known to the Line could get credit at any of its houses, by being regis-tered on identifying cards.

She decided to capture Mr. Sidney. She made plans.

In the spring she took a mysterious two weeks' leave of absence and journeyed through New York State, Pennsylvania, Ohio, and Indiana. The woman who had quite recently regarded it as an adventure to go to Brook-lyn was so absorbed in her Big Idea that she didn't feel self-conscious even when she talked to men on the train.

If they smacked their lips and obviously said to themselves, "Gee! this is easy—not a bad little dame," she steered them into discussing hotels; what they wanted at hotels and didn't get; what was their favorite hotel in towns in from fifteen hundred to forty thousand inhabitants, and precisely what details made it the favorite.

She stayed at two or three places a day for at least one meal—hotels in tiny towns she had never heard of, and in larger towns that were fumbling for metropolitanism. She sought out all the summer resorts that were open so early. She talked to travelers, men and women; to hack-drivers and to grocers supplying hotels; to proprietors and their wives; to clerks and waitresses and bell-boys, and unconsidered, observant porters. She read circulars and the catalogues of furniture establishments.

Finally, she visited each of Mr. Bob Sidney's White Line Hotels. Aside from their arrangements for "accommodations" and credit, their superior cleanliness, good mattresses, and coffee with a real taste, she did not find them preferable to others. In their rows of cuspidors and shouldering desks, and barren offices hung with insurance calendars, and dining-rooms ornamented with portraits of decomposed ducks, they were typical of all the hotels she had seen.

On the train back to New York she formulated her suggestions for hotels, among which, in her own words, were the following:

"(1) Make the offices decent rooms—rem. living-room at Gray Wolf Lodge. Take out desks—guests to register and pay bills in small office off living-room—keep letters there, too. Not much room needed and can't make pleasant room with miserable old 'desk' sticking out into it.

"(2) Cut out the cuspidors. Have special room where

drummers can play cards and tell stories and *spit*. Allow smoking in 'office,' but make it pleasant. Rem. chintz and wicker chairs at $3 each. Small round tables with reading-lamps. Maybe fireplace.

"(3) Better pastry and soup and keep coffee up to standard. One surprise in each meal—for example, novel form of eggs, good salad, or canned lobster cocktail. Rem. the same old pork, beans, cornbeef, steak, deadly cold boiled potato everywhere I went.

"(4) More attractive dining-rooms. Esp. small tables for 2 and 4. Cater more to local customers with a la carte menus—not long but good.

"(5) Women housekeepers and pay 'em good.

"(6) Hygienic kitchens and advertise 'em.

"(7) Train employees, as rem. trav. man told me United Cigar Stores do.

"(8) Better accom. for women. Rem. several traveling men's wives told me they would go on many trips w. husbands if they could get decent hotels in all these towns.

"(9) Not ape N. Y. hotels. Nix on gilt and palms and marble. But clean and tasty food, and don't have things like desks just because most hotels do."

§ 4

Three hours after Una reached New York she telephoned to the object of her secret commercial affections, the unconscious Mr. Robert Sidney, at the White Line Hotels office. She was so excited that she took ten minutes for calming herself before she telephoned. Every time she lifted the receiver from its hook she thrust it back and mentally apologized to the operator. But when she got the office and heard Mr. Bob Sidney's raw voice shouting, "Yas? This 's Mist' Sidney," Una was very cool.

THE JOB

"This is Mrs. Schwirtz, realty salesman for Truax & Fein. I've just been through Pennsylvania, and I stayed at your White Line Hotels. Of course I have to be an expert on different sorts of accommodations, and I made some notes on your hotels—some suggestions you might be glad to have. If you care to, we might have lunch together to-morrow, and I'll give you the suggestions."

"Why, uh, why—"

"Of course I'm rather busy with our new Long Island operations, so if you have a date to-morrow, the matter can wait, but I thought you'd better have the suggestions while they were fresh in my mind. But perhaps I can lunch with you week after next, if—"

"No, no, let's make it to-morrow."

"Very well. Will you call for me here—Truax & Fein, Zodiac Building?"

Una arose at six-thirty next morning, to dress the part of the great business woman, and before she went to the office she had her hair waved.

Mr. Bob Sidney called for her. He was a simple, energetic soul, with a derby on the back of his head, cheerful, clean-shaven, large-chinned, hoarse-voiced, rapidly revolving a chewed cigar. She, the commonplace, was highly evolved in comparison with Mr. Sidney, and there was no nervousness in her as she marched out in a twenty-dollar hat and casually said, "Let's go to the Waldorf—it's convenient and not at all bad."

On the way over Mr. Sidney fairly massaged his head with his agitated derby—cocked it over one eye and pushed it back to the crown of his head—in his efforts to find out what and why was Mrs. Una Schwirtz. He kept appraising her. It was obvious that he was trying to decide whether this mysterious telephone correspondent was an available widow who had heard of his charms. He finally stumbled over the grating beside the Waldorf and bumped into the carriage-starter, and dropped his dead cigar. But all the while Una steadily kept the conversation to the vernal beauties of Pennsylvania.

Thanks to rice powder and the pride of a new hat, she looked cool and adequate. But she was thinking all the time: "I never could keep up this Beatrice-Joline pose with Mr. Fein or Mr. Ross. Poor Una, with them she'd just have to blurt out that she wanted a job!"

She sailed up to a corner table by a window. The waiter gave the menu to Mr. Sidney, but she held out her hand for it. "This is my lunch. I'm a business woman, not just a woman," she said to Mr. Sidney; and she rapidly ordered a lunch which was shockingly imitative of one which Mr. Fein had once ordered for her.

"Prett' hot day for April," said Mr. Sidney.

"Yes. . . . Is the White Line going well?"

"Yump. Doing a land-office business."

"You're having trouble with your day clerk at Brocken-felt, I see."

"How juh know?"

"Oh—" She merely smiled.

"Well, that guy's a four-flush. Came to us from the New Willard, and to hear him tell it you'd think he was the guy that put the "will" in the Willard. But he's a credit-grabber, that's what he is. Makes me think— Nev' forget one time I was up in Boston and I met a coon porter and he told me he was a friend of the president of the Pullman Company and had persuaded him to put on steel cars. Bet a hat he believed it himself. That's 'bout like this fellow. He's going to get the razoo. . . . Gee! I hope you ain't a friend of his."

THE JOB

Una had perfectly learned the Bœotian dialect so strangely spoken by Mr. Sidney, and she was able to reply:

"Oh no, no indeed! He ought to be fired. He gave me a room as though he were the superintendent of a free lodging-house."

"But it's so hard to get trained employees that I hate to even let *him* go. Just to show you the way things go, just when I was trying to swing a deal for a new hotel, I had to bust off negotiations and go and train a new crew of chambermaids at Sandsonville myself. You'd died laughing to seen *me* making beds and teaching those birds to clean a spittador, beggin' your pardon, but it certainly was some show, and I do, by gum! know a traveling-man likes his bed tucked in at the foot! Oh, it's fierce! The traveling public kicks if they get bum service, and the help kick if you demand any service from 'em, and the boss gets it right in the collar-button both ways from the ace."

"Well, I'm going to tell you how to have trained service and how to make your hotels distinctive. They're good hotels, as hotels go, and you really do give people good coffee and good beds and credit conveniences, as you promise, but your hotels are not distinctive. I'm going to tell you how to make them so."

Una had waited till Mr. Sidney had disposed of his soup and filet mignon. She spoke deliberately, almost sternly. She reached for her new silver link bag, drew out immaculate typewritten schedules, and while he gaped she read to him precisely the faults of each of the hotels, her suggested remedies, and her general ideas of hotels, with less cuspidors, more originality, and a room where traveling-men could be at home on a rainy Sunday.

"Now you know, and I know," she wound up, "that

[321]

the proprietor's ideal of a hotel is one to which traveling-men will travel sixty miles on Saturday evening, in order to spend Sunday there. You take my recommendations and you'll have that kind of hotels. At the same time women will be tempted there and the local trade will go there when wife or the cook is away, or they want to give a big dinner."

"It does sound like it had some possibilities," said Mr. Sidney, as she stopped for breath, after quite the most impassioned invocation of her life.

She plunged in again:

"Now the point of all this is that I want to be the general manager of certain departments of the Line—catering, service, decoration, and so on. I'll keep out of the financial end and we'll work out the buying together. You know it's women who make the homes for people at home, and why not the homes for people traveling? . . . I'm woman sales-manager for Truax & Fein—sell direct, and six women under me. I'll show you my record of sales. I've been secretary to an architect, and studied architecture a little. And plenty other jobs. Now you take these suggestions of mine to your office and study 'em over with your partner and we'll talk about the job for me by and by."

She left him as quickly as she could, got back to her office, and in a shaking spasm of weeping relapsed into the old, timorous Una.

§ 5

Tedious were the negotiations between Una and Mr. Sidney and his partner. They wanted her to make their hotels—and yet they had never heard of anything so nihilistic as actually having hotel "offices" without "desks." They wanted her, and yet they "didn't quite know about adding any more overhead at this stage of the game."

Meantime Una sold lots and studied the economical buying of hotel supplies. She was always willing to go with Mr. Sidney and his partner to lunch—but they were brief lunches. She was busy, she said, and she had no time to "drop in at their office." When Mr. Sidney once tried to hold her hand (not seriously, but with his methodical system of never failing to look into any possibilities), she said, sharply, "Don't try that—let's save a lot of time by understanding that I'm what you would call 'straight.'" He apologized and assured her that he had known she was a "high-class genuwine lady all the time."

The very roughness which, in Mr. Schwirtz, had abraised her, interested her in Mr. Sidney. She knew better now how to control human beings. She was fascinated by a comparison of her four average citizens— four men not vastly varied as seen in a street-car, yet utterly different to one working with them: Schwirtz, the lumbering; Troy Wilkins, the roaring; Truax, the politely whining; and Bob Sidney, the hesitating.

The negotiations seemed to arrive nowhere.

Then, unexpectedly, Bob Sidney telephoned to her at her flat one evening: "Partner and I have just decided to take you on, if you'll come at thirty-eight hundred a year."

Una hadn't even thought of the salary. She would gladly have gone to her new creative position at the three thousand two hundred she was then receiving. But she showed her new training and demanded:

"Four thousand two hundred."

"Well, split the difference and call it four thousand for the first year."

"All right."

Una stood in the center of the room. She had "succeeded on her job." Then she knew that she wanted some one with whom to share the good news.

She sat down and thought of her almost-forgotten plan to adopt a child.

§ 6

Mr. Sidney had, during his telephone proclamation, suggested: "Come down to the office to-morrow and get acquainted. Haven't got a very big force, you know, but there's a couple of stenographers, good girls, crazy to meet the new boss, and a bright, new Western fellow we thought we might try out as your assistant and publicity man, and there's an office-boy that's a sketch. So come down and meet your subjects, as the fellow says."

Una found the office, on Duane Street, to consist of two real rooms and a bare anteroom decorated with photographs of the several White Line Hotels—set on maple-lined streets, with the local managers, in white waistcoats, standing proudly in front. She herself was to have a big flat-topped desk in the same room with Mr. Sidney. The surroundings were crude compared with the Truax & Fein office, but she was excited   Here she would be a pioneer.

"Now come in the other room," said Mr. Sidney, "and meet the stenographers and the publicity man I was telling you about on the 'phone."

He opened a door and said, "Mrs. Schwirtz, wantcha shake hands with the fellow that's going to help you to put the Line on the map—Mr. Babson."

It was Walter Babson who had risen from a desk and was gaping at her.

CHAPTER XXIII

"BUT I did write to you, Goldie—once more, anyway —letter was returned to me after being forwarded all over New York," said Walter, striding about her flat.

"And then you forgot me completely."

"No, I didn't—but what if I had? You simply aren't the same girl I liked—you're a woman that can do things; and, honestly, you're an inspiration to me." Walter rubbed his jaw in the nervous way she remembered.

"Well, I hope I shall inspire you to stick to the White Line and make good."

"Nope, I'm going to make one more change. Gee! I can't go on working for you. The problem of any man working for a woman boss is hard enough. He's always wanting to give her advice and be superior, and yet he has to take her orders. And it's twice as hard when it's me working for you that I remember as a kid—even though you have climbed past me."

"Well?"

"Well, I'm going to work for you till I have a job where I can make good, and when I do—or if I do—I'm going to ask you to marry me."

"But, my dear boy, I'm a business woman. I'm making good right now. In three months I've boosted White Line receipts seventeen per cent., and I'm not going back to minding the cat and the gas-stove and waiting—"

"You don't need to. We can both work, keep our jobs,

and have a real housekeeper—a crackajack maid at forty a month—to mind the cat."

"But you seem to forget that I'm more or less married already."

"So do you! . . . If I make good— Listen: I guess it's time now to tell you my secret. I'm breaking into your old game, real estate. You know I've been turning out pretty good publicity for the White Line, besides all the traveling and inspecting, and we have managed to have a few good times, haven't we? But, also, on the side, I've been doing a whale of a lot of advertising, and so on, for the Nassau County Investment Company, and they've offered me a steady job at forty-five a week. And now that I've got you to work for, my *Wanderjahre* are over. So, if I do make good, will you divorce that incubus of an Eddie Schwirtz and marry me? Will you?"

He perched on the arm of her chair, and again demanded: "Will you? You've got plenty legal grounds for divorcing him—and you haven't any ethical grounds for not doing it."

She said nothing. Her head drooped. She, who had blandly been his manager all day, felt managed when his "Will you?" pierced her, made her a woman.

He put his forefinger under her chin and lifted it. She was conscious of his restless, demanding eyes.

"Oh, I must think it over," she begged.

"Then you will!" he triumphed. "Oh, my soul, we've bucked the world—you've won, and I will win. Mr. and Mrs. Babson will be won'erfully happy. They'll be a terribly modern couple, both on the job, with a bungalow and a Ford and two Persian cats and a library of Wells, and Compton Mackenzie, and Anatole France. And everybody will think they're exceptional, and not know they're really two lonely kids that curl up close to each other for comfort. . . . And now I'm going home and do a couple miles publicity for the Nassau Company. . . . Oh, my dear, my dear—"

§ 2

"I will keep my job—if I've had this world of offices wished on to me, at least I'll conquer it, and give my clerks a decent time," the business woman meditated. "But just the same—oh, I am a woman, and I do need love. I want Walter, and I want his child, my own baby and his."

THE END